The Vampire in Science Fiction Film and Literature

ALSO BY PAUL MEEHAN
AND FROM MCFARLAND

Horror Noir: Where Cinema's Dark Sisters Meet (2011)

Cinema of the Psychic Realm: A Critical Survey (2009)

Tech-Noir: The Fusion of Science Fiction and Film Noir (2008)

The Vampire in Science Fiction Film and Literature

PAUL MEEHAN

McFarland & Company, Inc., Publishers
Jefferson, North Carolina

LIBRARY OF CONGRESS CATALOGUING-IN-PUBLICATION DATA

Meehan, Paul.
The vampire in science fiction film and literature /
Paul Meehan.
p. cm.
Includes bibliographical references and index.

ISBN 978-0-7864-7487-5 (softcover : acid free paper) ♾
ISBN 978-1-4766-1654-4 (ebook)

1. Vampire films—History and criticism.
2. Science fiction films—History and criticism.
3. Science fiction, American—History and criticism. I. Title.
PN1995.9.V3M44 2014 809.3'9375—dc23 2014018064

BRITISH LIBRARY CATALOGUING DATA ARE AVAILABLE

On the cover: Poster art for the 2004 film *Dracula 3000*
(Lionsgate Films/Photofest)

Printed in the United States of America

McFarland & Company, Inc., Publishers
Box 611, Jefferson, North Carolina 28640
www.mcfarlandpub.com

Table of Contents

Introduction

Vampires, those ubiquitous children of the night, are a product both of ancient legends and the 19th century gothic imagination. As originally conceived, they are *nosferatu*, immortal beings who inhabit a twilight world of darkness, and are usually found lurking in graveyards, ruined castles and abandoned churches.

Because of the popularity of vampire tales in our culture, everyone is familiar with their nature and the classic "rules" of vampirism. They are undead corpses who feed upon the blood of the living and must lie in their coffins in the daytime. Having the power of shapeshifters, they can transform into wolves, bats, or even mist. Possessed of eternal life, they do not die or age and can only be destroyed by a stake through the heart or by being exposed to sunlight. They have pale skin and prominent canine fangs that are used to extract blood from their victims. Religious objects such as the crucifix, holy water or a consecrated host, as well as herbs such as garlic and wolfbane, repel them. Mirrors do not reflect their image. They possess superhuman strength as well as hypnotic and telepathic powers. Those who die from the vampire's bite become vampires themselves.

But these rules, formulated by Bram Stoker in his seminal vampire novel *Dracula* (1897), have altered considerably over time. As the myth evolved, later writers and film-makers have adopted or rejected the rules as they have seen fit in order to offer new versions of vampirism. In Anne Rice's screenplay for *Interview with the Vampire* (1994) for instance, the vampire Louis (Brad Pitt) dismisses Stoker's vampiric strictures as "the vulgar fictions of a demented Irishman." By the 1980s the vampire film revival, pioneered by England's Hammer Films and other British studios in decades past, had run its course. The gothic formula had become passé, and audiences demanded fresh interpretations of the nature of vampirism, in films like *The Hunger* (1983), *Fright Night* (1985) and *The Lost Boys* (1987).

Over many decades the vampire has changed its form, not into bat or wolf but instead has metamorphosed into new, technological mutations more in keeping with our scientific age: aliens, psychics, futuristic warriors, plague bearers and mad scientists. As vampire scholar J. Gordon Melton observes, "As the vampire myth developed and went through a rationalizing/secularizing process, various authors have posed alternative, nonsupernatural theories for the origin of vampires—from disease to altered blood chemistry. Eventually, at the height of interest in flying saucers in the 1950s, it was inevitable that the idea of vampires as space aliens would be posed."[1] Similarly, in his book *Vampire Forensics*, Mark Collins Jenkins points out: "Science fiction, in fact, has extended and elaborated the vampire myth for years. Shunning the supernatural, it has offered ingenious empirical explanations of the phenomenon, ranging from bizarre psychological conditions to alien species to literal vampire plagues."[2]

In truth, however, despite their occult pedigree the literary vampire which first emerged during the 19th century has always embodied an element of science fiction. As students of the horror genre well know, both the Frankenstein monster and the vampire story were conceived during the infamous literary soiree held on the shores of Lake Geneva in the summer of 1816. In attendance were the famous British poets Percy Bysshe Shelley and Lord Byron, along with Shelley's wife, Mary Godwin, and Byron's physician, John Polidori. After reading horror tales to amuse themselves, Byron proposed that they should each write a ghost story. The result was Polidori's story, "The Vampyre," the first such story in the English language, and Mary Shelley's famous novel *Frankenstein* or *The Modern Prometheus*, published in 1818.

While Polidori's vampire character, Lord Ruthven, was a supernatural creature, Mary Shelley's creation represented a new, realistic development of the gothic novel. As Raymond T. McNally and Radu Florescu write in their book *In Search of Dracula*: "Mrs. Shelley achieved horror and mystery through the use of science.... The agent of horror in her book was no spook, no supernatural being, nor the illusion of such. It was a real monster manufactured by the technical expertise of a Dr. Frankenstein."[3]

Likewise, McNally and Florescu continue, when *Dracula* came along 80 years later, "it was solidly in the tradition of Mary Godwin Shelley ... that Bram Stoker wrote his own horror story. Like them, he presented the vampire as an actual phenomenon.... Moreover, Stoker made Dracula a contemporary, a vampire who lived in, and walked the streets of Victorian England."[4] In his book on the history and development of the science fiction genre, *Trillion Year Spree*, sci-fi author Brian Aldiss offers that the SF genre can trace its origins back to *Frankenstein*. He writes, "Science fiction is the search for a definition of mankind and his status in the universe ... and is characteristically cast in the Gothic or post–Gothic mode.... We look at the dream world of the Gothic novel, from which science fiction springs; we identify the author whose work marks her out as the first science fiction writer."[5]

Indeed, Stoker's inspired point of departure from the gothic formula was to move Count Dracula out of his medieval castle in Transylvania and into the age of the machine. Horror historian David Skal notes: "Once Dracula relocates to England, the story's primary setting is a true bastion of 'mad' science: a lunatic asylum near Purlfleet. *Dracula*'s late–Victorian scientists are Dr. John Seward, proprietor of the madhouse, and Professor Abraham Van Helsing, an eccentric Dutch alienist."[6] Echoing the notion of the vampire as a real-world phenomenon, the 1931 Universal film version of *Dracula* contained an epilogue in which Dr. Van Helsing (Edward Van Sloan) directly addresses the audience and asserts that "there are such things" as vampires.

The perennial vampire slayer, Dr. Abraham Van Helsing, represents Stoker's attempt to link the notion of the vampire to the world of science. Van Helsing is portrayed as a medical doctor and a scientist who brings the scientific method to bear on the study of the supernatural. He is assisted by fellow physician/scientist Dr. Seward, whose skepticism concerning matters of the occult he must overcome. Regarding extraterrestrial vampires, this idea also harks back to the Victorian period. The very first alien invaders in fiction, H.G. Wells's octopus-like Martians in *The War of the Worlds* (1898), were blood drinkers. This seminal portrayal has provided inspiration for alien vampires in science fiction films and literature ever since.

As the horror and science fiction genres developed, it was also inevitable that the technological terrors unleashed by 19th century mad savants, such as Dr. Frankenstein, Dr. Jekyll and Dr. Moreau, would intersect with the domain of the vampire. Science and technology were transforming the world, and the idea of the vampire along with it. Advances in medicine, especially hematology, had fictional mad scientists puzzling over the mysteries of blood and devising new modes of medical vampirism.

In a parallel development, research into ESP phenomena conducted during the new century began to redefine the vampire's psychic dimension. Their hypnotic and telepathic powers were now seen in a scientific context. The idea of the "psychic vampire" was born, conceived as a creature that possessed paranormal powers and used them to extract, not blood, but the very life force from their victims.

Envisioning the future has always been the purview of science fiction writers and film-makers, and as the genre developed the vampire was thrust into the realm of high technology, a gothic anachronism set against a future-noir backdrop. These futuristic bloodsuckers stalked their prey through tomorrow's mega-cities while morphing into sci-fi action figures reminiscent of superheroes and villains with special powers.

In adapting the 19th century literary vampire into a more modern milieu, some writers and film-makers chose to import Stoker's supernatural vampires wholesale into later centuries. A prime example is Stephen King's novel *Salem's Lot*, in which all the classic "rules" of vampirism still apply in the late 20th century, as a *Nosferatu*-like creature invades a New England town. Others, however, have chosen to eschew the traditional supernatural formula in favor of more scientific (or quasi-scientific) concepts that allow the vampire to credibly exist in our secular, technological world. The vampires in the *Twilight* saga, for instance, can go out in sunlight, do not sleep in coffins (in fact, they do not sleep at all), do not breathe or have a heartbeat, have impervious, stone-like skin, possess superhuman strength and agility, and have psychic powers. No explanation is offered, however, for how the *Twilight* vampires can perform their feats without benefit of a functioning respiratory or circulatory system. This vision of the vampire, therefore, ultimately falls back on supernatural concepts despite its scientific gloss.

This book examines the metamorphosis of the vampire from religious and magical beings into creatures of science fiction. It will analyze the role of science in the origin of the legendary and literary vampire, and examine the scientific and pseudo-scientific milieu of the late Victorian period from whence the literary vampire emerged in the "sensation fiction" of J. Sheridan Le Fanu, Bram Stoker, Arthur Conan Doyle and H.G.

Wells. In the years that followed, writers of both pulp and modern science fiction developed the theme of the sci-fi vampire in memorable stories and novels by such luminaries as A.E. Van Vogt, Richard Matheson, Fritz Leiber, William Tenn, Tanith Lee and Brian Aldiss. Particular attention will be paid to the works of the crypto–Nazi German writer Hanns Heinz Ewers, whose early novels frame the science fiction vampire in terms of Nazi eugenics ideology, and American author Whitley Streiber, who connects the vampire with his alleged experiences of alien abduction.

The book's film section will analyze the myth in terms of five specific themes that had been developed in the literature. Historically, vampires have long been connected to plague and disease. This theme has been reflected in a number of films, going back to F.W. Murnau's silent German classic *Nosferatu* (1922) and continuing in later works such as *The Last Man on Earth* (1965), *I Am Legend* (2007) and *Daybreakers* (2010), in which vampiric blood plagues threaten the very existence of mankind.

Psychic vampires are only human and not undead creatures, but they retain the vampire's hypnotic, psychological and telepathic powers of mind, which they use to dominate and manipulate ordinary humans and steal their life force. Examples include *Svengali* (1933), *The Climax* (1943) and *The Shout* (1974).

As previously noted, extraterrestrial beings have long been associated with vampirism. During the science fiction film boom of the 1950s, alien vampires descended to planet Earth from outer space in movies like *The Thing from Another World* (1951), *Not of this Earth* (1956) and *It—The Terror from Beyond Space* (1958). The trend continued in later decades in works by famed horror and science fiction directors such as Curtis Harrington's *Queen of Blood* (1966), Mario Bava's *Planet of the Vampires* (1968), Tobe Hooper's *Lifeforce* (1985), and Stephen Spielberg's *The War of the Worlds* (2005).

Mad scientists are, of course, a staple of both the horror and science fiction genres, and there are a number of films in which vampirism and mad science intersect, beginning with *The Vampire Bat* (1933) and continuing through the classic horror movie cycle in films like *The Return of Dr. X* (1939) and *House of Dracula* (1945). The trend continued in the 1950s and '60s in such sci-fi horror fare as *The Vampire* (1957), *Blood of Dracula* (1958), *Blood of the Vampire* (1966) and *Atom Age Vampire* (1960). Count Dracula himself appears as a mad scientist in works as diverse as *Abbott and Costello Meet Frankenstein* (1948) and *Van Helsing* (2006).

Another take on the science fiction vampire occurs in films in which they must confront some aspect of human technology. This approach has flourished in the era of hi-tech cinema and digital special effects adaptations of comic books and graphic novels. Vampires who used to slink through graveyards in slow motion dressed in evening clothes have been superseded by athletic bloodsuckers in tight-fitting outfits, performing impossible martial arts routines and wielding exotic weaponry in contemporary metropoli or in the shadows of the mega-cities of the future. Recent examples include the popular *Blade* and *Underworld* franchises as well as *Ultraviolet* (2005) and *Priest* (2011).

Science fiction vampires can even assume more exotic, non-human forms. They can be protoplasmic parasites, as in *The Quatermass Experiment* (1956), *First Man into Space* (1958) or *Goke, Body Snatcher from Hell* (1969). They can be giant mutant bats or swarms of bats, like those depicted in *The Devil Bat* (1941) or *Nightwing* (1979). Or they can be monstrous shambling extraterrestrials, such as the alien bloodsuckers in *First Man into Space* (1956) and *It! The Terror from Beyond Space* (1958).

The science fiction idiom has also freed the vampire from its Eastern European, gothic milieu. Instead of traipsing around in moldering Transylvanian castles, sci-fi vamps have been propelled into outer space in films like *Queen of Blood* (1966), *Lifeforce* (1985) and *Dracula 3000* (2004), or even to distant alien worlds beyond Earth in genre fare such as *Planet of the Vampires* (1965) and *Vampire Men of the Lost Planet* (1970).

The concept of the vampire has gone a long way, from its origin as a complex of ancient superstitions, to Victorian gothic nobility, to tech-noir action figures in an urban landscape, that have evolved in ways that reflect our culture. As critic Nina Aurebach observes, "Every age embraces the vampire it needs."[7] Our technological age demands a hi-tech version of the myth, and this melding of science fiction and gothic horror is likely to be the dominant form of vampire fiction in the 21st century. As Matthew Beresford observes in his book *From Demons to Dracula*, "Gone are the 'old world' qualities and associated images; there are no graveyards, no castles, no rising from the dead, no sleeping in coffins. Instead, we are introduced to a gleaming, cutting edge cyber-vamp who exists on the borders of reality."[8]

In truth, science has always been part of vampire literature and film, but this relationship has never been explored. Until now.

Within these pages lurk time-traveling vampires, spacefaring vampires, future-noir hemophages, giant mutant bats, vampiric plants, blood-drinking mad scientists, cyber-vampires, half-human hybrid *dhampirs* and bloodsucking extraterrestrials. *The Vampire in Science Fiction Film and Literature* chronicles a new chapter in the history of these children of the night.

Part I

Origins

Chapter One

The Scientific Origins of the Vampire Myth

While folklore beliefs and myths about vampire-like creatures can be traced as far back as ancient Mesopotamia, Greece and Rome, the history of the vampire as we know it properly begins in Central and Eastern Europe in the 18th century. During the early 1700s, reports of outbreaks of vampirism in these regions would eventually reach Western Europe and introduce the concept into Western culture.

By the early 18th century, the influence of the Turkish Ottoman Empire was on the wane in these lands after a series of military defeats and treaties, and the Austrian Hapsburgs began to absorb vast swaths of formerly Ottoman territories. The Hapsburg Empire assumed control over the provinces of Hungary, Serbia, Moravia, Slovakia and Slovenia, where age-old superstitious belief systems still flourished. One of these was a belief in vampires.

These Eastern European vampires were a variant of the folk idea of the *revenant*, that is, a ghost being a reanimated corpse instead of an immaterial specter. They were thought to be created from people who were victims of suicide, or who had died unnatural or unusual deaths, and returned from their graves to plague the living, usually their relatives, by visiting them at night to suck their blood. Those who died from the vampire's bite would become vampires themselves, and these newly undead could only be neutralized by being disinterred, decapitated and staked through the heart. When exhumed, their corpses were found to be bloated with the blood of their victims and their mouths likewise smeared with blood.

Epidemics of vampirism reportedly occurred in Istria in 1672, Hungary in 1725–30, Silistria in 1755 and Wallachia in 1756. These outbreaks, usually occurring in remote areas, became the subject of controversies regarding the existence of the phenomenon. In this age of enlightenment in Western Europe, science would be brought to bear in shedding light on the reality or non-reality of the vampire. Accordingly, those newly minted Hapsburg subjects living in these provinces began to call upon the authorities in Vienna for help in combating the plague.

In the summer of 1725 a number of mysterious deaths occurred in the Serbian village of Kislova on the Danube east of Belgrade that were believed to be the work of a vampire. The suspect was an individual named Peter Plogojowitz, recently deceased, who posthumously appeared to several villagers, all of whom subsequently died. The chief magistrate of the village requested assistance from the Austrian authorities, and an official, Imperial Provisor Frombold, was dispatched to Kislova to investigate.

By the time Provisor Frombold reached the village, Plogojowitz's body had already been exhumed. In his report on the incident, Frombold noted that the corpse was found to be in an unusual state of preservation. The body was ruddy and swollen, its hair, beard, nails and skin were growing, but most tellingly, there appeared to be fresh blood around the mouth. This was enough proof of vampirism for the villagers, who promptly drove a stake through the corpse's heart, whereupon blood gushed forth from the mouth and ears. Frombold also reported that the body exhibited "wild signs," a euphemism for having an erection. Possessed by fear over the unnatural event, the villagers quickly burned Plogojowitz's body. The bodies of the other villagers who had died suddenly were also exhumed, but no signs of vampirism were found.

The Imperial Provisor's report on the Plogojowitz case would wend its way into the Western European press and become one of the major exhibits in the case to be made for the existence of vampires in the 1730s. It was followed by an even more sensational case just a few years later.

In this case, the vampire in question was an individual named Arnold Paul (sometimes spelled Paole), who had been a Turkish conscript in Kosovo and had returned to his home in the Serbian village of Medvegia in 1727. Paul married and tried to settle down to a new life as a farmer, but confided to his bride that he was troubled by an incident that had occurred during his military service. He claimed that he had been attacked by a vampire, but had followed it to its grave and killed it. Although he had taken the ritual precautions of eating dirt from the vampire's grave and bathed his wounds in its blood in order to cleanse himself, Paul felt he had been cursed by his strange experience.

Unfortunately, Paul's premonition seems to have been correct, because shortly thereafter he was killed when he fell from a haywagon and broke his neck. A few weeks after Paul had been buried, some of the villagers claimed that he had visited them at night and attempted to strangle them. When four of the villagers and some of the local livestock died, Austrian officials were summoned from Belgrade to combat the wave of vampirism. With two Austrian military surgeons present, Paul's grave was opened forty days after his death. His body, like that of Plogojowitz, was found to be in a state of preservation. The skin and nails were apparently still growing and blood trickled from the corpse's mouth. A stake was driven through Paul's heart, causing blood to gush forth and a groan to issue forth from his lips. As a further precaution, Paul's head was cut off and his body was cremated. The four townspeople who had died were similarly exhumed, staked, decapitated and burned.

Four years later, a new epidemic of vampirism hit Medvegia. Seventeen people in the village had died under mysterious circumstances, and after a preliminary report by a contagious disease specialist, officials decided that further action was necessary. In January of 1732, Regimental Field Surgeon Johannes Fluckinger, two medical examiners and two Austrian army officers were dispatched from Belgrade to the Serbian village.

Fluckinger had the bodies of the seventeen recently deceased villagers exhumed and he and his team performed autopsies on the corpses. A dozen out of the seventeen alleged victims of vampirism were found to be in a state of preservation and were bloody and bloated. These twelve individuals were thought to have been infected through eating a sheep that Paul had supposedly killed, and through being bitten by two of Paul's female victims. The locals wasted no time in decapitating the twelve bodies and cremating them, while the five properly decomposed corpses were re-interred in the village cemetery.

Upon returning to Belgrade, Fluckinger wrote an official report, which he titled "Visum et Repertum," Latin for "Seen and Discovered." The report was sealed, notarized by the two surgeons and army officers, and sent to Hapsburg emperor Charles VI in Vienna. Soon afterward, the report was reprinted in a Nuremberg scientific journal and caused a sensation at the 1732 Leipzig Book Fair. Although strange goings-on had been reported from the hinterlands for generations, this report was different. In his book *Vampire Forensics*, Mark Collins Jenkins notes, "But 'Visum et Repertum' was not just another compendium of fantastic tales; there was no fiendish corpse in it. Rather, as a report of scientific observations, it appealed to Enlightenment scholars precisely because Fluckinger's conclusions amounted to a medical acknowledgement that a phenomenon called vampirism might exist. It thus kindled a fierce debate throughout the German academic and medical establishment."[1]

The Fluckinger report set off a firestorm of controversy in the capitals of Western Europe. Numerous learned treatises and dissertations on vampirism were published in the years following its release. Journalists picked up on the story and disseminated it widely throughout France, England, Italy and other European countries, and for the first time the word "vampire" entered Western parlance.

The great European vampire debate would rage on for two decades, yet the matter would not be settled by appeals to either science or superstition, but by religion, as learned religious scholars and theologians weighed in on the reality of the phenomenon. Chief among these was the respected French biblical scholar Dom Agustin Calmet, abbot of the Benedictine Abbey at Senones. Calmet championed the cause of the vampire in a treatise he authored in 1746, which became a bestseller and was reprinted in revised editions in 1749 and 1751 and later translated into German and English. He collected reports on numerous cases of European vampirism and helped to popularize the phenomenon.

But Calmet's advocacy of the vampire would run up against stiff opposition within the Catholic Church. His primary theological adversary was Monsignor Giuseppe Davanzati, the archbishop of Trani in Southern Italy. Davanzati's main objection concerned the desecration of corpses, which was regarded as anathema to Christian teachings, and he denounced the outbreaks of vampirism as dangerous hysteria in his 1746 exposé, *The Vampires*. Eventually, Davanzati's skeptical view would prevail when Pope Benedict XIV, in 1749, expressed the opinion that vampires were "fallacious fictions of human fantasy."

In 1755, the Hapsburg Empress Maria Theresa, devout in her Catholic faith, denounced belief in vampires as superstition and fraud, and decreed criminal penalties for the exhumation, staking and burning of corpses. There would be no further official investigations into the phenomenon by the Austrian government. The controversy was at an end, but the concept of the vampire had been seeded into Western culture, and would emerge into the literature of the following century.

In the 18th century, science, or more properly, the application of scientific methodology, was a relatively new discipline, and science was pushing up against a wall of superstition and irrationality. Medical scientists of the time were challenged to either prove or disprove the existence of the vampire, and struggled to do so. In his book *From Demons to Dracula*, Matthew Beresford states, "Given the emerging scientific abilities of the period, this should have been a straightforward task, and yet in carrying it out scientists were somewhat hampered by society's refusal to abandon superstition and mysticism."[2] What, then, can 21st century science reveal about the nature of the vampire plagues?

Forensic scientists have had more than two hundred years to advance medical understanding of the processes involved in the decomposition of corpses. Many of the signs that were alleged to indicate vampirism by superstitious peasants have conventional explanations.

In his book *Vampires, Burial and Death*, folklorist Paul Barber argues that the belief in vampires originated in misunderstandings about how human bodies decay. Barber defines a vampire as a body that, in all respects, appears to be dead except that it does not decay as we expect, its blood does not coagulate, and it may show changes in dimension and in color. In the cases of Peter Plogojowitz and Arnold Paul, the suspected vampire corpses were well preserved, the hair, nails and skin were still growing, they were bloated, supposedly with the blood of their victims, and there was blood around their mouths as evidence of their evil repast.

Bodies buried in the ground decay more slowly than those exposed to air and bacteria on the surface. During the colder months the decaying process is further slowed. Some buried bodies are subjected to a process called *saponification*, in which body fats are rendered into a substance called adipocere, a waxy material sometimes called "corpse wax" or "grave wax" that encases the corpse in a layer of preservative. Muscular tissues that have been subjected to saponification can appear newly dead, even if the body has been interred for a century or more.

Likewise, the appearance of hair, teeth, skin and nails growing after death is an illusion caused by the skin and gums shrinking back to make them more prominent. Layers of skin can slip away, creating the impression that the corpse is growing new skin. Bloating is caused by the production of methane gas by bacteria in cavities inside the body that can puff it up to two or three times normal size. The reddish appearance of the suspected vampire is part of the normal decay process in which the skin changes color from red to green to purple to brown as part of what pathologists call the chromatic stages of decomposition.

The most damning evidence of vampirism was thought to be blood around the mouth of the deceased, or a coffin seemingly filled with blood. In reality, the red fluid is not blood, but a dark-colored liquid called "purge fluid," which is produced by the decay of the internal organs. Purge fluid may seep out of the corpse's mouth, and could gush forth if a stake was driven into the chest. It can also seep out and pool inside the coffin to make it appear that the body is wallowing in blood. The vampire shrieking as the stake is pounded into its heart is probably an embellishment of the sound of gas suddenly being expelled through the corpse's windpipe.

Vampires have always been associated with illness and plague, and modern-day scholars have suggested a variety of diseases that mimic their appearance and habits. In the wake of the conquest of the New World in the 16th century, corn was introduced into areas of Eastern Europe as a food crop to replace wheat. The problem is that corn is lacking the nutrients niacin and tryptophan in comparison to wheat, and a diet overly reliant on corn will cause a vitamin deficiency disease called pellagra. The disease causes the skin to become scaly and inflamed, lending the sufferer a grotesque appearance. Pellagra is a wasting illness that causes brain functions to deteriorate, leading to bizarre, irrational behavior, dementia and death.

The genetic blood disorder called porphyria may also have a connection with vampirism. A rare disease carried by one in every 200,000 people, porphyria is caused by an inability of the body to produce heme, the red pigment in the blood's hemoglobin. It can cause hypersensitivity to sunlight so extreme that severe lesions can form on the skin exposed to ultraviolet rays (think of Christopher Lee's skin flaking off when exposed to the morning sun in *Horror of Dracula*). The gums recede, making the teeth appear more prominent, and the lack of heme makes the blood assume a purplish color. Today, the disease can be treated with direct injections of heme, but in times past porphyria sufferers may have been motivated to drink blood in order to injest heme through the stomach to relieve their symptoms.

Anemia is another disease of the blood connected with vampires. The illness is caused by a lack of hemoglobin, the oxygen-carrying component of the blood, or by a lack of red blood cells. Those who suffer from anemia typically have a pale complexion, are physically listless, and sometimes have fainting spells, all symptoms associated with victims of vampirism. In the novel *Dracula*, for instance, the Count's victim, Lucy Westenra, exhibits these symptoms, which Dr. Van Helsing at first diagnoses as anemia before determining that Lucy is suffering from a lack of whole blood.

In addition to these non-infectious conditions, there are also a number of infectious diseases that are associated with vampirism. Foremost among these is plague, sometimes referred to as the Black Plague or the Black Death. The disease originated in Asia and migrated to Europe in the 14th century, where it killed off half of the population of Europe, between 1348 and 1350, before eventually dissipating. Symptoms include dark spots on the skin, swollen lymph glands, coughing up blood from the lungs, coma and death. Vampires are frequently associated with rats, and the plague is spread by rats, or more precisely by the rat flea, a bloodsucking organism whose bite transfers the bacillus (*Yersinia pestis*) into either the blood or the lymph glands. People suffering from what is called the pneumonic form of the disease expel blood from their lungs, which can be seen around the mouth to create the false impression that the person has been drinking blood.

The term *nosferatu* is generally thought to derive from the Greek word *nosophorus*, which translates as "plague carrier." In one famous scene in *Dracula*, the Count unleashes a swarm of rats against Van Helsing and his team of vampire hunters. Fortunately, they are dispersed by some well-trained rat terriers. There's also the mad Renfield's vision of "rats, hundreds, thousands, millions of them," inspired by the vampire. In F.W. Murnau's *Nosferatu*, the vampire is accompanied to the city of Bremen by a ship full of rats that also bring the plague to the city.

Rabies is another disease thought by medical experts to explain the vampire myth. There were severe outbreaks of rabies in Hungary and areas of the Balkans between 1721 and 1728, a time period which correlates with the vampire epidemics in Eastern Europe. The disease can be spread through the bites of wolves and bats, two animals which are associated with vampires. Rabies is a viral disease transmitted through saliva, and rabid people, like vampires, are compelled to bite others to pass the disease along. The illness causes a bloody frothing at the mouth and bared teeth in sufferers, and other symptoms include an aversion to strong odors (like garlic), a disruption of the sleep cycle leading to nocturnal habits, and a heightening of the sex drive. Left untreated, rabies invariably results in mania, dementia and death. The invention of a rabies vaccine by Louis Pasteur in 1885 has practically eradicated the disease among humans in the modern world.

Perhaps the most controversial disease associated with vampirism is syphilis because of its alleged connections with Bram Stoker by literary scholars. A number of Stoker's biographers have asserted that the author died of syphilis, which was incurable in the late 19th century. While this assertion cannot be proven conclusively, a number of writers have interpreted the text of *Dracula* as a cautionary tale about the disease.

In his book on the history of science fiction, *Trillion Year Spree*, British SF author Brian Aldiss states, "My own theory is that in fact *Dracula* is only metaphorically and euphemistically about vampirism. Its real subject is that obsession of the *fin de siècle*, syphilis. *Dracula* is the great Victorian novel about VD, for which vampirism stands in as Stoker's metaphor...Van Helsing is the doctor with the syringe. The Count, largely off-stage, represents the disease itself, Renfield, the lunatic, its tertiary stage. The women, Lucy Westenra and Mina Murray, are the vectors of syphilis."[3] Aldiss carries this theory over into his science fiction novel *Dracula Unbound*, which features Stoker himself as a character who has contracted the disease.

Horror historian David J. Skal concurs in his book *Hollywood Gothic*, noting, "*Dracula* can be read as an almost transparent syphilis parable; its images of wanton women, contaminated blood, telltale skin lesions, and pseudoscientific 'remedies' all resonate powerfully with Victorian panic about sexual contagion, the scapegoating of prostitutes, and the attendant rise of blood-purifying quack cures."[4] Even if Stoker did not contract the disease himself, like other Victorians he would have been aware of its sexual means of transmission and fatal consequences.

Another medical condition that may have contributed to the origin of vampire myths is catalepsy, or narcosis, a state in which the body's vital functions slow down to a state indistinguishable from death. Respiration may become so shallow as to be imperceptible, body temperature may fall, pulse can become undetectable, yet the person may still be alive. Cataleptic states have been known about as far back as ancient Rome, where bodies were forbidden to be buried for eight days after apparent death. Reports of catalepsy have persisted into the modern world. In one case, doctors in Sheffield, England, who brought a portable cardiograph machine into a local mortuary, detected signs of life in a woman who had been declared dead of a drug overdose. In another incident, a physician was conducting an autopsy on a cadaver at a New York City morgue. As he made his first incision the "corpse" suddenly woke up and grabbed the doctor by the throat, causing him to die of shock.

During the 18th and 19th centuries, before embalming had become a standard post-mortem procedure, many lived in mortal fear of being interred prematurely. This is vividly reflected in several of the works of Edgar Allan Poe, including "The Premature Burial," "The Fall of the House of Usher" and "Ligeia." The phobia was so widespread that it affected famous people. The composer Chopin, for instance, had his heart cut out as a precaution, while the Duke of Wellington remained unburied for two months to ensure that he was really dead.

During those times, bodies were sometimes buried in shallow graves that were no more than six- to eighteen-inches deep, and under these conditions it is possible that a person who had been prematurely buried could claw his way out of the earth and return from the "dead." Mark Collins Jenkins writes, "The idea of premature burial prefigured the larger idea of reanimated corpses, and for that reason, it was inevitably invoked as an explanation for vampirism... Indeed, the whole vampire legend might be based on dim memories of living people who had actually returned from the grave."[5] In his non-fiction book on the zombie phenomenon in Haiti, *The Serpent and the Rainbow*, ethnologist Wade Davis recounts his quest among voodoo practitioners for the "zombie poison," a toxic substance called tetrodotoxin, which is derived from the liver of the puffer fish. Voodoo priests reputedly use poison to induce a cataleptic state of "voodoo death," and subsequent reversal of this state after burial by means of an antidote.

Vampires are associated with sleep, and are fond of attacking their victims in their beds. They are obliged to slumber in their coffins during the day in what has been called "vampiric sleep." It is therefore not surprising that there is a connection between vampires and certain sleep disorders that are referred to collectively as *parasomnia*.

Probably the most obvious of these is somnambulism, or sleepwalking. Sleepwalkers typically get out of their beds and roam around performing simple, repetitive tasks, called *automatisms*, as if they are fully awake, but can sometimes accomplish more complex tasks, including homicide. The somnambulist's eyes remain open, but are dull and glazed, and they generally have no memory of what has occurred during their sleepwalking episode. It was once thought that somnambulists were acting out desires in their dreams, but modern research has shown that these fits occur when the brain is not in a dreaming state. Sleepwalking is a hereditary condition.

In centuries past, sleepwalking was surrounded by an aura of mystery and the supernatural. Curiously, Lord Byron's physician John Polidori, one of the attendees at the famous 1816 gathering between Byron and Percy and Mary Shelley that produced *Frankenstein*, obtained his medical degree from the University of Edinburgh by writing a treatise on sleepwalking. Polidori went on to write "The Vampyre," the first vampire story in the English language, although somnambulism does not figure in his story.

It does, however, figure prominently in Stoker's *Dracula*, in which Lucy Westenra is induced to sleepwalk by the Count as he approaches on the doomed ship *Demeter*. As Mina Murray writes in her journal, "Then, too, Lucy, although she is so well, has lately taken to her old habit of walking in her sleep. Her mother has spoken to me about it, and we have decided that I am to lock the door of our room every night ... and she tells me that her husband, Lucy's father, had the same habit; that he would get up in the night and dress himself and go out, if he were not stopped."[6] Then, on the stormy night when Dracula and the *Demeter* reach England, Lucy resumes her sleep-walking. "Strangely enough," Mina writes, "Lucy did not wake; but she got up twice and dressed herself. Fortunately, each time I awoke in time and managed to undress her without waking her, and got her back to bed. It is a very strange thing, this sleep-walking, for as soon as her will is thwarted in any physical way, her intention, if there be any, disappears, and she yields herself almost exactly to the routine of her life."[7]

Unfortunately, once the Count has established himself in Whitby, Mina fails to prevent Lucy from sleepwalking to a deadly tryst with the vampire. In one of the most eerily effective scenes in the novel, Mina wakes in the middle of the night to find Lucy missing, and goes looking for her. She spies Lucy in the distance, slumped on her favorite bench overlooking the sea, with a dark form bent over her. The vampire flees upon Mina's approach, and she leads a somnolent Lucy back to the safety of the house.

The nocturnal ramblings of Lucy and other female victims of vampirism would become a cinematic staple of vampire films, from *Nosferatu* (1922) to *Bram Stoker's Dracula* (1992). Although Lucy has been sleepwalking since childhood, Dracula is able to use this propensity to exert a hypnotic and telepathic control over his victim. Thus, in *Dracula*, somnambulism is connected with supernatural and psychic phenomena. Hypnotism and somnambulism are also central features of one of the most influential horror films in cinema history, *The Cabinet of Dr. Caligari* (1919). Modern critics have pointed out that Stoker correctly noted that sleepwalking has a hereditary component, a medical fact that he probably learned from his brother, the knighted physician William Thornley Stoker.

Somnambulism is linked to another enigmatic sleep disorder called night terrors, or *pavor nocturnus* in Latin. This condition mostly affects young children, but can also occur in adults. During an attack, the person will wake up screaming in the middle of the night, bolting upright in bed with wide-open eyes in a state of confusion and fear, sweating, breathing hard, and with a rapid heart rate. Unlike a typical nightmare, the sufferer will not remember any dream content, as night terrors, like sleepwalking, do not occur in a state of dreaming sleep. Night terrors are linked to somnambulism, and both afflictions tend to run in families.

In Whitley Strieber's seminal science fiction vampire novel *The Hunger* (1981), the female vampire Miriam Blaylock feigns being afflicted with night terrors in order to contact Dr. Sarah Roberts, a medical expert in the condition, whom she wishes to turn into a vampire companion. Miriam checks herself into a sleep-research center at Sarah's hospital, knowing she is the only physician who specializes in treating the illness. According to Strieber, "Medicine knows night terrors in adulthood as one of mankind's most frightening problems. Miriam could have quoted Sarah Roberts: 'These terrors arise from the primordial depths and induce in the sufferer perhaps the most intense fear that a human being can know. In quality and intensity they are to nightmares as a typhoon might be to a spring shower.'"[8] Miriam undergoes nocturnal monitoring at the sleep-research center, where the doctors observe her entering an REM (rapid eye movement) dream state while she is experiencing night terrors, although this is not medically accurate. She is also able to recall the content of her dream, which is likewise inaccurate.

Strieber explains Miriam's night terrors as an aspect of his concept of "vampiric sleep," which, in turn, is related to the vampire's longevity. Her vampire companion, John, loses his immortality due to problems with insomnia. Strieber's acquaintance with parasomnia issues may also reflect on his alleged experiences of alien abduction in his non-fiction book *Communion*, which the author claims are related to his vampire fiction. The author's experiences will be discussed in depth in later chapters.

Sleep paralysis is another sleep disorder that is highly relevant to the origin of vampire legends. It is related to hypnagogic and hypnopompic hallucinations that occur in states between sleeping and wakefulness. During an episode of sleep paralysis the sleeper will believe that they are fully awake when they are actually still in a dream state. The body will remain paralyzed in a condition that is referred to as muscle atonia, or muscle weakness, which is designed to prevent the body from physical actions during dreaming, something that might prove dangerous to a sleeper. Unlike somnambulism or night terrors, sleep paralysis takes place during dreaming REM sleep.

While lying in bed in a state of paralysis, the sleeper will typically experience hallucinations that a presence or entity has entered the room. It is usually perceived as an evil or malignant creature that intends to do harm to the sleeper. The entity will then approach the bed and press down upon their body, usually in the chest area, then begin choking, strangling or suffocating them. Strange sounds, smells, or anomalous light phenomena can be observed. The experience ends when the terrified sleeper struggles into full wakefulness to find that the invading entity has vanished.

In his seminal study of this phenomenon, *The Terror That Comes in the Night*, author David Hufford cites a number of first-hand accounts of this terrifying experience. One case involved a young woman named Sharon, who was hospitalized with a herniated disc and laid up in traction. As she closed her eyes to get some sleep, she heard the door to her room open and heard the sound of several pairs of stockinged feet shuffling across the carpet, although no one could be seen. Hufford writes: "Naturally this alarmed her, but when she attempted to reach the call button to ring for the nurse, she found that she could not move.... Then she suddenly saw a bearded, male face suspended in mid-air.... It was totally unfamiliar to her, and it struck her as being malevolent. It was staring intently at her. As she looked at this threatening face, she felt a very intense pressure forcing her head down into her pillow. She described this force as violent and painful."[9] Paralyzed with terror, she heard the door open a second time. A nurse had come into the room to check on her, and as soon as this occurred, all features of the experience disappeared. It took the nurse a while to calm a hysterical Sharon down after this frightening experience.

Another one of Hufford's informants was a young man named Jack, who described an episode that occurred when he was younger and sleeping in the same bed as his brother. As Jack drifted off to sleep, he became aware that there was a presence in the room. Unable to move anything but his eyes, he watched as the "person" glided over to the bed. Jack recounted that "it was very dark and shadowy, you know. Just like a silhouette. But it did have, like, a cape. A very transparent, like dark cape, you know, that just hung down. The face wasn't a clear face, but what it did have ... was two very dark eyes.... They were piercing. They were just looking at me. It wasn't just like two dots. They were eyes, and it sent a chill up my spine.... I didn't want to breathe or move in any way. I felt this hardness on my chest, you know, pressure was there."[10] Fortunately, his brother noticed that Jack was breathing very heavily and woke him, whereupon the bedroom invader with the scary eyes abruptly vanished.

Now consider this passage from *Dracula*, in which the Count seems to materialize in Mina Harker's bedroom as she is trying to fall asleep: "There was in the room that same white mist that I had before noticed.... I felt the same vague terror which had come to me before and the same sense of some presence.... Then indeed my heart sank within me: Beside the bed, as if he had stepped out of the mist—or rather as if the mist had turned into this figure, for it had entirely disappeared—stood a tall, thin man, all in black. I knew him at once from the description of the others.... For an instant my heart stood still, and I would have screamed out, only that I were paralyzed."[11]

It's not difficult to see how an episode of sleep paralysis could be interpreted as a visitation by a ghost, an incubus or a vampire. Bedroom apparitions abound in vampire literature and film, beginning with J. Sheridan Le Fanu's *Carmilla* (1871). The features of sleep paralysis are remarkably consistent over time and place. Hufford cites a case from the Philippines in which the sleeper is haunted by a vampire being known as an *aswang*: "At about one o'clock, Aguas felt that somebody was staring at him. He opened his eyes and looked around. At the window he saw an old woman, the lower part of her body missing, staring at him, her greying hair standing up and with her lips open in a devilish grin. Her eyes were bloodshot and big. He was so frightened that he tried to scream but nothing came out of his mouth. He tried to wake his companion up but he could not move. He tried to close his eyes but couldn't. After a few minutes the *aswang* flew away."[12] As is evident from these examples, sleep paralysis provides yet another scientific explanation of the vampire legend.

Animals that suck blood to live are readily observed in nature. Most of these are invertebrate pests such as mosquitoes, fleas, leeches and lice. But there are also some vampires among the higher animals. One exotic example is the vampire finch (Geospiza difficilis septentrionalis), a small bird native to the Galapagos Islands that subsists on the blood of other birds. The most infamous of these is the vampire bat (*Desmodus rotundus*), which is native to Mexico, Central and South America. While most bats' diets consist of insects or fruit, the vampire bat stealthily laps up the blood of other mammals while they sleep, cutting into the skin with a pair of razor-sharp incisors. Their saliva contains an anticoagulant substance that keeps the blood flowing freely as they feed. They have also been known to carry rabies, a disease associated with vampirism. Bats are the creatures most associated with vampires, and, like vampires, they sleep during the day and feed at night.

The literary vampire emerged in the 19th century, in the aftermath of the Age of Enlightenment, and the vampire genre is most closely associated with the late Victorian era (1837–1901) in England. The Victorian period was a time of technological ferment, when many novel advances in science and medicine began to improve the lot of the common man. The Victorians were great believers in progress and technology, yet it was also a time that witnessed a movement away from the rationalism of earlier times and toward romanticism and mysticism with regard to social values, religion and the arts.

Steam power came into its own, with railroads and steamships providing new avenues of rapid transportation and commerce. Gas lighting was installed in London and in townships across England, providing illumination for darkened streets and gas heating for Britain's notoriously cold, damp climate. Electrical power began to be exploited at this time, with the first electric streetlights installed in London in 1882, although it would be decades before electric lights completely supplanted gaslight. The invention of the telegraph, and later the telephone, provided a revolution in communication. Other technological innovations of the period included subways, elevators, the telegraph, pneumatic tires, the sewing machine, the bicycle, modern sanitation and photography.

Some noted scientific luminaries of Victorian times included mathematician Charles Babbage (1791–1871) the inventor of the "difference engine," the world's first analog computer; Lord Kelvin (1824–1907), who formulated the modern laws of thermodynamics; and Michael Faraday (1791–1867), who discovered benzene and then explored the qualities of electromagnetic fields. The most infamous savant of the period was Charles Darwin, whose books *The Origin of Species* (1859) and *The Descent of Man* (1871) outlined the theories of evolution and natural selection, theories that contradicted the biblical narratives concerning the creation of the world and humankind.

Darwin's controversial writings created a schism between science and religion and led to the creation of a new discipline, paleontology, the study of the life forms of the past. Some critics postulate that Darwin's theories may have also had an influence on the conception of the vampire in Stoker's *Dracula*, who possesses the qualities of a degenerate, de-evolved being.

There were significant advances in medical technology as well. Anesthesia came into widespread use and was utilized on Queen Victoria herself during the birth of her eighth child, Prince Leopold. The British physician Joseph Lister (1827–1912) introduced the use of antiseptics to the operating room. Anesthetic and antiseptic techniques revolutionized surgery and greatly increased the life spans of the Victorian populace. Another novel life-saving medical technique, one that had a significant relationship to the creation of the literary vampire, was blood transfusion. British obstetrician James Blundell performed the first successful transfusion of human blood in 1818, but the process was still not well understood by the late 19th century, prior to the discovery of human blood types and cross-matching between donors and receivers. Blood transfusions are conspicuously featured in *Dracula* and in the pre-*Dracula* science fiction vampire story "Good Lady Ducayne."

Running counter to these vistas of scientific progress, however, was a vein of mysticism and anti-rationalism in the Victorian psyche that found expression in two popular pseudo-sciences of the time, mesmerism and spiritualism. Mesmerism was named for the German doctor Franz Anton Mesmer (1734–1815), who devised novel methods of treatment for his patients. Mesmer believed that the human body possessed a magnetic force or fluid that could be manipulated through the application of magnetic fields. Accordingly, one of his healing techniques involved placing magnetized metal plates on his patient's limbs. He developed a theory of "animal magnetism," which has come to be associated with the kind of sexual charisma possessed by Count Dracula.

Franz Anton Mesmer (1734–1815), the inventor of mesmerism.

Mesmer experimented with inducing trance states by staring deeply into his patient's eyes (another trait associated with vampires) and by the use of "passes," vigorous gestures performed over the patient's body that were designed to rearrange the body's magnetic fluids, although these passes strongly resembled the theatrical gestures used by magicians in performing stage magic. Once entranced, individuals could be given suggestions to carry out all sorts of actions. It was observed that certain entranced persons, referred to as *somnambules*, or somnambulists, seemed capable of performing paranormal feats and became renowned psychic celebrities. Thus, mesmerism became connected with the occult and the preternatural.

In 1778, Mesmer left Vienna and migrated to Paris, where he set up a practice and attempted to gain scientific respectability for his unorthodox healing methods. Many of his patients claimed to have been cured of all manner of ailments, giving him the aura of a miracle man. As patients flocked to his hospital, he soon became a wealthy and influential man, and was rumored to have been initiated into several occult and esoteric societies. Eventually, he would become the leader of a cult as adherents of his philosophy spread the word about mesmerism throughout Europe. His fame, however, was to be short-lived, for in 1784 the French government convened a commission to evaluate the medical efficacy of Mesmer's treatments. After due deliberation the commission ruled that his methods amounted to little more than quackery, and in the aftermath he was forced to leave Paris. He wandered around Europe for the rest of his life, trying to gain scientific respectability for his theories, but this goal would forever elude him.

Despite this fall from grace, Mesmer's ideas continued to resonate in the public mind. By the 1840s there were hundreds of wandering mesmerists traveling throughout England, exhibiting mesmeric phenomena in public shows before paying audiences. Charles Dickens, who was England's most popular writer of the mid–19th century, reportedly dabbled in mesmerism in the 1840s. Edgar Allan Poe wrote about it in macabre tales like "The Facts in the Case of M. Valdemar" and "Mesmeric Revelation." Trances and somnambulism are featured in *Dracula*, but mesmerism is also a key theme in earlier works depicting psychic vampires such as George du Maurier's novel *Trilby* (1894) and Arthur Conan Doyle's short story "The Parasite" (1894).

Spiritualism was another mystical movement that achieved vast popularity in the Victorian consciousness. The movement drew inspiration from the works of the Swedish mystic Emanuel Swedenborg (1688–1772), whose writings posited a spirit world in which discarnate souls inhabit multiple heavens and hells and sometimes communicate with the living. Historically, the movement had its genesis in 1848, when two sisters, Margaretta and Catherine Fox, reported a series of strange rapping noises on their farmhouse in Hydesville, New York. These anomalous raps were allegedly communications from spirit beings, who could, in this way, answer "yes" or "no" to questions put to them. Later, the sisters devised a code to correspond to individual letters of the alphabet in order to facilitate more elaborate communications from the spirit world.

The rapping spirits soon spread from the Fox household to the surrounding communities, as people set up their own séance groups and found that they could produce similar phenomena. Spiritualism, as the new movement was called, was the belief that

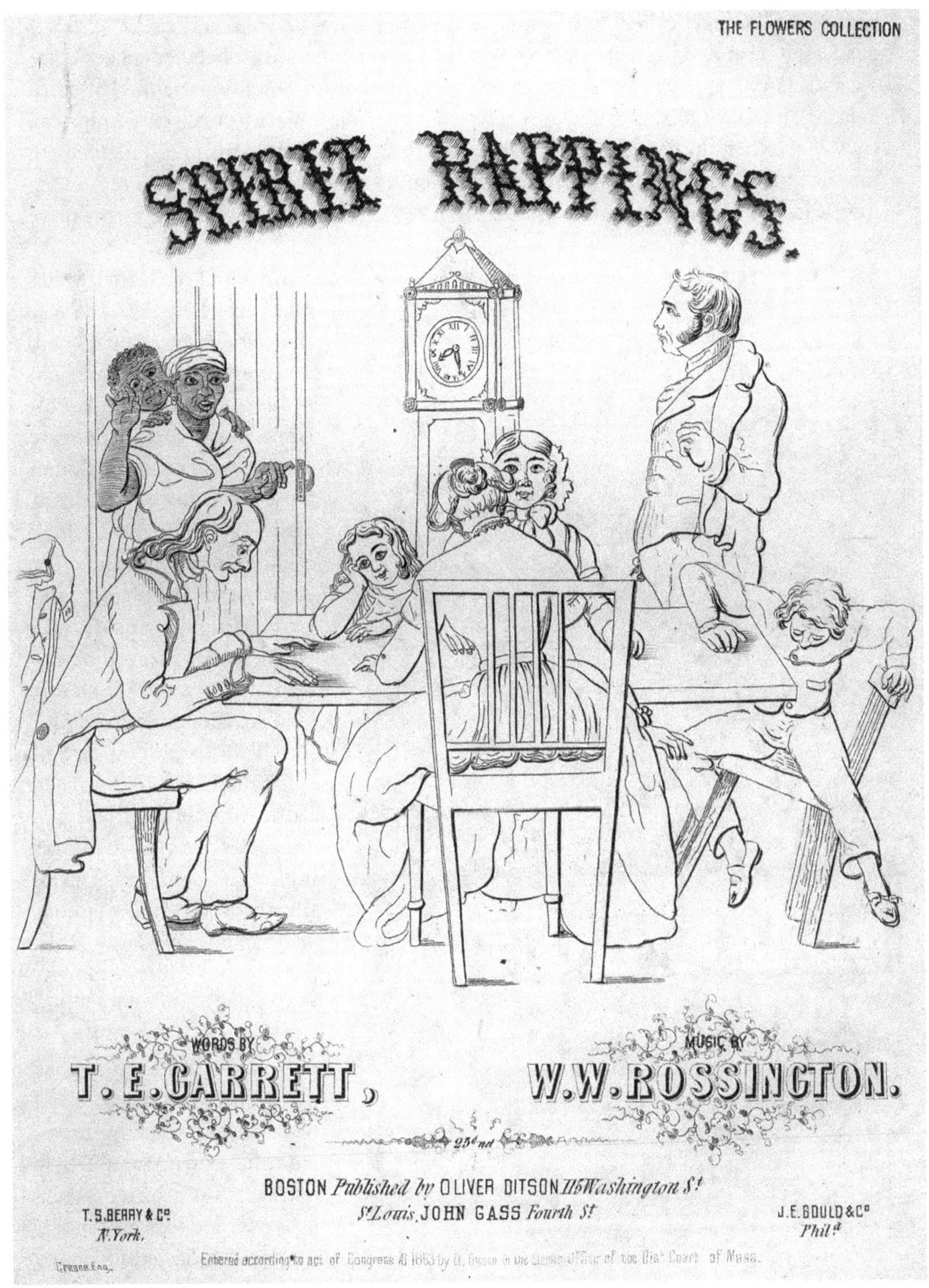

This 1853 sheet music cover page illustrates the Spiritualism fad of the mid–19th century.

psychic individuals called "mediums" could enter a trance state and speak with the dead, levitate and materialize objects by means of a diaphanous substance called "ectoplasm," clairvoyantly reveal hidden information, and produce writings penned by spirit beings. The spiritualist movement received a surge of popularity during the American Civil War, when the families of soldiers killed in the war wished to communicate with their loved ones in the afterlife. Abraham Lincoln's wife, Mary Todd Lincoln, grieving for the loss of her son, held séances in the White House that were attended by the president.

The movement quickly gained popularity as it spread throughout the United States and Europe. By 1897, the year that *Dracula* was published, it was estimated to have eight million followers. Spiritualism's most vocal advocate was the writer Arthur Conan Doyle, creator of the ultra-rational detective Sherlock Holmes, who would fully embrace the movement later in his life. Doyle's second wife, Jean Leckie, claimed to be a medium and frequently held séances on their estate.

During the 1920s, the famous stage magician Harry Houdini campaigned against the excesses of Spiritualism.

The proliferation of spirit mediumship, however, led to widespread fraud and abuse as bogus mediums bilked the credulous out of their life savings. The famous stage magician Harry Houdini would emerge as the most outspoken opponent of spiritualism, conducting a personal crusade to expose phony mediums that received wide coverage in the press. Houdini and Conan Doyle entered into a bitter public feud over the reality of mediumship that lasted for many years. Despite the fact that Margaretta Fox had recanted in 1888 and admitted that their séances were a fraud, the belief in spirits and mediums remained popular into the next century, especially in England.

Ironically, advances in communications technology during Victorian times may have aided the notion of communication with the dead. If disembodied voices could speak from a phonograph or telephone, might not the voices of the departed be heard in the séance room? Note that the phonograph, the telegraph and the telephone are all featured prominently in Stoker's *Dracula*. In 1882, psychic researcher F.W.H. Myers coined the term "telepathy," which was defined as direct communication between two minds. Telepathy is also a plot element in *Dracula*, especially in the later chapters in which Mina Harker's telepathic link with the Count is used to locate him as he is fleeing back to Transylvania.

Like mesmerism, spiritualism also contributed to the creation of the vampire myth. Horror scholar David J. Skal observes that "the 'experiments' of spiritualism rose, in part, to provide some quasi-scientific justification for the traditional Christian concept of an afterlife, under mortal siege by rapid advances in science and an ever-encroaching materialism. The trappings of spiritualism are discernable in *Dracula*; since the Count is dead, the hypnotic trances of Lucy and Mina are, ipso facto, mediumistic. Like spiritualism, Dracula himself emerges as a kind of fantastic bargained compromise between science and religion, however hellish and grotesque."[13]

The Victorian dichotomy between logic and the irrational would produce a creature that partook of both science and the supernatural, a being with a foot in both worlds—the vampire.

Chapter Two

The Science Fiction Vampire in Literature

The vampire plagues of the 18th century had introduced the concept of the vampire to Western Europe, and it wasn't long before they would be incorporated into literary works of fantasy and horror. Some of the greatest poets of the time were inspired by the theme, including Samuel Taylor Coleridge in "Christabel" (1798–1800) and Lord Byron in "The Giaour" (1813). Byron was also present at the famous literary soiree attended by the poet Percy Shelley, his wife, Mary Godwin, and Byron's physician, John Polidori, in the Villa Diodati, overlooking Lake Geneva, in June 1816. Forced indoors by inclement weather, Byron proposed that they entertain themselves by having each of them write a ghost story.

This story-writing contest would produce Mary Shelley's seminal gothic science fiction novel *Frankenstein*. Byron contributed the outline for a vampire story he left unfinished, but Polidori appropriated Byron's plot fragments and fleshed them out into a short story entitled "The Vampyre," published in 1819. The first vampire story in the English language, "The Vampyre" featured an aristocratic bloodsucker named Lord Ruthven, who is reckoned by vampirologists to be the progenitor of Stoker's Count Dracula.

Polidori's grim tale of blood, madness and death was at first ascribed to Lord Byron's authorship, which attracted wide attention in literary circles. The French playwright Charles Nodier adapted the story for the Parisian stage in his production of *Le Vampire* in 1820. It was later adapted into a German opera, *Der Vampyr*, by Heinrich August Marschner in 1829. The acclaimed French novelist Alexandre Dumas, *père*, penned his own theatrical adaptation of the work in 1851. Another offspring of Polidori's vampire was the British novel *Varney the Vampire: Or The Feast of Blood*, by James Malcolm Rymer. Published as a 900-page "penny dreadful" in 1847, Rymer's lurid potboiler was nonetheless the first vampire novel in the English language.

The first truly significant vampire story in English, however, was Irish writer J. Sheridan Le Fanu's novella *Carmilla*, published in book form in an anthology of the author's weird fiction entitled *In a Glass Darkly* in 1872. *Carmilla* takes place in Styria, a bucolic province in southeast Austria, where the narrator, a young woman named Laura, lives in a deserted *schloss* with her father and a governess. One night a carriage breaks down near the castle and a mysterious noblewoman and her daughter emerge from the wreck. The mother claims to be on an urgent mission that will brook no delay, and while the carriage is being repaired she convinces the family to look after her daughter, Carmilla, until her business is concluded.

Carmilla is a strange and languid young woman who quickly becomes a companion to Laura in her solitude. She seems to have an unwholesome fascination with Laura, and there are hints of a lesbian attraction between the two. Soon, Laura is having nightmares about being visited in her bedroom by a supernatural intruder and begins to waste away. As the story progresses, Carmilla is revealed to be a 150-year-old vampire, Mircalla, Countess of Karnstein. Her tomb is located, she is exhumed and found to be in a coffin floating in blood, whereupon she is staked, beheaded and burned.

Written twenty-five years before *Dracula*, Le Fanu's vampire tale provided inspiration for fellow Irishman Stoker's more famous creation, and contained many of the basic elements of vampire lore. Le Fanu is credited as being the inventor of the modern ghost story, and *Carmilla* is considered one of the finest vampire stories in the English language. The novella was adapted for a number of films, beginning with Carl Theordor Dreyer's classic *Vampyr* (1932) and continuing with the Hammer productions of *The Vampire Lovers* (1970), *Lust for a Vampire* (1970) and *Twins of Evil* (1971). As their lurid titles suggest, the Hammer "Karnstein" series emphasized and amplified the lesbian overtones implicit in the plot of *Carmilla*, and the work would continue to provide inspiration for generations of Sapphic bloodsuckers in the cinema, from *Dracula's Daughter* (1936) to *The Hunger* (1983).

In order to provide a sense of unity to the five weird tales in *In a Glass Darkly*, which had originally appeared as separate magazine stories, Le Fanu created a framing narrative. Each story began with a prologue, presenting it as a case history from the voluminous files of Dr. Martin Hesselius, physician, occultist and practitioner of "metaphysical medicine." The prologues are related by an unnamed narrator, an admiring fellow doctor who acts as medical secretary and custodian of Hesselius's records. In the prologue to *Carmilla* he writes, "Upon a paper attached to the Narrative which follows, Doctor Hesselius has written a rather elaborate note, which he accompanies with a reference to his Essay on the strange subject which the MS. Illuminates. This mysterious subject he treats, in that Essay, with his usual learning and acumen, and with remarkable directness and condensation.... I have determined, therefore, to abstain from presenting any *precis* of the learned Doctor's reasoning, or extract from his statement on a subject which he describes as 'involving, not improbably, some of the profoundest arcana of our dual existence, and its intermediates.'"[1]

Hesselius appears as a character in only one story in the collection, "Green Tea," in which a staid English clergyman is haunted by the eerie phantasm of a monkey. The story is presented in the form of letters written to the doctor's fellow savant, Professor Van Loo of Leyden, described as "a chemist, and a man who read history and metaphysics and medicine." Unfortunately, Hesselius is unable to affect a cure for the reverend's haunting. Tortured by visions of the phantom monkey, the clergyman takes his own life, while the doctor delivers the posthumous diagnosis that his affliction was caused by overindulging in green tea.

Hesselius is the first man of science to be connected with vampirism in horror literature. He provides the obvious blueprint for Stoker's vampire hunter, Doctor Abraham Van Helsing in *Dracula*, and for a slew of psychic sleuths and scientific ghostbusters that followed. The framing device in *Carmilla* presents vampirism as a real-world phenomenon, its use of medical language and science-laden jargon lending it a modernistic air of verisimilitude that Stoker would adopt a quarter of a century later.

While vampires are almost always associated with members of the animal kingdom, the first vampiric plant in literary history appeared in "The Man-Eating Tree," a short story by Phil Robinson from his collection entitled *Under the Punkah* (1881). It's presented as a traveler's tale, narrated by the author's uncle as a true account of one of his journeys into the wilds of Africa. On a hunting trip in the land of Nubia in Central Africa, the narrator and his native attendant, a young lad named Otona, are stalking antelope through a fern forest. He shoots a young animal and sends Otona to fetch the wounded fawn, but when the boy passes near an odd-looking tree it suddenly moves its foliage to envelop both hunter and prey. There is a strangled scream from the boy and then the forest is silent.

Thinking that Otona may be alive, or that a giant snake concealed among the branches may account for an illusion of movement, the hunter approaches the tree. He perceives that it has "great waxen flowers" and succulent-looking fruit that hang on its branches like "glorious golden ovals." Its leaves are equipped with sucker-like cups designed to drink its victim's vital fluids. As he gets closer, the tree's foliage becomes more agitated, quivering "through every branch, muttering for blood." The fleshy leaves reach their horrid lips out toward him in anticipation of the vampiric embrace.

Fascinated and terrified by the sight, the hunter is stunned into immobility, but as the vampire tree strains to reach him he comes to his senses and starts firing his rifle into the monster. The shots have an immediate effect, causing wounds on the trunk and boughs, and before long the tree is reduced to a dead, shattered trunk. For the *coup de grâce*, the hunter plunges his hunting knife deep into the tree's central bole, as if staking a vampire. Inside, the ruined foliage the corpse of Otona is discovered, with "a hundred vampire leaves still clinging to it."

Robinson's tall tale is a highly effective exercise in storytelling. His lurid descriptions imbue the vampire tree with a nightmarish life, allowing the images to linger disturbingly in the reader's mind. The story was so compelling that it inspired the myth of the "Man-Eating Tree of Madagascar," a hungry plant whose human-devouring exploits were chronicled in many traveler's tales of the period. A few years later, Sir Arthur Conan Doyle had written "The American's Tale," a cowboy story which featured a man-eating plant (in Arizona, no less!), but Robinson's bloodsucking tree is a true vampire.

Oddly, the concept of vampires in the plant kingdom can be found in Eastern European folklore, where it was believed that vinous plants such as the pumpkin and the watermelon could become vampires, but "The Man-Eating Tree" represents the first non-human vampire in literary history. Vampire plants would later appear in the film *The Thing from Another World* (1951) and in Brian Aldiss's novel *Dracula Unbound* (1992).

Another variety of vampiric flora would show up a few years later in H.G. Wells's short story "The Flowering of the Strange Orchid" (1894). The story's protagonist is a Britisher by the name of Mr. Winter-Wedderburn, a milquetoast chap who laments his humdrum existence where "nothing ever does happen to me." Wedderburn's obsession is cultivating orchids, and his only excitement comes from the possibility of discovering a rare new species.

One day he brings home the rhizome of a rare orchid from the Andaman Islands that he has purchased from a botanical house. The orchid collector, a man named Batten, had been found dead next to the specimen in a mangrove swamp, his body drained of blood, presumably by tropical leeches. Wedderburn fusses over the plant in his hothouse, nurturing it with all his horticultural skills until it begins to flourish. His housekeeper, however, does not like the look of the orchid, which is growing a set of aerial rootlets that resemble clutching fingers and has sharp, red-tipped leaves.

Wedderburn's ministrations are rewarded when the mystery orchid finally blooms. Overjoyed, he examines the white, gold and purple flowers, but as he admires the blossoms the room begins to sway and he loses consciousness. When he doesn't show up for tea-time, the housekeeper goes looking for him in the hothouse, where the air is thick with a strange perfume. She finds him prone upon the floor, with the orchid's aerial rootlets firmly attached to his chin, neck and hands. Then she notices a trickle of red liquid on his cheek and realizes that the plant is siphoning off his blood. Staggering from the overpowering effects of the soporific fragrance, she manages to break a window, letting fresh air into the hothouse. She drags Wedderburn outside, with the orchid's tendrils still attached, and begins to break off the rootlets and destroy the plant. After a visit from the doctor, Wedderburn is none the worse for wear, and basks in the excitement of his strange adventure.

The story is an uneasy amalgam of social satire and horror, as the sole purpose of the weird encounter seems to be to provide the bland Mr. Wedderburn with an "adventure" to enliven his otherwise dull, middle-class existence. Its tone is lighthearted rather than melodramatic. This theme clashes with the horror element, which is the true core of the story. Wells's bloodsucking orchid, like Robinson's man-eating tree, is a totally alien, non-human take on the vampire concept that is much more in the realm of science fiction than gothic horror. The plot embodies the familiar sci-fi notion of "nature gone mad" that would blossom during the next century. The strange orchid finds a distant correspondence to Audrey, the monstrous plant featured in Roger Corman's cult film *The Little Shop of Horrors* (1960) and its subsequent filmic and theatrical iterations.

The late Victorian period was a time when the romantic imagination flowered and brought forth masterpieces of fantasy, horror and science fiction that still resonate. The impressive list of Victorian fantasia includes Robert Louis Stevenson's *The Strange Case of Dr. Jekyll and Mr. Hyde* (1888), H. Rider Haggard's *She* (1886), Oscar Wilde's

The Picture of Dorian Gray (1890), J.M. Barrie's *Peter Pan* (1904), the science fiction novels of H.G. Wells, the gothic mysteries of Sir Arthur Conan Doyle, and, of course, *Dracula* (1897). But, prior to *Dracula*, a number of vampire stories appeared that had a science fiction twist.

One of the most popular novels of the era was George du Maurier's *Trilby* (1894), a strange and tragic tale of psychic vampirism and mesmeric transformation set in the 1850s. The main characters are three Britishers, described as "the Three Musketeers of the Brush," who have come to Paris to study painting. These musketeers include the strongman Taffy, a mellow Scot called the Laird, and the young and naïve Little Billee. While pursuing their muse, the three friends lead a carefree bohemian existence in a studio they share in the Latin Quarter. Various eccentric characters continually drift in and out of the studio.

Trilby O'Ferrall, a beautiful half-Irish young woman who is their laundress, attaches herself to the trio. Her special favorite, however, is Little Billee, for whom she develops an infatuation, and the feeling is mutual. Another visitor to the studio is Svengali, an Eastern European Jew who is a brilliant musician. Svengali also becomes infatuated with Trilby, who is tone deaf and possesses no musical talent, but who possesses a marvelous set of vocal cords.

The maestro sees an opening, however, when he cures Trilby of a terrible eye pain by placing her in a mesmeric trance. He stares deeply into her eyes, and then "he made passes and counterpasses on her forehead and temples and down her cheek and neck. Soon her eyes closed and her face grew placid."[2] But while she is spellbound he takes the occasion to plant a post-hypnotic suggestion that, "you shall see nothing, hear nothing, think of nothing but, Svengali, Svengali, Svengali."[3]

After she is brought out of her trance, the Laird warns Trilby about the dangers of mesmerism. "He mesmerized you," he declares; "that's what it is—mesmerism! I've often heard of it, but never seen it done before. They get you into their power, and just make you do any blessed thing they please—lie, murder, steal—anything! And kill yourself into the bargain when they've done with you!"[4]

Billee is charmed by Trilby's beauty, and not only as a suitor. He derives creative

Trilby is mesmerized by the evil hypnotist Svengali in George du Maurier's illustration for his novel *Trilby* (1894).

inspiration from the girl that brings his artistic talents to fruition. The young painter proposes marriage, and Trilby accepts, but before the engagement can proceed, Billee's mother, Mrs. Bagot, arrives from England to check out her son's fiancée. She is appalled to find that Trilby has a checkered past, which includes having worked as a nude model. After a confrontation with the girl, Mrs. Bagot convinces Trilby that she will not be a fit wife for her son. As a consequence, Trilby abruptly leaves Paris and Billee, who knows nothing about the reason for her disappearance, is heartbroken, falls ill, and nearly dies. In the aftermath, he returns to Devonshire with his mother and, after awhile, Taffy and the Laird also return home to England.

Years later, the three friends are reunited in London, where they attend a musical performance featuring the diva called "La Svengali," the "wonder of the hour," a songstress whose voice has created a sensation throughout Europe. Billee is astonished to discover that La Svengali is in fact, Trilby, who is now married to Svengali, although she seems like an entirely different person; she does not even recognize her former fiancé.

Svengali's hypnotized slave is transformed into a diva in this du Maurier illustration for *Trilby* (1894).

Billee happens to encounter Svengali at a post office, where the maestro attacks him for no apparent reason. The stalwart Taffy intervenes and then publicly humiliates Svengali, who is too cowardly to defend his honor in a duel. The three friends contrive to bring matters to a head by purchasing front-row tickets to La Svengali's next performance, where Billee will be clearly visible to Trilby. When Svengali perceives their presence he is so upset that he retreats from the conductor's podium to a booth high up in the theater, where he goes into an apoplectic fit and dies of a heart attack. Suddenly freed from the maestro's mesmeric influence, Trilby reverts back to her original self and is unable to sing. Her career as La Svengali is over.

Trilby has no memory of her life while under Svengali's mental domination, and now that she is free from his influence her health rapidly deteriorates. It soon becomes apparent that she is dying, and the three friends lovingly care for her during her final months. On her deathbed, Trilby seems to fall back into a mesmeric trance, and dies calling out, "Svengali, Svengali, Svengali." After her death, Billee is so bereft that he dies of a broken heart.

The story of Trilby and Svengali takes up only a portion of the novel; the rest is devoted to Parisian travelogue, various Gallic character studies and the travails of the three musketeers in their bohemian Latin Quarter existence. Subsequent theatrical and cinematic adaptations have focused on the Trilby/Svengali narrative and discarded the rest. George du Maurier (the grandfather of gothic novelist Daphne du Maurier) was a caricaturist for *Punch*, and *Trilby* is lavishly illustrated by the author in the manner of a modern graphic novel. Despite the work's unusual premise, there is no attempt at creating a mood of the fantastic or horrific; instead, the book tends to concentrate on bohemian rhapsody and the dramatic interplay between the various eccentric characters.

Trilby was an enormously popular success and was adapted into a long-running play on the London stage in 1895, in which Herbert Beerbohm Tree played Svengali. Tree's production was so popular that the proceeds enabled him to establish Her Majesty's Theater and the Royal Academy of Dramatic Arts. The play soon migrated to America, where its popularity continued for decades. Warner Bros. produced a screen version, entitled *Svengali*, in 1931, which was directed by Archie Mayo and starred the distinguished actor John Barrymore in the title role.

Unlike many of the other Victorian era classics, however, *Trilby* has fallen into relative obscurity. Part of the reason for its present inaccessibility may be due to the rambling, unfocused nature of the narrative and writing that frequently shifts from English to French and other languages, thereby confusing monolingual readers. Another reason is the rabidly anti–Semitic depiction of Svengali, who is portrayed as a diabolical figure with a hook nose and pointed ears and beard in the author's illustrations that would be right at home in a Nazi-era anti–Semitic tract.

The Svengali character represents the first example of a psychic vampire in a major work of literature. He not only mesmerizes his victim but drains the life force out of her as well. Du Maurier never explains, however, how Svengali has acquired his hypnotic acumen. His sinister qualities are not overly emphasized, and he is presented as a cartoonish buffoon, a caricature of a degenerate Jew rather than an evil mastermind with supernatural powers.

Literary critics have pointed out similarities between *Trilby* and *Dracula*, citing du Maurier's novel and its theatrical adaptation as a major influence on Stoker's vampire tale. Tree's major theatrical rival was the renowned Victorian actor Henry Irving, whose manager was Bram Stoker. Svengali and the Count have a lot in common, including their Eastern European origin, their degenerate appearance, their choice of female victims, and their mesmeric powers. Both novels feature sainted female characters suffering through wasting illnesses while surrounded by groups of adoring men. In his book *Hollywood Gothic*, David J. Skal notes that du Maurier "describes Svengali as an 'incubus,' and in one memorable illustration depicts him as half-human and half-spider—just as Stoker would present Dracula as a creepy amalgam of man, lizard and bat. In his human form, Svengali provides a much closer physical model for Dracula than any of Irving's characterizations. He has the profile of a predatory bird, not to mention pointed ears. Svengali sports a beard, a style Dracula adopts for a couple of scenes."[5] Other literary historians have pointed out that Stoker was well into the writing of *Dracula* when du Maurier's novel appeared, but it seems reasonable to assume there was some cross-pollination, even on an unconscious level, between the two works.

Another weird tale of psychic vampirism by a major Victorian writer was published in 1894, when Sir Arthur Conan Doyle's story "The Parasite" appeared. The narrative unfolds in the form of the diary entries of one Austin Gilroy, a professor of physiology at an unnamed university. Devoted to reason and the scientific method, Gilroy stands in opposition to his fellow academic, Professor Wilson, a psychologist who studies psychic phenomena, a subject that the pragmatic Gilroy disdains.

Wilson invites Gilroy and his fiancée, Agatha Marden, to a party at his home where he hopes to demonstrate the reality of the psychic realm to the skeptical professor. At the party, they are introduced to Miss Penclosa, a dowdy, fortyish woman with a crippled leg, who has recently arrived in England from Trinidad. Wilson informs Gilroy that Miss Penclosa possesses the power of mesmeric trance, and arranges for her to demonstrate her mental powers upon Agatha.

The mysterious Miss Penclosa rises to the occasion by putting Agatha into a state of "mesmeric sleep," and gives her a secret post-hypnotic suggestion, a "private test" that will be enacted at ten o'clock on the following morning. She also gives Gilroy a note, to be read after the test has taken place. The next day, at nine-thirty, Agatha pays a visit to the professor and explicitly tells him that their engagement is off. Despite Gilroy's entreaties, Agatha is adamant, leaving him dumbfounded. Then, at ten o'clock, he remembers Miss Penclosa's note, and reads therein that his fiancée's odd behavior was merely a demonstration of her hypnotic abilities, and that Agatha will remember nothing of the incident afterwards, which proves to be true.

His scientific world-view having been turned on its head, Gilroy pays a visit to Miss Penclosa, who indulges his curiosity by explaining the basis of her hypnotic powers. She claims to be able to project her consciousness inside another person's body during the mesmeric trance in order to control the actions of people at a distance. While she is thus engaged, her body falls into a state of lethargy which can become life-threatening. Intrigued by this strange phenomenon, the professor arranges to be placed into a trance in order to study the mesmeric effect subjectively.

Gilroy's experiment proceeds as Miss Penclosa conducts numerous sessions in which he is put into a mesmeric sleep. At first the experiences are exhilarating as he glimpses visions of dreamlike worlds, but he soon becomes tired and drained as a result of the sessions. The mesmerist, meanwhile, seems to gain in vitality, as if she is absorbing his life force. Finally, it becomes obvious to Gilroy that Miss Penclosa has fallen in love with him. The professor is appalled, but the mesmerist's psychic hold on him is so strong that he cannot help but continue with the experiments.

The hypnotist exerts all her powers to pry Gilroy away from Agatha as they become locked in a battle of wills. She clouds his mind to such an extent that he is unable to deliver his lectures coherently and is soon in danger of losing his professorship along with his marriage. But the energy she has expended in controlling Gilroy's actions start to take a toll on Miss Penclosa's health. In a final, desperate attempt to strike out at her rival, she compels the professor to bring a bottle of sulfuric acid into Agatha's room with the aim of disfiguring her for life. The effort proves to be too great for the mesmerist, who has expended all her powers. Miss Penclosa dies suddenly, freeing Gilroy from her spell.

Occult scholar Montague Summers was the first to note that "The Parasite" was a vampire story in a survey of the literature in his book *The Vampire: His Kith and Kin* (1928), describing Miss Penclosa as "a human vampire or psychic sponge." Of course, all vampires are parasitic in nature. In 1924, Conan Doyle wrote the Sherlock Holmes story "The Adventure of the Sussex Vampire," in which the case turns out to have a conventional explanation and Holmes scoffs at the notion of vampires. "The Parasite" reveals the author's intense interest in occult and psychic phenomena, a fascination that would consume him later in his life.

Like *Trilby*, "The Parasite" presents a psychic individual with mesmeric powers who is able to control others and force them to perform self-destructive acts, although Miss Penclosa is a much more sympathetic character than Svengali. Both works exhibit a Victorian fascination with mesmerism that would culminate in *Dracula*. The protagonist, Professor Gilroy, is a man of science whose skepticism is challenged only after personal experimentation and direct observation of the phenomenon in question. Like Sherlock Holmes, he has no use for illogical thought or intuition. "I have trained myself to deal only with fact and with proof," he narrates. "Surmise and fancy have no place in my scheme of thought. Show me what I can see, with my microscope, cut with my scalpel, weigh in my balance, and I will devote a lifetime to its investigation."[6] In this case, however, the scientific method comes up wanting as Gilroy ultimately cannot reconcile Miss Penclosa's powers with the material world of science.

As is evident from the continuing popularity of his fiction, Conan Doyle knew how to spin a good yarn, and "The Parasite" offers up a suspenseful, inventive narrative that remains fresh, even by today's standards. The psychic vampire, Miss Penclosa, is drawn both as a pathetic, lovelorn figure and as a threatening psychic menace, while the plight of the hapless Professor Gilroy is truly horrendous. This early story was one of a number of science fiction and horror tales concocted by Conan Doyle during his long literary career.

Another Victorian author, popular at the time but who has fallen into relative obscurity, was Mary Elizabeth Braddon (1835–1915). A prolific novelist who is estimated to have penned over ninety books, she was the most popular female author of the period. She wrote "penny dreadfuls," serialized novels of mystery, sensation and adventure that touched on themes of crime, medicine, science and horror. In 1896, her tale of scientific vampirism, entitled "Good Lady Ducayne," was published in *The Strand Magazine*.

Miss Bella Rolleston is the story's protagonist, a young ambitious London woman who is living in poverty and striving to support herself and her mother. She registers with an employment agency that procures a position for her as a companion for a rich, elderly gentlewoman, the Lady Adeline Ducayne, for the princely sum of a hundred pounds a year. Lady Ducayne gives the impression of advanced age, with "a face so wasted by age that it seemed only a pair of eyes and a peaked chin.... Claw-like fingers, flashing with jewels, lifted a double eyeglass to Lady Ducayne's shining black eyes, and through the glasses Bella saw those unnaturally bright eyes magnified to a gigantic size, and glaring at her awfully."[7] Bella's lack of references and other considerations are waived in favor of the young woman's robust good health.

Bella accepts the position, and the pair travel to Italy, where the Lady lives in seclusion in a hotel in the backwater town of Cap Ferrino. At first Bella is charmed by her surroundings, and her duties attending to Lady Ducayne are minimal, allowing her ample free time. She makes the acquaintance of another young English woman, Lotta Stafford, and Lotta's brother, Herbert, who has just passed his physician's exams. But when Lotta and Herbert leave to tour Genoa and Pisa, Bella falls into a state of melancholy. Cooped up with the old woman, her health begins to fail. She is further chagrined when she accidentally overhears two hotel guests discussing the fact that Lady Ducayne's previous two companions had been healthy young women who suddenly became ill and died. Needing the money for her impoverished mother, she decides to stay on with her employer despite her misgivings.

Fearing for her health, she begins receiving treatments from Ducayne's Italian physician, Dr. Paravicini, a seemingly harmless, inoffensive man who has a private sitting-room, where he experiments "in chemistry and natural science—perhaps in alchemy." But the doctor's treatments don't work, and Bella begins to have disturbing dreams and awakens the following morning, only to discover strange wounds on her arms. Paravicini ascribes the wounds to "mosquito bites."

By a fortuitous circumstance, Herbert and Lotta return to Cap Ferrino, and the young doctor is appalled by Bella's listless condition. He examines her and finds the wounds, and the young doctor realizes the truth. Dr. Paravicini has been drugging Bella and transfusing her blood into the veins of Lady Ducayne in order to keep the withered crone alive beyond her natural years. In this manner she has killed many young girls over the years and used their blood to extend her life span. Herbert confronts Lady Ducayne with this scenario and threatens to expose her to the authorities, whereupon she releases Bella from her service and vows to abandon her vampiric pursuits. Bella is given a sum of money to assure her silence and she winds up marrying Herbert.

The story is presented as a gothic mystery that suggests an occult agency is at work, but ultimately unravels into a non-supernatural dénouement. Like *Carmilla* and *Trilby*, the plot of "Good Lady Ducayne" centers around the slow, wasting illness of the primary female character, a motif that will later appear in *Dracula*. As in Polidori's "The Vampyre," the villain is an aristocrat, and the Lady Ducayne is a particularly loathsome one, as she literally sucks the lifeblood from a helpless member of a lower social class. There are historical echoes of Elizabeth Bathory (1560–1614), the infamous Hungarian "blood countess" who reportedly bathed in the blood of her servant girls in order to preserve her youth. Bathory has been the subject of a number of vampire films, including *Countess Dracula* (1970), *Daughters of Darkness* (1971) and *Immoral Tales* (1974).

Mary Elizabeth Braddon's mysterious tale of black medicine and scientific vampirism is told in crisp, clear prose, with a finely drawn cast of characters involved in an intriguing plot. "Good Lady Ducayne" is the first story to explicitly link those two mainstays of horror cinema and literature: the vampire and the mad scientist. Indeed, vampires and laboratories would prove to be a heady mix. Blood transfusion, still a novelty to Victorian medical science, is one of the story's key plot elements, and the procedure would also figure in several scenes in *Dracula*. The story seems to have been the inspiration for Ricardo Freda's *I Vampiri* (a.k.a. *The Devil's Commandment*, 1956), a gothic horror film in which a doctor uses blood to restore the youth of a decadent countess, as well as other sci-fi horror films in which a mad doctor must extract some vital fluid from a living person in order to preserve a woman's youth, such as *The Corpse Vanishes* (1942) or *The Leech Woman* (1960).

The year 1897 witnessed the publication of Abraham "Bram" Stoker's *Dracula*, the most famous vampire tale in history, and the inspiration for a seemingly endless number of plays, movies, literary sequels, comic books and sundry other cultural manifestations. Stoker's novel begins with the journey of English solicitor Jonathan Harker to Count Dracula's castle in Transylvania to conclude the sale of Carfax, a house in the London suburb of Purfleet. Harker soon learns that the Count is an inhuman creature with supernatural powers as he observes Dracula skittering down the vertical face of the castle like a gecko and summoning the wolves of the forest. It becomes apparent that Harker is a prisoner in Castle Dracula as he helplessly watches the vampire depart for England along with boxes of his native earth.

The scene then shifts to England, where Harker's fiancée, Mina Murray, awaits Jonathan's return by visiting her friend Lucy Westenra in Whitby, a seaside town in North Yorkshire. Miss Westenra has three suitors: Dr. John Seward, the head of a mental hospital; Texan Quincey Morris; and Arthur Holmwood, whom she chooses to marry. During her visit, a violent storm blows a derelict Russian schooner, the *Demeter*, into Whitby harbor. A searchlight trained on the ship reveals a ghastly scene: the ship's captain, dead, lashed to the wheel. As the *Demeter* sails eerily into the harbor, Dracula, in wolf form, leaps off the ship and goes bounding away into the woods. A boarding party finds the entire crew missing, and the ship's log documents the presence of a mysterious stowaway on board, a strange man who is responsible for the disappearance of the crew.

Soon afterward, Lucy begins to walk in her sleep and is lured out of the house one night to a rendezvous with Dracula. After her encounter with the vampire, she begins to suffer from a mysterious wasting illness similar to severe anemia, although no physiological cause can be found for her condition. In the meantime, Jonathan turns up in a hospital in Budapest suffering from a brain fever, with no knowledge of how he escaped from Dracula's castle. Mina hastens to join her fiancé, and while she is nursing him back to health, the two are married.

Failing to find an effective treatment for Lucy, Seward calls in Dr. Abraham Van Helsing, an eccentric Dutch physician and expert on rare diseases, who has suspicions about the nature of her illness. After several blood transfusions, Lucy expires. After her death, a strange woman begins preying on children in the area and draining them of their blood. Jonathan and Mina return to London, where Mina comes down with symptoms identical to Lucy's. Van Helsing is now convinced that the women are the victims of a vampire, and that Lucy has become one of the undead. In a grisly scene, he leads Holmwood, Morris and Seward to Lucy's tomb, where they find she has indeed become a vampire, and drive a stake through her heart.

Once Jonathan has regained his strength, he joins the vampire hunters in their search for Dracula's boxes of native earth, which are essential to his sustenance. Mina, for her protection, is moved to Dr. Seward's asylum, but the feeble-minded mental patient Renfield lets Dracula inside, where the vampire forces Mina to drink some of his blood before he is chased away by Van Helsing and his crew. The vampire hunters are successful in neutralizing all of Dracula's earth boxes except one, which the Count uses to aid him in his escape from England. He charters a ship to take him back to Transylvania, but fearing that Mina will become a vampire even if Dracula returns to his native land, the team sets out in hot pursuit.

Dracula uses his powers of sorcery to speed the ship on its way by controlling the winds, but Van Helsing, Jonathan, Mina and the others use the telegraph, the railway system, a steam launch and other modern inventions to aid them. In addition, Van Helsing is able to hypnotize Mina, who has a telepathic mind link with the Count, to help ascertain Dracula's whereabouts. The team manages to catch up with the vampire on the road to Castle Dracula, where they dispatch the Count to the netherworld, thereby freeing Mina from the vampire's spell.

Dracula, and the similarly themed *Trilby,* were the most widely read novels of the period, and both went on to highly successful adaptations on the stage. Stoker's novel is written in the "epistolary" style, that is, as a collection of letters, diary entries, telegrams, newspaper clippings and so forth, a literary form that was popularized in 19th century novels, such as Wilkie Collins's *The Woman in White* (1860) and Robert Louis Stevenson's *The Strange Case of Dr. Jekyll and Mr. Hyde* (1888), but can be off-putting to the modern reader. As many critics have noted, Stoker's skills as a writer leave much to be desired. His characters, with the exception of the Count himself, are weak and forgettable, the dialogue is stilted and frequently lapses into passages written in laughable dialect (such as Van Helsing's fractured English), and many descriptive passages are flat and have an indistinct sense of place. Yet there are also scenes of nightmarish horror that still have the power to shock, such as Jonathan's ordeal in Castle Dracula, the entrance of the ghost ship into Whitby harbor, and the staking of Lucy.

In the novel, the vampire is clearly a creature of the supernatural realm. Van Helsing enumerates some of the Count's occult powers thus: "This vampire which is among us is of himself so strong in person as twenty men ... he have still the aids of necromancy ... the divination by the dead, and all the dead that he can come nigh to are for him at command; ... he can, within his range, direct the elements; the storm, the fog, the thunder; he can command all the meaner things: the rat, and the owl, and the bat—the moth, and the fox, and the wolf; he can grow and become small; and he can at times vanish and come unknown."[8] Thus the vampire partakes of the folkloric powers of both the ghost and the shape-shifting sorcerer. Yet Dracula does not inhabit the mythical realm of the past; he is a denizen of the scientific age.

His chief opponents are both scientists, Dr. Seward, the psychiatrist who records his diary on a phonograph machine (a science fictional device circa 1897), and Dr. Van Helsing, who is described as "a philosopher and a metaphysician, and one of the most advanced scientists of his day." Van Helsing is clearly a descendent of Le Fanu's Dr. Hesselius, who was also a physician, occultist and practitioner of "metaphysical medicine," as well as a student of vampirism. Stoker's vampires are presented as a real-world phenomenon, akin to an exotic, malignant disease. "The strength of the vampire," Van Helsing explains, "is that no one will believe in him," in the secularized culture of 19th century England. Only a man with a foot in both worlds, like Van Helsing, can recognize, diagnose and cure the illness of vampirism.

Stoker even suggests that the Count himself is a variety of scientist. "He was in life a most wonderful man," Van Helsing explicates. "Soldier, statesman and alchemist—which latter was the highest development of the science-knowledge of his time. He had a mighty brain, a learning beyond compare.... He dared even attend the Scholomance, and there was no branch of knowledge of his time that he did not essay."[9] The Scholomance was a school for evil magicians, located among the mountains over Lake Hermanstadt, where, according to legend, the devil claims the tenth scholar as his due. One of the primary skills taught there was the manipulation of the weather, a skill that Dracula may have acquired through its teachings. Van Helsing also speaks of Dracula "experimenting, and doing it well" in his dealings with the vampire hunters and with Renfield.

Dracula can be read as a parable of science against sorcery as the vampire pits his supernatural powers against the 19th century technology of his foes. From the moment that Dracula reaches England he is confronted with this technology, as his ship, the *Demeter*, is caught in the glare of an electric searchlight as it glides into Whitby harbor. When the vampire drains Lucy's blood, it is replenished by Van Helsing's blood transfusions. In the final chapters, as the Count is using his occult powers to speed his ship back to Transylvania, Van Helsing's team counters by racing ahead via the Orient Express, using a steam-powered launch to navigate the local rivers, and employing the instantaneous communications of the telegraph system to keep track of Dracula's whereabouts. In the end, science triumphs over sorcery.

The Count has many attributes of the super-powered characters that would later emerge in pulp fiction and comic books. Like Superman, he has a clearly defined set of supernormal powers (super-strength, shape-shifting, control of the weather, etc.) and weaknesses (garlic, the cross, sunlight, and so forth), and can be considered the world's first super-villain. Dracula would be transformed into a superhero during the 1960s in a Dell Comics series, and as a Marvel Comics villain in the 1970s, and this concept would provide the basis for the super-vamps featured in the *Blade* and *Twilight* movies of the 21st century.

In the year after *Dracula*'s publication, England was again invaded by vampires, but of a very different sort, in H.G. Wells's classic alien invasion novel *The War of the Worlds* (1898). The story is told through the viewpoint of an unnamed science journalist who is researching a series of anomalous events observed on the surface of the planet Mars by astronomers. Shortly thereafter, a cylindrical projectile lands in a field near his home village of Woking, Surrey, and the narrator hastens to investigate the strange occurrence. He watches as the cylinder unscrews and disgorges Martians, who resemble bug-eyed octopi.

The Martians' intent is soon made manifest as they proceed to slaughter a group of curious onlookers with a heat ray. Soon, other cylinders are landing around the countryside, and giant tripod war machines stride about, wreaking havoc. The aliens cut a wide swath of destruction through England as British 19th century military technology proves to be powerless against the Martian heat ray and poison-gas weaponry. An apocalyptic holocaust ensues as London is decimated and millions flee in panic and are cut down by the invaders. The narrator watches as one of the tripods gathers up a group of humans with its metal tentacles and deposits them alive inside a utility basket. "It was the first time I realized," he observes, "that the Martians might have any other purpose than destruction with defeated humanity."[10]

After witnessing these horrible events, the narrator and a curate take refuge in an abandoned house near the village of Sheen, but they are trapped inside the house when a Martian cylinder lands nearby. They manage to stay hidden for almost two weeks while the narrator observes the Martians at close range. He soon learns that the creatures are vampires who directly transfuse the blood of humans into their bodies. "They were heads—merely heads," the narrator explains. "They did not eat, much less digest. Instead, they took the fresh, living blood of other creatures and *injected* it into their own veins ... blood from a still living animal, in most cases from a human being, was run directly by means of a little pipette into the recipient canal."[11]

On Mars, the vampiric aliens subsist on blood from a race of bipedal, vaguely humanoid creatures, a few of which were taken along for the interplanetary journey and drained en route. The Martians make a hideous hooting noise as they are preparing

A Martian war machine searches for blood donors in this 1906 illustration for a Belgian edition of H.G. Wells's novel *The War of the Worlds* (1897) by artist Henrique Alvim Correa.

to ingest blood. "Their peculiar hooting invariably preceded feeding; it had no modulation, and was, I believe, in no sense a signal, but merely the expiration of air preparatory to the suctional operation."[12] From his hidden vantage point the narrator observes the Martians feeding upon a middle-aged man they have captured. One of the tripods extracts the unfortunate individual from a cage-like structure on its back with a tentacle and hurls him into a pit. "He vanished behind the mound, and for a moment there was silence. And then began a shrieking and a sustained and cheerful hooting from the Martians."[13]

Eventually their sanctuary is discovered, and the Martians invade the house where the narrator and the curate are hiding. The curate is dragged outside by a war machine's tentacle, while the narrator manages to hide in a coal cellar. After a few days he emerges to find the Martians have withdrawn from their nearby encampment. Wandering around the countryside, he finds it empty of both man and Martian. When he reaches London he finds the city mostly deserted and the great tripod war machines standing idle. The Martians have succumbed to diseases caused by earthly germs, for which the aliens have no acquired immunity.

The mother of all alien invasion epics, Wells's novel contains vivid scenes of mass destruction that achieved even more cultural resonance in Orson Welles's infamous 1938 radio broadcast that panicked America, and in George Pal's 1953 blockbuster version made during the early years of the atomic age. Neither of these iterations, however, touched on Wells's concept of the Martians as extraterrestrial vampires, although this was depicted in the 2005 Steven Spielberg adaptation.

Like Count Dracula, Wells's Martians are described as being degenerate creatures that have devolved from a previously human state. The author explains that their evolution into blood-drinking organisms has simplified their internal anatomy.

> Strange as it may seem to a human being, all the complex apparatus of digestion, which makes up the bulk of their bodies, did not exist in the Martians.... The physiological advantages of the practice of [blood] injection are undeniable, if one thinks of the tremendous waste of human time and energy occasioned by eating and the digestive process. Our bodies are half made up of glands and tubes and organs, occupied in turning heterogeneous food into blood. The digestive processes and their reaction upon the nervous system sap our strength and color our minds. Men go happy or miserable as they have healthy or unhealthy livers, or sound gastric glands. But the Martians were lifted above all these organic fluctuations of mood and emotion.[14]

Wells seems to look approvingly upon the Martian anatomy, and speculates that mankind may someday evolve into similar organisms without the burdens of human feelings.

Wells's depictions of Martian blood drinking are as horrific as the vampiric exploits of Count Dracula. His alien vampires were the precursors of a long line of extraterrestrial bloodsuckers appearing in films such as *The Thing from Another World* (1951), *Not of This Earth* (1956), *Plan 9 from Outer Space* (1959), *It! The Terror from Beyond Space* (1958), *Planet of the Vampires* (1965) and *Queen of Blood* (1966). A full-scale invasion by alien vampires, however, didn't occur onscreen until the release of Tobe Hooper's *Lifeforce* (1985).

On the literary scene, however, more vampires were on their way over from Mars in a pair of novels by French science fiction writer Gustave Le Rouge, *The Prisoner of Planet Mars* (*Le Prisonnier de la Planète Mars,* 1908) and its sequel, *The War of the Vampires* (*La Guerre des Vampires,* 1909). In *Prisoner,* protagonist Robert Darvel, an

American engineer obsessed with communicating with other worlds, travels to the Chelambrum monastery in Tibet to meet with Prince Ardavena, a ruler and mystic who has similar interests. Ardavena convinces Darvel to construct a "psychic energy condenser," a device which will focus the paranormal energies of a thousand Hindu holy men into a metal chamber, which will enable communication with other planets. When Darvel attempts to use the energy condenser, instead of merely sending a message to Mars he is catapulted bodily through the void to the Red Planet.

Darvel finds that much of Mars is swampland, the remains of the planet's oceans. He encounters many fantastic creatures in this alien landscape, including giant crabs, giant clams and giant moles, and is almost killed by a predacious squid-like monster with bloodsucking tentacles. He also comes across a docile group of diminutive, pre-technological humans who are dominated by the Erloors, a race of nocturnal, bat-winged, humanoid vampires. These bat people are subservient to another vampire race of invisible Erloors, who, in turn, are dominated by a bodiless Great Brain, an intelligence who rules the planet from a fortress concealed inside a crystal mountain. Darvel attempts to pull the plug on the Brain's power source and almost succeeds, but at the last minute the Brain responds by sending him back to Earth.

Alien vampires from Mars are pictured in this early cover illustration for H.G. Wells's *The War of the Worlds* (1898).

In the sequel, *The War of the Vampires*, Darvel learns that fifteen of the invisible Erloors have accompanied him back to Earth. Fortunately, Darvel has devised a special helmet that enables him to see the invisible vampires, who have large, bulbous heads, bulging eyes, diaphanous wings and tentacle-like fingers. These Erloors want Darvel to return to Mars to finish off the Great Brain, who holds them enslaved, and when he refuses they wreak havoc, abduct his fiancée and hide her in a cave. Darvel manages to track the creatures to their lair, dispose of them, and rescue his beloved.

An explorer from Earth encounters a bat-winged Martian vampire in this illustration for Gustave Le Rouge's interplanetary adventure *The Prisoner of Planet Mars* (1908).

Obscure today, Le Rouge was a popular science fiction writer of his time who is credited with moving sci-fi away from the juvenile adventure fiction of Jules Verne and toward a more mature form. His fantastic Martian landscapes have been compared to those of C.S. Lewis in his novel *Out of the Silent Planet* and may have inspired Edgar Rice Burroughs's Red Planet romance, *A Princess of Mars*. Martian slaves ruled by a disembodied brain would later appear in William Cameron Menzies's classic sci-fi film *Invaders from Mars* (1953).

Taking his cue from Wells, Le Rouge offers up an entire planet dominated by vampires. His Erloors are wonderfully imaginative creations that unite the traditional bat-winged imagery of the supernatural vampire with the science fiction concept of the alien. He vividly describes their dirty yellow-colored membranous wings, their protruding, blood-red lips and the eyes, which are "scarlet-rimmed like those of an albino, set in a bloodless face." Le Rouge's extraterrestrial vampires are more anthropomorphic and more vivid than the big-brained, bug-eyed Martian octopi depicted in *The War of the Worlds*.

Another European writer of the early 20th century whose work has become undeservedly obscure today is the German novelist and scenarist Hanns Heniz Ewers. Widely considered one of the modern masters of macabre fiction, his writings have been suppressed because of his association with the Nazis. Ironically, Ewers's works were banned in Germany during the mid–1930s for their moral depravity, and his assets and property were seized. He died in poverty in Berlin in 1943.

Earthling scientists capture a Martian vampire in Gustave Le Rouge's sequel *War of the Vampires* (1909).

Ewers wrote the screenplay for one of the first works of German Expressionist cinema, *The Student of Prague*, directed by Stellan Rye in 1913 and starring the acclaimed German actor Paul Wegener. An eerie Faustian tale of a deal with the Devil and man haunted by his evil *doppelgänger*, it was remade by Henrik Galeen in 1926 and stars Conrad Veidt and Werner Krauss in the main roles. He also authored the memorable ghost/vampire short story "The Spider." Today, Ewers is best known for his trio of novels featuring a decadent antihero protagonist named Frank Braun, a world traveler, philosopher, and, ultimately, a vampire. The first book in the Braun trilogy, *The Sorcerer's Apprentice* (1910) does not concern vampirism, but the sequel, *Alraune*, is Ewers's most enduring work and a classic of vampire literature.

As the story begins, Frank Braun is discussing folklore concerning the mandrake plant with his uncle, Professor Jacob ten Brinken, an eminent man of means who is a privy counselor, a medical scientist and an ugly old lecher. According to legend, the mandrake plant (*alraune* in German) was thought to spring from the death ejaculation of an executed criminal. The mandrake was thought to have magical aphrodisiac qualities, but eventually brought pain, misfortune and miserable death to whoever possessed it. Braun has a brainstorm that ten Brinken should use his scientific skills to "create an alraune, one that will be alive, one of flesh and blood, a magic creature."

Enthralled by Braun's demented suggestion, ten Brinken concocts a bizarre experiment. He enlists the most debauched prostitute in the city, whose name, coincidentally, happens to be Alma Raune, to be artificially inseminated with the sperm of notorious rapist and murderer Peter Noerrissen, which is obtained upon his execution on the guillotine. Alma is sequestered in a clinic as the child is brought to term, but dies giving birth to a female, who is given the name Alraune.

The child is taken to ten Brinken's house, where she is to be brought up as his adopted daughter, but the girl soon shows signs of a cruel and unusual nature. When she is old enough to leave home, she is sent to a convent school, where she is eventually expelled for sleepwalking, torturing small animals and making a schoolmate swallow poison. Alraune comes to maturity in the Professor's household, where she dominates the old man and turns him into a shadow of his former self. She causes the death of the family coachman and manipulates two of her suitors into a fatal duel as her evil feminine persona comes into full maturity. Like her namesake, the mandrake plant, she spreads death and destruction around her.

Continuing her domination of the Professor, she acts seductively toward him, playing upon his depraved, incestuous lust. Manipulating his affairs, she brings him to financial and legal ruin. Facing imprisonment, for crimes of which he is innocent, ten Brinken opts to commit suicide. Before hanging himself he changes his will, appointing Frank Braun as his executor, in the hopes of ruining the man who suggested this folly to him.

Braun returns from lengthy travel in the Orient and assumes his duties as executor of the ten Brinken estate. Moving into the Professor's house, he is brought into close contact with the unnatural woman, but Alraune has met her match in the decadent, worldly Braun, and the two quickly become lovers. Braun then initiates her into practices of erotic vampirism with which he has become familiar on his travels. "It was he who had first taught her how pleasant was the drunkenness induced by sipping little drops of blood of one's beloved. Her thirst, however, was unquenchable, her desire insatiable."[15]

One night she wounds Braun with a knife and nearly sucks him dry. Their erotic liaison begins to degenerate into a love/hate relationship fraught with mistrust as each plans the death of the other. Finally, Alraune, seized in a fit of somnambulism, sleepwalks naked out onto the roof of the house, and when someone shouts her name she awakens and falls to her death.

Unlike the staid world of British Victorian fiction, Ewers's story unfolds in the decadent demi-monde of fin-de-siècle Germany, a milieu more depraved than anything in Oscar Wilde's fiction. Ewers's demented tale of tainted love, medical experimentation, incest, morbidity, suicide and vampirism is nonetheless a fascinating excursion into the macabre. *Alraune* combines elements of both *Frankenstein* and *Dracula* in its depiction of an artificial being of pure evil who has a taste for blood. The mandrake woman provided the template for many science fiction *femmes fatales* that followed, including Miriam Blaylock, the alien bloodsucker in Whitley Streiber's seminal sci-fi vampire novel *The Hunger* (1981). Pre-Nazi eugenics figures largely in the plot, the moral of the story being that people with undesirable genetic traits should not be allowed to breed.

In spite of its depravity, *Alraune* struck a chord with the German public, being

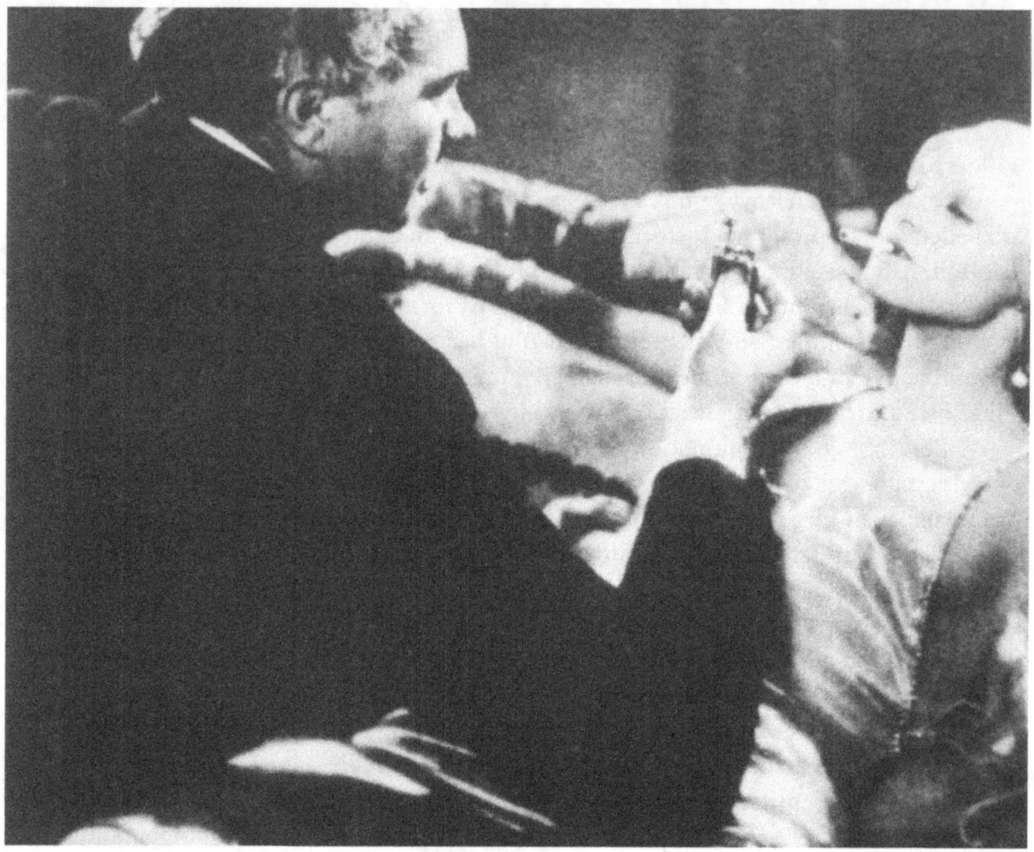

Paul Wegener as Professor Ten Brinken and Brigitte Helm as Alraune in the 1928 film version of the Hanns Heinz Ewers novel *Alraune*.

adapted for the screen numerous times, beginning with the first film version lensed in 1918, followed by a Hungarian version directed by Michael Curtiz in 1919. The best-known versions were made in Germany during the Weimar period, including a 1928 silent film entitled *Unholy Love* directed by Henrik Galeen starring Brigitte Helm as Alraune and Paul Wegener as Professor ten Brinken, and *Daughter of Evil*, a sound version which also starred Helm, directed by Richard Oswald. Another German adaptation, *Unnatural* (1952), was filmed by Arthur Maria Rabenalt, starring Hildegard Knef as Alraune, and Erich von Stroheim as ten Brinken.

All of the screen adaptations of the novel, however, focused on the relationship between ten Brinken and his creation, so the Frank Braun character was written out along with Alraune's vampirism. The Alraune character was surely the inspiration for the robot Maria in Fritz Lang's 1926 dystopian classic *Metropolis*, a soulless artificial woman who inspires men to acts of lust and violence, who was also played by Brigitte Helm. Helm also starred as the immortal psychic vampire queen of Atlantis in G.W. Pabst's *L'Atlantide* (1932). More recently, the deadly, genetically engineered alien beauty

Syl (Natasha Hentsridge) in *Species* (1995) is a direct descendent of the mandrake woman.

Vampire (1921), the third novel in the Frank Braun trilogy, continues Braun's misadventures after *Alraune*. As the novel opens, our antihero is traveling around the world in a tramp steamer when World War I breaks out. Unable to return to Germany, Braun manages to jump ship in San Francisco and travels to New York, where he becomes a political activist on behalf of pro–German groups in the United States. In New York he runs into a former lover, Lotte Levi, a beautiful, highly sensual Jewess, and the two resume their erotic relationship. But Braun has acquired a compulsion to drink blood, and experiences somnambulistic episodes during which he satisfies his bloodlust and has total amnesia afterwards. In order to allow Braun to further the cause of the Fatherland, patriotic German Lotte freely offers him blood from her breasts so that his vampirism will not compromise his duty.

Unlike *Alraune*, there's no science fiction element in the novel, as the vampirism is depicted as being psychological and erotic in nature. There is an eerie prescience, however, about the notion of a German vampire draining the blood of a Jew in a book written years before the Nazi regime came to power. Braun's political escapades in *Vampire* are an autobiographical reflection of the author's activities in America during World War I.

British writer Algernon Blackwood, whose forte was short stories dealing with supernatural topics such as "The Wendigo" and "Ancient Sorceries," turned to the subject of psychic vampirism in "The Transfer" (1912). The story is narrated by Miss Gould, a young woman who is employed as a governess at the country estate of the Frene family. The youngest of the Frene children, seven-year-old Jamie, has a fascination with a section of the garden dubbed the "Forbidden Corner," a barren patch in the garden in which nothing will grow. Jamie contends that there's something "bad" about the spot because it's not "fed" and can't get the food it wants. He brings the bare patch offerings of dead birds and mice he finds around the property, but the spot is still not nourished.

One summer day Mr. Frene's brother, Uncle Frank, is due to pay a visit to the Frene household. Miss Gould, who has the ability to clairvoyantly see inside of people, perceives that Uncle Frank feeds off the energy of others while draining their life force in the process. With her insight she observes that "he absorbed into himself all loose vitality that was to be had. His eyes and voice and presence devitalized you.... So this is how I saw him—a great human sponge, crammed and soaked with the life, or proceeds of life, absorbed from others—stolen. My idea of a human vampire was satisfied."[16]

During Uncle Frank's visit, he is inexplicably drawn to the Forbidden Corner, where he confronts a power similar to his own, only stronger, and gets caught in a spell that Miss Gould alone can perceive. "What actually happened, I clearly understood, was that all this vitality and life he had transferred from others to himself for years was now in turn being taken from him and transferred—elsewhere."[17] Uncle Frank loses consciousness, and is never the same afterwards, but the empty patch is revitalized, and becomes a section of the garden that is "very strong, full-fed, and bursting with life."

Blackwood, like his fellow British writer Arthur Conan Doyle, was fascinated by psychic phenomena. He would later create an ESP-enabled psychic detective named John Silence as a counterpoint to the psi-agnostic Sherlock Holmes. Like Conan Doyle's "The Parasite," Blackwood's story is also about psychic vampirism, but "The Transfer" presents two psychic vampires in conflict with one another. The human "psychic sponge," Uncle Frank, must contend with a psychic vampire from the vegetable kingdom. Oddly, the reader's sympathy is with the "Forbidden Corner" that gives Uncle Frank his comeuppance, and the unfortunate man becomes a kind of human sacrifice to the forces of nature. A third psychic viewpoint is that of Miss Gould, who is able to perceive the vampiric contest by means of her clairvoyant vision.

By the end of the Victorian Era, most of the basic science fiction vampire themes had been established. These would include vampires versus technology (*Dracula*), alien vampires (*The War of the Worlds, Prisoner of Mars*), mad scientists and vampires (*Good Lady Ducayne, Alraune*) and psychic vampires ("The Parasite," "The Transfer"). Some of the most inventive writers of the period, including H.G. Wells, Bram Stoker, Arthur Conan Doyle, Hanns Heinz Ewers and Algernon Blackwood, created works that continue to resonate today.

Moving into the 20th century, science fiction literature, which had been conceived in Europe, started to blossom into a distinct genre in America during the Golden Age of the pulp magazines. Printed on cheap, wood-pulp paper, these popular periodicals offered up sci-fi action and adventure stories to a mass audience on a monthly basis. Editor Hugo Gernsback published the first science fiction pulp, *Amazing Stories*, in 1926, which was followed by *Astounding Stories* in 1930 and a raft of imitators. Pulp writers would continue to explore the theme of the science fiction vampire in novel and interesting ways.

Unlike the fantasies of Verne and Wells, proponents of rocket science, such as the American Robert Goddard and the Germans Willy Ley and Herman Oberth, posited a practical means of transportation to neighboring worlds. Before the advent of unmanned interplanetary probes showed Mars and Venus to be lifeless worlds with hostile environments, it was taken for granted by science fiction writers that mankind would someday explore and colonize these nearby planets, which became the settings for all manner of sci-fi pulp adventures. Mars was thought to be an ancient desert planet well past its prime, while Venus was frequently depicted as a steaming-hot world of oceans and jungles.

One of the first female science fiction writers of the pulp era was Catherine Moore, who wrote under the name C.L. Moore. The wife of (and frequent collaborator with) fellow SF writer Henry Kuttner, Moore authored a series of tales about a Han Solo–type interplanetary outlaw and adventurer named Northwest Smith. In her first published story, "Shambleau" (1933), we are introduced to the steely-eyed Smith, who is concocting some illegal scheme in a Martian frontier town when he encounters a lynch mob in hot pursuit of a woman, whom they refer to as "Shambleau." Having pity on the victim, Smith faces down the crowd with heroic bravado and decides to take the woman, who possesses a strange kind of attraction, home with him.

Once they are safe in his lodgings, Smith takes a closer look at her. Shambleau has velvety brown skin, green eyes with pupils like a cat's that can see in the dark, clawed hands and hair concealed beneath an elaborate turban. Her command of language is limited, and she can only converse haltingly with him. Smith makes sexual advances toward the alien woman, but is repulsed by some animal quality about her. Nonetheless, he allows her to remain with him while he conducts his shady business dealings around town during the day, but at night he has strange dreams that some paralyzing force is enfolding him in an ecstatic but smothering embrace.

He awakens one night in a half-dreaming state, in which he observes the creature removing her turban, whereupon a torrent of blood-red, worm-like tendrils, writhing as if horribly alive, cascade down to the floor. The obscene tentacles, wet and slimy as entrails, enfold him as he lies helpless in a state of paralysis. He is transported into a state of ecstasy as he stares into Shambleau's green eyes, while her telepathic voice murmurs inside his mind, in a manner that is "promising, caressing, alluring, sweeter than honey." As he endures the obscene pleasures of her embrace, Smith is vaguely aware that she is sucking the very life force out of his body. Fortunately, his business partner, Yarol the Venusian, comes looking for Smith at his apartment and stumbles upon the horrific scene. While Smith pleads with Yarol to go away, the Venusian somehow breaks free of Shambleau's hypnotic control and dispatches her with a blast from his ray gun. Afterward, they speculate that the Shambleau race had traveled to Earth in antiquity and inspired the ancient Greek legends of the gorgon, Medusa.

Moore's short story is a tour de force of sci-fi horror that blends the two genres seamlessly into genre-blending unity and is even more remarkable for being her first published effort. The story first appeared in the November 1933 issue of *Weird Tales*, a pulp more associated with Lovecraftian horror than science fiction, and has been anthologized many times since. Like most vampire fiction, *Shambleau* deals with themes of sexuality and addiction as the male protagonist is drawn into a deadly web of desire and ecstasy from which he is only extricated by a fortuitous circumstance. Like her supernatural brethren, Shambleau possesses the power to hypnotize and immobilize her victims, and the story's climax, in which Smith is helplessly paralyzed as the creature preys on him, has the ambience of an episode of sleep paralysis. The Shambleau is a marvelous creation, a mythical creature that is part lamia and part gorgon, and arguably the most memorable alien vampire in all of SF literature. *Shambleau* may have provided the inspiration for the alien vampire woman in films, like Curtis Harrington's *Queen of Blood* (1966) and Tobe Hooper's *Lifeforce* (1985).

A subsequent Northwest Smith adventure, *Black Thirst* (1934), also deals with an alien vampire. This time Smith is on Venus pursuing one of his usual illegal ventures in a waterfront area when he encounters a fantastically beautiful alien woman. The bronze-haired beauty is a *minga*, one of a race of genetically engineered courtesans bred in a secret stronghold. The minga woman, whose name is Vaudir, convinces Smith to accompany her inside the stronghold, with promises of gold.

He follows as Vaudir leads him inside and through its twisty corridors to a room ominously draped in black velvet. There he confronts the master of the minga, an imposing male entity called the Alendar, who is lounging on a throne. The Alendar prevents Smith from using his ray gun via a telepathic command, and a lengthy monologue ensues. Smith is duly informed that the palace is a spawning ground for feminine beauty, upon which the Alendar, the last of an ancient race of psychic vampires, feeds. When the Alendar tells Smith he intends to feed upon Smith's male beauty, he somehow recovers his volition and blasts the vampire into oblivion, while Vaudir is also killed in the mêlée. Although *Black Thirst* is well-plotted and has plenty of creepy atmosphere, the story's main premise is not well developed, as no explanation is given as to how the psychic vampire "feeds" on beauty. There is also a hint of homoeroticism in the Alendar's threat to feed on Smith's male beauty.

Another pulp science fiction writer who explored the alien vampire theme was A.E. Van Vogt, author of such celebrated SF novels as *Slan* (1946), *The World of Null-A* (1948) and *The Voyage of the Space Beagle* (1950), this last providing some inspiration for both the *Star Trek* and *Alien* franchises. His story "Asylum" (1942) takes place on a future Earth in which there is a one-world government, interplanetary space travel and war and homicide have been eliminated by means of hypnotic mind-control techniques. Unknown to earthlings, a superior civilization called the Galactics has colonized Earth, which they judge to be in the third degree of development, and is secretly watching and guiding it toward joining the larger federation of worlds.

As the story opens, Earth is discovered by two alien vampires, Merla and Jeel, as their spaceship enters the solar system. They are Dreegs, a spacefaring race without a home planet who search for primitive, developing worlds to plunder. The Dreegs, who are super-intelligent, have lightning-fast reflexes and hypnotic powers of mind, and subsist on the blood and life force of less-advanced races. Merla and Jeel alert the Dreeg tribe to the location of Earth, where they hope to harvest several tankers of blood. First, however, they must find and neutralize a Galactic Observer, an official who is working incognito somewhere on Earth and can foil their plans.

The vampire couple lands on Earth and promptly slake their bloodlust by committing a double murder, the first homicides on the North American continent in twenty-seven years. The mysterious murders create a sensation, and William Leigh, ace news hound for the Planetarian News Service, is called in to report on the case. Merla and Jeel decide to exploit Leigh's information connections to discover the identity of the Observer, and soon have the hapless earthman in their power. Merla, however, forges an erotic bond with the reporter and relishes draining his blood and life force when their task is completed.

They find out that the Observer is Professor Garret Ungarn, an eccentric scientist who lives an isolated existence on a meteorite orbiting near Jupiter. The Dreegs hypnotize Leigh and send him on a mission to infiltrate Ungarn's home in Jupiter space and disable the energy screens that protect the Galactic outpost. Leigh manages to accomplish this, but when the vampires arrive on the meteorite they are in for an unpleasant surprise. As Merla is about to drain his blood, Leigh's personality is subsumed by a powerful Galactic being who drains the female vampire of most of her life force and makes the now-docile Dreegs leave the solar system, thus averting the bloodsuckers' invasion of Earth.

Van Vogt's space opera is a lively bit of pulp science fiction that caroms from a vampire ship in deep space to a futuristic Earth, and finally, to the lonely Galactic outpost near Jupiter. The best feature of "Asylum," however, is the alien vampire couple, Merla and Jeel, who are beautiful, sleek predators who revel in erotic murder. In this, they resemble the vampire duo in Whitley Streiber's novel *The Hunger* (1981). The Dreegs were the first vampiric extraterrestrials to invade Earth from outside the solar system, and may have provided inspiration for the space invaders in Roger Corman's *Not of This Earth* (1956) and Tobe Hooper's *Lifeforce* (1985).

Fritz Leiber is best known for his sword and sorcery tales featuring the heroic duo of Fafhrd and the Gray Mouser, and for his science fantasy novel *Conjure Wife* (1943), which was the basis for the acclaimed British horror film *Burn, Witch, Burn* (1962). In addition to his work in the horror and fantasy genres, Leiber also wrote science fiction novels such as *The Big Time* (1961), *The Silver Eggheads* (1962) and *The Wanderer* (1964). Leiber's short story "The Girl with the Hungry Eyes" (1949) is a classic tale of psychic vampirism.

As the story opens, Dave, a down-and-out professional photographer, is visited in his hole-in-the-wall studio by a model, referred to only as "the Girl," a young woman who is unusually photogenic and possesses a pair of peculiarly mesmerizing eyes. On a whim he shoots a photo spread of the Girl, which goes over big with his clients. Soon, advertising agencies are clamoring for the Girl's image, and ads featuring her visage are soon proliferating in magazines and on billboards. Dave's photography business is suddenly doing very well, but the Girl is not at all interested in the profits.

Outside of her camera-friendly qualities, the Girl seems to be completely ordinary, although she does make a number of peculiar demands on the photographer. She will work only with him, and will not reveal her name, her address, phone number or any personal details about her identity. She also insists that their business relationship be strictly platonic. He is even forbidden from following her once she leaves his studio.

Forced into a professional, non-sexual relationship with the enigmatic woman, Dave becomes obsessed with her. He comes to believe that she is able to telepathically focus men's desires on her image and feed upon their hungers. "There's vampires and vampires," he muses, "and not all of them suck blood."[18] Around this time a half-dozen mysterious deaths occur around the city. In all cases the victims are perfectly healthy men who die of apparent heart attacks. Mad with curiosity, Dave is finally motivated enough to break their pact and follow her. He watches as she picks up a gentleman, who drives away with her in his car. The next day the man's picture is in the newspaper, having been found in his car with his heart stopped in the same fashion as the other victims.

Compelled by some self-destructive urge, he demands to leave one night with the Girl. She consents, and they walk to a nearby park and find a deserted place, but instead of making love, she focuses her hungry eyes on him and starts telepathically absorbing his life force. "I want you," she says. "I want your high spots. I want everything that's made you happy and everything that's hurt you bad ... I want your wanting me. I want your life. Feed me, baby, feed me."[19]

Horrified, Dave finds the strength to free himself from her embrace and runs for his life. He never sees her again, but realizes the depth of her powers, which have been amplified by the arts of modern advertising. "She's the eyes that lead you on and on, and then show you death," he explains. "She's the creature you give everything for and never really get. She's the being that takes everything you've got and gives nothing in return. When you yearn toward her face on the billboards, remember that. She's the lure. She's the bait. She's the Girl."[20]

Leiber paints the nameless Girl as one of the most banal vampires in sci-fi literature, who possesses none of the aristocratic hauteur of Count Dracula or his ilk, but instead comes off as a proletarian. Her lack of breeding, however, does not make her any less deadly. Leiber builds a fine sense of mystery into the story while satirically portraying the Madison Avenue advertising industry as practicing a kind of psychic vampirism. The story was allegedly the basis for the 1993 film *The Girl with the Hungry Eyes*, directed by Jon Jacobs, but the movie bears little resemblance to Leiber's work.

Another memorable sci-fi take on the psychic vampire theme was C.M. Kornbluth's "The Mindworm" (1950). In the story's prologue, a naval officer and a nurse observe a nuclear test on a deserted Pacific atoll and afterwards have sex. The casual liaison leads to an unwanted pregnancy, but their reproductive systems have been irradiated and, as a result, the woman gives birth to a mutant male child, the Mindworm of the title, who possesses strange telepathic abilities.

The boy is sent to an orphanage, where he grows into a sickly, antisocial child. After a botched adoption, the Mindworm sets out on his own, living by his wits and his mind-reading powers. He finds he can kill people by exciting their emotions and telepathically draining their life force, an exchange which gives him sustenance. By probing inside their minds, he is able to manipulate their hopes and fears and create situations that enable him to suck the life out of them. He visits a craftsman and deliberately destroys his finest work, causing the man to go into a spasm of fury as the Mindworm feeds off his rage. Another victim is a young Hispanic girl he picks up who thinks he is a rich man who wants to marry her, but who suffers the same fate as he consumes her dreams along with her life.

After killing eight people in a movie house as their emotions surged while being moved by the film, the Mindworm is forced to leave the city as a police investigation closes in on him. He gets on a train at random and winds up in a West Virginia coal-mining town inhabited mostly by recent Eastern European immigrants. After feeding on one or two of the locals, he finds that he likes the flavor of the townspeople better than that of city folk and decides to stay awhile. The trouble is, he is unable to wrap his mind around the thoughts of the townsfolk because they are in a foreign language. After he kills an immigrant girl the community is aroused, and a group of older men take the matter into their own hands.

The Mindworm perceives their jumble of thoughts as the men approach: gobble-gobble whampyear—Whampyir—WAMPYIR! As the story concludes, "The sharpened stake was through his heart and the scythe blade through his throat before he could realize that he had not been the first of his kind; and that what clever people have not yet learned, some quite ordinary people have not yet entirely forgotten."[21]

"The Mindworm" is one of the first stories to re-invent the supernatural vampire in science fiction terms. Thus, the undead creature of sorcery is transformed into a genetic mutant with telepathic powers, a product of the atomic age. Kornbluth deftly takes the reader inside the mind of the psychic vampire as he trolls through the thoughts of the people around him, picking up random snatches of interior monologue in his effort to stalk his prey and evade the law. Like Leiber's Girl, the Mindworm is a stone cold murderer, a psychopath, and a serial killer who feeds on strong human emotions.

By the 1950s science fiction literature had moved beyond the pulp fiction phase and entered a new level of maturity and respectability. The lurid pulps had given way to slick SF magazines like *Galaxy*, and small presses had to contend with mass-market publishers like Doubleday and Ballantine. Space opera adventures had been replaced by thoughtful tales that revolved around hard scientific concepts, and a new generation of SF writers had arisen, including such luminaries as Isaac Asimov, John Wyndham, Ray Bradbury and Arthur C. Clarke. Another writer of the period whose work continues to have a deep resonance in popular culture is Richard Matheson, who worked extensively in film and television and penned some of the most memorable episodes of *The Twilight Zone*. Matheson's first SF novel, *I Am Legend* (1954), remains one of the classic works of science fiction horror.

As the novel opens, it is the year 1976. The last man on Earth, Robert Neville, is the only survivor of a plague that has turned every other human being into a vampire. Every night the vampires emerge from their hiding places to besiege his house, which has been built into a fortress designed to withstand their onslaughts. Neville, forced to endure the unendurable, is tormented by his loneliness, drinks heavily, and generally tries to cope with his horrific situation as best he can in his self-contained existence.

During the daylight hours Neville hunts down the vampires, who are allergic to garlic and the cross and can be killed by exposure to sunlight or a stake through the heart. In flashbacks he reveals how a germ, which may have been genetically engineered as a biological weapon by the U.S. government, was spread throughout the population by flies and mosquitoes, and how his wife died of the plague and returned as a vampire a year later.

Striving to understand his situation, he becomes an amateur scientist and begins to study the disease and discovers a bacterium that is responsible for the vampire plague. The bacillus re-animates the human body after death, creating the illusion of the living dead. It also keeps the host body away from sunlight, which is deadly to the germ. "And all without blood-eyed vampires hovering over heroines' beds," he muses. "All without bats fluttering against estate windows, all without the supernatural. The vampire was real. It was only that his true story had never been told."[22] In addition to the undead hordes, there are also "living vampires," demented individuals who are immune to the plague but merely believe themselves to be vampires.

One day Neville spots a feral dog that has somehow survived the plague. Desperate for companionship, he begins leaving food out for the animal and finally succeeds in luring it into his house. Despite his best ministrations, however, the dog soon dies, but Neville is now hopeful that there are other survivors of the vampire disease. His hopes are soon realized when he discovers a young woman, apparently alive, walking around in the sunlight. Stunned, he manages to cajole the reluctant woman into accompanying him back to his home. He learns that her name is Ruth, and that she has been on the run for a week after her husband was killed by the vampires. Neville is suspicious of her story, however, as she flinches when exposed to a plate of garlic. His fears are soon justified, for she turns out to be one of a new race of mutant vampires whose brains are unimpaired, and who can survive for short periods in the sunlight.

The mutant vampires come for him, invading his house and dragging him off to confinement, where he is condemned to death. Awaiting execution, he realizes that he is now the abnormal one, an "invisible specter who had left for evidence of his existence the bloodless bodies of their loved ones."[23] He is now the monster, the legend in a world of vampires.

Matheson's chilling post-apocalyptic tale is a gut-wrenching story of isolation, survival and terror as the reader becomes immersed in the yearnings and sufferings of the last human being on Earth, Robert Neville. Alone in a world of bloodsucking fiends, Neville displays forthright courage and ingenuity while battling intense guilt over his perceived failure to protect his wife and daughter from the plague. For these reasons, *I Am Legend* remains the most emotionally moving work of science fiction literature to date. The reader hopes and grieves along with Neville in his quest to understand and cope with his unbearable situation as he is ultimately transformed into a monster in a brave new world of vampiric humanity.

I Am Legend presents a highly detailed conception of the science fiction vampire as Neville becomes an amateur scientist trying to understand the nature of the problem through observation and experimentation. In line with folklore traditions, vampirism is presented as a product of a disease vector, and Matheson traces its origins to the historic outbreaks of bubonic plague in Europe and Asia during the Middle Ages. He also presents a plausible theory of the rapid spread of the disease via insect bites. But some of the author's concepts are stretched a bit too far in order to accommodate as many of the traits of the traditional vampire as possible. For instance, he creates the idea of "living" vampires, who are plague survivors suffering from mental illness which causes them to *think* they are vampires, to account for the aversion of certain vampires to the cross. The efficacy of garlic in repelling vampires remains unexplained.

Matheson's novel was a seminal work that has, to date, been filmed three times: as *The Last Man on Earth* (1964) starring Vincent Price; as *The Omega Man* (1971) with Charlton Heston; and as *I Am Legend* (2009) featuring Will Smith. The film versions vary widely in quality and fidelity to the book, with the 2009 version being the best on both counts. In addition, the novel was the inspiration of a plethora of "zombie apocalypse" movies and TV shows, beginning with George Romero's classic *Night of the Living Dead* (1968).

Another writer of the period, Fredric Brown, was known for his short-short stories with trick endings. In "Blood" (1954), Vron and Dreena are the last two vampires who have survived into the 22nd century after a series of pogroms has eliminated the rest of their race on Earth. Seeking to escape annihilation, they construct a time machine to take them into the far future, where all memory of vampires has been forgotten, so that they can breed and regenerate themselves.

Fleeing into the future in their time machine, they stop several times, only to find that vampires have *not* been forgotten. At one time stop, they find the world has been taken over by a race of intelligent dogs, but when they feed on one of these they are chased back to their time machine. Finally, far in the future, the time machine runs out of fuel. After stopping, they find that the canine race is gone and has been supplanted by a new breed of telepathic beings. Approached by one of the telepaths, the creature reads their minds and informs them that all memory of vampires has been forgotten. Thinking that they have finally reached their goal of a blood-rich environment, their hopes are dashed when the being informs them that all life on Earth is now vegetative, and that he has evolved from what was once called a turnip.

In Brown's story the vampires are both sympathetic and comical, although their situation will eventually lead to a slow, wasting death. Once again vampires are somehow connected with horticulture. Time-traveling vampires would also appear in Brian Aldiss's 1991 novel *Dracula Unbound.*

William Tenn's story, "She Only Goes Out at Night" (1956), posits a medical explanation for vampirism. The story unfolds in rural Groppa County, where several children have been victimized by someone who has taken their blood, although not fatally. Tom, the narrator of the story, works for the local physician, Dr. Judd, who is trying to find a solution for the mysterious attacks. Half Romanian by birth, Tom recalls folk legends told to him by his Transylvanian mother, and believes the attacks are the work of a vampire. His suspicions fall on Tatiana Latianu, a Romanian girl from a neighboring township whom Dr. Judd's son, Steve, has begun dating. Tatiana is a troubled young woman who has attempted suicide, refused to marry Steve, and, as the story's title suggests, only goes out at night.

As Steve and Dr. Judd investigate, they learn that Tatiana is indeed the vampire who has been taking the children's blood, and has suffered terrible remorse for doing so. She is not, however, an undead, supernatural creature, but merely suffering from a rare disease. Once Dr. Judd has diagnosed her condition as "a sickness like any other sickness," he devises a treatment regimen to combat it. She is given hormone injections and is put on a diet consisting of a "daily blood toddy," a formula concocted from dehydrated blood, which is readily available from pharmaceutical companies. In addition, she is instructed to wear dark glasses that enable her to move around in the daytime. Thus cured of her vampiric disease, she is free to marry Steve instead of being staked by the superstitious locals.

Like Matheson's *I Am Legend*, Tenn's story treats vampirism not as a supernatural curse, but rather as a disease treatable by science, enabling Tatiana to lead a normal life by means of a relatively simple treatment regimen. While the narrator, Tom, jumps to a supernatural explanation for the attacks, Dr. Judd brings the cold light of reason to bear on the problem and all but guarantees a happy ending. Tatiana's insistence on drinking the blood of children without fatal results recalls the similar habits of Lucy Westenra, the vampire lady of Stoker's *Dracula*. "She Only Goes Out at Night" was followed by medical vampire tales such as Simon Raven's *Doctors Wear Scarlet* (1960) and Theodore Sturgeon's *Some of Your Blood* (1961), which attempt to explain vampirism as a psycho-sexual mental disorder.

Roger Zelazny, who is best known for his science fantasy novel *Lord of Light* (1967) and his heroic fantasy Amber series, penned a delightfully satiric short story entitled "The Stainless Steel Leech" (1963). The story takes place in a post-human world in which mankind is extinct and robots are the only extant life form. Our first-person narrator is a defective "werebot," a machine that drains energy from other 'bots, and who is no longer connected to central control. The Werebot likes to hang around human cemeteries, and in one of the graves he discovers Fritz, the last vampire on Earth, who is so decrepit from lack of blood that he cannot get up from his casket.

One day Fritz requests that the Werebot put flowers on the grave of his adversary, Kensington, who had been the last man on Earth and with whom he had fought many duels. While the Werebot is going about his task he is apprehended by a robot overseer, or "Over" and five assistant 'bots who mark him as a defective unit to be junked, but the Over is unable to drain his power. Fortunately, Fritz comes to the Werebot's rescue, rising from his grave in sunlight in a final effort. The Over and his assistants take him for a human being, whereupon Fritz orders the assistant 'bots to stake the Over. Exposure to sunlight causes poor Fritz to turn to ashes as the Werebot muses, "I, the unjunked, am legend."

Zelazny's comical short story nevertheless introduces a new concept of sci-fi vampirism: a robot vampire who drains electrical energy from other robots and hangs around a cemetery. Oddly, the last vestige of humanity in the story's posthuman future world is a vampire, and the alliance between the Werebot and the undead vamp is another original idea.

British author Colin Wilson is best known for his non-fiction books on the occult, but he also writes science fiction novels from time to time. Wilson combined a number of occult concepts with vampire lore and sci-fi in his novel *The Space Vampires* (1976).

Set in the near-future of the late 21st century, the story begins with the crew of the British deep space probe *Hermes* discovering a fifty-mile-long derelict alien ship drifting in the asteroid belt between Mars and Jupiter. Olof Carlsen, commander of the *Hermes*, and his crew explore the immense spaceship, which they believe has been floating among the asteroids for thousands of years. They discover the bodies of a number of humans entombed inside the ship and bring three of them, two women and a man, back to Earth for study.

Once they are back on Earth, the corpses are placed in a hi-tech space laboratory. Without warning, one of the females awakens and literally sucks the life out of an unfortunate reporter who has trespassed into the facility. Carlsen witnesses the resurrection and has his mind probed by the alien woman, but manages to resist her telepathic urgings. Soon, all three of the aliens have escaped, leaving a trail of dead bodies in their wake. The authorities duly deputize Carlsen to locate and neutralize the creatures. The astronaut teams up with celebrity criminologist Dr. Hans Fallada, who explains his theory that the extraterrestrials are psychic vampires who acquire sustenance by extracting the "lambda force," or life force, from their victims.

Fallada and Carlsen travel to a remote castle in Sweden to consult vampire expert Count Ernst von Geijerstam about the problem. Considered a crank psychologist, the Count nonetheless provides useful theoretical information about psychic vampirism, including the notion that the space vampires have the ability to jump from body to body. During the visit, Carlsen discovers that he himself is a kind of human vampire who can extract the life force from others, and acquires a telepathic link with the female vamp who attempted to drain him. Using the mind meld, he locates the alien by remote, viewing her environs in a small town in Yorkshire.

Carlsen and Fallada immediately return to England, where they are joined by Scotland Yard inspector Hesseltine. The trio of investigators trace the alien to a nearby insane asylum, where the alien has taken over the body of one of the nurses. Trying to escape, the vampire jumps into the body of the head of the hospital, Dr. Armstrong, but the team manages to trap the alien by giving Armstrong a strong sedative. They transport him to London, but unfortunately one of the other vampires has possessed the British prime minister, Jamieson, and is plotting to bring the alien ship to Earth so that the space vampires can overwhelm humankind. A telepathic battle of wills ensues between the Commander and the aliens, which only ends when a higher alien being inhabits Carlsen's body and uses overwhelming psychic force to exorcise the vampires and send them back to their home planet.

The Space Vampires begins well, with evocative opening scenes depicting the discovery of the enormous alien spaceship and its monstrous cargo that recall similar scenes in Ridley Scott's *Alien*, released just three years later. When the action returns to Earth, however, the focus of the narrative shifts from science fiction to criminal detection and police procedural. The book's middle section digresses into a discussion of psychic topics, such as spirit possession, Kirlian photography, drowsing with pendulums, clairvoyance, et cetera, topics that are only tangentially related to vampirism.

On the other hand, Wilson explores the concepts of alien and psychic vampires simultaneously, and his ideas concerning the exchange of psychic energies between organisms in nature are original and provocative, especially when he suggests that all acts of sex contain an element of vampirism. The telepathic link between Carlsen and the female vamp recalls the similar mind meld between Mina Harker and the Count in Stoker's *Dracula*.

Wilson freely acknowledges that *The Space Vampires* is a reworking of A.E. Van Vogt's "Asylum." Both works feature ruthless alien vampires who absorb their victims' life force, a relationship between an earthman and a female extraterrestrial vampire, a plan for the vampiric invasion of Earth, and a denouement in which the hero becomes possessed by a higher alien force and defeats the vampires. The novel was filmed by director Tobe Hooper under the title *Lifeforce* (1985), and the movie version adds epic scenes of a zombie apocalypse in London that do not appear in the book.

Another British writer, Tanith Lee, has contributed a number of memorable works of vampire fiction in a fantasy/horror vein, including *Kill the Dead* (1980), *The Blood of Roses* (1990) and *Dark Dance* (1992). She also authored one of the finest works of vampire science fiction, *Sabella: Or the Bloodstone* (1980). Sabella Quey (a.k.a. Bella), the first-person narrator, is a young woman who lives a solitary existence on a lonely plateau on Novo Mars, a Mars-like world that has been terraformed and colonized by Earth. Sabella is a vampire who drinks blood, avoids sunlight and wears dark glasses and black goth attire. Being a vampire, she is irresistibly attractive to males, who die in ecstasy during sex as she sucks their blood. But, more recently, she has taken to feeding on the blood of animals rather than human victims. She wears a curious crimson gemstone, which she found as a child, in a pendant around her neck.

One day Sabella receives a letter informing her that her aunt Cassi has died, and that she will receive an inheritance if she attends Cassi's funeral in a nearby city. After the ceremony she is given a small casket containing a crucifix and a note from her aunt, accusing her of being a vampire. The cross is intended to cripple her in her bloodsucking endeavors, as Cassi had become a convert to a Christian religious sect in her final days. During the trip she meets a young man named Sand Vincent, who insinuates himself into her company, and they promptly fall into bed and begin an erotic relationship.

Sand follows Bella back to her isolated home on the Hammerhead Plateau, where they continue their lovemaking and bloodletting. As he falls under Bella's spell, he reveals that he is actually a private investigator hired by Cassi to expose her as a vampire. Unfortunately, she overindulges her thirst and inadvertently kills Sand. She disposes of his body in an incinerator, but soon afterward Sand's brother, Jace, shows up and discovers Sand's burned remains. Seeking vengeance, Jace keeps Bella a prisoner in her home. But she manages to steal a car and escape to the city, where she goes underground and makes her living as a prostitute.

Following a clue in her aunt's note, Bella is drawn to a museum in the town where she had lived as a child. The museum houses artifacts of the indigenous civilization of

Novo Mars, an alien race of vampires who became extinct a thousand years earlier. She recalls an incident from her childhood when she had found the bloodstone in her pendant in a mining tunnel, and learns that the bones of a little girl were found at the same site. The truth is that she is not the real Sabella Quey, but an alien doppelgänger who assumed her identity. It turns out that Jace is also a regenerated Novo Martian, and the two are destined to lead a symbiotic relationship, wherein he will offer her his blood as sustenance and feed without killing him, a survival strategy adopted by the aliens as the environment on their planet degraded.

Told first-person through the eyes of the vampire, *Sabella* unfolds as a mystery that gradually reveals the truth about the alien nature of Bella and Jace, who are not revealed as alien doppelgängers until the very end of the novel. *Sabella* paints a portrait of the title character that is at once sympathetic and disturbing, as desire and death interweave themselves inside her mind. As she wryly observes, "We're all bloodsuckers one way or another." The novel's mood reeks of isolation and melancholy as the vampire ekes out a lonely existence without human companionship while being threatened by her own family.

Sabella is reminiscent of another female vampire story set in a Martian environment and written by a female author, namely C.L. Moore's "Shambleau." The book's Christian religious angle has affinities with the theological musings of the vamps in Anne Rice's *Interview with the Vampire* (1976) and its sequels. The novel may have provided inspiration for elements of the *Twilight* saga in the name of its heroine, Bella, and in the notion that the vampires subsist by hunting wild animals and drinking their blood rather than claiming human victims.

The novelist Whitley Strieber occupies a unique place in the history of science fiction vampire literature, as he claims that his vampire tales allegedly originate with his experiences of alien abduction. Strieber's breakthrough vampire novel, *The Hunger* (1981), updated the myth into 1980s New York, and while it contains a number of science fiction elements, aliens are not mentioned; the E.T. connection would only become apparent later.

Strieber's protagonist is wealthy New Yorker Miriam Blaylock, an exquisitely beautiful vampire woman who is immortal and completely inhuman. She lives in a fortress-like townhouse in the exclusive Manhattan neighborhood of Sutton Place with her consort, John. Even though she is immortal she is obsessed with mortality, taking elaborate precautions to ensure her survival. Miriam possesses strength and agility superior to humans, has telepathic abilities and an enhanced immune system. Members of her race sleep during the day to revive themselves after feeding, but are not bothered by sunlight. They are able to reproduce, but remain very few in number. For this reason she is obliged to create companions by turning her lovers into human vampires. This is accomplished by transfusing her blood into their systems. Unfortunately, the vampires she creates in this fashion have an extended life span, but do not share her immortality and tend to suddenly age after a few hundred years.

This is the fate that has befallen her present companion, John, whom she turned into a vampire in the 18th century. Realizing that their longevity is related to vampiric sleep, Miriam approaches Sarah Roberts, a doctor who is conducting ground-breaking research into the relationship between sleep and aging at the Riverside Sleep Research Center in Manhattan. Posing as a patient who suffers from the sleep disorder called night terrors in adulthood (see Chapter One), Miriam seeks out Dr. Roberts at the center, beguiling Sarah with her telepathic sexual attractions while she is being studied. Drawn to the mysterious woman, Sarah makes a house call at Miriam's home and winds up being seduced by the vampiress, who also transfuses some of her blood into Sarah's veins.

As the doctors at the Sleep Center study Miriam more closely, it soon becomes apparent that she is not a human being. She is subjected to X-rays, EEGs, chromosomal studies and blood analysis, which reveals that her's is unlike human blood, having additional types of cells that bolster her immune system and contribute to her longevity. After being transfused with the alien blood, Sarah's own blood begins to mutate as she transforms into a vampire. She starts to experience the Hunger, the overwhelming desire to drink blood, but is restrained by having taken the Hippocratic Oath. In the end, however, she gives in to the unholy urge when she drains the blood from her fiancé, Tom, and afterwards slits her wrists in despair. But because she can no longer die a human death, she becomes one of Miriam's undead lovers that are kept in a shrine in her attic.

Strieber's novel vividly portrays the homicidal world of the vampire as we follow Miriam's amoral and murderous exploits and experience Sarah's transformation into her newfound, ecstatic existence. The fierce, predatory creatures are described as being "part of the justice of the earth," superior beings that prey upon mankind and cull the human herd. *The Hunger* paints a convincing portrait of vampires living secretly in late–20th century New York by conjuring a realistic, gritty sense of place combined with scientific verisimilitude that updates the vampire myth. The gothic supernatural vampire is dispensed with in favor of a science fiction approach grounded in the real world. At the same time, the narrative careens around through the centuries, from ancient Rome to London in 1430, to Swabia in 1724, in order to provide a backstory for Miriam's eternal existence, a literary technique that smacks of time travel.

The Hunger was made into a stylish motion picture adaptation in 1983 by British director Tony Scott (brother of Sir Ridley Scott) in his directorial debut. Its stellar cast included French actress Catherine Deneuve as Miriam, British pop star David Bowie as Miriam's consort, John, and Susan Sarandon in an early role as Sarah Roberts (see Chapter Three).

Miriam Blaylock is the novel's most memorable creation, an exquisite demigoddess who is more than human, although her origin and inhuman nature are not explained in *The Hunger*. X-rays reveal that her skull is a different shape than ours. She is obliged to wear makeup, special lenses that darken the color of her eyes, a wig and facial prosthetics to mimic the appearance of a human being. In one scene she deliberately reveals her true appearance to Sarah as a transcendentally beautiful creature: "Miriam did not look a thing like a human being, but she was *beautiful*! ... This was the goddess Athena, Isis—Sarah could not find a word, a name. The eyes were not pale gray at all, but shining, piercingly bright. The skin was as white and smooth as marble. There were no eyebrows.... The hair, which had been concealed by a wig, as gold as the eyes, was soft, almost like smoke, finer than the hair of a baby."[24] The pale skin, bald head and shining, compelling eyes fit the general description of the "gray alien" that had entered our culture in the 1970s during a rash of UFO abduction reports. Also, like the UFOnauts, Miriam possesses telepathic powers. This similarity would come to be highly significant in light of future events in Strieber's literary career.

In 1985, just four years after the publication of *The Hunger*, Strieber reportedly began to experience anomalous events, strange lights and sounds, in a cabin he owned in upstate New York. Troubled by these events, he was inspired to write a strange short story entitled "Pain," which was published in 1986. The story is told by a nameless first-person narrator, a horror novelist who is a thinly veiled stand-in for Strieber himself. The novelist is conducting research about prostitution, perversion, and their relationship to pain and death. As the story opens, the narrator conducts a rambling discourse concerning his morbid preoccupations with suffering, human sacrifice, global climate change, political conspiracies and UFOs, and expresses a belief that an alien race is secretly preying upon our suffering while our government covers up the existence of the extraterrestrial presence.

In the course of conducting research on sadomasochistic prostitutes in New York, he is brought into contact with a beautiful young woman named Janet O'Reilly, who claims to be a dominatrix who indulges her client's masochistic penchants for erotic suffering. Intrigued by Janet's beauty and by her philosophy of pain, he decides to submit to her ministrations.

He is drawn by degrees into Janet's world of suffering in spite of being a conventional family man with children. She proceeds to torture him in a series of sexless rituals that make him experience unbelievable physical and mental torments, which she insists will ultimately "lift the burden of self from your shoulders." After being subjected to a mock execution and nearly suffocated and burned to death while locked inside a metal box, he suffers a mental breakdown. He has a vision of the destruction of the world in a nuclear war that will be secretly provoked by the aliens as part of a transformation of mankind. Her "lessons" completed, Janet departs from his life, but he secretly yearns for her return, which will mean his death.

In "Pain," Strieber puts forth the theory that the aliens are a race of psychic vampires who are feeding upon humankind's tragedies in order to transform our race through suffering: "They love us. They do. We are their grass, their trees, their rooting piglets. They have grown immense on us, sapping us, whipping us with war and famine and pestilence, designing brain and body for more and more breeding, until the world is choked with billions upon billions of shining, brilliant human souls ready for the slaughter. Ready also, for growth."[25]

He further elaborates on the alien's motives thus: "The obvious conclusion is that they use us for their own reasons, gaining something we do not understand from our suffering and slaughter, gaining strength perhaps, or pleasure, or maybe even the fundamental energy of their civilization. As the burning of oil fuels human civilization … so also the carnage of human beings might provide this invisible higher civilization with its prime energy source."[26] In other words, he is presenting a vision of an entire race of psychic vampires who are covertly absorbing our energies on a massive scale.

This bleak and disturbing story of extreme sadomasochism, psychic vampirism, UFO conspiracy lore and spiritual transformation was written as Strieber reportedly started to recover memories of his alien abductions. In 1986, he began to undergo hypnotic regression therapy to recover the memories of his abductions, and in due course he acquired total recall about his close encounters with a number of alien life forms who allegedly took him on board a spacecraft, induced him to have hallucinatory visions, stuck a needle into his brain and subjected him to a humiliating rectal probe.

Strieber wrote an allegedly non-fiction account of his abduction exploits, which was published as *Communion: A True Story*, in 1987, in which he relates how he formed a special mental bond with one of the creatures whom he perceived to be female. According to his description, "She's … bald.… She's got a big head and her eyes have bulges. She's sort of brown-skinned, not like a black person but like leather. Yellow-brown."[27] The entity attempted to sexually arouse Strieber, but he was unable to respond under the circumstances. He did, however, reportedly experience a profound telepathic mind-meld with the alien lady while staring into her eyes. "She had those amazing, electrifying eyes, the huge staring eyes of the old gods.… She was undeniably appealing to me. In some sense I thought I might love this being—almost as much as I might my own anima."[28] An iconic picture of this creature, painted by portrait artist Ted Jacobs, appeared on the cover of *Communion*.

As the therapy unfolded, Strieber came to believe that he had been abducted a number of times during his life, going back to his childhood, by what he termed the "visitors." He also speculated that unconscious material from his abduction experiences might have found its way into his fiction. Referring to "Pain," he explains, "What is most interesting to me about this story is that it continues imagery that is present in my early horror novels. The visitors could be seen … as Miriam Blaylock in *The Hunger*. The theme is always the same: Mankind must face a harsh but enigmatically beautiful force that, as Miriam Blaylock describes herself, is 'part of the justice of the world.'"[29] Here Strieber is suggesting that his fictional female vampire was inspired by his real-world encounters with the femalien creature described in *Communion*.

The abduction book was a bestseller and Strieber authored several follow-up accounts relating his further experiences with the visitors before returning to horror novels and writing a sequel to *The Hunger*. Miriam Blaylock re-appears in *The Last Vampire* (2001), in which her extraterrestrial origin is finally revealed. In the sequel, an international group of vampire hunters, led by CIA agent Paul West, is decimating the vamp population, using specially designed hi-tech weapons. Miriam is hunted through the streets of Bangkok, Paris, and, finally, New York by the vampire slayers. It turns out that West is actually a human-vamp hybrid, who tracks Miriam to her New York lair, an exclusive nightclub called the Veils, where elite patrons are catered to with excessive doses of sex, drugs and rock 'n' roll. Instead of dispatching West, however, Miriam is drawn to him sexually, and the CIA stud winds up impregnating her after a bout of wild sex. The novel ends with Miriam on the run once more as the vampire hunters invade her Sutton Place townhouse and rescue West from her clutches.

Whereas Miriam is the only vampire extant in *The Hunger*, in *The Last Vampire* there are small populations of the creatures living in Asia, Europe and America. They are the remnants of an alien race from another star system that arrived on Earth fifty thousand years earlier and genetically engineered the human race from simian progenitors (à la *2001*). The vampires refer to themselves as the "Keepers," while the humans are simply "Prey." The Keepers taught mankind agriculture and civilization and ruled over the Prey during the dynasties of ancient Egypt, but over the centuries the vampires went into decline, slowly abandoning their technology while humans developed theirs. By the early 21st century the Keepers have become a decadent race of outcasts; the former masters of the planet are reduced to leading a tenuous existence inside secret underground tunnels, where they must conceal themselves from humans. They also have reproductive problems that have brought them to the brink of extinction. The notion of humans and aliens mating and producing hybrid offspring is another theme appearing in UFO abduction lore.

In *The Last Vampire*, Strieber never explains how the alien vampires traveled to Earth through interstellar space, nor does he indicate their point of origin. Likewise, the reason and circumstances of the vampire race's abandonment of their high technology is also left unexplained. Smug in their physical superiority to Homo sapiens, the vampires are unable to adjust to the idea that the race they created as prey animals are now capable of hunting and killing them with hi-tech weapons.

Dan Simmons's short story "Carrion Comfort" (1983) is a chilling tale of psychic vampirism. The main characters are three psychic and psychopathic vampires, Melanie Fuller, Nina Drayton and Willi Borden, who use what they call "the Ability" to manipulate humans into committing murder and suicide and then "Feed" on their life force. These Feedings have extended their life spans to over a century, although they are all showing signs of age. They have been using their mind-control powers for years in what they call "the Game," in which they compete with one another to see who can commit the most horrific acts, which have included the Charles Manson mass-murders and the killing of John Lennon. The three vampires meet once a year to compare notes on who has caused the most death and mayhem. That vampire is then declared the winner of the Game.

Melanie is the first-person viewpoint character, and the story begins in her old-fashioned house in Charleston, South Carolina, as the three psychic vampires hold their annual contest. Willi and Nina bring scrapbooks documenting their horrible crimes and gloat among one another over their homicidal deeds and manipulation of human "cattle." But they are shocked to learn that Melanie has tired of the Game and will no longer participate, even though her lack of Feeding is causing her to age more rapidly.

Willi and Nina are somewhat chagrined over Melanie's lack of enthusiasm for continuing the Game, but they part amicably when the meeting is concluded. Soon afterward, however, Melanie learns that Nina has murdered Willi by causing his death in a plane crash and knows that she will be Nina's next victim in her plan to eliminate them both. The two psychic vampires play a murderous game of cat and mouse as they use the Ability to psychically manipulate humans in their homicidal war for supremacy.

Simmons crafts a masterful tale of psychic vampirism that removes the supernatural element from the myth while retaining all of the horror. The vampires exhibit a chilling psychopathology and commit their foul deeds against a backdrop of outward respectability. The first-person narration allows the reader direct access to Melanie's sociopathic and narcissistic thought process, revealing the vampires to be arrogant, cruel, and self-pitying. "Of all mankind's self-inflicted terrors," Melanie muses, "of all its pathetic little monsters, only the myth of the vampire had any vestige of dignity. Like the humans it feeds on, the vampire must respond to its own dark compulsions. But unlike its petty human prey, the vampire carries out its sordid means to the only possible ends that could justify such actions—the goal of literal immortality. There is a nobility there. And a sadness."[30]

Like the vampires of old, Simmons's psychic vamps possess hypnotic and telepathic powers, feed on their victim's life force and are unnaturally long-lived. The notion that three amoral people could play with human lives and secretly and capriciously mold events on the world stage is especially disturbing. The author expanded this basic story into a 900-page novel with the same title, which was published in 1989. *Carrion Comfort* introduced a number of new characters and subplots, but the concept of the psychic vampire remained the same as in the short story. The title is a reference to a verse by horror writer Manly Wade Wellman.

British SF writer and science fiction historian extraordinaire Brian W. Aldiss, who is perhaps best known for his story "Super Toys Last All Summer Long," which was filmed by Steven Spielberg as *A.I.: Artificial Intelligence* (2001), also wrote a gothic time-travel novel titled *Frankenstein Unbound* (1973), which was made into a movie by Roger Corman in 1990. In the novel, Aldiss's protagonist, inventor/industrialist Joe Bodenland, time-travels to the past, where he encounters Mary Shelley, as well as Dr. Frankenstein and his monster. Aldiss wrote a sequel in 1991 entitled *Dracula Unbound*, in which Bodenland once more ventures back through the ages, this time to come face to face with Bram Stoker and Dracula.

Dracula Unbound begins with a prologue set in the very distant future, where the sun has dimmed to a perpetual twilight. Vampirism is so rampant that even the plants drink blood. A race of humanoid bat-winged vampires called the "Fleet Ones" has enslaved mankind and forced them to use their superior human intelligence to harness technology. A group of scientists devise a plan to send one of their number back through time to warn humankind of the vampire threat.

Back in the year 1999, paleontologist Bernard Clift discovers a fossilized human-like skeleton in the Utah desert that is 65 million years old, far older than any fossil primates heretofore discovered. It is found in a stratum just below what is called the K-T barrier, a geologic line that indicates the catastrophic event that killed off the dinosaurs. Clift approaches millionaire industrialist Joe Bodenland for financial support for his excavation of the momentous find. When Bodenland visits the burial site, he and Clift observe a strange phenomenon: a UFO-like, glowing object passing overhead. On subsequent nights Bodenland and Clift chase the object in a helicopter until they finally manage to slip aboard the mysterious craft.

The object turns out to be a "time train" that shuttles the Fleet Ones back and forth from the future to the past on a pre-programmed route to vital points in the vampire's time stream. Clift is killed by one of the time-traveling Fleet Ones but Bodenland manages to continue on while learning how to control the train. After traveling to the prehistoric past, the train arrives in London in 1896, right in the backyard of Bram Stoker. The author has contracted syphilis, which is incurable in his day, from his adventures with prostitutes. He periodically drops in on Renfield, a patient in a nearby hospital, who is in the degenerative tertiary phase of the disease and receives quack treatments from his physician, Dr. Van Helsing.

After fending off attacks from a vampire lady named Bella, who has been sent by Dracula to seduce him, Bodenland has a vision that reveals that the vampire race evolved from parasitic pterodactyls, huge bat-winged flying reptiles, during the age of the dinosaurs. He convinces Stoker to board the time train and travel to 1999, where his disease can be cured by antibiotics. But in order to destroy the vampire threat, they first decide to journey to the year 2599, where he has learned from Bella that humankind has invented the ultimate weapon against the vampires, a super-fusion bomb called the "F-bomb," which will also destroy most of humanity if detonated.

Riding the time train to 2599 they arrive at the "Silent Empire," the last outpost of humanity in the city of Tripoli, Libya. They are pursued by Lord Dracula, who can also use the train due to a time paradox. Dracula wants to detonate the F-bomb so that the Fleet Ones can take over the earth, but is ultimately outfoxed and outfought by Bodenland and Stoker, who manage to obtain the bomb and take it with them on the time train. In order to destroy the vampire threat once and for all, they go back 65 million years to the late Cretaceous era and set off the bomb, destroying the pterodactyl-vampires along with the dinosaurs in a world-changing nuclear conflagration. In the aftermath they return to 1999, where Stoker is cured of his venereal disease and returns to his own time to write *Dracula*.

As is evident from this summary, which has omitted several subplots and minor characters, the plot of *Dracula Unbound* is cumbersome and overly complex. The narrative plays out over millions of years, sometimes shifting confusedly between eras. With the exception of Stoker and Dracula, Aldiss's characters are lackluster and one-dimensional. His characterization of Stoker is particularly uncharitable. In his non-fiction book on the history of SF, *Trillion Year Spree* (see Chapter One), he expresses the idea that *Dracula* is really about Stoker's having contracted syphilis. While there is some historical evidence to suggest this, it is controversial and far from proven. In one particularly egregious scene in the novel, Stoker is shown having sex with a teenaged, menstruating prostitute, reflecting Stoker's supposed sexual obsession with blood. In spite of this character assassination, Stoker the "Ginger Man" emerges as a charming and even heroic figure.

Dracula himself makes only sporadic appearances in the narrative, wherein he is portrayed as a majestic, satanic figure, complete with horns: "Count Dracula appeared, horned and gigantic, more devil than man. His face was like a painted skull.... Dracula's brow was rocky and brutal, a mere base from which two short horns curled. The horns were crusted like a goat's. Nor was the head noble. It was brachycephalic, with no curve at its rear, so that its peak fell straight down to the neck. Lower and upper jaws were remarkably pointed.... Only the lips held color. Of a mauvish red, they expressed at once *luxuria* and cruelty, round which the teeth were glimpsed like fingers clutching a curtain."[31]

Putting these flaws aside, *Dracula Unbound* does present an interesting sci-fi take on the vampire concept. Aldiss's vampires are essentially reptiles, a species of parasitic pterosaur that evolved during the Mesozoic Age. In one scene the Fleet Ones are shown herding a group of duckbilled dinosaurs into a pen for a bloodsucking repast. The primitive limbic, reptilian brains of the dinosaurs are in conflict with the more advanced neo-cortical mental architecture of the humans who oppose them. As in other works of vampire fiction, the Fleet Ones are unable to grasp or manipulate technology, instead relying on their superior natural endowments in their battle against the human species. In spite of all the science, however, the vampires are sometimes described as "the Un-Dead," who can be dispatched by a stake through the heart. The science fiction concept of time travel combined with a vampire story is a novel idea that could have been used to greater effect.

The late science fiction writer George Alec Effinger was best known for a trio of novels and a number of short stories set in a nameless North African city in the early 22nd century. Beginning with *When Gravity Fails* (1987), Effinger chronicled the exploits of his half–Arab, half–French semi-hero, Marid Audran, who inhabits the world of the Budayeen, a futuristic Kasbah populated by prostitutes, transvestites, transsexuals, drunks, drug addicts, hustlers and all manner of sci-fi ne'er do wells. One feature of this cyberpunk futureworld is the use of plug-in personality modules, or "moddies," that interface directly with the brain and enable the wearer to temporarily experience being another person, either real or fictional. Chipping a moddie into your skull socket can make you believe you are James Bond, Sherlock Holmes or 22nd century porn starlet Honey Pilar, and act accordingly.

In "Marid and the Trail of Blood," Audran is confronted by what appears to be a vampire stalking the streets of the Budayeen. One of the district's strippers is killed, followed by the homicide of a street urchin, and both victims have been drained of blood. Audran's suspicions fall on another exotic dancer, Sheba, who has stopped appearing during the daytime. Gaining entrance to Sheba's apartment, he finds the place deserted and discovers a wrapper from a shop that sells illegal bootleg moddies of a violent variety. At the store, he finds a set of *Dracula* moddies for the novel's major characters, including Jonathan Harker, Lucy Westenra, Renfield and Dr. Van Helsing, but the Count Dracula moddy has been stolen from the set.

Marid buys the remaining set and chips in the Van Helsing module in order to find the Dracula persona. Immediately Audran's personality becomes subsumed by that of the Dutch vampire hunter, who promptly goes off in search of a little girl who has been kidnapped from the Budayeen. But the poorly written moddy software transforms the Van Helsing character from a kindly doctor to a vicious monomaniac. Before long, Van Helsing/Audran locates Dracula/Sheba in the district's cemetery, where vampire and vampire slayer go *mano a mano*. Sheba has been transformed into a horrific creature, sporting prosthetic canine fangs and possessing augmented strength as she grapples with her nemesis. Van Helsing finally gains the upper hand, but as the homicidal Dutchman is about to drive a stake through Sheba's heart, Audran comes to his senses and pops out his and Sheba's moddies, returning them to their true selves. He rescues the little girl from one of the nearby tombs, destroys the ultra-violent moddies and decides that Sheba is not responsible for the deeds she committed while under the influence of the device.

Like Fredric Brown's "Blood" and Roger Zelazny's "The Stainless Steel Leech," "Marid and the Trail of Blood" takes a humorous approach to the subject matter while neatly fitting the story into the Marid Audran cycle of tales. One of the interesting facets of this sci-fi take on the vampire is the moral equivalence drawn between Dracula and Van Helsing, who are both depicted as homicidal maniacs. Effinger's cyberpunk conception of Dracula as a software module is both hilariously original and horribly feasible. "Beneath Van Helsing's overwhelming presence," he writes, "Audran realized that the vampire moddy was constructed with an endocrine controller, letting a flood of adrenaline loose in Sheba's bloodstream. Whoever was correct—Audran or Van Helsing, believer in natural law or in evil magic—it made no difference. The ultimate effect was the same."[32] The Dracula moddy is the ultimate extension of present-day vampire role-playing computer games.

Guillermo del Toro is best known for his cinematic excursions into horror and fantasy in an impressive body of film work that includes the Oscar-winning *Pan's Labyrinth* (2006). Del Toro has also ventured into the realm of sci-fi vampirism in his films *Cronos* (1993) and *Blade II* (2002). Along with co-author Chuck Hogan, the acclaimed director has written a trio of novels, *The Strain* (2009), *The Fall* (2010) and *The Night Eternal* (2011) that constitute science fiction vampire literature's equivalent of J.R.R. Tolkien's trilogy *The Lord of the Rings*.

The epic begins with a intercontinental flight from Germany, landing at Kennedy Airport in New York City. As the plane taxis toward the gate, it stops dead, with all interior lights extinguished and all window shades pulled down. The authorities are concerned that the mysterious event may have been caused by some new disease or plague, so doctors and technicians from the Center for Disease Control are called in to investigate Upon entering the airplane, the CDC team finds all of the passengers and crew dead except for four individuals who have no knowledge of what happened during the final moments of their flight. Another mystery surrounds the disappearance of a large coffin-shaped box from the plane's cargo hold.

It isn't long before the corpses from the plane begin to rise up from the morgue as vampires and start attacking the living. All hell breaks loose in the Big Apple as the infection spreads exponentially and soon engulfs the entire city in chaos. Scientists studying the pandemic find that the vampire plague is caused by a virus carried inside parasitic capillary worms Upon entering the human body, the parasite physically alters it from the inside, changing the internal organs to suit its purpose and substituting a white ichor for blood. A new organ is formed in the mouth, a whip-like "stinger" that extends several feet, an elongated tongue through which the vampire siphons up blood. The vamps can see in the dark, are stronger and more agile than humans, have a kind of passive telepathy and are allergic to ultraviolet light and silver. They are also unable to cross bodies of running water of their own volition. Their accelerated metabolism produces high body temperatures and demands frequent feedings. As the vamps mature they acquire a pale skin and lose their hair and genitalia. They are immortal unless they are decapitated, exposed to strong ultraviolet light or starved of blood.

The vampires are ruled by a deathless creature called the Master, who is able to move from body to body and has been on the earth for millennia. For the last hundred years or so the Master has resided inside the body of Jusef Sardu, a terrifying, freakish giant. The creature has telepathic powers that are used to control the vampires and can also tap into human minds if they are in close proximity. Its ultimate goal is the total subjugation of mankind in order to usher in a vampire-ruled order, a new world wherein humans will be farmed for their blood.

The Master's chief opponent is Professor Abraham Setrakian, a Jewish survivor of Treblinka concentration camp during World War II, where he first encountered the creature. Setrakian has devoted his life to tracking down the Master, and has become well-informed in the lore of vampires. After being academically disgraced by the Master's agents he has been stripped of his professorship and is reduced to running a seedy pawn shop in Spanish Harlem, where he studies the forbidden science of vampirology in secret.

As the vampire virus spreads through New York and the rest of the world in a plan devised by the Master, civilization begins to collapse and various characters are drawn to align themselves with Setrakian or with the Master. Setrakian's allies include Dr. Ephraim "Eph" Goodweather, a doctor working for the Center for Disease Control and his assistant, Dr. Nora Martinez; macho rat exterminator Vasily Fet; Mexican-American gangbanger turned vampire hunter Augustin "Gus" Elizalde; and Mr. Quinlan, a.k.a. "The Born," a renegade vampire who fights with the humans. Opposing them are Eldritch Palmer, a sickly wheelchair-bound billionaire who yearns to be relieved of his humanity; Gabriel Bolivar, a vampire rock star; Dr. Everett Barnes, Goodweather's former boss at the CDC; and Kelly, Eph's former wife, who has been turned into a vampire. The vampire slayers must manage to stay alive while searching for clues about how to destroy the Master in an ancient book called the *Ordo Lumen*.

Like many other science fictional takes on the vampire in books and films, *The Strain* provides a scientific basis for vampirism. In nature, parasites have been known to change the biology of the host organisms that they invade, and once again it is a plague virus that transforms humans into vamps. The authors present scientific rationales for silver affecting the vampires (although silver is usually fatal to werewolves, not vampires, in occult lore) by claiming it has special disinfectant properties, and for the effect of UV light (it destroys the virus). Other science fiction elements include a space station whose flaming re-entry provides an omen, and the use of an atomic bomb as an anti-vampire weapon.

The trilogy draws upon a number of well-known vampire texts in formulating its plot. Stoker's *Dracula* is invoked in the early chapters dealing with the mysterious arrival of the ghostly jetliner and in the monstrous, inhuman nature of the powerful vampire figure. The character of Abraham Setrakian is obviously modeled on Stoker's primordial vampire hunter Abraham Van Helsing. Richard Matheson's *I Am Legend* is also referenced in the concept of a viral vampire plague that spreads throughout the world. Several themes have also been borrowed from del Toro's vampire films *Cronos* and *Blade II* (see Chapter Six). *The Strain* and its sequels draw inspiration from popular "zombie apocalypse" sci-fi horror fare such as *World War Z* (2013). As of this writing (2013), *The Strain* is under development as a TV miniseries for the FX cable channel and is scheduled to air in 2014. Del Toro is slated to direct the series and the cast reportedly includes actors John Hurt and Sean Astin.

Science fiction concepts have been a component of vampire literature from its inception. The psychic vampire appeared during the Victorian period in *Trilby* and "The Parasite," "The Flowering or the Strange Orchid" featured a non-human vampire, while "Good Lady Ducayne" was a tale of mad science and vampirism. All of these works predate the publication of *Dracula* in 1897, and the first extraterrestrial bloodsuckers invaded Earth in the following year in *The War of the Worlds*. Even *Dracula*, the most influential vampire novel of the 19th century, contains a number of science fiction elements.

SF stories that brought the vampire into the orbit of science continued in the pulp magazine period and beyond. Works such as *I Am Legend* and "She Only Goes Out at Night" explained vampirism as a medical condition. "The Girl with The Hungry Eyes," "The Mindworm" and "Carrion Comfort" further explored the concept of the psychic vampire. "Asylum," *Sabella: Or the Bloodstone*, *The Space Vampires* and *The Hunger* all posited alien vamps. And science fiction literature developed new concepts of vampirism, such as the robot vampire in "The Stainless Steel Leech" and Dracula-on-a-microchip in "Marid and the Trail of Blood."

Although the male vampire, typified by Count Dracula, is the vampiric archetype prevalent in horror cinema, the majority of vampires in science fiction literature are female, as evidenced by the femme vamps in "The Parasite," "Good Lady Ducayne," *Alraune*, "Shambleau," "Asylum," "The Girl with the Hungry Eyes," "She Only Goes Out at Night," *The Space Vampires, Sabella: Or the Bloodstone, The Hunger*, "Pain," "Carrion Comfort" and "Marid and the Trail of Blood." While only three of the authors cited are women (M.E. Braddon, C.L. Moore and Tanith Lee), one may speculate that male SF writers are drawn to create female vamps who were more exotic, liberated and seductive. In any event, the likes of Alraune, Shambleau, Sabella Quey and Miriam Blaylock constitute vital and memorable examples of the science fiction vamp.

By the end of the Victorian Period all of the basic templates for the science fiction vampire concept had been created. These themes were elaborated on by science fiction writers, from the pulp era to the present. The following chapters will explore the appropriation of these themes in popular science fiction literature and horror films.

PART II

The Films

CHAPTER THREE

Plagues of Blood

As discussed in Chapter One, 19th century vampire literature emerged as a result of the "vampire plague" during the previous century. The word *vampire* entered the English language at this time, along with the concept of vampirism as a disease process that was supernatural in nature, yet amenable to scientific analysis. Stoker's novel *Dracula* depicted the vampire-hunting medico Dr. Van Helsing offering a heady mix of superstition and science as a cure for the bloodsucking plague that had invaded England.

The first significant screen version of *Dracula* personified the vampire as a vector of plague. Acclaimed director F.W. Murnau's unauthorized iteration of the Stoker novel, entitled *Nosferatu* (1922), was filmed during the period of German Expressionist cinema, a style that had been ushered in by Robert Weine's film *The Cabinet of Dr. Caligari* (1919). Because *Nosferatu* was made without permission of the Stoker estate, it was a very loose adaptation of the novel and the names of the principal characters were changed. This did not prevent Stoker's widow from suing the film's production company for copyright infringement, however.

Nosferatu begins with a prologue title that states (in the English-language version), "From the diary of John Cavallius, able historian of the city of Bremen. Nosferatu? Was it he who brought the plague to Bremen in 1838?" As the film opens, the Jonathan Harker character, renamed Waldemar Hutter (and played by Gustav von Wangenheim), journeys to Transylvania to close a real estate deal, leaving his wife Ella (Greta Schroeder-Matray), in Bremen. Upon reaching an ancient castle, he swiftly concludes the business but is victimized and imprisoned by the vampire Count Orlock (Max Schreck). While Hutter watches helplessly, Orlock departs for Germany in a coffin along with several boxes of his native earth.

Orlock plans to travel to Bremen via ship, and when his boxes are being loaded on board they are found to be swarming with rats. In spite of this, the boxes are placed in the cargo hold and the ship sets sail for Bremen. Meanwhile, Hutter escapes from Orlock's castle, taking a book about vampires with him, and sets out for home. Back in Germany, Ella senses his impending return in somnambulistic trances. Aboard the ship, the vampire kills off the crew one by one, and the ghost vessel sails eerily into Bremen harbor. Orlock stashes his coffin in a nearby building while rats swarm out of the hold of the ship and invade the city, bringing the plague with them.

Inserts depict a local savant, Professor Bulwer (the Van Helsing character, played by John Gottowt), who is conducting a course "on the secrets of nature and their strange correspondences to human life." The professor is shown lecturing his students about the carnivorous venus flytrap. "Astonishing, isn't it, gentlemen?" he asks rhetorically as the plant munches on a fly. "That plant is the vampire of the vegetable kingdom." He then exhibits a microscopic organism, which is projected on the screen in the act of trapping and consuming another microbe. "And now, gentlemen, here is another type of vampire, a polyp with claws," he proclaims, "transparent, without substance, almost a phantom."

Soon, processions of townsfolk are carrying coffins through the streets of Bremen. A newspaper headline reads: "New Plague Baffles Science," as the text continues, "A mysterious epidemic of the plague has broken out in eastern Europe and in the port cities of the Black Sea, baffling the medical profession." By this time Hutter has returned home and is reunited with Ella. She begins reading from the book of vampires that her husband has brought home from Orlock's castle, and learns that the nosferatu can be destroyed by a virtuous woman who offers herself to him and entices him to remain with her until dawn. In the film's climax she offers herself to the vampire, who feeds on her blood. Upon sunrise, he fades away into the sunlight as the plague on the city is lifted.

Murnau's innovative directorial techniques, which included optical superimposition, accelerated motion (under-cranking), negative printing and stop-motion animation, as well as the director's eye for pictorial composition, made *Nosferatu* into a classic of silent film horror that still retains the power to frighten viewers. Eschewing the studio-bound artificial environment of expressionist films like *Caligari* and most other German cinema of the period, Murnau took his camera outdoors and shot much of the film in naturalistic settings. Scenes like Orlock's first attack on Hutter and the black ghost ship gliding into Bremen harbor are unforgettable and capture some of the imagery in Stoker's novel in a uniquely disturbing fashion. The film's most memorable aspect, however, is Max Schreck's appearance as the gaunt, bald-headed, clawed Count Orlock, which is truly nightmarish and was later replicated for *Salem's Lot* (1979), *Shadow of the Vampire* (2000) and Werner Herzog's 1979 sound remake of Murnau's 1922 silent.

Although Count Orlok is clearly a supernatural creature of the night, he also represents a visual metaphor for the plague itself. Schreck's cadaverous body, his rodent-like features and bat-like ears all suggest the iconography of the disease and the animal vectors that spread it. Orlok is surrounded by swarms of rats that he leads into the city like a demonic Pied Piper in reverse. It is the disease, a pestilence that baffles medical science, that is responsible for killing large numbers of people rather than the blood-sucking attacks of the vampire. The film references the outbreaks of alleged vampirism and bubonic plague in Eastern Europe in the 18th century, as discussed in Chapter One, and the word *nosferatu* is thought to derive from the Greek term *nosphoros*, which translates as "plague bearer." While the Van Helsing character plays no significant role in the film's narrative, he is on hand to scientifically demonstrate the existence of vampirism in the natural world.

Count Orlock (Max Schreck) emerges from the hold of the doomed ship to spread the plague throughout Bremen in F.W. Murnau's *Nosferatu* (1922). Note the rat perched on the vampire's shoulder.

Richard Matheson's science fiction novel *I Am Legend* (1954) revolved around the idea of vampirism as being caused by a plague. The book provided inspiration for three film adaptations, the first of which was *The Last Man on Earth* (1964), a low-budget horror picture co-scripted by Matheson himself and shot in Italy. Vincent Price stars as scientist Robert Morgan, the sole human survivor following the outbreak of a virulent disease three years earlier. But he is hardly alone. The disease turned humans into living-dead vampires. Morgan is shown performing his daily routines, sharpening stakes, tooling around the city to pick up groceries, transmitting signals on his short-wave radio, searching out the undead to drive stakes through their hearts, and dumping their bodies into a garbage pit on the edge of town. At night the vampires assault his fortress-like home and taunt its barricaded inhabitant. Clearly, Robert Morgan is living a nightmarish existence, one he describes as "a heartbeat away from hell."

In flashbacks, we see Morgan in the earliest days of the plague, when he and his assistant Ben Cortman (Giacomo Rossi-Stuart) were working to stem the spread of the disease. Despite their best efforts, the populace begins dying off by the thousands.

Morgan alone has acquired an immunity to the disease, having been bitten by a vampire bat in Panama years earlier. Inevitably, Morgan's daughter, Kathy (Christi Courtland), and then his wife, Virginia (Emma Danieli), die of the plague. After he buries Virginia she returns from the grave seeking his blood, and although this is not actually shown, he is forced to stake her. In the aftermath of this horror he has become dedicated to eradicating the undead vampires, including his erstwhile friend and colleague, Ben, who now leads the undead hordes who assail Morgan's house every night.

Returning to the present, Morgan finds a wild dog roaming around his house and tries to befriend it, but the animal soon dies of the plague, dashing his hopes for finding any companionship in his misery. As he is burying the dog he meets a living woman, whom he convinces to return home with him. Her name is Ruth Collins (Franca Bettoia). Although Ruth claims to be immune to the plague, Morgan soon learns that this is not the case. In fact, she is one of a new society of plague survivors who consider him a monster. As she tells him accusingly, "Many of the people you destroyed were still alive."

Soon, a group of the black-clad paramilitary forces of the new-world order arrive. They slaughter Ben Cortman and the other undead vamps besieging Morgan's house, and pursue him to an abandoned church, where he is cornered on the altar. "Freaks, all of you," he shouts as they surround him. "I'm a man! The last man!" Ironically, he is killed by a metal spear through the heart cast by one of the vampires. As the last man on Earth expires on the altar, the crying of a baby presages the coming of a new human race.

The Last Man on Earth is an eerily effective low-budget sci-fi horror thriller that vividly portrays the nightmarish existence of its isolated protagonist In contrast to many of his hammy performances in other 1960s-era horror flicks, Vincent Price delivers a serious, measured portrayal of the title character. Shot in Rome by director Sidney Salkow, the film makes effective use of its locations. Much of the film is shot in interiors that create a disturbingly claustrophobic setting. Images of corpses lying in the streets and army trucks piled high with the bodies of plague victims add an economical, yet effective, sense of horror.

Oddly, *I Am Legend* author Richard Matheson disavowed the film over changes to his screenplay made by co-scripter William F. Leicester. Matheson was also reportedly dissatisfied with the film's direction and Price's performance. He was obliged to receive screen credit, using the pseudonym "Logan Swanson." Ironically, *The Last Man on Earth* remains the most faithful screen version of his novel to date. The screenplay improves on the book's narrative by making the protagonist into a scientist instead of an amateur savant, and by expanding the flashback scenes to create a deeper emotional backstory for the Robert Morgan character. There are thematic correspondences with another classic Matheson science fiction novel and screenplay, *The Incredible Shrinking Man* (1957), which also featured an isolated hero struggling to survive in a world filled with monsters (in this case, spiders and a house cat). The film's vampires (who are never shown actually drinking blood), provided a template for the ghouls of later films,

Scientist Robert Morgan (Vincent Price) contends with a group of plague-ridden vampires in the first screen version of Richard Matheson's novel *I Am Legend, The Last Man on Earth* (1964).

from George Romero's *Night of the Living Dead* (1968) to AMC's current hit cable TV show *The Walking Dead.*

Matheson's novel was transmogrified into a vehicle for action star Charlton Heston in its second filmic incarnation, *The Omega Man* (1971). The film is set in a deserted post-apocalyptic Los Angeles in the year 1975, where last man on Earth Dr. Robert Neville (Heston) passes the time tooling around town in a convertible, firing an automatic weapon at a shape glimpsed behind a window and watching *Woodstock* in an empty movie theater. Before sundown, however, he must return to his swanky, fortress-like townhouse to enjoy a rare vintage from his wine cellar, watch himself on a giant screen closed-circuit TV and play chess with a mannequin companion as bands of mutated humans roam the streets below, besieging his *sanctum sanctorum.*

The creatures are human survivors of the plague who have entered the disease's "tertiary phase," which turns them into albino bleached blondes who cannot tolerate light. In order to accommodate their photosensitivity, they wear monk-like robes with hoods and sunglasses. The plague survivors call themselves "the Family," and are led

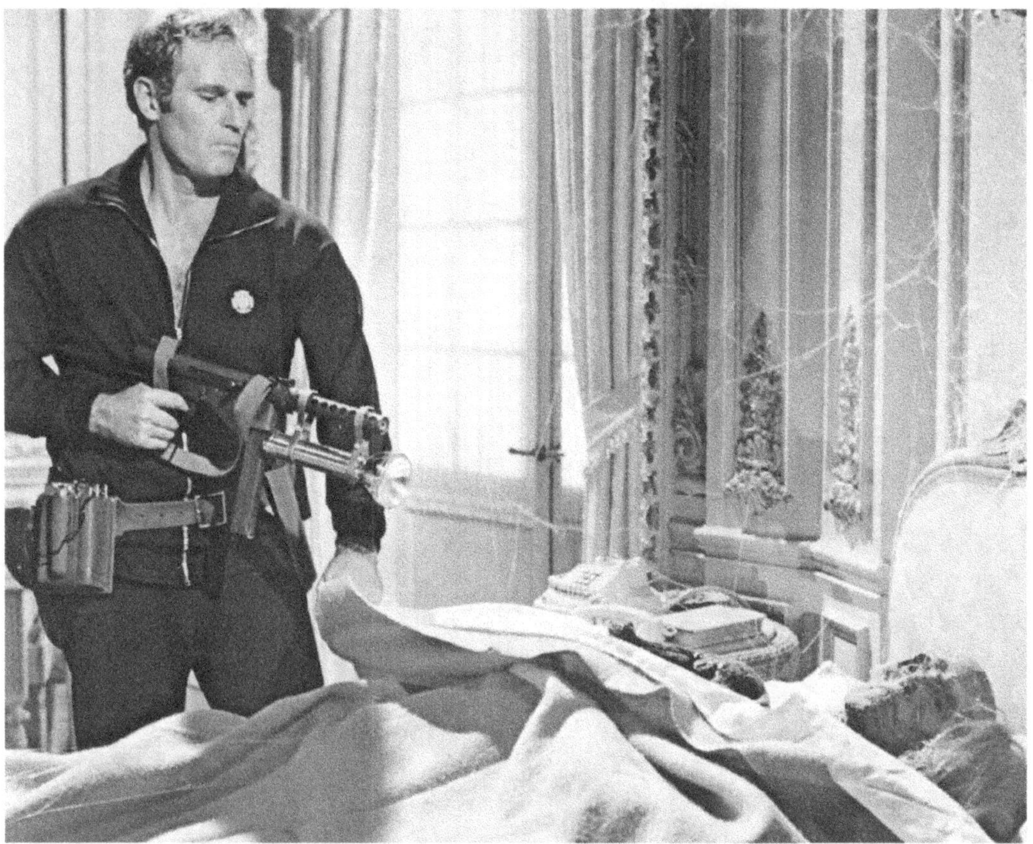

Dr. Robert Neville (Charlton Heston) searches for plague survivors in a post-apocalyptic L.A. in the second version of *I Am Legend*, *The Omega Man* (1971).

by former TV newscaster Jonathan Matthias (Anthony Zerbe), who now leads a crusade against Neville as the last of the "users of the wheel," the technocrats that destroyed the world by unleashing the plague during a world war. In flashbacks we learn that Neville was a military scientist who gave himself an injection of an experimental vaccine that rendered him immune to the plague.

Matthias and the Family manage to capture Neville and are preparing to burn him at the stake in Dodger Stadium when he is rescued by Lisa (Rosalind Cash) and Dutch (Paul Koslo), two apparently normal humans who take him to their secret hideout where there are a number of child survivors. It turns out, however, that they only have a limited immunity and will eventually contract the plague. Neville proposes that he create a serum derived from his own blood that will contain antibodies that should confer his immunity upon them. While they are working on the serum, romance blossoms between Lisa and Neville, but when their task in completed, Lisa inexplicably turns into one of the Family and betrays him. The final battle takes place just before dawn as Lisa is rescued from the mutants, but Neville is impaled with a spear hurled

Neville (Charlton Heston) is taken prisoner by robed members of "the Family" in *The Omega Man* (1971).

by Matthias. As the sun rises, Dutch arrives to take possession of the serum and save Lisa and the rest of humanity, while Neville expires in a pool of blood, his arms outstretched in a crucifixion-like pose.

Without doubt, the most off-the-wall version of the Matheson novel, *The Omega Man* is *I Am Legend* for the Woodstock generation. The screenplay by John William and Joyce C. Corrington is as much about the race, class and anti-establishment preoccupations of the era as it is about plagues, mutants or the end of the world, and has dated badly. Heston, who had morphed into Hollywood's number one sci-fi star of the period in memorable outings like *Planet of the Apes* (1968) and *Soylent Green* (1973), delivers a breezy portrayal of Robert Neville that actually makes being the last man on Earth seem like a lot of fun. Tough mama Rosalind Cash, as Lisa, spouts black power slogans and seems like a refuge from a contemporaneous blaxploitation flick. The plague being a result of germ warfare reflects the rampant anti-military sentiment of the times.

Worst of all, *The Omega Man* transforms the novel's vampires into a group of mutant Luddites who are much more interested in burning books and trashing museums than they are in drinking Robert Neville's blood. The robed, photophobic albinos of the Family do share some of the traits of vampirism, however, and Lisa cuts a wickedly vampish figure once she turns into one of them. Neville's offering his blood to save the world becomes sort of a vampire in reverse, and his Christ-like death by impalement recalls the religious overtones of the title character's death in a church at the conclusion of *The Last Man on Earth*.

By the late 1990s, actor Will Smith had become what Charlton Heston was to the 1970s: the big screen's number one science fiction action star. After headlining in sci-fi blockbusters like *Independence Day* and two *Men in Black* films, Smith was ready to follow Heston and assume the mantle of Robert Neville as *I Am Legend* (2007) was finally lensed under its own title. This time, however, a big budget and 21st century CGI special effects would bring Matheson's science fiction vampire story to life with a cinematic hyper-reality never dreamed of in the earlier versions.

The story line has been updated to the year 2012, where former military scientist, Dr. Robert Neville (Smith), is the lone human inhabitant of Manhattan Island after a genetically engineered virus (designed to cure cancer) has mutated into a plague germ and wiped out most of the population of the world. Amid spectacularly realistic scenes of a post-human New York overgrown with weeds and decay, Neville, accompanied by his German Shepherd, Sam (dogs are immune to the airborne strain of the disease), hunt deer in Times Square, play golf on the Intrepid Air & Space Museum and race up and down Park Avenue in Neville's roadster. The lone scientist sends out radio broadcasts announcing that he will be at the South Street Seaport every day at noon, but nobody ever shows up. During contemplative moments he is haunted by memories of the death of his wife and son in a helicopter crash when Manhattan was being quarantined three years earlier.

Neville and Sam live in a fortified town house across from Washington Square Park in Greenwich Village, where they take nightly refuge from the depredations of monstrous vampiric mutants intent on draining their blood. The vampires are gaunt and bald-headed, possess superhuman strength and agility but have only rudimentary reasoning powers. Ultraviolet energy in sunlight will destroy them, so during the day they are confined to communal "hives" located in dark, secret places. When Neville accidentally discovers one of the hives, he manages to capture one of the creatures, using a vial of his own blood as bait. He brings the vampire to his hi-tech basement laboratory, where he is experimenting with vaccines he hopes will cure the disease.

One day, in a curious reversal, the vampires manage to catch Neville in a clever snare trap. As he races against the sun to free himself, twilight descends as Sam is attacked by three vampire dogs and gets bitten. As dogs are not immune to the contact strain of the plague, he becomes infected and Neville is forced to kill him with his bare hands as the beloved pet transforms into a vicious vampire hound. Devastated by the loss of his only companion, he drives out to inflict vengeance on the vampires, but winds up getting attacked at the South Street Seaport and trapped in his car by the

creatures. As he sinks into unconsciousness, he has vague memories of having been rescued.

The following morning he awakens in his townhouse to find that a woman, Anna (Alice Braga), and her son, Ethan (Charlie Tahan), have made themselves very much at home. They are plague survivors who had honed in on his radio signal, traveled to New York from Brazil, and waited for him at the Seaport. It was Anna who saved him from the "darkseekers," as she calls them. She is on her way to a survivors' colony she has heard about in a safe zone in Vermont, and she wants Neville to go with her, but he insists on staying in his lab at "ground zero" to continue seeking a cure for the plague.

Unfortunately for them, the darkseekers have followed Anna's car and have discovered Neville's secret lair, and when the sun goes down they attack the townhouse in large numbers. Even the townhouse's fortifications cannot keep them out, and Neville, Anna and Ethan are forced to take refuge in the basement, although this will not hold them off for long. At this point the scientist examines the vampire he had captured earlier and treated with a serum derived from his blood and finds it has returned to a normal state of humanity. Realizing that his blood contains a cure for the plague, he quickly draws a sample and gives it to Anna. As the darkseekers crash through the final barriers, Neville explodes two grenades, sacrificing himself for the woman and her son and preserving the blood serum that will save all of humankind from the vampires' curse. An epilogue shows Anna and Ethan reaching the Vermont colony, a bucolic land of normalcy far away from the urban vampires of the ruined city. Neville's legend is the gift of his blood that will restore the human race.

The most expensive and elaborate version of Matheson's novel, *I Am Legend* captures much of the book's nightmarish, post-apocalyptic ambience. Shot on location in New York by director Francis Lawrence, the film reputedly sported a budget of $150 million, including a crowd scene shot at Brooklyn Bridge that, alone, cost $5 million. Armies of digital effects technicians painstakingly scrubbed all the people out of the New York backgrounds, then inserted new digital elements to create the fantastic illusion of a dead and rotting city. Yet all this visual splendor does not overwhelm the human element, as Will Smith delivers a solid dramatic portrayal of Robert Neville in his tragic struggle to survive, persevere and ultimately become a legend in a one-man show that carries the movie. The film conjures an eerie mood of dread in its early scenes set in a haunted landscape where unknown terrors are lurking and are only gradually revealed to the viewer. Long stretches of "pure cinema" with minimal dialogue tell the story powerfully in pictures and also serve to heighten the sense of the character's abysmal loneliness.

Strangely, *I Am Legend* owes as much to *The Omega Man* as it does to the Matheson novel. The screenplay was penned by Mark Protosevich and Akiva Goldsman, but a

***Opposite:* Dr. Robert Neville (Will Smith) and his canine companion, Sam, hunt for game on Manhattan Island in the third version of Matheson's novel, *I Am Legend* (2007).**

screen credit also reads: "Based on the screenplay by John William and Joyce H. Corrington," the writers who scripted *The Omega Man*. The two films have a number of plot points in common, including Neville's townhouse/fortress, the colony of uninfected humans and the salvation of the world through Neville's blood. Many critics felt that *I Am Legend* had a "third act problem," and the film does seem to lose its focus when Neville suddenly acquires a surrogate family and finds himself in a conventional domestic situation. The syrupy ending, in which Anna and Ethan find their way to a picture-postcard Vermont town that looks like something out of a Norman Rockwell painting, is particularly discordant.

The vampiric "darkseekers" (referred to as "hemocytes" in the script) are not well developed conceptually and are shown very sparingly in the early reels. Our first glimpse comes when Neville comes upon a vampire hive in the darkened interior of a building, his flashlight briefly revealing a cluster of darkseekers standing in a circle facing each other in their daylight torpor. They are portrayed as sub-human troglodytes, bald, skinny and uniform in size, not unlike insects. They have only rudimentary intelligence and lack the power of speech, using their oversized mouths only to scream like banshees. In keeping with the concept of vampires in the 21st century, they are super-athletic and possess augmented speed, strength and agility. The only way we know they are vampires is when, in one scene, Neville lures them with the scent of his blood.

The three screen iterations of Matheson's seminal science fiction vampire novel belong to different decades and reflect different sensibilities. Budget-wise, *The Last Man on Earth* is the most humble of the three, yet is the most faithful adaptation of the book. It belongs to the milieu of Vincent Price Euro horror flicks of the early '60s. *The Omega Man* injects counterculture racial and antiwar sentiments into the narrative, while *I Am Legend* reflects fears of terrorism in a post–9/11 America. Strangely, although the basic story is ostensibly about vampires, no actual bloodsucking is ever depicted in any of the screen versions, or in Matheson's novel, for that matter.

Vampire plagues continued to infest movie screens during the 1970s. In *The Bat People* (1974), physician Dr. John Beck (Stewart Moss) and his wife, Cathy (Marianne McAndrew), are enjoying a belated honeymoon vacation, but while taking a guided tour of some scenic caverns in the area, Dr. Beck gets bitten by a bat. He is concerned that the animal may have been rabid, but knowing that the disease has an incubation period of at least thirty days, he refuses to cut the vacation short. Still, to be on the safe side, he begins the lengthy Pasteur treatment for the disease. Unfortunately, he has an adverse reaction to the initial injection and starts to have seizures and experiences vivid nightmares. The doctors chalk it up to an allergic reaction to the serum, which can sometimes mimic the symptoms of rabies.

A series of grisly murders has struck the little resort town, and Beck's erratic behavior draws the attention of Sheriff Ward (Michael Pataki), who suspects him of the crimes. Beck himself doesn't know if he is having hallucinations when he perceives himself turning into a humanoid vampire bat man who may be responsible for the killings. After breaking into a hospital blood bank and downing a pint to slake his thirst, he steals an ambulance and heads for the bat cave, with the sheriff in hot pursuit. Ward hunts the bat creature through the stalactites and stalagmites of the cavern, but Beck manages to elude him. That night, as Ward is staking out the cave in his police cruiser, vampire bats swarm out of the cave and attack his car. Then Cathy, who appears to be in the thrall of the bats, throws the car door wide open, allowing the bats to drain the sheriff's blood, after which she joins her husband in the cave.

A swarm of killer vampire bats descends upon an unsuspecting humankind in this poster for *The Bat People* (1974).

This exercise in low-budget film-making by director Jerry Jameson and writer/producer Lou Shaw is indifferent drive-in fare with little to recommend it beyond the contribution of makeup artist Stan Winston in his first feature film effort. Winston, who created the film's bat man, would go on to win Oscars for his creature creations in *Terminator 2*, *Aliens* and *Jurassic Park*. Otherwise, it's pretty dull stuff, filled with revolting close-ups of live bats, hokey subjective camera shots and execrable dialogue.

Although many species of bats can carry rabies and transmit the disease through a bite, no explanation is offered as to why or how a bat bite could transform a human being into a were-bat, and a vampire bat man to boot. Like the rat man in *Nosferatu*, the vampire in *The Bat People* sends forth hordes of plague-carrying animals to spread disease. The film explicitly links vampirism to rabies, one of the illnesses linked to the vampire outbreaks of the 18th century. Vampire bats are indigenous to Central and South America and are not found in the United States, nor do they attack humans in swarms and kill them by draining their blood.

Rabies-infected vampires of an entirely different stripe appeared in Canadian cult director David Cronenberg's science fiction horror movie *Rabid* (1977). The film stars former porn actress Marilyn Chambers as Rose, a young woman who sustains serious injuries in a motorcycle crash along with her boyfriend, Hart Read (Frank Moore). While Hart's wounds are not life-threatening, Rose is in need of immediate treatment to save her life, and is rushed to the nearest medical facility at the Keloid Clinic, a private plastic surgery hospital that is very close to the scene of the accident. The clinic's head physician, Dr. Dan Keloid (Howard Ryshpan), employs a radical surgical technique involving grafts of "morpho-genetically neutral tissues" in an emergency operation that restores Rose's internal organs.

Unfortunately, the experimental surgery has changed Rose into a carrier of an extremely virulent strain of rabies. She is also a vampire, with an insatiable thirst for human blood. She now possesses a vagina-like cavity underneath her armpit, from which a penis-like probe with a barbed tip emerges to penetrate her victim's bodies and siphon off their blood. Her vampiric predations also infect them with the super-rabies virus, but Rose does not consciously remember any of this. After feeding on several people in the clinic, including Dr. Keloid, she checks herself out of the hospital and hitchhikes to Montreal to link up with Hart.

Most of Rose's attacks are not fatal, but the people whose blood she sucks soon come down with the highly contagious rabies-like disease that transforms them into homicidal maniacs, frothing at the mouth like mad dogs. Once she returns to Montreal, she continues her depredations among the urban population, who then bite others and infect them until there is an epidemic in the city. Attacks by the rabid occur on a crowded subway train and at a shopping mall, and martial law is soon declared by the authorities. The Department of Health figures out that those who have contracted the disease cannot be cured, and soldiers are given orders to shoot the rabid on sight. Garbage trucks, manned by soldiers wearing hazmat gear, patrol the streets, picking up the bodies of dead plague victims.

Rose takes refuge with a friend, Mindy Kent (Susan Roman), but is unable to control her lust for blood. Hart enters Mindy's apartment and catches Rose in the act of absorbing Mindy's blood. Horrified at the sight, he tells her that she is the carrier of the disease that has infected everyone in the city, and then bolts. Still having no memories of her blood-letting episodes, she is determined to prove him wrong. She picks up a guy (Allan Moyle) she meets in the lobby of the apartment building and brings him upstairs with her to see if she will give him the disease. She puts her vampire armpit on him, but he responds by going rabid and kills her in a homicidal rage. The film ends with an army patrol dumping Rose's body into a garbage truck along with the corpses of other plague victims.

Rabid, Cronenberg's second feature, was shot in Montreal on a modest budget of 560,000 Canadian dollars (in 1977 dollars), and the director makes effective and economical use of the city's locations. Cronenberg's direction and screenplay display his signature use of "body horror" derived from fears about disease, deformity and physical degeneration, as evidenced in some of his later films, such as *The Fly* (1986), and his obsession with monstrous medical malpractice, as in *Dead Ringers* (1988). Marilyn Chambers acquits herself well, delivering a competent performance in a sympathetic yet horrific role as the befuddled but promiscuous Rose.

All in all, however, while competently made, *Rabid* is not one of Cronenberg's better efforts, being virtually a remake of his first feature, *They Came from Within* (1975). The screenplay never explains why Rose becomes a vampire after the operation, where the rabies-like disease comes from, how she acquires her mutant bloodsucking organ, or the reason behind her convenient lapses of memory. Vampires are once again associated with disease, as rabies has been linked to the historical outbreaks of pseudo-vampirism in the 18th century. Scenes of martial law and the bodies of plague victims being collected by soldiers in trucks recall similar ones in *The Last Man on Earth*. The film also reflects upon the emergence of AIDS and other blood-borne, sexually transmitted diseases during the 1970s as a kind of vampirism. *Rabid*'s star, Marilyn Chambers, is herself an icon of the changing sexual mores that helped enable the spread of these illnesses. Rose's bloodletting organ is at once a vampiric phallus and a grotesque *vagina dentata*.

Killer vampire bats are on the loose once again, in *Nightwing* (1979). Nick Mancuso plays New Mexico Masaki tribal cop Youngman Duran, who is investigating some mysterious animal deaths out on the reservation. The livestock have been found drained of blood and smelling of ammonia, with no tracks of predators evident. But Duran soon has bigger worries when his kinsman and renegade Masaki shaman Abner Tasupi (George Clutesi) lets loose a magical curse upon the whites who are planning to desecrate tribal lands by mining for oil shale. As if in response to Abner's ceremony, a large colony of vampire bats descends upon the small community and begins draining the blood of humans and animals alike.

Soon a self-styled "exterminating angel," a Britisher named Phillip Payne (David Warner), shows up on the rez and starts taking samples from the carcasses. "I kill vampire bats, that's what I do," he helpfully explains to Duran. "I kill them because they're evil." Payne has it in for the bats big time and drives around in a van sporting radar and other hi-tech bat detection gear and a fully equipped laboratory. Funded by a grant from the World Health Organization, Payne uses his "batmobile" as a command post while waging his one-man war against the nightfliers. Payne tells Duran that the deceased have been sucked dry of their blood by a colony of sixty thousand vampires holed up in a cave somewhere in the desert. Even worse, the little varmints are spreading bubonic plague, which could start an epidemic in the area.

When Duran's main squeeze, reservation doctor Anne Dillon (Kathryn Harrold), is trapped in the desert by the bats, he and Payne locate and rescue her. They take refuge inside an electrified cage as the deadly critters try their best to gnaw their way through the mesh. When daylight comes, Payne manages to locate the bat cave and starts to implement his plan to poison the colony, using cyanide gas. Meanwhile, Duran has eaten some hallucinogenic datura root and is engaged in a battle of Indian magic with Abner's ghost. Unfortunately, Payne's plans go awry, and Duran, his mind expanded by the datura, comes up with plan B. Trapping the bats inside the cave, he ignites the oil shale deposits in the cave, burning the colony to death in a conflagration of fiery wings.

Obviously influenced by Steven Spielberg's mega-hit *Jaws* (1975) and the raft of nature-strikes-back thrillers that followed in its wake, *Nightwing* fails to generate much interest, due to lackluster direction by Hollywood veteran Arthur Hiller and an unfocused screenplay by Steve Shagan. Adapted from a novel by *Gorky Park* author Martin Cruz Smith, the film incorporates themes from Native American religion and spirituality that were popularized at the time by books like *Black Elk Speaks* and the anthropological ramblings of Carlos Castaneda. The bat hunter, played by David Warner, is shamelessly stolen from the similarly obsessed shark killer played by Robert Shaw in *Jaws*, although the script never reveals exactly why Warner has gone bats over the creatures. The unconvincing mechanical bats were created by creature maker Carlo Rambaldi, who fabricated the aliens for Spielberg's *Close Encounters of the Third Kind* and *E.T.*

The film presents a number of outright falsehoods about vampire bats to make them seem more menacing. *Nightwing* conjures up images of tens of thousands of bats swarming over man and beast alike, draining their victims of all their blood. Bat killer Payne speaks of the "foul syrup of digestive blood" excreted by countless thousands of the vampires befouling the floor of their caves. At the film's conclusion, an end title drolly reports that "in recent years, vampire bats were discovered and destroyed in a cave in Val Verde County, near Del Rio, Texas." This ominous statement seems to suggest that swarms of vampire bats were poised to invade the United States. In the real world, these bats inhabit tropical regions of the Americas and typically exist in colonies of a thousand or less. They do not drain their victims of all their blood, but instead gently lap the blood from humans, cattle and other mammals while they are sleeping, taking only small amounts of blood. Once again, the vampire is associated with plague and disease, although vampire bats do not carry or spread bubonic plague. The film also makes a connection with the "animal mutilation" phenomenon of livestock being found dead under mysterious circumstances that emerged into popular culture in the 1970s and was usually associated with UFO activity.

Whitley Strieber's vampire novel *The Hunger* was brought to the big screen in 1983 by MGM with an unusual cast that included French glamour actress Catherine Deneuve, rock star David Bowie and American actress Susan Sarandon in an early role. The film begins with vampires Miriam Blaylock (Deneuve) and her consort John (Bowie) picking up a couple in a chic New York club and going back to the couple's apartment, ostensibly for some kinky sex. As foreplay commences, however, the unfortunate pair are vampirized by Miriam and John, who use small knives instead of fangs to open their victim's throats. This violent scene is intercut with shots of monkeys tearing one another apart during an experiment in sleep deprivation and longevity being conducted by Dr. Sarah Roberts (Sarandon) at the nearby Park West Clinic.

After their feeding, John is unable to enter into the vampiric sleep that maintains his youth. Although he is more than two hundred years old, he appears to be only thirty, but when he is sleep deprived he starts to age rapidly. While waiting to see Dr. Roberts at the clinic, he becomes an old man in a matter of hours. The doctor believes he has a condition called *progeria*, in which his blood cells can no longer retain oxygen, but before she can treat him he returns to the Manhattan townhouse he shares with Miriam. His condition is incurable, however, and all she can do is place him in her attic along with the living dead remnants of all the other lovers she has had over the centuries.

Motivated by professional curiosity, Sarah goes looking for John at his address, but encounters Miriam instead. Soon, she comes under the hypnotic spell of the vampire woman and is seduced in an explicit lesbian love scene. During their tryst, Miriam transfuses some of her blood into Sarah's veins with the intent of making her into a long-lived companion to replace John. Sarah's transition is traumatic, however, as she is unable to eat and begins experiencing symptoms that mimic those of hard drug withdrawal.

Examined by the doctors at Park West, including her boyfriend, Dr. Tom Haver (Cliff De Young), Sarah is informed that there are two strains of blood fighting it out inside her circulatory system. An alien strain of weird, inhuman blood is consuming her own, yet the new strain is stronger and more disease resistant than her own. Tom notices an odd wound on her arm, and knowing she has visited Miriam, suspects foul play. Sarah returns to the townhouse to confront Miriam, but is unable to control her hunger for blood. When Tom follows Sarah to the Blaylock townhouse, Sarah is overcome with bloodlust and drains his blood, but she is so overcome by remorse that she tricks Miriam into nearly killing her. In the confusing climax, Miriam takes Sarah up to the attic to be with the others, whereupon John and the undead wraiths come back to life and destroy the vampire woman. A brief epilogue shows Sarah, who is now presumably a vampire, living in London with a female lover.

The movie version of *The Hunger* is a pale adaptation of Strieber's vampire novel. Despite some deft art house flourishes by neophyte director Tony Scott (brother of acclaimed film-maker Sir Ridley Scott), the film is shot in cold blue and gray tones that lend an emotional distance to the proceedings. At times, the movie has the ambience of a 1980s MTV music video, but these visual stylistics are not enough to sustain the film's horrific mood. Catherine Deneuve brings a sophisticated sensuality to the role of Miriam Blaylock, but otherwise fails to embody the inhuman perversity of the character. Brit rocker David Bowie delivers a solid yet understated performance as Miriam's doomed acolyte, John. For her part, Susan Sarandon drew kudos from the gay community for her steamy, semi-nude love scenes with Deneuve. Despite its flaws, however, *The Hunger* is a seminal vampire film that moved the genre away from Transylvania, wolfbane, garlic and graveyards and into a modern milieu of sex, drugs and rock 'n' roll. Bauhaus's vampire anthem, "Bela Lugosi's Dead," played over the opening credits, ushered in a new era of pop vampirism.

Streiber's novel was adapted for the screen by Ivan Davis and Michael Thomas, who simplify the plot while keeping only the bare bones of the story and tossing out most of the science. The Miriam Blaylock character has been stripped of her alien qualities, and most of the book's exquisite explanations of vampire hematology have been excised. Likewise, Strieber's theories concerning the relationship between longevity and vampiric sleep have been muddled, although some of the author's scientific rationale about how humans become vampires is mentioned briefly, although not explored. The film depicts vampirism as a medical condition that causes longevity but also rapid aging, a "blood borne metabolic aging disease."

Swarms of diseased killer bats invaded movie screens once more in *Bats* (1999). Sci-fi femme Dina Meyer (*Johnny Mnemonic, Starship Troopers*) stars as wildlife zoologist Dr. Sheila Casper, a bat expert who is recruited by the Center for Disease Control as part of a government team investigating a series of animal mutilations and human deaths near the West Texas town of Gallup. She is aided by her African-American sidekick Jimmy Sands (Leon), local sheriff Emmett Kinsey (Lou Diamond Phillips) and eccentric government scientist Dr. Alexander McCabe (Bob Gunton) as the team attempts to isolate and neutralize the vicious creatures.

McCabe reveals that the plague is the result of two bats mutated by an experimental virus that escaped from a CDC research facility and have infected the local species. The experiment was designed to increase the bat's natural intelligence and aggressiveness because, as McCabe explains, "I'm a scientist. It's what we do." Although the virus cannot infect humans, the fear is that the disease will spread throughout the bat population of the United States, creating hordes of the flying killers.

The team is tasked with locating the roost and exterminating every last bat. Without warning, however, a swarm of bats attacks Gallup that night while the redneck townsfolk vainly try to fight off the flying creatures with guns. The next day the Army is called in and Dr. Casper requests a special weapon to fight the bats, a super-cooling unit that will lower their body temperatures to the point of causing death. Using satellite imagery, the military has tracked the colony to an abandoned mine and is bivouacked nearby, ready for further action, and the refrigeration machine is lowered into the roost.

Unfortunately, the soldiers underestimate their adversaries, as the bats swarm the next night and decimate the unit. The team takes shelter in a local school and survives the attack, but Dr. McCabe goes bonkers and attempts to sabotage the mission. He reveals that he released the mutant bats on purpose and believes that he has a special bond with his creations and does not want them to be destroyed. But when he tries to demonstrate his control, the bats kill him. When the sun comes up, Dr. Casper and Sheriff Kinsey don protective suits, equipped with body armor and self-contained breathing apparatus, to insulate them from the poisonous ammonia fumes generated by concentrated bat droppings. They invade the roost and must wade, waist-deep, through a lake of bat guano in order to manually activate the machine that will freeze the bats to death.

On the surface, *Bats* seems like a rehash of *Nightwing*. Common plot elements between the two films include the southwestern U.S. location, a bat-obsessed scientist and a small-town sheriff tricked out in a cowboy hat. Although there are some derivative elements, *Bats* is a superior movie thanks to a more focused screenplay by John Logan and smoother execution by director Louis Morneau. The Native American mysticism angle is discarded in favor of science fiction; the final result exploits some of the menace of flying creatures from Alfred Hitchcock's *The Birds* (1963). The bats themselves are a lot larger and more realistic than their counterparts in *Nightwing*, eclipsing the full moon with their numbers in one memorable scene. Principals Dina Meyer and Lou Diamond Phillips turn in rather uninspired performances.

Mad science is represented by Bob Gunton's Dr. McCabe, who believes he has a special rapport with his creations that enables him to communicate with and control them; ultimately, he suffers the fate that these mentally unbalanced savants usually suffer for their hubris. Although the virus cannot infect humans, it does affect other bats, turning them into a ravenous flying plague. There is a suggestion that McCabe's experiments were designed to exploit the mutant bats as a weapon. Oddly, research scientists did contemplate using bats as weapons against the Japanese during World War II. Incendiary devices were attached to the bats' bodies that were designed to go off after the animals were released over Japanese cities and roosted on their flammable paper houses. In practice trials, however, after the bats were released they managed to chew off the firebombs, causing damage to nearby buildings, and the bizarre plan was shelved.

Vampires take over the world in the Australian action thriller *Daybreakers* (2010). The film is set in a near-future dystopia, in the year 2019, after a mutant virus spread by bats has turned almost all of the world's human population into vampires. These future noir vampires have fangs and light-reflective eyes, are immortal, and burst into flame when exposed to sunlight. Trouble is, there are too few humans left to supply the vamps with blood. These potential victims are ruthlessly hunted down by special army units and placed in commercial "blood farms," mass harvesting facilities where they are maintained in a comatose state and slowly bled to provide sustenance for the vampire population. As the blood supply dries up, unfed vampires degenerate into "subsiders," bald, bat-winged mutants who lose all capacity for rational thought and must be exterminated. This vampire society inhabits a dark city, where everyone hides from the sun and wears black clothing.

Edward Dalton (Ethan Hawke) is chief hematologist at the Bromley Marks pharmaceutical firm who is desperately working to create a synthetic blood substitute for his boss, Charles Bromley (Sam Neill), but, so far, all efforts have failed. Dalton is sympathetic to the plight of the humans, but Bromley was cured of terminal cancer when he turned and he enjoys being a vampire. Dalton's younger brother, Frankie (Michael Dorman), is one of the army's human hunters and also relishes his existence as a vamp. One night Dalton gets into a driving accident with a car full of humans and shields them from a group of vampire troopers. Soon afterward he is visited at home by Audrey

The vampire futureworld's industrial blood farms are pictured in this poster for *Daybreakers* (2009).

Bennett (Claudia Karvan), one of the people he protected. She intimates that a hidden colony of humans has found a cure for vampirism, and convinces him to accompany her to the colony.

At the colony, Dalton is introduced to Lionel "Elvis" Cormac (Willem Dafoe), an eccentric character who was once a vampire but is now human. He tells Dalton how he was cured by being exposed to a limited amount of sunlight during a car accident, and suggests that Dalton undergo an experimental procedure designed to make him human again. Dalton undergoes the treatment, which involves being bombarded with short bursts of ultraviolet light, and is cured. Unfortunately, they are tracked down by vampire troops from the government, and flee back to the city as the vamps destroy the colony. Frankie tracks down his brother and Cormac and bites Elvis in order to change him back to being a vampire, but the opposite result ensues as Frankie is changed back to being human. It turns out that treated blood is the cure to vampirism.

Riots have broken out in the city due to severe shortages of blood, as the vampire's world collapses. According to plan, Frankie delivers Dalton and Cormac to Bromley at the drug company's headquarters, where Audrey has been taken captive by the big pharma mogul. Bromley informs them that researchers have produced the long-sought-after synthetic blood substitute, but that humans will continue to be farmed because some vampires will always prefer "the real thing." "What's to cure?" he gloats triumphantly, but when he puts the bite on Dalton to change him back to a vampire, he is in for a rude surprise: he has become human again. He is then hoisted by his own petard as his vamp soldiers, driven mad by blood thirst, drain him dry. Audrey, Cormac and Dalton are poised to suffer a similar fate when Frankie drives to the rescue and sacrifices himself to save them. As the vamp troopers drain his blood they all become human *en masse*, setting off a chain reaction that will reverse the infection. A brighter day dawns for humanity's survival.

A highly original blend of action thriller, horror and science fiction, *Daybreakers* revamps elements from *I Am Legend* (a worldwide vampire plague and humans struggling to survive in a world of vampires) and Roger Corman's *Not of this Earth* (industrial blood farms). The writer/director team of brothers Peter and Michael Spierig, create a believable, yet surrealistic, future netherworld where vamps rule. Urban Brisbane locations were skillfully combined with digitally generated exteriors to build a glittering city of night, a black dystopia where coffee shops serve up cups filled with blood, humans hang like cattle as their veins are slowly emptied, and troops in futuristic battle gear chase down mutant bat creatures. The fine cast, including Ethan Hawke, Sam Neill, Willem Dafoe and Aussie actress Claudia Karvan, turn in lively and earnest performances, making the most of this unusual material. Dafoe's portrayal of the gritty Lionel "Elvis" Cormac, however, dominates much of the film, with pithy lines of dialogue such as: "Being human in a world of vampires is about as safe as barebacking a five-dollar whore."

The film departs from the contemporary notion of the superhuman vamp to depict vampires living everyday lives in a society largely similar to our own. Apart from their immortality they have no super powers, although they do burst into flames when destroyed. As in *The Bat People* and *Nightwing*, vampirism is once more the result of a disease spread by bats, and a cure is once again found in the blood of a human who sacrifices himself to save humankind from the plague, as in *The Omega Man* and *I Am Legend*. Critics have pointed out that the vampire civilization's dependence on blood is a metaphor for modern society's addiction to fossil fuels, and the film's scenes of vamps rioting as the scarce, non-renewable resource dries up is a reflection of our own dire situation, giving new meaning to the phrase, "No blood for oil."

For nearly a hundred years the cinematic vampire has been portrayed as the bringer of plagues, which are spread by their animal familiars, the rat and the bat. In some ways this motif is a reflection of the historical vampire epidemics of the 18th century, but it also reflects the rise of contemporary blood-borne diseases such as hepatitis B and AIDS, as well as exotic new diseases such as the hanta virus, which is spread by rodents and genetically engineered diseases reputedly produced in government laboratories as germ-warfare weapons. It is to be hoped that new plagues of blood will not arise, like vampires, to threaten the existence of the human race.

CHAPTER FOUR

Mad Scientists and Vampires

The figure of the mad scientist is one of the mainstays of both the science fiction and the horror film. These self-obsessed and slightly crazy savants continually strive to push the boundaries of knowledge forward, but usually wind up creating monsters instead. Some of them begin as compassionate idealists, but some are just plain nuts.

Mad scientists were created in the 19th century, in nascent works of science fiction, and are still with us two centuries later. The three archetypal mad doctors were Mary Shelley's Dr. Frankenstein in *Frankenstein* (1818), Dr. Jekyll in Robert Louis Stevenson's *The Strange Case of Dr. Jekyll and Mr. Hyde* (1886) and H.G. Wells's *The Island of Dr. Moreau* (1896), all of whom created memorable creatures that graced the printed page as well as the silver screen.

During the silent film era, American film-makers occasionally dabbled in movies featuring mad scientists. John Barrymore's version of *Dr. Jekyll and Mr. Hyde* (1920) and the Lon Chaney vehicle *The Monster* (1925) come to mind, but the mad doctor character really came of age during the period of expressionist cinema in Germany, after World War I. Early science fiction thrillers such as *Homunculus* (1916), *The Cabinet of Dr. Caligari* (1919), *The Hands of Orlac* (1924) and *Alraune* (1928) all featured mad scientists and their diabolic creations. The most memorable of all, however, was Rotwang, played by Rudolf Klein-Rogge, the evil genius who creates a robot woman in Fritz Lang's future noir epic *Metropolis* (1926). Mad scientists relocated to America with a vengeance during the early sound period with popular Hollywood fare such as *Frankenstein* (1931), *Dr. Jekyll and Mr. Hyde* (1932), *Doctor X* (1932), *The Island of Lost Souls* (1933), *The Invisible Man* (1933), *Mad Love* (1935) and *The Invisible Ray* (1936).

The vampire was poised to encounter mad scientists on the screen during this period, but hardly for the first time. Sheridan le Fanu's Dr. Hesselius and Bram Stoker's Dr. Van Helsing have some of the eccentric traits of the mad doctor, and although they do not create monsters, they are certainly associated with them. As recounted in Chapter Two, M.E. Braddon's short story "Good Lady Ducayne," published a year before Stoker's *Dracula*, was the first work to explicitly link the vampire theme to a mad scientist.

Universal's film version of *Dracula* in 1931 kicked off the horror movie wave of the 1930s. In its wake came *The Vampire Bat* (1933), a modest production filmed by indie studio Majestic Pictures on the Universal backlot. The movie takes place in the little village of Kleinschloss, where a series of grisly murders has occurred. All of the

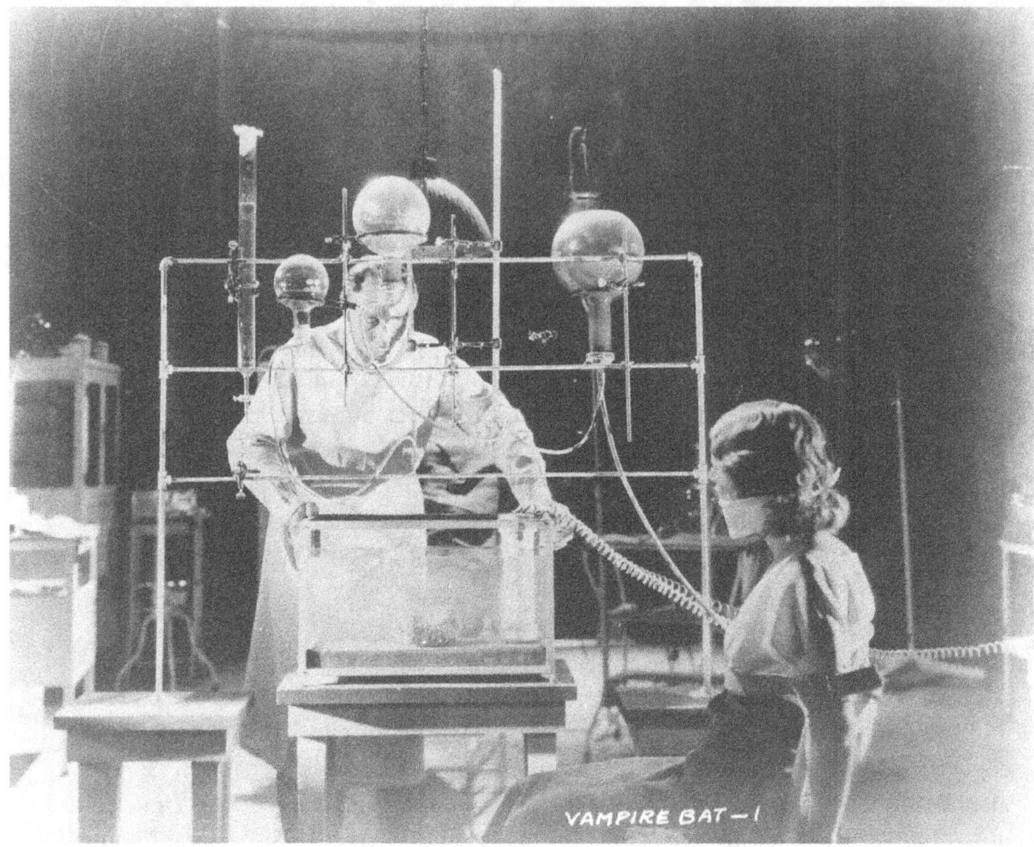

Dr. Otto von Nieman (Lionel Atwill) reveals the vampire lifeform he has created to his assistant, Ruth (Fay Wray), in *The Vampire Bat* (1933).

victims have been completely drained of blood and each victim has two puncture wounds on the throat. In addition, swarms of bats have descended on the town. Local authorities are certain that the killings are the work of a vampire, but the town's level-headed police inspector Karl Bretschneider (Melvyn Douglas) is not so sure. "I'm looking for a human being," he steadfastly proclaims to the superstitious villagers. But the town's resident physician, Dr. Otto von Nieman (Lionel Atwill), subscribes to the vampire theory, citing vamp attacks from the 17th and 18th centuries. Von Nieman is an odd bird who maintains an extensive laboratory where he conducts unusual experiments, aided by his young assistants Ruth (Fay Wray) and Emil (Ralph Howard).

Suspicions fall on Herman Glibe (Dwight Frye), a simpleton who makes pets out of bats. According to Herman, his little furry friends are not the culprits. "Bats no do," he insists, "They soft, like cat. They not bite Herman." As the mysterious murders continue, however, Herman, who has been seen skulking around town late at night, becomes the prime suspect. Inspector Bretschneider orders him brought in for questioning, but a group of overzealous villagers, wielding torches and pitchforks, cause him to jump into a chasm rather than be captured. The superstitious townsfolk drive a stake through his heart, just to be sure. But, when another victim is found drained of blood, it becomes obvious that Herman was not the culprit.

The truth is that von Nieman has created an artificial life form, a lump of pulsating protoplasm ensconced in a fish tank, that must be fed with human blood. The mad doctor has placed Emil under his hypnotic spell to help him obtain blood for his experiments, while espousing the vampire theory to muddy the waters. In order to harvest the blood from his victims, a suction device is placed against the neck, simulating the wounds from vampire fangs. Von Nieman kidnaps Ruth and the inspector and is preparing to drain their blood with the machine, when he loses his mental control over Emil. The two men struggle and manage to shoot each other to death.

Director Frank Strayer crafts a nifty little horror/mystery thriller from a screenplay by Edward T. Lowe. Strayer utilizes fluid camera shots, unusual in the static camera setups that prevailed during the early sound period, to create mood and move the narrative along. He also coaxes fine performances from leading man Melvyn Douglas, scream queen Fay Wray, horror heavy Lionel Atwill and the always-intense Dwight Frye. Frye, in particular, is at the top of his form in his over-the-top portrayal of the batty Herman Glibe, which is virtually a revamping of his role as Renfield, the Count's demented slave in Tod Browning's *Dracula*, made just two years earlier. Wray and Atwill had previously been paired in the 1932 thrillers, *Doctor X* and *Mystery of the Wax Museum*, both directed by Michael Curtiz.

The Vampire Bat substitutes science for the supernatural, explaining away the villagers' folk beliefs as mere superstition. The scientist, von Nieman, is able to use the supernatural as a distraction that conceals his homicidal deeds. His creation, the sponge-like mass of "living, growing tissue" that feeds on blood, is a unique type of science fiction vampire. In another sense, von Nieman is a techno-vamp, for it is he who drains the victims of their blood and exerts a Dracula-like hypnotic control over his cohort, Emil.

As the 1930s wore on, mad science horror movies continued to be profitable. Warner Brothers, not known for their horror product, got into the action in a sequel to their Technicolor horror hit *Doctor X*, prosaically titled *The Return of Doctor X* (1939). The sequel, however, had virtually nothing to do with the original, but was instead based on a short story entitled "The Doctor's Secret" by William J. Makin and adapted for the screen by Lee Katz. Humphrey Bogart, who was at that time a mere character actor at Warners,' was compelled to accept the part of the vampire, the titular Doctor X, by the studio heads. Bogart, who wound up with third billing on the picture, expressed the sentiment that he wouldn't mind playing a vampire if the blood was Jack Warner's.

The protagonist is Walt "Wichita" Garrett (Wayne Morris), a newspaper reporter for the New York *Morning Dispatch*, who is given a routine assignment to interview touring European actress Angela Merrova (Lia Lys). Upon arriving at her hotel room, however, he finds she has been murdered, killed by a stab wound to the abdomen.

Thinking he's got the scoop of a lifetime, Wichita phones the story in to his editor before going to the police. The presses stop, the story runs, but when the reporter and the cops revisit the scene of the crime, the body is no longer there. Worse yet, Merrova turns up at the newspaper office very much alive the following day, threatening to file a lawsuit over the story. To Garrett, however, she has an odd demeanor and an unnatural pallor, which is accentuated by her black dress.

Seeking an answer to the enigma, Garrett consults with a physician friend, Dr. Mike Rhodes (Dennis Morgan), at Jules Memorial Hospital, but he can offer no clues. Intrigued by the medical mystery, Dr. Rhodes discusses the matter with the hospital's senior hematologist, Dr. Francis Flegg (John Litel) who is similarly baffled by the strange sequence of events. Things get even weirder when one of the hospital's professional blood donors is found dead in his apartment with his body completely drained of blood. The donor had a rare group 1 (type AB) blood type, but police forensics experts find a few drops of blood at the murder scene that appear to be group 4 (type O), but which also display strange hematological abnormalities.

The rare group 1 blood is desperately needed for an operation to be performed by Dr. Flegg. Fortunately, a young nurse at the hospital, Joan Vance (Rosemary Lane), also has the rare blood type and volunteers to be an emergency donor for the patient. After the operation, Dr. Flegg waxes eloquent about the future of hematology. "The day is coming when man will be able to control blood," he proclaims, "and when that time does arrive he'll be able to control his destiny." He then quotes Scripture: "Remember the Bible—'and the life, which is the blood thereof.'"

Screen icon Humphrey Bogart as the resurrected vampire scientist Doctor Quesne (alias Doctor Xavier) in *The Return of Doctor X* (1939).

Dr. Rhodes examines the bloodstain found at the crime scene and finds that the substance does not appear to be human, but some kind of artificial blood. Baffled, Rhodes and Garrett take the specimen to Dr. Flegg's private office for a second opinion, where they encounter Flegg's creepy assistant, Dr. Quesne (Bogart). Excessively pallid, slightly effete and sporting a white "skunk stripe" through his hair, Quesne presents a ghastly appearance. Flegg emerges and dismisses Quesne, whom he claims to be treating for "a terminal case of primary anemia." Upon examining the blood sample, however, Flegg insists that it is normal group 4. After the interview, Rhodes leaves, but Garrett stays behind to

Walter Garrett (Wayne Morris, left) and Michael Rhodes (Dennis Morgan, center) confront Dr. Quesne (Humphrey Bogart) over the prone form of vampire lady Lya Lys (Angela Merrova) in *The Return of Doctor X* (1939).

snoop and watches as Merrova arrives and is given a blood transfusion by Flegg. She is subsequently found dead a second time, her body drained of blood.

Quesne's features have sparked a memory in Garrett, who digs through the newspaper's morgue until he unearths a series of stories about Dr. Maurice Xavier, the so-called "starvation killer" who starved children to death as part of some hideous experiment and he had been sent to the electric chair several years earlier. When confronted by Rhodes and Garrett, Dr. Flegg admits that he revived Xavier after his electrocution using an experimental technique involving synthetic blood, which he proceeds to demonstrate on a lab rabbit. Unfortunately, the process turned Xavier into a human vampire who can only subsist on the rare group 1-type blood; it is he who is responsible for the recent wave of vampire killings. Badly in need of another transfusion, Xavier kidnaps Joan, whom he knows, from reading Flegg's hospital records, has group 1 blood, and transports her to his ramshackle former lab, located in the wilds of New Jersey, to perform the operation. Garrett and Rhodes alert the cops, however, who rush to rescue her, and a typical Warner Brothers gunfight ensues between Xavier and the police, during which, Dr. X is shot dead.

This oddball meld of sci-fi, horror and crime melodrama is chiefly remembered for Humphrey Bogart's woeful miscasting in a role originally intended for Boris Karloff. Three years earlier, Karloff had played a similar role as a criminal brought back from the dead in Warners' *The Walking Dead* (1936), but the horror star was busy working on a series of mad doctor pictures for Columbia and declined the part. Who knew that Bogart was destined to become a Hollywood phenom just eighteen months later when he starred in Raoul Walsh's *High Sierra* and John Huston's *The Maltese Falcon*? Although it is painful to watch the future star running around in white makeup and a black cloak, Bogie comes through like a trouper, delivering a sinister performance as the dead/alive techno-vamp Quesne. Vincent Sherman, in his directorial debut, moves the action along briskly in typical Warner Bros. fashion, while adding some stylistic flourishes, but the film's main flaw is Lee Katz's unfocused screenplay, which careens from comedy to action to mystery, and the poorly conceived main character of "Wichita" Barrett, who brings a bit too much attempted comedy into the mix.

Despite its many flaws, however, *The Return of Doctor X* contains the first depiction of an actual science fiction vampire in screen history in the person of Xavier/Quesne. Like his supernatural brethren, he has come back from the dead and must have blood to live. The film contains a lengthy sequence in which Flegg brings a dead lab rabbit back to life using his experimental medical techniques, a notion gleaned from the popular culture of the time. During the early 1930s, California physician Robert E. Cornish claimed he could bring dogs back from the dead via a complex medical procedure he had developed. Cornish appeared as himself in the Universal feature film *Life Returns* (1935), in which he demonstrated his techniques on a dog, and also provided technical expertise for mad science thrillers, such as MGM's *Mad Love* (1935) and Warners' *The Walking Dead* (1936). Here science, not sorcery, was the vehicle for the resurrection of the dead.

Bela Lugosi, who had starred as the Count in the 1931 production of *Dracula* (the film that had kicked off the whole Universal Studios horror movie cycle), had fallen on hard times by the early 1940s and was reduced to making low-budget programmers at poverty-row studios like Producers Releasing Company (PRC). One such production was *The Devil Bat* (1940), a modest horror thriller that takes place in Heathville, a small town on the outskirts of Chicago. Lugosi plays Dr. Carruthers, a research scientist for Heath Cosmetics, a firm whose formula for a greaseless cold cream has made a fortune for the firm. Feeling he has been robbed of profits that are rightly his, Carruthers plans revenge on the company's CEOs.

Toward this end he toils in a secret laboratory in his home, creating a gigantic bat using "glandular stimulation through electrical impulses," a technique which involves passing a high-voltage current into the creature. In order to guide the bat to its intended victims, he uses a distinctive scent he has trained the bat to recognize. The fragrance is contained in an aftershave lotion that he gives to the victims. Once splashed on the neck, the bat will detect it and go for the jugular. The "devil bat," with a five-foot wingspan, dives on its prey and comes screeching out of the sky like the proverbial bat out of hell.

After one of the mad doctor's enemies is dispatched in this fashion (without the bat having been seen), Johnny Layton (Dave O'Brien), ace reporter for the Chicago *Daily Register*, is sent to Heathville, along with his sidekick, photographer "One Shot" McGuire (Donald Kerr), to investigate the mysterious murder. The next time the bat claims a victim, Layton catches a glimpse of the creature and reports the phenomenon to his paper, causing a rash of lurid headlines about the "devil bat." Sniffing around for clues, the intrepid newshound finds a bottle of the shaving lotion in the home of one of the deceased and fingers Carruthers for the crimes, although he has no proof. His suspicions are further aroused when the doctor gifts him with a bottle of the after-shave.

The doctor's next intended victim is Mary Heath (Suzanne Kaaren), daughter of the Heath Cosmetics magnate. This time he has spiked Mary's cologne with the formula. In the meantime, Layton breaks into the doctor's house and discovers his secret lab and knows with certainty that he is the killer. That night, when Carruthers lets loose the devil bat, he confronts the doctor and douses him with the shaving lotion, causing the bat to attack him and tear out his jugular. When the creature goes after Mary, Layton shoots it dead, ending the creature's reign of terror.

Widely considered one of the best horror films made at PRC during the '40s (although this isn't saying much), *The Devil Bat* soars on Lugosi's restrained performance as the vengeful mad savant, Dr. Carruthers. Bela spends a fair amount of screen time wearing welder's goggles and leering dementedly as he supersizes his bat with bolts of electricity. Director Jean Yarborough (spelled Yarbrough in the credits) shows a fine sense of pacing throughout, and he would later go on to direct horror thrillers and comedies at Universal. Scripter John T. Neville labors mightily to make this loopy melodrama plausible, and almost succeeds.

The film's chief drawback is its low-budget production values. When seen in long shots, the devil bat is clearly a prop hanging upside-down on what appears to be a clothes hanger, while in close-ups a live bat is used, jarring the viewer with the incongruity. In flight, however, the huge flying creature is especially menacing as it swoops down on its victims while shrieking hideously. Mad science is used to create a murderous monster, although in nature bats are harmless creatures. Still, the very idea of a giant bat preying on humans is the stuff of nightmares. Six years later, PRC produced a sequel entitled *Devil Bat's Daughter* (1946), but it had very little to do with the original film.

By 1945, the Universal horror movie cycle that began in 1931 with *Dracula* and *Frankenstein*, was coming to an end. The last film in the series was *House of Dracula* (1945), a monster rally that featured the Wolfman and Frankenstein's monster in addition to Count Dracula, with a mad doctor and a hunchbacked nurse thrown in for good measure. The story is set in the mythical realm of Vasaria, an eastern European

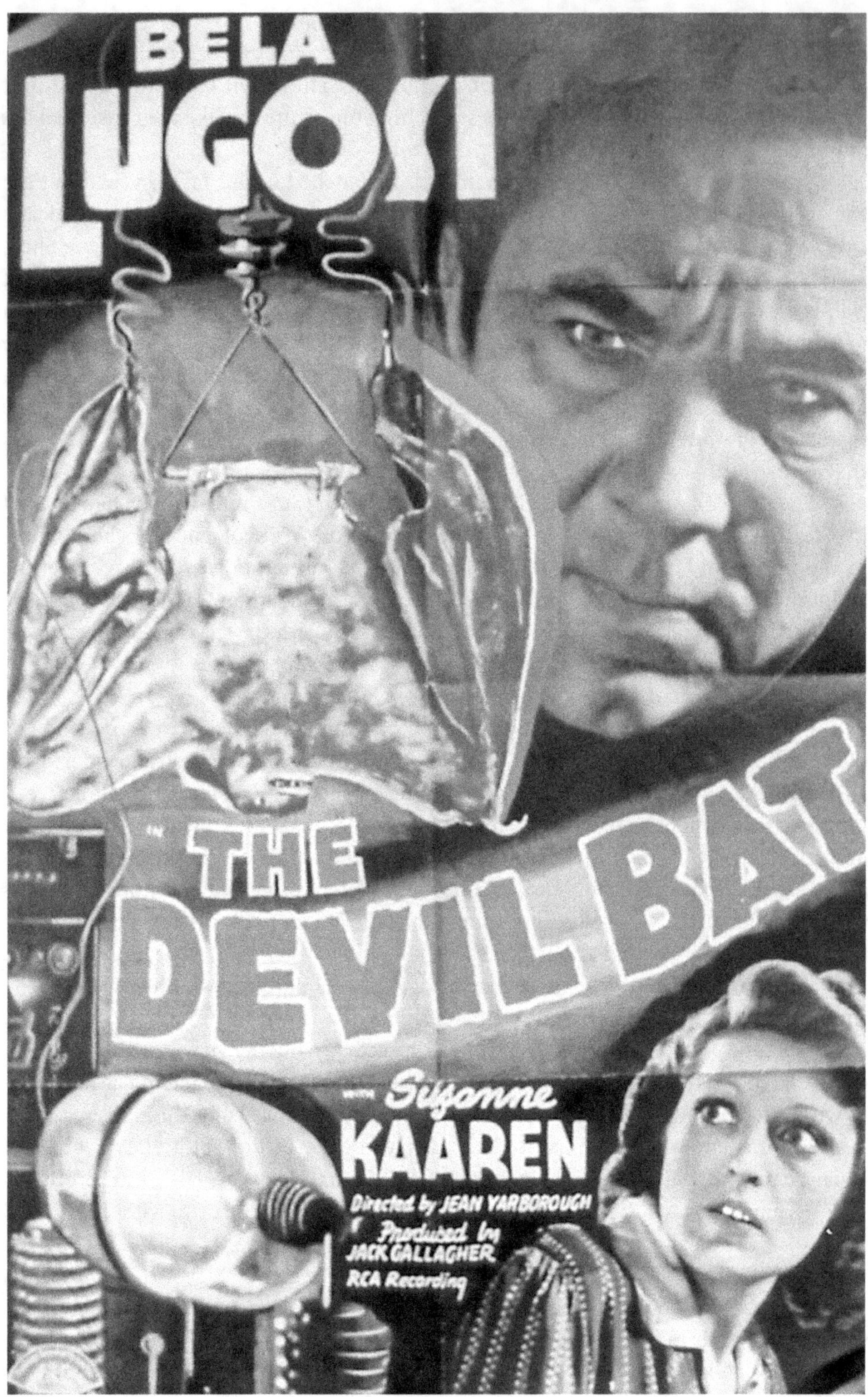

Mad scientist Dr. Carruthers (Bela Lugosi) and his monstrous creation are featured in this poster for *The Devil Bat* (1940).

locale used in several of Universal's horror pictures in lieu of Transylvania. The renowned physician and research scientist Dr. Franz Edelman (Onslow Stevens) resides in a gothic castle high on a hill overlooking the sea, where he has an extensive laboratory facility.

One night the doctor has an unusual walk-in patient—Count Dracula (John Carradine). The Count, who introduces himself at "Baron Latos," declares that he has decided "to seek release from a curse of misery and horror," and seeks Edelman's medical help in curing his condition. At first, the doctor dismisses the existence of vampirism, explaining that "cases have been recorded in which the victims, driven by some abnormal urge, actually believe that the blood of other people was necessary to keep them alive and became psychopathic killers in order to obtain it. These beliefs probably upset their metabolisms, induced fixations, lustful appetites." Nevertheless, Edelman accepts the Count as a patient because curing his condition represents "a challenge to medical science." While in the doctor's office, the vampire encounters his nurse, Milizia (Martha O'Driscoll), for whom he feels a sexual/vampiric attraction.

By some odd coincidence, a coffin containing earth from Dracula's grave is conveniently found in the cellar of Edelman's castle, allowing the vamp to stick around for his treatments. Taking a sample of Dracula's blood, Dr. Edelman discovers an unusual parasite in the specimen. With the help of his second nurse, Nina (Jane Adams) who is pretty but hunchbacked, the doctor prepares an antitoxin and administers it to the Count via blood transfusion. The doctor hopes to eventually cure the vampire with regular treatments of the antitoxin-laden blood.

In the meantime, Larry Talbot (Lon Chaney, Jr.) who turns into the Wolfman during nights when the moon is full, shows up and demands that the doctor treat him for his monstrous affliction. Edelman is skeptical again, but after watching Talbot transform, he theorizes that "pressure upon certain parts of the brain" is the cause of his lycanthropy. He proposes a cure, utilizing a serum derived from a mold produced by a rare plant, *clavaria formosa*, that he cultivates in a hothouse. The serum will dissolve some of the bone in Talbot's skull and relieve the pressure without resorting to surgery.

Complications arise, however, when Frankenstein's monster is discovered in a cave beneath the castle encased in mud after having been sucked into quicksand at the conclusion of the previous movie, *House of Frankenstein*. His scientific curiosity piqued, Dr. Edelman brings the monster, who is in a cataleptic state, into his laboratory but declines to revive him. Things go further awry when Dracula, who is lusting after Milizia, reverses the flow of blood during one of the treatments and transfuses some of his vampire blood into Edelman's veins. This causes the doctor to metamorphose into an evil version of himself in a Jekyll and Hyde–type transformation, but Edelman uses his will power to regain his proper senses. When the Count tries to put the bite on Milizia, the doctor interferes and destroys the vampire by dragging his coffin into the sunlight.

Dr. Edelman and his medical team race against time to collect enough of the mold

serum to treat Talbot before the next full moon, and they finally succeed. While Talbot is recuperating, however, the doctor reverts to his evil self and murders one of the villagers, then returns to the castle and becomes Edelman once more. When the night of the full moon comes, Talbot finds he is cured of his lycanthropy, but the doctor transforms again and commences to bring the Monster back to life. As sparks fly from the big machines in Edelman's laboratory, the villagers, under the leadership of Police Inspector Holtz (Lionel Atwill), march on the castle with torches and pitchforks. In the meantime, the doctor's evil self goes on a killing rampage and strangles Nina, but when he menaces Milizia, Talbot shoots him dead. Fortified with electricity, the Monster revives, but Talbot douses him with flammable chemicals. Talbot escapes with Milizia, and the villagers arrive to witness the doctor's laboratory being destroyed in a fiery conflagration.

Remembered chiefly as the swan song of the seemingly immortal Universal monsters, *House of Dracula* seems to be on autopilot under the indifferent direction of Erle C. Kenton, but the real culprit is screenwriter Edward T. Lowe, who devised the film's highly contrived plotline. Dracula's coffin, for instance, is conveniently found installed in Edelman's cellar, while Frankenstein's Monster just happens to turn up in a nearby cavern.

(Top to bottom) Glenn Strange as Frankenstein's Monster, Lon Chaney, Jr., as the Wolf Man, John Carradine as Dracula, Onslow Stevens as the Mad Doctor and Jane Adams as the Hunchback are pictured in this poster for *House of Dracula* (1945).

On the plus side, cinematographer George Robinson, who worked to create the distinctive look of many of Universal's horror classics, paints the film with dark shadows and serves up gobs of murky atmosphere.

John Carradine, reprising his role as the Count from the studio's previous monster rally *House of Frankenstein*, visually resembles Stoker's conception of the character, but portrays Dracula as a mannerly, well-spoken gent in evening clothes, a performance that lacks the on-screen menace of Bela Lugosi. Lon Chaney, Jr., in his fourth outing as the Wolfman, was reportedly struggling with alcoholism during filming. Glenn Strange as Frankenstein's Monster goes from resurrection to cremation in mere minutes of screen time at the film's conclusion, while horror movie veteran Lionel Atwill, in one of his final performances, has a throwaway part as Inspector Holtz.

In *House of Dracula* the supernatural is challenged by science, as represented by the kindly, rationalistic figure of Dr. Edelman, who attempts to treat the monsters using experimental medical techniques, with mixed results. Edelman rationalizes Dracula's vampirism as being a mere blood abnormality and Talbot's lycanthropy as the product of a brain disorder, but, ultimately, he is overwhelmed by the forces of darkness. As Susannah Clements notes in *The Vampire Defanged*, "Although humans might try to understand the supernatural through the lens of a scientific worldview, science is never enough to fully understand and address the supernatural power. In *House of Dracula*, science might have cured the Wolf Man, but it also ended up contaminating the scientist with vampire blood and turning him into a monster. Science might help, but it simply is not enough in the fight against sin and evil."[1] In fact, Edelman, transformed into the Mr. Hyde–like mad doctor character, was billed as one of the film's monsters alongside Dracula and the other tenants of his "house." The notion of a vampire seeking medical help to escape from the curse of vampirism had been borrowed from the sequel to *Dracula*, *Dracula's Daughter* (1936, see Chapter Six). The plot of *House of Dracula*, however, does not make it clear whether the Count is really seeking a cure from Dr. Edelman, or if it is merely a ploy to get close to Milizia.

The end of World War II also rang down the curtain on the horror film until well into the 1950s, as war-weary movie audiences turned away from the escapist fantasies of the genre toward more realistic film fare. But the three Universal monsters had one more appearance to make three years later—opposite screen funnymen Bud Abbott and Lou Costello in *Abbott and Costello Meet Frankenstein* (1948). Lon Chaney, Jr., and Glenn Strange would reprise their roles as the Wolf Man and the Monster, while Bela Lugosi would portray the role of Count Dracula for his second and last time in a motion picture. And, as in *House of Dracula*, the Count would once again be involved with mad science.

Chick Young (Abbott) and Wilbur Gray (Costello) are postal workers in the town of La Miranda, Florida, where two large crates containing the purported remains of Count Dracula and the Frankenstein Monster arrive by special delivery. The grisly cargo is bound for a local sideshow, McDougal's House of Horrors, where they are to be placed on display. Wilbur nearly goes postal when the reanimated Count emerges

Funnymen Bud Abbott and Lou Costello are menaced by (left to right) Glenn Strange as the Monster, Bela Lugosi as Dracula and Lon Chaney, Jr., as the Wolf Man in Universal's final monster rally, *Abbott and Costello Meet Frankenstein* (1948).

from his coffin and revives the Monster. The two creatures stalk off into the night, leaving the boys to take the rap for the theft of the valuable shipment, but they are bailed out of jail by Joan Raymond (Jane Randolph), a canny insurance investigator who pretends to have a romantic interest in Wilbur in the hope that he will lead her to the missing property.

Wilbur is also being courted by Sandra (Lenore Aubert), but for an entirely different reason. She is, in reality, one Dr. Cassandra Mornay, a scientist who is on the run from European authorities after conducting a series of unorthodox experiments. Now continuing her work in a laboratory located inside a gothic castle on a nearby island, Dr. Mornay is collaborating with Count Dracula, who has assumed the identity of a visiting scientist named Dr. Lajos. Their goal is to transplant Wilbur's brain into the skull of the Monster in order to make it more docile.

Soon afterward, Larry Talbot, who has been in pursuit of Lajos/Dracula, shows up in La Miranda and enlists the aid of Wilbur and Chick. After a series of comic misadventures everyone winds up on the island, where Wilbur is captured and prepped for radical brain surgery by Dr. Mornay and the Count. All hell breaks loose when the full moon rises and transforms Talbot into the Wolf Man, who goes after Dracula while the monster chases Chick and Wilbur around the castle. Dracula tries to escape by turning into a bat, but the Wolf Man grabs it and they both tumble into the sea. The Monster is consumed by flames yet again, but this time it's for good.

Widely considered one of the comedy duo's best efforts, the film would inspire a series of horror/comedy sequels, as Abbott and Costello met with the rest of the monster menagerie, including the Invisible Man, the Mummy, and Dr. Jekyll and Mr. Hyde. A sparkling script by John Grant, Fredric I. Renaldo and Robert Lees, and flawless execution by director Charles T. Barton, create a perfect meld of laughter and the macabre. Bud and Lou are at the top of their game, while Lugosi, Chaney and Strange provide just the right amount of menace as counterpoint to the comic hi-jinks.

Bram Stoker hinted that Count Dracula had a scientific disposition in *Dracula*, and Lugosi had previously played a Dracula-like mad scientist in Columbia's *The Return of the Vampire* (1943), but this was the first onscreen portrayal of the Dracula character as an evil savant, a role he would later assume in *Van Helsing* (2004). As Dr. Lajos, the Count is shown working in the lab while performing the techniques that will revive the Monster. As vampirologist David J. Skal observes, "*Abbott and Costello Meet Frankenstein* is of some interest today for its superimposition onto Dracula of both the vampire and mad scientist traditions; the time-honored opposition of science and the supernatural settles down for a cheerful codependency."[2]

Horror and science fiction films were on hiatus between 1945 and 1951, but mad science came back in a big way in the atomic '50s. England's newly minted Hammer Studios got into the game in the middle of the decade with a series of sci-fi films based on the exploits of intrepid rocket scientist Dr. Bernard Quatermass, a character that had been created by scenarist Nigel Kneale for a series of popular television melodramas broadcast on the BBC. While not an evil or schizophrenic scientist in the classic sense, Quatermass invariably stirred up a mess of trouble while exploring the unknown reaches of the universe.

In the first movie in the series, *The Quatermass Xperiment* (1955), released in America as *The Creeping Unknown*, Dr. Quatermass (Brian Donlevy) has sent a rocket into outer space with a three-man crew that has crash-landed near a small town in rural England. Only one of the astronauts, Victor Caroon (Richard Wordsworth) is found inside the spaceship, while the fate of the other two men remains a mystery. Caroon is in a state of shock and is hospitalized, but Police Inspector Lomax (Jack Warner) suspects that Caroon may have murdered the other two crewmen, and begins an investigation. Rather than working at cross-purposes, Quatermass teams up with Lomax in order to solve the mystery.

Caroon remains in a catatonic state and his wife, Judith (Margia Dean), wants to get him away from Quatermass and the government doctors that she feels are acting against his best interests. She hires Christie (Harold Lang), a private investigator to smuggle him out of the clinic, but as they are hustling down the hospital elevator, Caroon suddenly strikes out. The P.I.'s corpse is later found to be a dried-out husk from which all the bodily fluids have been extracted. Caroon stumbles out into the night and finds his way to a drug store, where he seeks something that will help him end his life, but instead winds up confronting the pharmacist, who is found in the same desiccated state as the first victim. Prowling around the London docks, the infected astronaut encounters a little girl playing with her doll, but the last vestige of his humanity prevents him from taking her life.

A massive manhunt ensues that leads Quatermass and Lomax to the city zoo, where several animals have been found dead, along with a slime trail. Following the trail around town, the investigators arrive at Westminster Abbey, where they find that Caroon has morphed into an inhuman monster that resembles a giant octopus clinging to a metal scaffolding. Quatermass is concerned that, if the creature is shot, it will release a cloud of spores that will enable it to reproduce, so a high-voltage cable is attached to the scaffold and the monster is electrocuted. In the aftermath, Quatermass stalks off to start another science project that will surely involve more extraterrestrial mischief.

Nigel Kneale's original story is vastly more intelligent and mature than the typical '50s-era horror/sci-fi movie product, and the basic material is further burnished by the deft screenplay contributions and inspired directorial flourishes of Val Guest. The director shoots in a documentary style, using real locations as a backdrop to the fantastic goings-on. Hammer cast American character actor Brian Donlevy as Quatermass to make the film more palatable to U.S. audiences, and Donlevy plays the character with brusque aloofness. Richard Wordsworth steals the show, however, as the doomed Caroon, his angular features twisting into a mask of bewilderment and pain during his horrific ordeal. The scene in which he confronts the little girl is especially well acted and recalls a similar monster/child confrontation, in James Whale's *Frankenstein* (1931).

The infected astronaut, who is the film's vampire, fuses the science fiction notions of the vampiric plague carrier and the extraterrestrial bloodsucker into a single character. In addition to blood, Caroon extracts all the fluids from his victims, even turning bone to powder. *The Quatermass Xperiment* prefigures the alien vamps in Tobe Hooper's space opera epic *Lifeforce* (1985), who similarly turn their human victims into dried-out husks. Made before manned spaceflight became a reality, the film reflects anxieties about the exploration of the cosmos and what kind of micro-organisms might be found lurking, not on other planets, but in near–Earth space, a theme picked up on in similarly themed sci-fi films, such as *First Man into Space* (1958) and *The Andromeda Strain* (1971). Three sequels followed: *Quatermass II* (1957), *Quatermass* and the Pit (1968) and *The Quatermass Conclusion* (1979), but none of them involved vampires.

Meanwhile, back in Hollywood, producer Herman Cohen was busy churning out cheesy, low-budget horror flicks for another fledgling studio, American International Pictures. Cohen's *I Was a Teenage Werewolf* (1957), starring a young Michael Landon, was a box-office hit for AIP, so Cohen commissioned screenwriter Ralph Thornton to script a follow-up featuring a female vampire. The result was *Blood of Dracula* (1957), which could have more accurately been titled, "I Was a Teenage Dracula."

Teenage vampire Nancy Perkins (Sandra Harrison) demonstrates the possibilities of ludicrous makeup in *Blood of Dracula* (1957).

As the film opens, teenager Nancy Perkins (Sandra Harrison) is being sent off to the Sherwood School for Girls, a boarding school, by her father. Nancy has issues with her family because her father has remarried only six months after her mother's death, and arrives at the school full of smoldering resentments at being uprooted from her former life. She soon falls under the spell of Miss Branding (Louise Lewis), the school's chemistry teacher, who harbors resentments of her own against the patriarchy. Miss Branding has been working on a revolutionary thesis for years that is always rejected by the male-dominated scientific community. "We live in a world ruled by men for men," she grouses, adding, "They'll destroy the world through their reckless experiments." Her research involves finding a "power strong enough to destroy the world buried within each of us."

Miss Branding hits on the rebellious Nancy as a subject for her unorthodox experiments. Befriending the girl, she uses hypnotism in conjunction with the occult force contained in an ancient amulet "from the Carpathian Mountains," the legendary realm of Dracula, to put Nancy into an altered state of consciousness. Using a combination of ancient and modern techniques, Nancy is transformed into a vamp with a bad hairdo, bad eye makeup, bad teeth and a bad attitude. Victims of the teenage monster start to pile up, their bodies drained of blood, with puncture marks on their throats, as the cops mutter about tales of vampires from the Old Country.

Nancy has no memory of the killings, but disturbing images begin to surface in her consciousness. When her former boyfriend, Glen (Michael Hall), unexpectedly shows up at the school, she nearly transforms into the creature, but uses her willpower to change back before she can put the bite on him. Confronting Miss Branding about her hypnosis treatments, Nancy turns into the vampire once more and attacks the scientist, who can no longer control her with the medallion, and both of them are killed in the homicidal mêlée.

Blood of Dracula is typical Cohen drive-in fare aimed at a juvenile audience. Following the template laid down in *Teenage Werewolf*, the movie contains large doses of teen angst, violence, monstrosity, and music, as each of Cohen's productions usually included an obligatory rock 'n' roll number, in this case an especially insipid song called "Puppy Love" (not to be confused with the '50's hit tune of the same name). Herbert L. Strock's pedestrian direction is adequate, but Ralph Thornton's screenplay contains some execrable lines of bad dialogue such as, "The power to kill is never pretty," and, "You can't laugh away murder." Principals Sandra Harrison and Louise Lewis do their best with this weak material, and there is perhaps a hint of lesbianism in their master/slave relationship.

The film associates vampirism with social rebellion and 1950s-era juvenile delinquency. Protagonist Nancy Perkins is an angst-ridden societal outcast who abandons her mascara and lipstick to become a murderous, uglified *femme fatale*. Supernatural and science fiction themes are mingled as the occult power of the Carpathian amulet, presumably imbued with the vampire magic of the Dracula clan, is combined with hypnotism to transform Nancy into a vampire. Science is very much in evidence, however, as amateur scientist Miss Branding is shown surrounded by bubbling chemical retorts and handling hazardous materials in protective gear in her laboratory. Vampirism is also associated with feminism, as the female scientist laments that her male counterparts are "reckless fools" who will turn the people of Earth into "monsters; grotesque, frightening fiends," a process that she will rectify with her feminine savantry. The creation of the female vampire is presented as a feminist parallel development to the masculine science of the atomic bomb.

Vampirism and mad science were also paired in the United Artists sci-fi horror film *The Vampire* (1957). The story takes place in a sleepy suburb of Los Angeles, where physician Paul Beecher (John Beal) leads a comfortable, if uneventful, existence as the town doctor, along with his adolescent daughter, Betsy. Everything changes when he makes a house call on a colleague, Dr. Matthew Campbell (Wood Romoff), a research psychologist who is seriously ill. Dr. Campbell has been conducting experiments on animals, including a cage full of vampire bats. Before dying of a heart attack, Campbell gives Dr. Beecher a bottle of pills he has produced from an experimental formula, and Beecher, who suffers from migraines, mistakes the bottle for his headache medication and pops one of Campbell's tablets by accident.

The medicine helps his migraine but also causes Beecher to have an episode of amnesia. Soon, he is downing more of the pills, which seem to have an addictive quality. Next, an unidentified prowler is seen skulking around the neighborhood, and one of Beecher's patients is discovered dead, under mysterious circumstances. The town's detective, Buck Donnelly (Kenneth Tobey), is called in to investigate, but although strange bite marks are found on the victim, the police inquiry fails to reach any conclusions. When Dr. Will Beaumont (Dabs Greer), one of Campbell's colleagues from a nearby university, arrives to check on Campbell's laboratory, Beecher learns the true nature of Campbell's experiments.

Dr. Paul Beecher (John Beal) is transformed into a bloodsucking fiend in this poster for *The Vampire* (1957).

The dead scientist had been working on a formula designed to speed up, or even reverse, the effects of evolution. Unfortunately, the formula, derived from vampire bats, is highly addictive and causes rapid "capillary disintegration" in experimental subjects. The vampire bat pills are causing Beecher to transform into a Mr. Hyde–like bloodsucker who has been victimizing the townsfolk, and later has no memory of the murderous episodes. As the bodies pile up, Beecher comes to realize his predicament, but he is unable to break his addiction to the medication. Further research reveals that the victims do not die from lack of blood, but from a bat-borne virus contained in Beecher's saliva that is injected during his vampire bites. In the final reel, Beecher transforms in front of his girlfriend, Carol Butler (Coleen Gray), but Buck and his police squad arrive in time to shoot the human vampire dead.

This obscure UA programmer is a lively exercise in '50s sci-fi horror that is utterly devoid of AIP's light touch. Paul Landres's direction of Pat Fielder's screenplay plays like high tragedy without comic relief, songs or loopy comic dialogue. Lead actor John Beal's tortured performance as the vampiric medico carries the film, even when he has to act while wearing mediocre monster makeup that makes him look like he has a bad case of psoriasis. The rest of the cast, including Kenneth Tobey and Colleen Gray, turn in adequate but uninspired performances.

Like *House of Dracula, The Vampire* combines mad science and vampirism in a character who is both physician and monster in a Jekyll/Hyde–type relationship, although poor Dr. Beecher is merely a small-town doctor who accidently gets involved with an insane research project. The vampire is also connected to the degenerative viral disease transmitted from the bats into the formula, and with drug addiction, as Beecher succumbs to the habituation syndrome caused by the ingestion of pills. This film should not be confused with a Mexican production with the same title released in the same year, directed by Fernando Mendez, that featured a supernatural vampire.

By the late 1950s, Hammer Studios had revolutionized the horror film with the first in a series of Universal monster movie retreads filmed in lurid Technicolor, *The Curse of Frankenstein* (1957) and *Horror of Dracula* (1958). Another fledgling British studio, Artistes Alliance, tried to steal some of Hammer's thunder with a color horror film of their own, entitled *Blood of the Vampire* (1958). Screenwriter Jimmy Sangster, who had written the Hammer Frankenstein and Dracula flicks, was hired on to script and hopefully provide some Hammer-inspired horror movie magic.

The film begins with a pre-credit sequence set in Transylvania in 1874, where a title card informs the audience that "the most loathsome scourge ever to afflict this earth was that of the vampire." A body is shown being staked and buried in a graveyard by a group of grim-looking men. Afterward, a deformed hunchback, Carl (Victor Maddern), exhumes the vampire's corpse and delivers it to a local physician, along with instructions for a heart-transplant operation. After performing the procedure, Carl brutally knifes the doctor to death for his troubles.

Six years later, in the city of Carlstadt, a young physician, Dr. John Pierre (Vincent Ball), is on trial for medical malpractice after one of his patients dies from a blood transfusion (an uncommon practice in 1880). Dr. Pierre is found guilty, but instead of being jailed in a regular prison, he is remanded to an asylum for the criminally insane run by one Dr. Callistratus (Sir Donald Wolfit). Callistratus is, in fact, the "vampire" who was resurrected in Transylvania six years earlier, using advanced medical techniques, and is now draining the inmates of their blood for his unorthodox experiments. He enlists Dr. Pierre's aid in performing what he is told is humanitarian research in blood transfusion and in determining the variety of different human blood types. In exchange for his co-operation, Pierre is spared from the drudgery and routine punishments doled out to the other inmates.

Pierre soon learns that the asylum director's motives are not as pure as he has been led to believe. He joins with a fellow inmate, Kurt Urach (William Devlin), in an escape scheme, but Callistratus foils their plan. Kurt is severely wounded, and Pierre is locked in the mad doctor's basement laboratory, while Callistratus informs the authorities that both men have died in the escape attempt. Pierre's fiancée, Madeleine Duval (Barbara Shelley), however, is not convinced, and executes a plan to infiltrate the asylum by taking a job as a domestic servant. Her true identity is soon discovered, however, and she winds up chained next to Pierre in the doctor's dungeon.

Callistratus explains to the hapless pair that the Transylvanian peasantry believed him to be a vampire because of his blood transfusion experiments, and he cheated being staked by transfusing himself with a rare blood type that kept him in a state of suspended animation until he received the heart transplant. Unfortunately, the transfusion caused him to acquire a degenerative blood disorder, and he has been secretly bleeding the asylum's inmates in order to keep himself alive. His next step will be to perform a total transfusion of blood between Kurt, whom he has infected with his diseased blood, and Madeleine. When Carl hears this, the hunchbacked servant, who has taken a shine to the girl, attacks the mad doctor and gets shot. Kurt suddenly revives and goes after Callistratus and, with Pierre's help, overpowers him. As Madeleine, Kurt and Pierre are escorting Callistratus to the authorities, the dying Carl lets loose a pack of the asylum's savage guard dogs, who attack Callistratus and tear him limb from limb.

Packed with the blood, gore and sadism of Jimmy Sangster's script, *Blood of the Vampire* is practically indistinguishable from the Hammer horror product. Sangster's approach, however, departs from the supernatural vampire formula of the Hammer Dracula series by grafting an element of science fiction onto the traditional notion of vampirism, thereby fusing elements of both the Frankenstein and Dracula myths. Director Henry Cass moves the plot along vigorously while providing effective gothic atmosphere. The acclaimed British Shakespearean actor Sir Donald Wolfit delivers a fine performance as Dr. Callistratus, and is ably assisted by Hammer horror heroine Barbara Shelley. Victor Maddern prevails over his grotesque makeup as the sympathetic Carl in a role that recalls J. Carol Naish's similar part as a lovesick hunchback in Universal's *House of Frankenstein* (1944).

As in *The Return of Dr. X* and *House of Dracula*, the mad doctor character becomes transformed into a vampire. The film's pseudoscience, such as the do-it-yourself 19th century heart-transplant surgery and suspended animation, strains credulity while reaching for a scientific rationale for vampiric resurrection. Vampirism is again associated with a rare blood disorder and transfusions. For modern day viewers, the film's technology represents an example of "Steampunk," a sub-genre of science fiction that evokes the 19th century sci-fi of Jules Verne and H.G. Wells, although this retro approach was not a category of SF when the film was made.

The Hammer horror films were part of a gothic cinema revival in Europe that also became popular in Italy. Films such as Ricardo Freda's *The Devil's Commandment* (1957) and Mario Bava's *Black Sunday* (1960) ushered in a new wave of continental horrors. Italian director Giorgio Ferroni entered this neo-gothic territory in an offbeat French/Italian production with the enigmatic title *Mill of the Stone Women* (1960).

The film is set in 19th century Holland, where a young art student, Hans von Arnim (Pierre Brice), travels to the tiny hamlet of Veeze to confer with art professor Gregorius Wahl (Herbert Böhme) about writing a monograph commemorating the

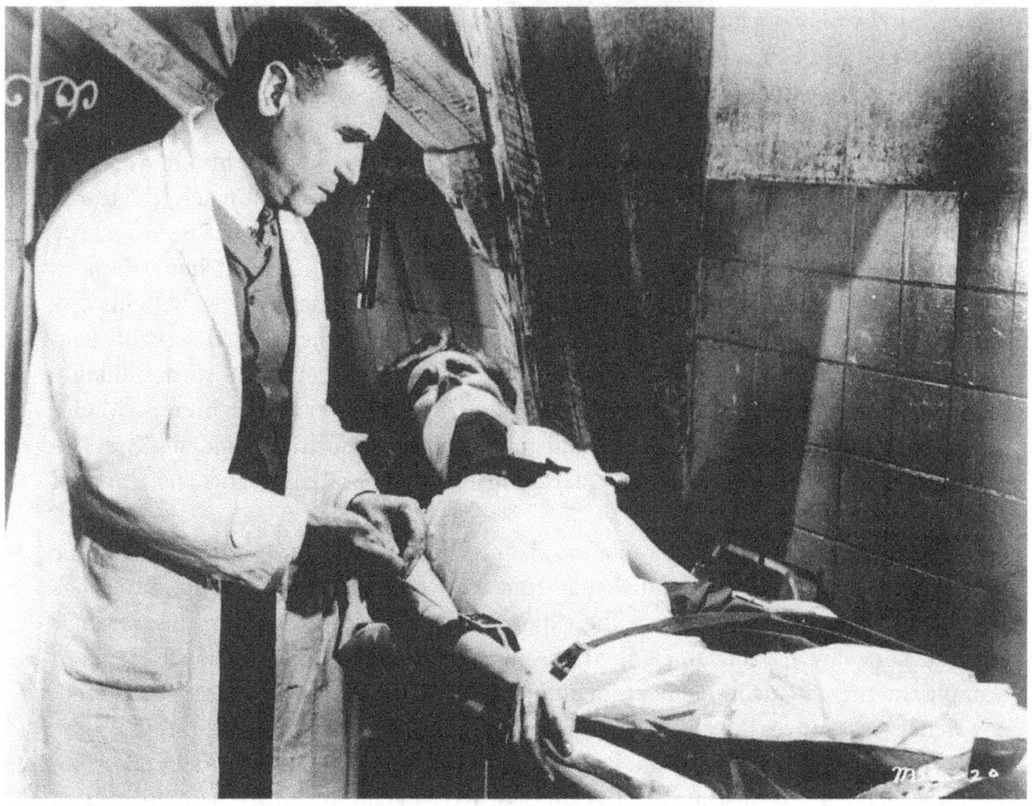

Dr. Loren Bohlem (Wolfgang Preiss) prepares to drain the blood from Annelore (Liana Orfei) and petrify her in *Mill of the Stone Women* (1960).

centennial of "the Carousel." This is a kind of mechanized wax museum where grotesque stone statues representing the most notorious *femmes fatales* of history parade around a stage on a set of tracks, a contrivance that was created by Wahl's father. Mechanical power to animate the figures is provided by a windmill, which also serves at the professor's abode. While working on the article at the spooky old mill, Hans encounters a beautiful and mysterious young woman whom he learns is the professor's daughter, Elfie (Scilla Gabel). Elfie is said to be a convalescent suffering from an unspecified wasting disease and is being treated by live-in physician Dr. Loren Bohlem (Wolfgang Preiss).

Although Hans is engaged to his sweetheart, Liselotte Kornheim (Dany Carrel), he soon falls prey to the seductions of the sensuous Elfie. When Dr. Bohlem learns of their tryst, he warns Hans that she has a serious congenital illness, and that one more crisis in her life could cause her death. Hearing this, Hans dutifully breaks off his affair with Elfie, causing her to collapse as if dead. Confused and distraught, Hans wanders around the mill in a hallucinatory state and catches a glimpse of a model at Wahl's art school, Annelore (Liana Orfei), tied up in the basement. The following evening, upon returning to the mill, Hans is yet more bewildered to encounter Elfie seemingly alive and well once more.

It turns out that Elfie has a rare blood disorder that causes her to go into death-like cataleptic fits until her sick blood is replaced by a total transfusion from a healthy person. Dr. Bohlem is keeping her alive by performing these procedures in a laboratory in the mill's basement, using a suction-pump mechanism. Annelore, who has been kidnapped for this purpose, is drained of her blood as Elfie is restored to life, and once she is dead the professor treats her body with a special compound that petrifies her skin. All of the stone figures on the carousel are the mummified corpses of victims of the fiends.

Dr. Bohlem tells Wohl that he has concocted a serum that will cure Elfie's condition permanently, but she needs one last transfusion from a donor with a rare blood type that happens to belong to Liselotte. When Liselotte comes up missing, Hans recalls seeing Annelore tied up, and he and his stalwart buddy Ralf (Marco Guglielmi) decide to pay the mill a visit. As Liselotte is being prepped for the operation, Bohlem tells Wahl that he will only give him the serum if he will consent to let Elfie marry him. Horrified by the thought, the professor stabs Bohlem to death, only to find that the glass vial containing the serum has been shattered. In despair, Wahl torches the mill, but Hans and Ralf arrive in a timely manner to rescue Liselotte while the professor is immolated and the corpses on the carousel melt horribly in the conflagration.

One of the true classics of '60s Italian gothic cinema, *Mill of the Stone Women* is a beautifully atmospheric exercise in horror and mystery. Director Giorgio Ferroni effectively utilizes subdued colors to create a gothic mood of morbidity and decay, and makes fine use of picturesque European locations to obtain a period flavor. Released in the same year as Mario Bava's horror classic *Black Sunday* (1960), the film also exhibits the gothic influences of Hammer and of Roger Corman's American International Poe series. The screenplay by Remigio Del Grosso, Ugo Liberatore, Giorgio Stegani and director Ferroni was supposedly adapted from an eponymous story from the book *Flemish Tales* by a writer of the macabre named Pieter Van Weigen. Van Weigen turns out to be a fictitious author invented by the publicity department to manufacture a Poe-esque connection to the AIP movies, the first of which, *House of Usher* (1960), was released in the same year. Regardless of its origin, the film's screenplay is entirely original and somehow plausible, despite its outré subject matter. The principal actors turn in restrained, intelligent performances, especially Scilla Gabel's sensuous, ethereal Elfie, while Wolfgang Preiss, who would go on to play the criminal mastermind Dr. Mabuse in Fritz Lang's sci-fi spy thriller *The Thousand Eyes of Dr. Mabuse* (1960), adds the right touch of Teutonic menace as the mad doctor Bohlem.

Mill of the Stone Women has an undeserved reputation as a "sex-horror film" due to a scene in which the audience catches a brief glimpse of one of French actress Dany Carrel's nipples while she is strapped to an operating table that looks more like a wardrobe malfunction than a deliberate nude scene. This partial appearance of a bare breast was cut for the American market. As in *Blood of the Vampire*, the 19th century blood transfusion equipment smacks of Steampunk, and recalls M.E. Braddon's Victorian-era science fiction vampire story *Good Lady Ducayne* (see Chapter Two), in which a sick woman is kept alive by periodic blood transfusions from young female victims. Here, vampiric resurrection is accomplished by scientific techniques as the vampire Elfie periodically "dies" and returns to life after partaking of blood pumped into her body in the laboratory. The film also combines the wax museum horror movie a la *House of Wax* (1953) with the vampire theme.

Another Italian sci-fi vampire movie released that year was *Atom Age Vampire* (1960). The film takes place in an unnamed French city during modern times, where exotic dancer Jeanette Moreneau (Susanne Loret) breaks up with her sailor boyfriend, Pierre (Sergio Fantoni), which causes her to get into a serious car accident. When Jeanette wakes up in the hospital, she finds that half her face is horribly scarred for life. Pierre, meanwhile, has shipped out on a long sea voyage and is unaware of her condition. One day she is paid an unexpected visit by a mysterious young woman named Monique Riviere (Franca Parisi), who makes her a strange offer. Monique is the lab assistant of the brilliant scientist Dr. Albert Levin (Alberto Lupo), who is working on a cancer cure. The doctor has heard about Jeanette's predicament and is offering to treat her in his home, but he demands absolute secrecy. Jeanette accepts the conditions, and abruptly leaves the hospital, telling no one where she is going.

Dr. Levin has discovered a substance called "Derma 28," that produces "the spontaneous reproduction of living cells," and has also isolated a second formula, dubbed "Derma 25," that produces deformities. After her first treatment with Derma 28, Jeanette's scar tissue completely disappears. Dr. Levin, beholding her loveliness for the first time, falls in love with her, much to the chagrin of Monique, who is carrying a torch for the doctor. Unfortunately, the effect of the serum is only temporary, and Jeanette's scars soon return. Derma 28 can only be obtained from the glands of a living woman, so Monique becomes the gland donor for a new batch. Her death is attributed to heart failure.

Subsequent applications of the formula have similar results, so Levin must murder local women in order to obtain their glands. To disguise himself, he takes injections of the other serum, Derma 25, which turns him into a monster; he must then enter a machine that emits clouds of radiation in order to become human again. Local law enforcement thinks the killings are the work of an escaped gorilla, while the press attributes the murders to an inhuman creature they call "Seddok." In the meantime, Pierre returns from his voyage and is desperately seeking Jeanette, whom he happens to run into one night on the waterfront. But the doctor and his mute servant, Sasha (Roberto Bertea), arrive and try to drown him by throwing him into the water, taking Jeanette back to Levin's and making her a prisoner.

Pierre goes to the police, who are beginning to suspect that Levin is Seddok. Exhuming Monique's body, they find evidence of foul play and prepare to arrest the doctor. Meanwhile, Jeanette is permanently cured of her scarification after one last application of the formula, but she still rejects Levin's romantic advances, causing him

Dr. Albert Levin (Alberto Lupo), transformed into the Seddok creature, menaces Jeanette Moreneau (Susanne Loret) in *Atom Age Vampire* (1960).

to spontaneously transform into the Seddok creature in a rage. Pierre, who has been staking out the doctor's house by himself, runs inside to aid her, but is knocked unconscious by the monster. Before Seddok can kill Jeanette, Sasha rebels and stabs the monster in the back, turning him back to Levin as the police arrive to take charge of the situation.

While it's not one of the better Italian forays into sci-fi horror, *Atom Age Vampire* is a fun romp, smoothly directed by Anton Julio Majano and produced by the master of Italian horror, Mario Bava. The mad scientist plot is clichéd and predictable, however, and sometimes veers into soap opera territory when explicating the dynamics of the love triangle represented by Jeanette, Monique and Dr. Leven. Set in an unspecified French city (probably Marseilles), director Majano uses outdoor locations to create a documentary look. In Italy the film was titled *Seddok, l'erede di Satana*, which translates as *Seddok, Heir of Satan,* which indicates that it originally had little or nothing to do with vampires until it became *Atom Age Vampire* in America. Some critics, however have pointed out that the removal of the vital essence of a woman to preserve and enhance the beauty of another echoes the real-world depredations of the "human vampire" Elizabeth Bathory (see Chapter One).

The European wave of techno-vamps continued with Tigon Studio's *Blood Beast Terror* (1967), starring the venerable Hammer horror actor Peter Cushing. The story unfolds in a village in 19th century England, where entomologist Professor Mallinger (Robert Flemyng) studies rare moths and conducts queer experiments on his secluded estate, assisted by his sultry daughter, Clare (Wanda Ventham). A series of mysterious vampire murders in the vicinity of Mallinger's manor have drawn the scrutiny of Police Inspector Quennell (Cushing), who sets out to investigate the enigmatic killings. A survivor of one of the assaults describes being attacked by a horrible winged creature with huge eyes. All of the victims are men, their bodies drained of blood and bearing strange wounds, and Quennell also discovers odd flakes of an unknown material at the murder scenes.

One day a professional insect collector named Britewell (William Wilde) arrives at the professor's with some rare moth pupae he has brought back from Africa. Invited to stay with Mallinger for a few days, Clare soon casts seductive eyes upon the young man. She invites him outside to play a game of hide and seek on the estate grounds one night, where he is attacked by a large flying creature and winds up like the other victims. Investigating Britewell's death leads Quennell to the professor's mansion, where he discovers the remains of a number of other victims. Learning that Mallinger and Clare have suddenly departed for the professor's second residence in the resort town of Upper Hyam, the inspector decides to follow his prime suspect incognito, and takes his daughter, Meg (Vanessa Howard), along as part of the ruse.

After they arrive at the inn in Upper Hyam, Meg takes up with a local lad, William (David Griffin), whose hobby is bug collecting. While chasing a Death's-Head moth through the fields, they accidentally trespass onto Mallinger's property and are warned off by an angry Clare. Soon afterward, Clare lures Meg into the professor's laboratory, where Mallinger places her in a hypnotic trance and transfuses some of her blood into a man-sized moth chrysalis, as it is revealed that his daughter is actually a vampire moth creature who can take on the appearance of a human being. The second mothman is being incubated to provide a mate for Clare. After extracting some blood, Mallinger induces hypnotic amnesia in Meg and sends her back to the inn, with orders to return later.

Things heat up when Quennell notices that scales from the wing of one of William's Death's-Head moth specimens resemble the flakes found at the murder sites when viewed under a microscope. Suspecting the truth, he travels out to the professor's place that night to bring the murderers to justice. Events have taken a terrible turn, however, as the professor, weary of his experiments with insect people, torches the chrysalis, whereupon Clare transforms into the moth woman and kills him. Quennell arrives to dispatch the creature by attracting it to the light from a fire and shooting it with his police pistol.

Peter Cushing reportedly thought that *Blood Beast Terror* was the worst film he had ever appeared in during his long career as a thespian, and it's easy to see why. The main problem is the hackneyed screenplay by Peter Bryan that fails to coherently establish the film's central premises. How did the professor turn an insect into a simulacrum of a woman? How does she metamorphose into her moth form and back again? Why does she need to drink blood? These questions are never answered, or even addressed, which makes for an incoherent plot. There are too many extraneous dialogue scenes that slow down the narrative, and some lame attempts at comic relief. Director Vernon Sewell does his best with this mediocre material, but is hampered by the truly awful moth woman costume that is shown onscreen as little as possible. Stalwart trouper Cushing crafts a dignified role as Inspector Quennell, and his performance is the film's only bright spot.

While the screenwriter deserves some credit for originality for coming up with a new idea for a science fiction vampire, any connection between moths and vampires is obscure other than the fact that they are both creatures of the night, although, in *Dracula*, Van Helsing lists the moth as one of the "meaner things," like the rat and the bat, that the vampire has the power to command. In Stoker's novel, plump Death's-Heads are vectored to Renfield by the Count for consumption by the insect-eating maniac. Moths are not known to be bloodsuckers in nature, but there is a species known as the Death's-Head, an insect that also features as a plot element in the psycho-thriller *The Silence of the Lambs* and in the Poe short story "The Sphynx." There's also a vague sci-fi connection to a creature called the "Mothman," a winged humanoid apparition said to have haunted the environs of Point Pleasant, West Virginia, in the late 1960s, a cryptic being that is sometimes associated with the UFO phenomenon. The movie's murderous moth lady has affinities with the killer insect women in science fiction horror films such as *The Wasp Woman* (1959) and *Invasion of the Bee Girls* (1973). *Blood Beast Terror* was also released under the alternate title *The Vampire Beast Craves Blood.*

As tastes in horror and science fiction films changed, it would be decades before mad science and vampirism would come together again, and when these themes merged once more, it would be in an entirely different idiom. South Korean director Park Chan-Wook's art-house vampire film *Thirst* (2009) is a case in point. It's the story of a Roman Catholic priest in contemporary Korea, Sang-hyun (Song Kang-ho), whose piety leads him to selflessly submit to an experimental treatment for an incurable disease called the Emmanuel Virus. Sang-hyun "dies" during the procedure, but later returns to life and is revered as a saint with healing powers. Attending to patients in a local hospital, he has a relapse and begins to suffer symptoms of the virus once more until he smells the blood of a hit-and-run victim one night and drinks some of that person's blood. Soon, he is siphoning off the fluid of unconscious patients and imbibing it through a plastic tube and stealing blood packs from the hospital's blood bank to avoid murdering people. After unsuccessfully trying to kill himself, Sang-hyun must face the truth that the experiment has turned him into a vampire.

One night the priest's childhood friend, Kang-woo (Shin Ha-kyun), who is suffering from cancer, invites him to participate in weekly games of mahjong at his home. Kang-woo lives with his wife, Tae-ju (Kim Ok-vin), and his mother, Lady Ra (Kim Hae-sook), and during these visits Sang-hyun and Tae-ju fall in love and begin an illicit love affair. Having sex in unused beds at the hospital, Tae-ju soon discovers the priest's secret when she finds him drinking the blood of one of the patients. Enthralled by Sang-hyun's vitality and his ability to run up and down walls, Tae-ju implores him to aid her by turning her into a vampire in order to escape her stultifying home life. "Vampires are cuter than I thought," she muses. She also suggests that they murder her husband so that they can be together, and also because he is mistreating her, and Sang-hyun agrees.

The couple lures Kang-woo out onto a lake in a small boat, where Sang-hyun drowns him and weighs down the body. They tell the police that the husband got drunk and accidentally fell out of the boat and drowned. With no suspicion of foul play, they wind up getting away with the murder. The priest leaves the monastery and moves in with Tae-ju, while Lady Ra, in her grief, drinks herself into a comatose state while helplessly watching the couple's perfidy in her own home. After witnessing terrifying apparitions of the ghost of Kang-woo, Tae-ju confesses that she had lied about her husband mistreating her, and begs Sang-hyun to kill her so that she can join her husband in death. Sang Hyun obliges, but then decides he does not want to live without her and uses his blood to turn her into a vampire while Lady Ra watches.

Tae-ju proves to be a more bloodthirsty vamp than the staid Sang Hyun, and has no compunction about taking human lives, which causes a rift between them. The vampire couple quarrel with each other as they leap like ghosts over the city's rooftops. When Lady Ra manages to communicate what has gone on to some of her mahjong partners, Tae-Ju ruthlessly kills them. Knowing that the authorities will soon be after them for the murders, Sang-hyun loads Lady Ra into a car and takes off into the night with Tae-Ju. She awakens from a short nap to find that he has driven them to a cliff overlooking the ocean, and that dawn is breaking. At first she tries to hide from the sun, but eventually accepts her fate as the vampire couple is burned to death by the rays of the rising sun as Lady Ra watches the double suicide.

One of a very few examples of an art-house vampire film (Carl Theodor Dreyer's *Vampyr* and Michael Almereyda's *Nadja* are two others), *Thirst* was adapted from French writer Emile Zola's notorious novel of depravity *Thérèse Raquin* (1867) by director Park Chan-wook and co-scripter Jeong Seo-Kyeong. As such, it's an uneasy mixture of family drama and the fantasy/horror film. Zola's basic plotline is horrible enough, and the addition of the vampire element adds nothing significant to the dramatic tension of the situation. Although the murdered husband's ghost appears in the Zola novel, the film's vampires and ghosts are of the variety typically found in Asian cinema: floating, vengeful, violent creatures The vampire pair dueling over the town's rooftops recalls a similar scene in Ang Lee's *Crouching Tiger, Hidden Dragon* (2000). Director Park Chan-wook creates some stylish visual compositions, but the film is overly long (at 134 minutes) and talky for a horror movie. Song Kang-ho delivers a fine performance as the vampire priest with a conscience, while Kim Ok-vin portrays the femme vamp Tae-ju as a lustful, bloodthirsty fiend. *Thirst* was awarded the Jury Prize at the 2009 Cannes Film Festival and nominated for the Palme d'or.

Although there's no mad doctor in evidence, the film's vampire is created via a scientific experiment gone horribly wrong, and once again vampirism is connected to a degenerative disease. In its early scenes at least, *Thirst* brings the vampire genre back to its religious roots, to the Catholicism of Stoker's *Dracula*. The film associates vampirism with piety and religious devotion on one hand, and with lust, murder and suicide on the other. As in many contemporary vampire movies, these vamps are abnormally strong and possess limited powers to defy gravity. The film's Korean title is *Bakjwi*, which translates as bat, a vampire reference. Vampires and priests would later appear in a sci-fi context in the sci-fi actioner *Priest* (2011).

Mad science and vampires were once again conjoined in *BloodRayne III: The Third Reich* (2010), the third in a series of films based on the *BloodRayne* video game. The main character is a buxom vampire slayer named Rayne, who is obviously a female version of the Blade character in the *Blade* series of comics and films (see Chapter Six). Like Blade, Rayne is a *dhampir*, a half-human, half-vampire hybrid who possesses some of the qualities of both species but uses her powers to hunt down and destroy vampires. And, like Blade, Rayne wields a sword against the undead. The series skips around in time: *BloodRayne I* (2005) takes place in 18th century Romania, while *BloodRayne II: Deliverance* (2007) is set in the Wild West, where the vampire killer rubs elbows with cowboy legends Pat Garret and Billy the Kid.

BloodRayne III takes place somewhere in Nazi-occupied Central Europe in 1943. A train carrying Jews to a concentration camp stops at a station and is attacked by Rayne (Natassia Malthe) and a group of freedom fighters, who take out the Germans and free their captives. Unfortunately, Rayne gets shot while taking out Nazi Commandant Ekart Brand (Michael Paré) and some of her mutant blood gets mingled with the officer's, turning him into a *dhampir* like herself. As he is undergoing his transformation he is attended to by SS doctor Mangler (Clint Howard), who realizes the potential of vampire blood and wants to capture Rayne in order to develop a serum from her blood that will make Hitler and the Nazi leaders immortal. The rest of the movie consists of gunfights, swordplay, mayhem, bloodletting and shots of Ms. Malthe's bare breasts as Rayne foils the evil SS plot.

This exercise in direct-to-video Euro trash was filmed on location in Zagreb, Croatia, by exploitation director Uwe Boll. The production's low budget gives it a drab, hurried look, while the cast seems to be going through their paces without much enthusiasm. Mad scientist Dr. Mangler (whose name is meant to suggest the real-life Nazi war criminal Dr. Mengele), hatches what is arguably the most bizarre plot in the annals of science fiction vampirism, namely the transformation of *Der Fuehrer* into a vampire. The film contains a hilarious dream sequence in which Rayne dreams she is being attacked by a vampire Hitler complete with fangs that is almost worth the rental price. Almost, but not quite.

The figure of the mad scientist has become somewhat passé as fear of technology has receded in the public mind in the hi-tech environment of the 21st century. The notion of a lone Byronic genius pushing the frontiers of knowledge has been replaced by corporate think-tanks and industrial conglomerates. A case in point is the army of scientists and technicians of the InGen Corporation that re-create the extinct dinosaurs in *Jurassic Park* (1993). Mad scientists were originally a fictional artifact of the late 19th century, as evidenced by the steampunk savants in *Blood of the Vampire*, *Mill of the Stone Women* and *Blood Beast Terror*. Making vampires the product of Victorian-era science injects imagery from the Frankenstein films, with its operating rooms, laboratories, bubbling chemical retorts and exotic medical paraphernalia. Mad science was responsible for creating a number of unusual vampiric creatures, including a giant bat, a blob of alien protoplasm, and a moth woman. Techno-vamps created in the laboratory by misguided scientists persisted into 20th century settings in films like *The Return of Dr. X*, *The Vampire*, *Blood of Dracula* and *Atom Age Vampire*, but seem to have become scarce in today's hi-tech world.

CHAPTER FIVE

The Psychic Dimension

"Psychic" is a term that denotes the preternatural powers of the human mind. It is derived from the classical Greek word *psyche*, meaning the soul or spirit. Since ancient times, mankind has believed that certain individuals possess special abilities that enable them to read the minds, foretell the future and control the actions of others.

Like the literary vampire, the concept of the paranormal was a product of the 19th century. As related in Chapter One, the discipline of parapsychology arose during late Victorian times as the influence of science grew and the dogmatic beliefs of religion waned. Parapsychology attempted to explain phenomena previously thought to be occult or supernatural in scientific terms. Mental telepathy, clairvoyance, telekinesis and other borderline experiences were subjected to the logical protocols of the scientific method. At the same time medical science was studying the use of mesmerism and hypnotism as a treatment for the mentally and physically impaired. It was believed that patients could be hypnotized and placed in a somnambulistic trance in order to achieve therapeutic results. Hypnotism was also thought to have a negative aspect in its potential for mind control of the hypnotic subject. The deeply entranced patient was referred to as a "somnambule" or somnambulist, and was believed to be capable of performing preternatural feats at the mental command of the hypnotist.

Vampires did not possess the psychic powers of telepathy and hypnotic mind control in European legends or in early vampire tales like Polidori's "The Vampire" or Le Fanu's *Carmilla*. The vampire's paranormal abilities originated with Stoker's *Dracula*, in which the Count, although clearly a supernatural being, has the powers of telepathy and hypnotic mind control seemingly inspired by parapsychology. But these themes had previously appeared in a non-supernatural context in George du Maurier's novel *Trilby* and Arthur Conan Doyle's short story "The Parasite," both of which had been published in 1894, three years prior to *Dracula*.

Related to the hypnotic powers of the vampire is a concept that has been referred to as "magnetic vampirism." The magnetic vampire, sometimes called a "psychic sponge," is an individual who is able to absorb the vitality, or life force, from another person by psychic means rather than sucking their blood. For example, parapsychologist D. Scott Rogo cites the case of a clairvoyant named Mollie Flancher who kept small animals as pets. The animals invariably died of no discernable cause, leading psychic investigators to believe she somehow absorbed their life force, not unlike a psychic Renfield. Psychic vampirism appears in a more science fiction context in the writings of mystical anthropologist Carlos Castaneda, who claims that humankind is surrounded by invisible spirit beings that continually drain us of our vital energies. It should be noted that modern-day members of vampire role-playing communities engage in magnetic energy exchange much more frequently than actually drinking blood.

In literature and film, hypnotic and magnetic vampirism are frequently combined. In *Trilby*, for example, Svengali uses his hypnotic powers to dominate Trilby but also drains her life force once his influence is removed. Similarly, in Fritz Leiber's "The Girl with the Hungry Eyes," C.M. Kornbluth's "The Mindworm" and Dan Simmons's "Carrion Comfort," the psychic vampires wield powers of hypnotic domination as they drain their victims of their vital forces.

Sometime after the First World War, two aspiring German writers, Carl Meyer and Hans Janowitz, visited a carnival sideshow where they were entertained by a circus act in which a man who claimed to be in a somnambulistic trance performed feats of strength while hurling prophetic utterances at the crowd. Meyer and Janowitz were so enthralled by this weird performance that it inspired them to write a screenplay involving a somnambulist and an evil hypnotist that was destined to become a classic of silent horror cinema, *The Cabinet of Dr. Caligari* (1919), directed by Robert Weine.

As originally conceived by Meyer and Janowitz, the film begins in the town of Holstenwall in northern Germany, where a fair is being celebrated and a traveling magician and hypnotist, Dr. Caligari (Werner Krauss) arrives to obtain permission to set up his attraction featuring Cesare, the Somnambulist (Conrad Veidt). Clad in a skin-tight black outfit, the entranced Cesare spends most of his time ensconced inside the doctor's coffin-like cabinet. When an arrogant town clerk insults Caligari, the official is found stabbed to death in his room the next day and the carnival proceeds as planned.

When the fair opens, two students, Francis (Friedrich Feher) and Alan (Hans Heinrich von Twardowski), attend the carnival and are attracted to Dr. Caligari's exhibit. They sit among the audience, entranced by the performance of the mesmerized Cesare, who seems to exhibit real prophetic powers under the doctor's hypnotic tutelage. "Cesare knows every secret," the doctor informs the crowd. "Cesare knows the past and sees the future." On a whim, Alan asks the somnambulist how long he will live, and Cesare curtly replies, "Until the break of dawn." The next day Francis learns that Alan has been knifed to death in his room in a manner similar to the official's murder.

Francis suspects that Caligari and Cesare are responsible for the murders, and convinces his fiance's father, Dr. Olsen (Rudolph Lettinger) to open an investigation into the doctor's activities. As they are investigating, another man, a petty criminal (Rudolph Klein-Rogge) is arrested for the two murders, drawing suspicions away from Caligari. In the meantime, Francis's fiancée, Jane (Lil Dagover), wanders into the carnival looking for her father and comes across Caligari's tent. Enticed inside by the doctor, she is introduced to Cesare, who awakens in his coffin and regards her with a lustful gaze, causing her to flee from the tent in horror.

That night, Caligari dispatches Cesare to murder Jane in her bedroom, but he is

Dr. Caligari (Werner Krauss, left), displays his carnival attraction, the somnambulist Cesare (Conrad Veidt), in *The Cabinet of Dr. Caligari* (1919).

smitten by an unholy desire and carries her off instead. Carrying her across the town's dizzily slanting rooftops, the somnambulist collapses from exhaustion and falls off the roof. Francis tracks Caligari to an insane asylum and is informed that the doctor is the director of the facility. While the doctor is asleep, Francis and the asylum staff go through his papers and discover a book about somnambulism that recounts a murder spree in 1783, committed by a certain Dr. Caligari and a mesmerized patient. The doctor's diary reveals that when Cesare was entrusted to his care, he conceived the idea of emulating his 18th century namesake. When the doctor awakens, the police confront him with Cesare's corpse, whereupon he goes mad and is placed in a straitjacket.

This core story was altered by director Weine, who shot additional sequences that were not in the original script. A framing story was added in which Francis is an inmate in a madhouse, inhabited by Jane and Cesare and presided over by a more beneficent Dr. Caligari, transforming the entire narrative into a demented fantasy concocted by a lunatic. With its painted shadows, oblique angles and twisted sets, *Caligari* conjures the demonic world of the nightmare, and despite its age, still engenders eerie feelings in the viewer. The film's evocative style inspired a revolution in German silent cinema by ushering in the expressionist movement, which was sometimes referred to derisively as "Caligarism." Producer Erich Pommer utilized the talents of members of the avant garde theatre group called Der Sturm to create the film's distinctive look. Painters Hermann Warm and Walter Rohrig created the distorted, visionary sets, while costumer Walter Reimann designed the characters' grotesque costumes. Werner Krauss, recruited from the famed Max Reinhardt theatrical company, is perfectly cast as the titular doctor and exudes a malignant screen presence, while fellow Reinhart alumnus Conrad Veidt provides the film's otherworldly screen menace as Cesare. *Caligari* created an international artistic sensation and is today considered one of the landmarks of the horror film. It would set the stage for the emergence of a wave of German science fiction, fantasy and horror cinema during the silent and early sound periods.

While the film's bizarre production design is meant to suggest a disquieting dreamscape, there's also an element of science fiction to *Caligari*'s visuals; its gravity-defying geometry seems to suggest the vistas of an alien world. Upon viewing the film, Russian director Yacov Protazanov was inspired to create a series of fantastic Caligari-esque sets representing a Martian city for his sci-fi epic *Aelita* (1924). While it is generally regarded as a horror film, *Caligari*'s themes of hypnosis and mind manipulation are not supernatural and bring the film into the realm of science fiction. It is the first film treatment of the psychic vampire theme as Cesare, the Somnambulist lies in his coffin during the day in a semblance of vampiric sleep and emerges at night to slink around on his murderous missions, while Dr. Caligari the hypnotist wields Dracula-like powers of mesmerism.

Beyond *Caligari*, German cinema of the silent period exhibited an avid interest in hypnotism and mind control. In F.W. Murnau's *Nosferatu* (1922), the vampire Count Orlok hypnotically induces somnambulistic trances. Fritz Lang's thriller *Dr. Mabuse, the Gambler* (1922) featured a super-criminal with the powers of mass-hypnosis, while in Lang's *Metropolis* (1927) an artificial woman incites proletarian crowds to riot. *Caligari*'s director Robert Weine followed up with a film entitled *Genuine: The Story of a Vampire* (1920), a fantastic, Arabian Nights–inspired tale about a malevolent slave girl who exacts revenge on the men around her, a Theda Bara–style vamp, but not a true vampire.

Horror films turned out to be big box office during the early sound era. In 1931, Universal kicked off the horror craze with *Dracula*, starring Bela Lugosi as the mesmeric Count. Warner Brothers entered the horror sweepstakes with their adaptation of George du Maurier's 1894 novel *Trilby*, a work that influenced Stoker's *Dracula* and featured an equally hypnotic personality. *Svengali* (1931), starred the acclaimed actor John Barrymore, known as "the Great Profile," as du Maurier's psychic vampire, and the screenplay adaptation by J. Grubb Alexander made the hypnotist/impresario the central character instead of Trilby and dispensed with most of the novel's complicated subplots.

In mid–18th century Paris, the eccentric, amoral musical maestro Svengali (Barrymore) ekes out a marginal existence as a music teacher and con man in the city's

Psychic vampire Svengali (John Barrymore) prepares to hypnotize his student, Madame Honori (Carmel Myers), into committing suicide in *Svengali* (1931).

bohemian Latin Quarter. The nature of his character is revealed in an early scene in which one of his students, Madame Honori (Carmel Myers), who has become infatuated with him, reveals that she has left her husband to become his lover. Because she is now penniless and possesses only mediocre singing gifts, she has become an impediment to his ambitions, so he callously uses his hypnotic powers to make her throw herself in the Seine. Afterward, he feels not the slightest remorse.

In need of a meal, Svengali pays a visit to the studio shared by three English painters, the Laird (Donald Crisp), Taffy (Lumsden Hare) and young Billee (Bramwell Fletcher). He also encounters Trilby O'Ferrell (Marian Marsh), their beautiful neighbor, an artist's model. When Trilby complains of headaches, Svengali convinces her to allow him to hypnotize her in order to cure them. He places her in a trance and examines her mouth, which is "like the roof of a cathedral" and perfect for singing. Then his eyes glow with an unearthly light as he commands that "you shall see nothing ... hear nothing ... dream nothing ... but Svengali!"

That night the mesmeric maestro exerts his control over Trilby in a beautifully realized sequence that begins with a close-up of Barrymore's face, his eyes glowing with hypnotic power, then pans slowly backward, through the window and out over the dark rooftops of Paris and into Trilby's room. As his influence over the hapless girl grows stronger, Trilby finally fakes her own death and disappears, leaving Billee confused and inconsolable. Several years later, after the three friends have returned to London, they attend a performance given by Svengali and his singing sensation, the operatic diva known only as "Madame Svengali," whom Billee recognizes as Trilby. When the trio try to link up with their old friends after the show, Trilby seems to recognize Billee and becomes herself again, if only momentarily, before being hustled into a waiting coach by Svengali and sinking back into her hypnotic fog. The meeting hardens Billee's resolve to pursue the couple in the hope that he can pry Trilby from Svengali's mental domination.

It soon becomes clear that Trilby and Svengali are married in name only during a scene in which the maestro nearly succeeds in hypnotizing Trilby into allowing him to consummate their marriage, but then relents. "But it is only Svengali talking to himself again," he muses as he breaks the spell. In the meantime, the meeting with Billee

Svengali (John Barrymore) uses his hypnotic powers on Trilby O'Ferrell (Marian Marsh) in *Svengali* (1931).

has loosened the hypnotist's hold on his subject, causing Trilby to lose her singing voice. After several cancelled performances the act is on the skids, and in due course Mr. and Mrs. Svengali are reduced from entertaining the crown heads of Europe to performing in a low-rent venue in Cairo, where Billee has followed them. It soon becomes apparent that Svengali's mind control efforts have taken a heavy toll on him, and he is, in fact, dying. During her final performance Trilby spots Billee in the audience and loses her power of song. Svengali's control is broken, and as he expires he petitions the Lord with prayer. "Oh, God," he intones, "grant me in death what you denied me in life—the woman I love." His wish is granted as Trilby murmurs, "Svengali," before falling dead upon the stage.

Virtually forgotten today, *Svengali* is just as impressive as Universal's horror hits *Dracula* and *Frankenstein*, which were also released in 1931. Barrymore is superb as the charismatic title character, his Rasputin-like onscreen persona alternating between the comedic and the horrifying. J. Grubb Alexander's script neatly removes the extraneous material from du Maurier's novel, a process which greatly improves the narrative's dramatic focus. Director Archie Mayo uses beautifully fluid camera work (a rarity in early sound cinema) while coaxing a fine performance from the notoriously mercurial Barrymore. Co-star Marian Marsh, only seventeen years old when the film was shot, provides a lively and enchanting screen presence. The evocative art direction of Anton Grot and cinematography of Barney McGill were nominated for Academy Awards, and the appearance of the actors and sets are derived from du Maurier's illustrations.

With Barrymore's forbidding appearance and Eastern European accent, the resemblance between the Svengali character and Count Dracula becomes more apparent on the screen. The film version accentuates Svengali's hypnotic mind control powers in a way that du Maurier's novel does not, and this change transforms him into a more sinister persona. Svengali is a hypnotic psychic vampire, but also a magnetic one, as he absorbs some of Trilby's life force in making her a diva of his creation, but the effort ultimately draws off all of his own vitality as well.

In 1919, French novelist Pierre Benoit published a novel entitled *L'Atlantide* (*Atlantis*), a science fiction adventure about three French Foreign Legionnaires who discover the remnants of the lost city of Atlantis beneath the sands of the Sahara desert. Benoit's novel borrowed heavily from H. Rider Haggard's *She*, which had been published in 1887. As John Baxter notes in his book *Science Fiction in the Cinema*, "Both books share a similar situation, the discovery in a remote part of the world ... of a lost civilization ruled by a white queen. In each, a number of men fall in love with the queen, but are destroyed by her.... And in each the queen is immortal, though successive filmmakers have varied on this point as the mood took them."[1] One of the main differences between the two books, however, is that Ayesha, the queen of the hidden kingdom in *She*, gains her immortality from a mystical flame, while Antinea, the ruler of Atlantis, derives her deathlessness by taking the lives of a succession of lovers throughout the ages. In Benoit's novel, the gold-plated corpses of fifty-three men who have given their lives for the queen's immortality adorn Antinea's palace.

L'Atlante has been filmed a number of times, the first being a silent version by Belgian director Jacques Feyder in 1920, but the most memorable version was lensed by the acclaimed Viennese director G.W. Pabst in 1932. Pabst is best known today for his silent classic about Lulu (Louise Brooks), a femme fatale, in *Pandora's Box* (1928). *L'Atlante* was shot simultaneously in English, French and German, a fairly common practice for European films of the early sound era, the English-language title being *The Mistress of Atlantis*. The narrative begins with two French Foreign Legion officers, Lt. St. Avit (Heinz Klingenberg) and Capt. Morhange (Gustav Deissl) getting lost in the Sahara Desert and being taken prisoner by the Tuaregs, a desert-dwelling Bedouin tribe. The Tuaregs take them to a strange underground city, which they learn is the remnant of the lost city of Atlantis, sunk, not beneath the ocean, but under the desert sands thousands of years ago.

The men are kept prisoner and separated, and Morhange is attended to by Hetman (Wladimir Sokoloff) an eccentric individual who acts as a mentor and kind of majordomo. Hetman informs Morhange that the city is ruled by a queen, Antinea, a goddess who devours her lovers. "There is no greater ecstasy," he tells Morhange, "nothing more sacred, than to die for a woman like that." Before long the Frenchman is taken to see Antinea (Brigitte Helm), a beautifully imperious but ice-cold monarch who invites him to play a game of chess. When the queen triumphs on the chessboard, Morhange realizes that his life has become forfeit.

The officer is held captive as he awaits Antinea's fatal summons, although he is somehow immune to the queen's feminine charms. In the meantime, Hetman regales Morhange with the tale (told in flashback) of how the present Antinea was the result of a union between a Tuareg chieftain and a Parisian can-can dancer. Finally, stung by Morhange's rejection of her advances, she compels him to murder St. Avit with her charismatic powers, and he obeys. Emotionally shattered, he manages to escape from the lost city and return to his unit, only to become obsessed with Antinea. He finally wanders out into the desert to return to Atlantis and its queen.

The Pabst version of Benoit's novel, as rewritten by scenarist Herbert Rappoport, dispenses with the queen's mummified victims and creates ambiguity about the true nature of Antinea's immortality. Likewise, the manner in which the queen dispatches her lovers in a surfeit of ecstasy is also unclear. Shot on location in the Haggar desert in Morocco, the underground city of Atlantis is presented in a minimalist fashion, as a maze of small, low-ceilinged rooms that imparts a claustrophobic mood to the proceedings. Pabst's fractured narrative unfolds obliquely and is often confusing, while there is little in the way of action in what is supposed to be an adventure story. Only the screen presence of Brigitte Helm as the Atlantean ice queen Antinea enlivens the film. The divine Ms. Helm, who had made a career out of playing fantastic parts such as the female android in Fritz Lang's *Metropolis* (1927) and the artificial woman in Henrik Galeen's *Alraune* (1928), lends her statuesque beauty to the role while reclining with her pet cheetah, or draped over a giant stone likeness of her immortal visage.

The deathless queen, subsisting on the life force of a succession of lovers, resembles the long-lived Count Dracula, a cruel nobleman who rules over an equally exotic foreign realm. While she does not subsist on the blood of her victims, Antinea consumes their lives in a similar ritual of erotic ecstasy. Benoit's novel would subsequently be filmed in 1948 as *The Siren of Atlantis*, with the sultry Maria Montez as Antinea, and by cult director Edgar G. Ulmer in a more science fiction iteration complete with helicopters and atomic bombs as *Journey Beneath the Desert* (1961).

In 1943, Universal produced a lavish Technicolor remake of Lon Chaney's 1925 silent horror classic *The Phantom of the Opera* starring Claude Rains. *The Climax* (1944) was originally conceived as a sequel to *Phantom*, which would feature the same sets, the same female lead and the same producer, but would star Universal's pre-eminent horror actor, Boris Karloff. Veteran screenwriter Curt Siodmak and co-scripter Lynn Starling composed a screenplay very loosely adapted from a play by Edward Locke that owed a greater debt to George du Maurier's psychic vampire novel *Trilby*.

Boris Karloff is pictured as evil hypnotist Dr. Friedrich Hohner in this poster for *The Climax* (1944).

Set during the late 19th century, Karloff plays Dr. Friedrich Hohner, physician for the Royal Vienna Opera, who is madly in love with prima donna Marcellina (June Vincent). When she spurns him, Hohner strangles her so that no one else will ever hear her heavenly voice again, and then installs her mummified body in a hidden shrine in his home. Ten years later a new diva, Angela Klatt (Susanna Foster), whose voice rivals that of Marcellina, is preparing to star in the Royal Opera's revival of *The Magic Voice*, which was Marcellina's opera, a work that has not been performed in the decade since she disappeared.

Piqued by the emergence of this new songstress, Dr. Hohner

resolves that Angela's talent will not challenge the posthumous musical fame of his beloved Marcellina. Using the pretext of a medical examination, he brings her to his private office and uses a hypnosis machine to place the singer under his control. "That voice belongs to Marcellina," he tells her, then adds commandingly, "You will never sing again." During rehearsal Angela becomes unable to sing when she spies Hohner peering at her with his hypnotic gaze from the audience. Claiming that Angela has suffered a mental breakdown, he helpfully volunteers to treat her in his home, much to the chagrin of her fiancé and vocal coach Franz Munzer (Turhan Bey), while the performance of *The Magic Voice* is postponed indefinitely.

Angela is kept in seclusion in the doctor's home, where, under Hohner's hypnotic spell, she becomes bedridden and mentally confused. His housekeeper, Luise (Gale Sondergaard), however, has become suspicious of the doctor's motives and conspires with Franz to have the girl vacate the premises. When their plan succeeds, Franz arranges to re-schedule the production of *The Magic Voice*. Hohner is unable to reassert his hypnotic control, and, hearing Angela's voice coming through the walls of the adjacent opera house, he becomes distraught. While seeking comfort at the shrine of the dead Marcellina, he accidentally sets off a fire that quickly consumes him and his dead love.

Like the 1943 *Phantom*, *The Climax* is an uneasy blend of horror movie and costume musical. The opulent sets (which were first used in the 1925 silent version of *Phantom*), the lush Technicolor cinematography and the elaborately staged musical numbers tend to overwhelm the film's horror content. In addition to the opera house sets, director George Waggner also reused European street sets from his production of *The Wolf Man* (1941). Scripter Curt Siodmak recycles plot elements from *Trilby* and its screen version, *Svengali*, in the story involving a mad hypnotist and his obsession with, and mental domination of, an opera singer. The film's most engaging aspect today is seeing Boris Karloff in his only performance in a color film during the classic Universal horror period.

Dressed in black evening clothes with a black opera cape, and sporting a mustache and a hypnotic stare, Karloff bears a close resemblance to John Carradine's portrayal of Count Dracula in Universal's monster rally *House of Frankenstein* (1944), released in the same year. Like Svengali, Dr. Hohner uses his hypnotic powers to dominate a young opera singer, diminishing her life force in the process. Hohner's strobing hypnosis machine was possibly inspired by a similar device featured in Universal's *Dracula's Daughter* (1936).

During the 1950s a hypnosis fad swept through American popular culture. Some of this interest in the phenomenon was revved up by a curious book entitled *The Search for Bridey Murphy* (1956) by Morey Bernstein, an allegedly non-fiction book in which a young woman was supposedly able to remember details of a previous lifetime in late 19th century Ireland. *Bridey Murphy* later turned out to be a fraud, but hypnosis, formerly a clinical medical technique, had become a mystical practice that had the potential of causing quasi-occult transformations in human beings. In sci-fi and horror films of the '50s, hypnosis became a plot device that turned humans into monsters or sent them into other realms. For example, as previously discussed in Chapter Four, an evil scientist hypnotizes a teenager into becoming a vampire in *Blood of Dracula* (1957), and hypnosis played a similar role in such genre fare as *I Was a Teenage Werewolf* (1957), *The She-Creature* (1956), *The Undead* (1957) and *The Alligator People* (1959). In these films hypnosis was just a subplot, but it took center stage in *The Hypnotic Eye* (1960).

The film opens with a horrible scene of self-mutilation as a young woman lights her hair on fire on a gas stove. It is one of a series of similar events where women have disfigured themselves by drinking lye, putting their face into the moving blades of a fan, cutting their face with a razor, etc. Detective Sergeant Dave Kennedy (Joe Patridge) is assigned to investigate, but neither he nor his colleague police psychiatrist, Dr. Philip Hecht (Guy Prescott), can ascertain any motive for the string of mutilations.

That night Dave takes his girlfriend, Marcia Blaine (Marcia Henderson) and another friend, Dodi Wilson (Merry Anders), to see a stage show featuring a hypnotist, The Great Desmond (Jacques Bergerac). Aided by his statuesque assistant, Justine (Allison Hayes), the hypnotist places four men in a trance and uses the power of suggestion to make one bark like a dog, another feel like he's cold, etc. Then he performs the pièce de résistance of the act. Using Dodi as a volunteer, Desmond hypnotizes the girl and seemingly levitates her body. Afterward, Dodi has no memory of having been hypnotized, but that night when she returns to her apartment she douses her face with concentrated sulfuric acid from a bottle she keeps in her bathroom (doesn't *everyone* keep a bottle of sulfuric acid in their medicine chest?).

After Dave and Marcia visit the disfigured Dodi in the hospital the next day, Marcia comes to believe that Desmond is causing the rash of disfigurements, using post-hypnotic suggestions and induced amnesia. Although Dave is skeptical, Marcia goes back to see Desmond's act again, during which the hypnotist brings her onstage and attempts to place her into a trance, using an eye-like hand-held device, but Marcia only pretends to be hypnotized. After the show, she tells Dave and Phil that Desmond gave her a post-hypnotic suggestion to return to his dressing room at midnight. Dave agrees to let her keep the rendezvous, but insists that he and Phil follow her.

When Marcia arrives at the hypnotist's dressing room, Desmond puts her into a trance, using the hypnotic eye device. He escorts her to a beatnik nightclub and then to her apartment, as Dave and Phil shadow them. Marcia allows Desmond inside her apartment, but he soon leaves and his assistant, Justine, inexplicably appears. Manipulating the hypnotized girl, Justine commands her to get into a scalding shower, but Dave arrives to interrupt her actions before another disfigurement can occur. This leads police investigators to suspect that Justine is the real power behind Desmond.

After interviewing the other disfigured victims, Dave and Phil decide to arrest the hypnotists, but, to their alarm, they discover that Marcia has been given a post-hypnotic command to return to the theater. As Desmond places the entire audience in a trance, Dave and Phil arrive to disrupt the performance and find that Justine has brought an entranced Marcia onto a catwalk, high above the stage. As Dave attempts to rescue

Marcia, Justine rips off a mask to reveal that her face is disfigured and expresses hatred toward the beautiful women that were their victims. When she commands Desmond to attack Phil, the cop shoots him dead, and Justine, driven mad with grief, throws herself from the catwalk to join her lover in death.

This oddball mixture of hypnosis, beatniks, horror and police procedural comes off as a goofy but entertaining bit of low-budget film-making from director George Blair and screenwriters Gitta and William Read Woodfield. Beat poet Ed "Big Daddy" Nord, the self-proclaimed "King of the Beatniks," gets to beat his bongos, while Allison Hayes, who portrayed the titular giantess in the 1958 sci-fi cult classic *Attack of the 50 Foot Woman*, provides the movie's cheesecake. The silliest scene, however, occurs during the final act when Desmond hypnotizes his audience, and, by extension, the movie theater audience, into following his loony suggestions. This gimmick was billed as "HypnoMagic, The Thrill You See and Feel" on ad copy for the picture.

The Great Desmond, played with cool Gallic aplomb by Jacques Bergerac, cuts a Dracula-like figure in his black evening clothes and presents a handsome, seductive appearance to the ladies. Like the Count, he is an attractive man with hypnotic powers and a suave European accent. Like a psychic vampire, he exerts hypnotic control over his female victims and takes away their beauty, which is the outward manifestation of their youth. In reality, Desmond himself is under the mental domination of his consort, Justine. The "hypnotic eye" device used to place people in a mesmeric trance is similar to the hypnosis machine used by the evil physician in *The Climax.*

By the early 1970s the gothic vampire revival, spearheaded by Hammer Films, had run out of steam, and the studio had begun to explore innovative ways to vary the formula. Christopher Lee's Dracula character was brought into the 20th century in *Dracula AD 1972* (1972) and *The Satanic Rites of Dracula* (1973), but the oddest take on the vampire theme was surely *The Legend of the Seven Golden Vampires* (1974), an uneasy blend of vampirism and Asian "chop-sockey" martial arts cinema. In a similar vein is *Captain Kronos, Vampire Hunter* (1974), an effort that attempted to combine vampires and swashbuckling swordplay.

Set during the Regency period in England, the film stars Horst Janson as Kronos, master swordsman of the King's Imperial Guard, who has been commissioned to rid the countryside of vampires. Kronos is assisted in his task by Professor Hieronymus Grost (John Cater), a hunchbacked version of *Dracula*'s Professor Van Helsing, who dispenses occult knowledge along with occasional bits of comic relief. The professional vampire hunters are called to the village of Durward by Kronos's old army buddy, Dr. Marcus (John Carson), to counter a series of baffling attacks on young women by a hooded figure in which the victims are not drained of their blood but have their youth and life force stolen. Grost observes that there are "as many species of vampire as there are beasts of prey," and speculates that they are up against psychic vamps rather than the conventional undead bloodsuckers. Local wench Carla (Caroline Munro) survives one of the hooded one's attacks, and, enamored of the dashing Kronos, joins the vampire hunting team.

(Left to right) Professor Hieronymus Grost (John Cater), Dr. Marcus (John Carson), Carla (Caroline Munro) and Captain Kronos (Horst Janson) of the King's Imperial Guard plan their next battle with a psychic vampire in Hammer's *Captain Kronos, Vampire Hunter* (1974).

Another girl is attacked in a church but manages to survive and describes her attacker as being someone very old, affirming Grost's theory that a psychic vamp is involved in the bizarre deaths. In the meantime, Dr. Marcus pays a visit to the home of his late friend, Lord Hagen Durward, to confer with the Lord's son, Paul (Shane Briant), and his sister, Sara (Lois Dane). Marcus learns that Lord Hagen had dabbled in the occult, but is unable to question Lady Durward (Wanda Ventham), who is bedridden with a mysterious wasting disease. He also learns that the Durward family is related to the Karnsteins, a bloodline of nobility who were reputed to be vampires. After leaving the Durward manor, Marcus is attacked by the robed, hooded figure and is turned into a vampire.

Seeking to be rid of the vampire's curse, Marcus implores Kronos and Grost to kill him, but this proves to be a difficult task. After staking and hanging fail to work, Marcus in finally dispatched when Kronos accidentally impales him on a cross made of iron. Knowing that the Durward family is the source of the vampire plague, Kronos obtains a large iron cross from a nearby cemetery and has Grost fashion it into a sword inlaid with a small mirror designed to reflect the vampire's psychic power back to its source. Gaining entrance to the Durward manor with a ruse, Kronos and Grost confront the family, where it is revealed that the psychic vampire is actually Lady Durward, who has killed the young girls to retain her youth. Even worse, she has used her powers to bring Lord Durward (William Hobbs) back from the dead. A duel ensues between the newly risen Lord and Kronos that ends in Durward being run through by the swordsman's iron blade. Lady Durward suffers a similar fate, and the vampire plague is ended. Their task completed, Kronos and Grost depart the village for their next adventure, journeying "wherever there is evil to be fought."

Some Hammer enthusiasts consider *Captain Kronos* one of the better films of the studio's late period, and it has achieved a certain cult status. Writer/director Brian Clemens deserves credit for attempting to break new ground by moving away from more traditional concepts of vampirism and introducing novel ideas concerning the psychic angle. The problem, however, is in the execution and meager production values. Most of the film is shot in the woods, with repetitive long shots of galloping horses and hand-held subjective camerawork depicting the vampire's attacks. Horst Janson as Kronos cuts a dashing figure as he swashbuckles through feats of swordplay and derring-do, while cult actress Caroline Munro is easy on the eyes as the peasant girl, Carla.

Captain Kronos was conceived as a TV pilot or the first in a series of films that would explore the concept that "there are as many species of vampire as there are beasts of prey." Unfortunately, Hammer would go into receivership in 1975, and no further variations on the vampire theme would be forthcoming. The film's concept of psychic vampirism is associated with the supernatural and occult rather than scientific parapsychology, as the Durward clan is related to the Karnsteins, the vampire aristocrats derived from le Fanu's *Carmilla* and featured in a number of Hammer productions of the early 1970s based on the classic work.

Another offbeat British production from the 1970s was Polish director Jerzy Skolimowski's *The Shout* (1978). Based on a 1929 story by classical scholar and mythographer Robert Graves, the film begins in a mental hospital, where an inmate named Charles Crossley (Alan Bates) relates his story to a man watching a cricket match at the asylum (Tim Curry). In flashback, Crossley tells of meeting Anthony (John Hurt), a church organist, in a rural seaside village in North Devon. Invited home for lunch by Anthony, Crossley regales him and his wife, Rachel (Susanna York), with tales from the Australian Outback, where he claims to have lived for eighteen years in complete isolation from white society. He unabashedly tells the couple that he murdered the three children he sired by an aboriginal woman just before his departure for England because they would be unable to fend for themselves in his absence. Crossley also claims to have learned the shamanic technique of the "terror shout" from the aborigines, and claims that it will kill any living thing within earshot.

Hearing about the shout fascinates Anthony, who is an electronic musician who uses sophisticated equipment to record exotic sounds, such as the buzzing of a fly or the magnified sound of stroking a dog's fur. The next day, as Anthony and Crossley are out walking in a deserted area of sand dunes, Crossley offers to demonstrate the shout after first advising Anthony to stop his ears with wax so that he will not be affected. Then Crossley unleashes the shout, which sounds something like a human cry blended with the noise of a jet plane taking off. Anthony is knocked unconscious by the force and a herd of sheep and their shepherd are found dead nearby.

Crossley moves in with the couple and uses his charismatic powers to seduce Rachel, while Anthony is fearful of Crossley's psychic abilities and remains a passive spectator. He is also obsessed with the notion of recording Crossley's terror shout on his audio equipment. There are also hints that Crossley possesses other telepathic and psychokinetic powers as well. Turned out of his home by the interloper, Anthony is forced to retaliate by utilizing special "sacred stones" to deflect Crossley's shamanic powers back at him, causing him to go mad. Flash-forward back to the cricket match at the insane asylum, where, at the conclusion of his tale, policemen arrive to arrest Crossley for child murder. Trying to defend himself using the terror shout, he is killed by its power instead of his intended victims.

Skolimowski's brooding mood piece, which he co-scripted with Michael Austin, falls somewhere between the horror and dramatic film genres, as its fantastic premise plays against what is essentially the story of a love triangle. The film's haunting landscape of tufted sand dunes and ragged seashore reflects the extreme isolation of the characters. A fine cast of distinguished British thespians acquit themselves well enacting this unusual material. The plot revolves around the concept of a preternatural sound, which is reflected in the film's evocative sonic atmosphere devised by Tony Banks and Michael Rutherford of the band Genesis. *The Shout* won the Grand Prix de Jury at the Cannes Film Festival and played to art-house audiences before sinking into an undeserved obscurity. It has recently been reassessed as one of the most stylish and effective British thrillers of the period.

Alan Bates dominates the film in his role as the enigmatic Crossley, his brooding performance hinting at his mystical and malefic powers. Clad in a black greatcoat, his dark, scowling features suggest the sorcerous majesty of a Count Dracula. Vampire-like, he uses his charismatic powers to manipulate and seduce those around him, and, like Dracula, he is a child murderer. Like *The Cabinet of Dr. Caligari*, *The Shout* utilizes a framing story set in a mental asylum, and, also like *Caligari*, the audience is unsure whether the events depicted are real or just the delusions of a madman.

Psychics, charismatics and evil hypnotists have fascinated screen audiences for decades. Towering figures of evil like Caligari, Svengali and Antinea draw their victims into webs of mental domination in which their minds and lives are bled dry. As the saying goes, there are vampires and there are vampires, and not all of them suck blood.

Chapter Six

Vampires vs. High Technology

At the movies, vampires usually have a highly ambivalent attitude toward technology. In *Bram Stoker's Dracula* (1992), for instance, the Count is impressed by the marvels of the Victorian "cinematograph" and exclaims, "Astounding! There are no limits to science!" In *Blood and Donuts* (1995) a vamp gets so upset about the Apollo 11 moon landing that he crawls into a hole and stays there for twenty-six years. In *Dark Shadows* (2012), vampire Barnabas Collins (Johnny Depp), resurrected from the 18th century, confronts a 1970s-era television set upon which Karen Carpenter is performing. "What sorcery is this?" he shouts, not realizing the nature of television. He then demands, "Reveal yourself, tiny songstress!"

As discussed in Chapter Two, the literary vampire was conceived against a backdrop of the emergence of modern technology during the Victorian Era. The Ur-text of the literary vampire, Bram Stoker's novel *Dracula*, depicts the supernatural Count in conflict with the forces of *fin-de-siècle* science as represented by his nemesis, Van Helsing. In Stoker's novel, Dracula is forced to square off against late 19th century medicine, communication and transportation technologies and is ultimately defeated.

Universal Studios brought the novel to the screen in a ground-breaking talkie version that would introduce American audiences to supernatural horror cinema for the first time. Universal's *Dracula* (1931) was derived from a popular 1927 stage adaptation by John L. Balderston and Hamilton Deane. In order to make the production more accessible to contemporary audiences, the playwrights shifted the novel's time period from gaslit Victorian London to the early 20th century, and the film's screenplay, penned by Garrett Fort, followed suit.

The film version dispensed with many of the novel's characters and changed the roles and relationships of others. Here Renfield (Dwight Frye), not Jonathan Harker, visits Castle Dracula to arrange the sale of Carfax Abbey and is put under the spell of the Count (Bela Lugosi). They journey back to England in the *Demeter*, which is discovered as a derelict with the captain and crew dead and Renfield found insane inside the ship's hold. The newly minted lunatic is placed in the insane asylum of Dr. Seward (Herbert Bunston) as Dracula takes up residence in the nearby ruins of the Abbey. Soon afterward the Count introduces himself to Dr. Seward, his daughter, Mina (Helen Chandler), and her fiancé, Jonathan Harker (David Manners), and Mina's friend, Lucy (Frances Dade), at the London Opera.

Lucy soon falls victim to the Count after several transfusions fail to reverse her

Professor Van Helsing (Edward Van Sloan, left) confronts the Count (Bela Lugosi) with his lack of a mirror image in *Dracula* (1931).

severely anemic condition. Dr. Seward is shown conducting an autopsy on her cadaver in a modern-looking medical theater, but he is mystified by the deadly illness. Seward consults a specialist in unusual diseases, Professor Van Helsing (Edward Van Sloan) about the mysterious death, which the Professor believes to be the work of a vampire. When Seward protests that "modern medical science does not admit to such a creature," Van Helsing replies, "The superstition of yesterday can become the scientific reality of today."

In the meantime, Dracula has bitten Mina and intends to make her one of the undead. Van Helsing is called in and confounds the Count with wolfbane, mirrors and crucifixes, but the vampire persists, sending out his slave Renfield to do his bidding by night. When Dracula abducts Mina and takes her to Carfax, Van Helsing and Jonathan follow Renfield to the vampire's lair. The Count savagely murders Renfield for this perceived betrayal, but must return to his coffin as day breaks. As Dracula lies helpless he is staked by Van Helsing and his spell over Mina is broken.

Directed by Tod Browning, who had lensed a number of Lon Chaney's silent horror vehicles, *Dracula* is enlivened by the evocative cinematography of the great German cameraman Karl Freund, who some film historians believe actually shot most of the picture. Lugosi, as Dracula, projected his signature malevolent screen presence in a role that would make him a star, and his villainy is contrasted with Dwight Frye's deliciously demented performance as Renfield and Edward Van Sloan's stolid portrayal of Van Helsing. The massive gothic set designs for Dracula's castle and Carfax Abbey were devised by Charles D. Hall, Hermann Rosse and John Ivan Hoffman, and are responsible for much of the film's total effect.

As it is in the novel, *Dracula*'s strongest scenes take place during the early reels in Transylvania and Castle Dracula, the eerie mood giving way to the stage-bound action transpiring in stuffy London drawing rooms. Whatever its faults, however, the film proved to be a surprise hit with Depression-era audiences and would usher in an entire generation of horror films produced by Universal and other studios during the 1930s and 1940s.

While the mysterious goings-on in *Dracula* are clearly the work of supernatural agency, the figure of Dr. Van Helsing stands in strong opposition to these forces, as his science is ultimately able to overcome the Count's arcane sorcery. In his first scene in the film he is shown analyzing a sample of Renfield's blood in a test tube in his laboratory, surrounded by microscopes, chemical retorts and other trappings of science. He utilizes the tools of empirical experimentation and scientific method to combat the vampire, no matter how outré. The film is set during the 1930s, in a modern 20th century world of automobiles, telephones and electricity, and preserves some of the novel's *frisson* between science and the supernatural. During the film's original release, the film contained a brief epilogue in which Van Sloan, playing Van Helsing, directly addressed the movie audience to suggest that vampires were a scientific reality.

After *Dracula*, Universal released *Frankenstein* (1931) in the same year, which led to a plethora of horror movie productions that earned the studio the sobriquet of "the house of horrors." A sequel to their premiere horror hit languished in development hell for a number of years, however, until Universal produced *Dracula's Daughter* (1936). The source material was reputedly Bram Stoker's short story entitled "Dracula's Guest," which was actually a deleted chapter from *Dracula*. In the original story, Jonathan Harker, while en route to Castle Dracula, catches a brief glimpse of a female vampire lying in a mausoleum. The film's convoluted writing credits indicate Garrett Fort as the screenwriter, and John L. Balderston as the story writer "based on a work by Bram Stoker, suggested by Oliver Jeffries."

The narrative of *Dracula's Daughter* commences where *Dracula* leaves off, as policemen arrive at Carfax Abbey to find Renfield dead of a broken neck and the Count (a wax dummy of Lugosi) lying in his coffin with a stake through his heart. The bobbies promptly arrest Professor Van Helsing (Edward Van Sloan) for murder and take him into custody while Dracula's corpse is carted off to the local jail. Scotland Yard inspector Sir Basil Humphrey (Gilbert Emery) is investigating the mysterious deaths, for which Van Helsing is the prime suspect. When the professor begins to expound on the subject of vampirism, Sir Basil derides his story as being "utterly mad." Van Helsing responds, "The strength of the vampire, Sir Basil, is in the fact that he is unbelievable." He further suggests that the inspector consult with one of his former students, the eminent psychologist Dr. Jeffrey Garth (Otto Kruger) on the matter.

In the meantime, Count Dracula's body is stolen from the jail by a mysterious woman, clad in black, who hypnotizes the guard. She is the Count's daughter, Countess Marya Zaleska (Gloria Holden), who has taken up residence in London, disguised as a Hungarian artist. Marya burns her father's corpse on a funeral pyre while performing a ritual intended to exorcise his power over her and release her from the curse of the undead. She exults to her human servant, Sandor (Irving Pichel), that she is finally "free to live as a woman," but her newfound humanity proves to be short-lived as she soon reverts to her former bloodsucking ways, claiming a young London toff as a victim.

As the whereabouts of Dracula's corpse are now unknown, the police are forced to drop murder charges against Van Helsing for lack of a *corpus dilecti* (Renfield's murder apparently having been forgotten). Dr. Garth meets with the professor concerning the death of the young man who has been found drained of blood with two fang marks on his neck. Van Helsing expresses his opinion that a vampire is responsible for the death, but his former pupil rejects the idea as preposterous. When urged to keep an open mind on the subject, Garth explains, "But it's a scientific mind and there's no place in it for superstition."

The professor replies, "Who can define the boundary between the superstition of yesterday and the scientific fact of tomorrow?"

Garth remains unconvinced.

Attending a party that night, Garth and his fiancée, Janet Blake (Marguerite Churchill) are introduced to the Countess. Marya is impressed by Dr. Garth's scientific acumen as he explains the principles of psychiatry and states that "sympathetic treatment will release the human mind of any obsession." Believing that the doctor can free her from the curse of the Draculas, she arranges a private consultation with him, much to Janet's consternation. During the session Marya is vague about the nature of her mental illness, but Garth diagnoses her affliction as being a psychological obsession and urges her to deliberately tempt herself in order to gain the willpower to resist her inner urges.

Following the doctor's orders, the Countess orders Sandor to bring a victim to her art studio in Chelsea, using the ruse of needing an artist's model. Sandor hits on a despondent young woman, Lily (Nan Grey), who is on the verge of throwing herself into the Thames, and convinces her to take the modeling gig. Unfortunately, Marya is unable to control her vampiric urges, and in a scene rife with lesbian sexuality she seduces Lily and drinks her blood. The girl is found on the street the next day barely alive and suffering from a massive blood loss and total amnesia about the night's events. She is taken to the hospital, where she is treated by Dr. Garth and given blood transfusions.

In an effort to recover Lily's memories, Garth brings her out of her coma with an injection of adrenaline and attempts to hypnotically de-program her, using "a mechanical means of inducing hypnosis," a portable device that focuses a strobing beam of light in her eyes. The technique enables Lily to briefly emerge from her trance and provide a clue that implicates the Countess as her assailant, but the strain is too great and Lily expires. Confronting Marya with his suspicions, the Countess demands that he travel back to Transylvania with her, and when he refuses she hypnotizes Janet and abducts her to the continent in an unmarked aircraft. Garth quickly charters a plane and sets off in hot pursuit, as Scotland Yard sends radio broadcasts about the kidnapping to European police agencies. Sir Basil, accompanied by Van Helsing, arrange their own air transportation and follow Garth and the Countess to Transylvania.

Managing to elude the international manhunt, Marya arrives at her ancestral homeland and takes up residence in Castle Dracula. When Garth arrives, he finds Janet in a catatonic trance as Marya offers him the choice of saving her life in exchange for his becoming her undead consort. "Let your science save her," she sneers, "or remain here." When medical science proves to be of no avail, Garth agrees to the unholy bargain, but Sandor, realizing he will be cheated out of Marya's promise to make him a vampire, kills Marya with a wooden shaft shot from a crossbow, but is himself shot by Sir Basil, who arrives in a timely fashion with the professor in tow. Janet is released from the spell of Dracula's Daughter, and Van Helsing reflects over Marya's corpse that the Countess is as beautiful as the day she died "a hundred years ago."

As a sequel to the studio's paradigm-shifting horror hit *Dracula*, *Dracula's Daughter* was a major comedown. Lacking the malefic screen presence of Lugosi, the film's star, Gloria Holden (who reportedly hated the part), projects little in the way of vampiric villainy, her bland performance devoid of any hint of supernatural dread. The plodding direction by Lew Landers does little to enliven the proceedings, although there are occasional flashes of visual brilliance provided by art director Albert D'Agostino, who would go on to do great work with RKO horror producer Val Lewton, and ace Universal cinematographer George Robinson. Lead actors Otto Kruger, Irving Pichel, and Marguerite Churchill go through their paces in uninspired fashion, while Edward Van Sloan, the previous film's only holdover, has his part considerably diminished in the sequel. Nan Gray as Lily, the poor waif seduced by the Countess, delivers the film's most memorable and sympathetic performance.

Lacking any real source material, Garrett Fort's screenplay fails to deliver much in the way of thrills and chills, although the film's lesbian subplot was provocative in the early days of Hollywood censorship. Fort's script portrays vampirism as a treatable condition, similar to drug addiction, that can be cured by modern medical science, a theme that would later be repeated in Universal's *House of Dracula* (1945). Marya views her treatment as pitting "the strength of the human mind against the powers of darkness." Ultimately, however, the dark arts prevail. While Van Helsing is relegated to a secondary role, Dr. Garth is depicted as a scientist toiling in a laboratory amid the trappings of science. The machine used to hypnotize Lily, described as "a mechanical means for inducing hypnosis," would later be used in Universal's *The Climax* (1944).

The pursuit of the vampire back to Transylvania that takes up the final chapters of Stoker's novel have been restored in the last reels of *Dracula's Daughter* in a more hi-tech iteration, with airplanes and radio broadcasts taking the place of steamships and telegraph messages.

Several years later, Lew Landers was back in the director's chair helming another *Dracula* semi-sequel, Columbia's *The Return of the Vampire* (1943). The old vampire himself, Bela Lugosi, put on the cape once more for this production, but since Universal still held the screen copyright to the Dracula character, Columbia screenwriters were obliged to give the lead character a different identity to avoid legal hassles. Thus, Lugosi played Armand Tesla, a vampire who is Count Dracula in everything but name.

The story begins in England in 1918 during the First World War, as narrated by Professor Walter Saunders (Gilbert Emery) of King's College, Oxford, as we observe werewolf Andres Obry (Matt Willis) skulking through fogbound Priory Cemetery and entering a tomb, where Tesla's coffin is ensconced. The vampire emerges and inquires about the whereabouts of his latest victim, Miss Norcutt (Jeanne Bates). Andreas informs him that she has been taken to a clinic run by local scientist Lady Jane Ainsley (Frieda Inescort).

Meanwhile, in a scene reminiscent of *Dracula's Daughter*, Lady Jane and the professor attempt to hypnotize the anemic Miss Norcutt at the clinic, hoping to discover the cause of her illness, but the unfortunate woman dies during the procedure. "I'm afraid it goes deeper than medicine," the professor laments, "deeper than science." That night, Professor Saunders reads a book on vampirism authored by Armand Tesla, a "depraved Romanian scientist," and deduces that Miss Norcutt was the victim of a vampire. The next day Saunders and Lady Jane discover the vampire's tomb and drive a stake through his heart, causing Andreas to be free of Tesla's spell and assume human form once more.

Twenty-four years later, in 1944, another world war is raging across Europe. Professor Saunders has died, and Scotland Yard Inspector Sir Fredrick Fleet (Miles Mander) has read the account of Tesla's staking in the professor's notes and commences an investigation. If it can be proved that Tesla was staked while still alive, Sir Fredrick will be forced to file murder charges against Lady Jane. Before the investigation can commence, however, the Luftwaffe bomb Priory Cemetery during an air raid and the vampire's body is unearthed. Two civil defense workers assigned to rebury the disinterred bodies find Tesla's corpse and remove the stake, thereby re-animating the vampire.

At the clinic, Lady Jane informs Andreas, who is now her lab assistant, that a famous scientist, Dr. Hugo Bruckner, has escaped from a Nazi concentration camp and is being brought to England by boat that night. She sends Andreas to meet the boat, but on the way he encounters the newly risen Tesla, who hypnotizes him and transforms him into a werewolf again. Andreas, the vampire's slave once more, secretly kills Bruckner and brings his clothes and identification papers to Tesla. The next day, Sir Fredrick and Lady Jane visit the cemetery to find Tesla's body missing, whereupon the inspector drops the murder charges against her for lack of evidence.

Lady Jane throws an engagement party for her son, John (Roland Varno), who has plighted his troth to Professor Sanders's daughter, Nicki (Nina Foch). Tesla arrives, pretending to be Dr. Bruckner, who is given a tour of Lady Jane's state of the art laboratory and "introduced" to Andreas. Sir Fredrick, who is also in attendance, grows suspicious of him, and of Andreas. On the morning following the party, Nicki is found lying unconscious on her bedroom floor with the marks of the vampire on her throat. In the meantime, Sir Fredrick assigns detectives to shadow Tesla/Bruckner and Andreas, and despite his skepticism, finds evidence that they are indeed a vampire and a werewolf.

Soon afterward, Tesla visits Lady Jane while she is playing the organ, gloating that he will have his revenge on her by turning both Nicki and John into vampires, but she responds by driving him off with a crucifix. Later that night, as Lady Jane is arguing with Sir Fredrick about the existence of vampires, Tesla remotely hypnotizes Nicki and commands her to come to him. Sir Fredrick and Lady Jane follow the entranced Nicki into the graveyard where the monsters are waiting for her, but, just then, air-raid sirens

Vampire scientist Dr. Armand Tesla (Bela Lugosi, right) summons his werewolf slave, Andreas (Matt Willisa), in *The Return of the Vampire* (1943).

sound and another German bombing raid commences. Nicki faints, but is picked up by Andreas, when he is shot by the Inspector. Gravely wounded, the werewolf still manages to carry the unconscious girl into Tesla's lair inside a ruined church. Andreas begs Tesla to save his life, but the vampire cruelly refuses to help him.

Resigned to his fate, the werewolf crawls into a corner to die, but instead finds a crucifix and renounces his evil ways, an act that transforms him back into human form. Before Tesla can vampirize Nicki, a bomb strikes the church, blowing gaps in the stone walls. As daybreak arrives, Andreas drags the torpid vampire out into the sunlight in a final act of redemption. Sir Fredrick and Lady Jane arrive to rescue Nicki and find the dead body of Andreas and the badly decomposed corpse of Armand Tesla sprawled in the rubble of the church.

Lugosi's star power drives the film, and while he's not as romantically charming as he was in *Dracula*, he's every bit as menacing. The actor had not donned the cape onscreen since he was featured in another *Dracula* rip-off, MGM's *Mark of the Vampire* (1935), nearly a decade earlier. Frieda Inescort, playing the part of the female Van Helsing, Lady Jane Ainsley, revitalizes the role of the scientist/vampire hunter, while Matt Willis's lycanthropic Andreas stands in for *Dracula*'s slave Renfield. On the minus side, Lew Landers's direction is pedestrian and slow-moving, making *The Return of the Vampire* seem more like a 1930s-era horror film than a product of the 1940s. Still, atmospheric set design by Louis Diage and art direction by Lionel Banks and Victor Greene create a fog-bound cinematic landscape that recalls the misty moors of Universal's *The Wolf Man* (1941) and help establish the film's eerie mood.

The story idea, conceived by Kurt Neumann and scripted by Griffin Jay and Randall Faye, is unique in the annals of 1940s horror films in that the movie's supernatural events take place against the realistic backdrop of England during the German Blitz, with its air-raid sirens, civil-defense workers, blackout curtains, bombed-out buildings and streets filled with rubble. Most horror films of the period were popular precisely because they provided escapist fantasy from the real-life horrors of World War II. Kurt Neumann would go on to direct science fiction horror films during the 1950s, such as *The Fly* (1958). The screenplay for *The Return of the Vampire* recycles plot elements cribbed from *Dracula's Daughter* (also directed by Landers), including the fatal hypnosis of the vampire's female victim and the vampire slayer character being accused of murder and later acquitted when the vampire's body disappears. This was the first movie to exploit an enmity between a vampire and a werewolf, a theme that would later be amplified into the vamp/lycanthrope conflicts featured in modern fare such as *Van Helsing* and the *Underworld* and *Twilight* series of films.

Lady Jane Ainsley, the film's Van Helsing character, represents the forces of scientific knowledge. She is seen toiling away in a typical 1940s-era laboratory, one of the first in a long line of female savants who would later blossom in the milieu of 1950s sci-fi flicks. The vampire in the film is impersonating a scientist, and the name Armand Tesla is a reference to Nicholas Tesla, the flamboyant real-life scientist/inventor who gave the world alternating current and remote control, and, according to apocryphal reports, also invented science fictional gizmos, such as death rays and earthquake machines. The storyline unfolds against the backdrop of the world's first hi-tech war, as the vampire's resurrection and death are partly enabled by fleets of German bombers.

In the late 1960s, television producer Dan Curtis brought forth the first gothic soap opera on TV, *Dark Shadows*. In 1967, the show attained great popularity when it introduced a vampire character named Barnabas Collins, played by Jonathan Frid, who had been resurrected from the 18th century to modern New England. The success of the show prompted Curtis to produce an ABC-TV movie of the week that also featured a vampire in contemporary America. Based on an unpublished novel by Jeff Rice, the telefilm was scripted by *I Am Legend* author Richard Matheson and featured veteran actor Darren McGavin as crusading news reporter Carl Kolchak.

Kolchak: The Night Stalker (1972) takes place in Las Vegas, where Kolchak, ace newshound for the *Las Vegas Daily News*, is investigating a series of baffling murders of young women who have been drained of blood. One of the victims was thrown thirty feet down a sand pit, without footprints of killer or victim, by an individual with seemingly superhuman strength. At a press conference, pathology experts are called in to explain that the victims died swiftly from a sudden, massive loss of blood, and that bite marks containing human saliva have been found on their throats. In addition, a hospital blood bank has been robbed of blood of all types and Rh factors.

As the bodies pile up, the hard-headed, cynical Kolchak reluctantly comes to believe that the murders have not been committed by "a nut who thinks he's Count Dracula," but that a real vampire is loose in Vegas. When his paper refuses to print his fantastic story, the irrepressible Kolchak refuses to break off his investigative journalism, and keeps chasing down clues gleaned from his contacts, including his girlfriend, casino worker Gail Foster (Carol Lynley), detective Bernie Jenks (Ralph Meeker) and real estate agent and chronic gambler Micky Crawford (Elisha Cook, Jr.). One night while cruising around the city in his convertible listening to the police radio, Kolchak picks up a call about a robbery in progress at another hospital blood bank. He arrives in time to witness a scuffle between police and hospital orderlies and a tall, cadaverous-looking individual who hurls his adversaries around with inhuman strength and is unaffected by a hail of bullets as he drives away with the pilfered blood.

At a news conference the next day, the police announce that they have identified the assailant by tracing the license plate number on the escape car. The suspect is an international fugitive, a Romanian named Janos Skorzeny (Barry Atwater), who was born in 1899, and is in his seventies. According to Scotland Yard and Interpol, Skorzeny inherited a fortune and immigrated to England during World War II, where he adopted the false identity of hematologist Dr. Paul Belasco and became a British citizen. As a blood specialist, Skorzeny/Belasco treated victims of the Blitz, and, after the war, an industrial-strength meat locker and an assortment of blood pumps were subsequently discovered in his medical office, an indication that he was extracting blood from his patients. Skorzeny later left England for Canada, where he was subsequently linked to a series of unexplained killings.

Proceeding under the assumption that his quarry is a real vampire, Kolchak packs a Van Helsing–type vamp-slayer kit, which includes wooden stakes, a mallet, a crucifix, etc., and goes looking for Skorzeny, although the police don't buy his theory. He gets a hot tip about a recent home sale of a decrepit fixer-upper from real estate agent Micky Crawford and goes looking for the vampire and what he hopes will be the biggest story of his career. After placing a call to Detective Jenks, he breaks into the house, which proves to be a gothic manse, complete with chandeliers and stained glass windows, in an advanced state of disrepair. Snooping around the place, he discovers a fridge filled with medical bottles of blood, a drawer containing various wigs, mustaches, theatrical make-up and other disguises, and, finally, a bound woman who is slowly being drained of her blood, a sort of living blood bank.

Intrepid newshound Carl Kolchak (Darren McGavin) wards off a vampire in modern Las Vegas in *The Night Stalker* (1972).

As Kolchak is freeing the woman, the vampire returns to his lair and attacks the reporter, who is at a severe disadvantage due to the vamp's unnatural strength. As they grapple, Detective Jenks shows up and aids in the struggle. Together, they manage to stake Skorzeny just as the police arrive in force. In the aftermath, Kolchak's scoop on the Vegas vampire killer is never published, and he is threatened with prosecution for first-degree murder unless he leaves town. Although the supernatural events are hushed up by the power structure, Kolchak notes that the bodies of Skorzeny and all of his victims were immediately cremated to ensure that they would not become members of the undead.

Curtis's contemporary vampire thriller proved to be a runaway hit with television audiences as the show garnered the highest ratings ever recorded for a made-for-TV movie. Matheson's teleplay sparkles with witty dialogue and terrifies with grisly chills that are beautifully realized through John Llewelyn Moxie's fluid direction. Darren McGavin's portrayal of the amiable but tenacious truth seeker Carl Kolchak injects a delightful element of humor to the otherwise-grim proceedings, and would prove to be one of the actor's most enduring roles. Barry Atwater's vampire Janos Skorzeny has no lines of dialogue, but nonetheless projects a dread screen presence. The film pays homage to the film noir cinema of the 1940s and '50s with its intensely urban setting, its wisecracking newshound protagonist, its mysterioso atmosphere, and in the deliberate casting of film noir actors, such as Ralph Meeker, Elisha Cook, Jr. and Charles McGraw, in supporting roles.

Like *I Am Legend, Kolchak: The Night Stalker* depicts the vampire as living in a modern milieu, existing within a 20th century technological world. Janos Skorzeny drives a car, steals blood from hospital facilities, employs elaborate disguises, must contend with law-enforcement forensic science and is tracked on international police force databases. Skorezny's curious backstory seems to reference plot elements from *The Return of the Vampire*, such as the vampire assuming the role of a distinguished foreign medical scientist operating in England during World War II. *The Night Stalker* inspired a follow-up ABC-TV telefilm entitled *The Night Strangler* (1973), in which McGavin returned as Kolchack, and a weekly TV series in 1975. Chris Carter has cited the Kolchak series as inspiration for his popular sci-fi–oriented show *The X-Files*, in which McGavin occasionally appeared as Arthur Dales, the "father of the X-files," as Kolchak was the precursor to psychic investigators Scully and Mulder.

Barry Atwater would reprise his role as vampire Janos Skorzeny later that year in another film that updated vampirism into the 1970s. At that time, Hammer Studios was attempting to revamp their Dracula franchise by bringing the Count into the 20th century. In a brief prologue to their seventh Dracula feature, *Dracula AD 1972* (1972), Skorzeny rises from a coffin and swears in the movie audience as members of the Count Dracula Society. The film reunited Christopher Lee, in the title role, and Peter Cushing as Van Helsing for the first time since the Hammer classic *Horror of Dracula*, in 1958.

The film begins in A.D. 1872 as the Count and the vampire slayer go *mano a mano* atop a speeding coach, outside London. When the coach crashes, Van Helsing manages to stake his nemesis with the broken spoke of a wheel before expiring from his wounds. Fast-forward a hundred years, to a group of hippies in London that includes Van Helsing's great-granddaughter, Jessica (Stephanie Beacham). A drugged-out reprobate, Johnny Alucard (Christopher Neame), dabbles in the occult and has obtained Count Dracula's ring. Johnny proposes that they conduct a magic ritual on the grounds of St. Bartolph's, a derelict church in the neighborhood slated for demolition.

Looking for occult thrills, the youths conduct the ritual, which involves Johnny giving a blood offering. The black magic ritual revives the Count, who kills one of the girls, Laura (Caroline Munro), as the others flee in terror. Laura's body is found in an adjacent lot the next day, and Scotland Yard inspector Murray (Michael Coles) is assigned to investigate the homicide. Noting that the body has been drained of blood and shows signs of a ritual murder, the inspector consults with Lorrimer Van Helsing (Cushing), who is the grandson of the original vampire hunter and an expert on the occult. Van Helsing is certain that a vampire cult is involved but has a hard time selling the idea to the skeptical Murray.

The risen Count turns Johnny Alucard into a vampire, who then helps him lure

A resurrected Dracula (Christopher Lee, left) squares off against Lorrimer Van Helsing (Peter Cushing) in the ruins of St. Bartolph's Church in *Dracula* AD *1972* (1972).

the other hippie victims into St. Bartolph's, one by one. His ultimate triumph, however, will be to bring Jessica to him and vampirize her, thereby having his revenge on Van Helsing. In the meantime, the vampire hunter traces Dracula to the ruined church and constructs a trap while he is out. When Dracula returns to his lair to consummate his unholy union with Jessica, Van Helsing springs the trap, causing the Count to fall to his doom into a pit lined with sharpened wooden stakes. The vampire is reduced to a crumbling skeleton as Jessica is freed from his mental domination.

While it's nice to have Hammer horror stars Lee and Cushing together again, *Dracula AD 1972* is not one of the studio's better offerings. The film's attempt at youth appeal has dated badly, and Johnny Alucard (spell his last name backwards) and his gang of youthful ne'er-do-wells seem like refugees from an *Austin Powers* comedy. In the brief screen time allotted Dracula, Lee has little to do except wear a cape, look sinister and bite necks. Cushing, on the other hand, delivers an impassioned performance as the film's next generation vampire slayer. Director Alan Gibson does a workmanlike job at the helm, but the result is not particularly distinguished.

One of the film's taglines was, "Past, present or future, never count out the Count." But Don Houghton's script confines the vampire to the gothic environs of St. Bartolph's ruined church. Thus, Dracula is never allowed to interact with 20th century science and technology. The film was reportedly inspired by the notorious case of the "Highgate Vampire," in which witnesses reported seeing apparitional figures inside the Cemetery of St. James in London's Highgate district (ironically, the graveyard in which vampiress Lucy Westenra in interred in Stoker's novel). Groups of self-proclaimed vampire hunters descended on the cemetery where the dead bodies of animals were found drained of blood and were thought to be the victims of a satanic cult. Later, the decapitated and partially burned body of a young woman was discovered on the grounds, leading to a media circus. The mysterious events at Highgate continued until 1983, and the case is considered by occultists to be the strongest modern evidence for the existence of vampires. The Hammer scriptwriters were also reportedly inspired by *Count Yorga, Vampire* (1970), a trendy, low-budget American vampire flick set in contemporary Los Angeles.

A sequel soon followed, entitled *The Satanic Rites of Dracula* (a.k.a. *Count Dracula and his Vampire Bride*, 1973). Lee and Cushing reprised their roles yet again, as did Michael Coles as Inspector Murray. Alan Gibson returned to direct a screenplay by Don Houghton that truly brought Dracula into the modern world by adding a touch of science fiction and James Bond–ish espionage intrigue.

As the film opens, British Secret Service agent Hanson (Maurice O' Connell) is being held prisoner by a satanic cult in Pelham House, a country estate outside London. The house is equipped with hi-tech surveillance equipment like electric-eye motion sensors, video cameras and a computerized control room. Hanson barely manages to escape from the manor while a black-magic ceremony is being conducted by cult leader Chin Yang (Barbara Yu Ling), bringing his superiors a tiny roll of microfilm recorded on a watch, which serves as a camera. Hanson dies of his wounds, but his superior, Torrence (William Franklyn), learns from the micro-photos that several prominent Britons, including a high government minister, a general and an eminent scientist are part of the cult. Fearing reprisals against their organization by the minister, the spies call upon Scotland Yard's Inspector Murray, who, in turn, refers them to Lorrimer Van Helsing.

Van Helsing suspects that the cultists have found a way to resurrect Count Dracula, using black magic. Torrence, Inspector Murray and Van Helsing's granddaughter Jessica (played here by Joanna Lumley) decide to infiltrate Pelham House to determine the truth. They encounter a group of female vamps in the building's cellar before being chased off the property by a gang of motorcycle thugs.

In the meantime, Van Helsing decides to pay a visit to an old friend (who happens to be one of the cultists), the Nobel Prize–winning biologist Dr. Julian Keeley (Freddie Jones), at the Keeley Foundation for Science. Keeley appears to be having mental problems that are linked to his work on creating a mutant bubonic plague bacillus that is far more virulent than any existing strain. The scientist also reveals that he has been

(Left to right) Jessica Van Helsing (Joanna Lumley), Inspector Murray (Michael Coles) and Lorrimer Van Helsing (Peter Cushing) draw their plans against the Count in *The Satanic Rites of Dracula* (1973).

under pressure from the cult to complete his work before the "Sabbath of the Undead" on the 23rd of the month. He claims to have accomplished his mission before the deadline, displaying a line of plague cultures on petri dishes. During their conversation, Van Helsing is shot with a tranquilizer dart by one of the cult's henchmen and loses consciousness. When he awakens, the bacteria samples are gone and Keeley's dead body is hanging from the rafters.

Van Helsing informs the other vampire hunters that he believes Dracula is behind a plot to release the plague to cause the mass extinction of mankind. He further speculates that the Count has a death wish, and that the extinction of humankind will ultimately release him from the curse of the undead. Learning that the Keeley Institute was funded by the reclusive real estate developer D.D. Denham, Van Helsing's suspicions are further aroused when he finds that the offices of the Denham Group are housed in a new skyscraper that has been built on the former site of St. Bartolph's, the church where Dracula had been destroyed in the previous movie.

Granted an audience with the secretive real estate tycoon in the ultra-modern office building, Van Helsing learns that he is in the presence of the reincarnated Dracula. He attempts to dispatch him with a silver bullet, but fails and is taken captive by the cultists. The Count orders that he be taken back to the manor. In the meantime, Murray, Torrence and Jessica are conducting surveillance of Pelham House when Torrence is killed by a sniper and Murray and Jessica are taken prisoner by the motorcycle thugs.

The Sabbath ritual commences that night with a hypnotized Jessica stretched out on the cult's altar as Van Helsing watches helplessly. Dracula tells his disciples that he intends to loose the plague that very evening, and when one of them balks that individual is exposed to the bacillus and suffers a hideous death. During the ceremony, Murray manages to escape from confinement and smashes the equipment in the computer room, causing a fire that destroys the plague germs along with many of the cultists. While Murray rescues Jessica, Dracula goes after Van Helsing, who escapes into the surrounding woods and manages to entangle the Count inside a hawthorn bush, a shrub that magically nullifies his vampiric powers. Thus imprisoned, Dracula is staked by Van Helsing for the last time in a Hammer horror film.

Scenarist Don Houghton, who worked on the BBC-TV sci-fi series *Doctor Who*, introduces several intriguing science fiction elements into the mix. For the first time Dracula exists within a hi-tech world of computers, electric eye sensors, spycraft gizmos, motorcycles and genetic engineering and is able to adapt these technological advances to his advantage. Conversely, Van Helsing has to rely on traditional supernatural remedies like silver bullets and hawthorn to triumph over his foe. Once more the vampire is connected with the spread of bubonic plague, but this time the disease vector is concocted in the laboratory.

This unlikely blend of supernatural horror, science fiction and espionage manages to live up to its high concept approach thanks to brisk direction by Alan Gibson. Stars Christopher Lee and Peter Cushing turn in fine performances in their final go-round as vampire and vampire slayer, and are ably assisted by the quirky portrayals of Freddie Jones and Barbara Yu Ling in supporting roles. Lee's Dracula has more lines of dialogue in *The Satanic Rites*, although this was not to the liking of all critics. Unlike *Dracula AD 1972*, the sequel truly moved the Dracula character into the modern world as part of Hammer's effort to reinvent the vampire genre in films such as *Captain Kronos: Vampire Hunter* (1972) and *The Legend of the 7 Golden Vampires* (1973). Alas, it was all for naught: audiences proved not to be receptive to these updated vampire myths, and the House of Hammer closed its doors just a few years later.

Writer/director Guillermo del Toro is perhaps the most acclaimed creator of fantastic films working today. His films, notably *Mimic* (1997), *The Devil's Backbone* (2001), *Hellboy* (2004) and *Pan's Labyrinth* (2006) have been critical and commercial successes that have elevated the creative stature of cinematic fantasy. Del Toro has shown a fondness for vampires by directing *Blade II* (2002) and authoring the science fiction vampire novel *The Strain* (2009) and its sequels. His first feature film, *Cronos* (1992), was a unique and highly original treatment of the vampire theme.

Cronos begins with a brief prologue set in 1536, in Veracruz, Mexico, where an enigmatic alchemist (Mario Ivan Martinez) is seeking to create an invention that will grant him eternal life. Centuries later, in 1937, a residential building collapses to reveal bowls full of blood, a human victim, and the remains of the alchemist, who had become a vampire and survived for hundreds of years. The items in the estate are put up for auction, and one of them eventually winds up inside a curio shop operated by elderly antiques dealer Jesus Gris (Federico Luppi). Señor Gris leads an idyllic life, running his little shop with the help of his mute granddaughter, Aurora (Tamara Shanath).

One day, Gris notices that a statue of an angel in his shop has a false bottom; upon opening it, he discovers an unusual object inside. It turns out to be the cronos device, an ornately carved golden box, roughly the size and shape of a human heart. It is an invention fashioned by the alchemist that enabled the vampire's immortality, although Gris knows nothing of this. Winding the mechanism while holding it in his hand, the device suddenly grips him with six insect-like claws and pricks him with a mechanical stinger that injects an unknown substance into his body.

Soon afterward a hulking thug named Angel (Ron Perlman) visits the shop and starts nosing around. He is acting as a lackey for his uncle, Dieter de la Guardia (Claudio Brook), a wealthy, dying businessman who has obtained the alchemist's diary and is obsessed with finding the cronos device, which he believes will cure him and extend his life span. In the meantime, Gris has become addicted to using the cronos, which is making him more youthful while instilling him with a taste for human blood. He opens up the shop one day to find it has been ransacked, with one of Angel's business cards left behind to indicate who is responsible.

Angel abducts Gris from a party and attempts to beat the location of the device out of him. When that fails, he places Gris's body inside his car and pushes it over a cliff. The vampire comes back to life in a funeral parlor and narrowly escapes being cremated. Returning to his shop, he finds he can no longer tolerate sunlight and must sleep in a coffin-like box during the daytime. Hoping to find out some information about the infernal machine, Gris brings it along on a visit to de la Guardia's factory, accompanied by Aurora. The ailing industrialist, who inhabits a suite inside his factory adorned with his X-ray negatives, parts of his body that have been surgically removed and preserved in jars, and arcane medical equipment, proceeds to enlighten Gris about the origin and nature of cronos, information gleaned from the alchemist's notebook. A living insect, he explains, is encased inside the device that is perfectly integrated into the mechanism's clockwork contents. It is this living creature that excretes the substance that transforms humans into long-lived vampires. He also reveals that if the device and the insect are destroyed, Gris will die.

De la Guardia stabs Gris and attempts to take the cronos, but Aurora whacks him on the head from behind, seriously wounding him. Then Angel shows up and chases Gris out onto the roof of the factory, where he mercilessly beats the old man. Gris retaliates by grabbing onto Angel as he jumps off the roof. Angel is killed in the fall but Gris is revived by Aurora, who uses the cronos device on him. Shamefully tempted to drink Aurora's blood to slake his vampire's thirst, Gris chooses instead to destroy the cronos, smashing it with a rock. Freed from the curse of the undead, he returns home to die peacefully.

Like del Toro's other cinematic works, *Cronos* is more of a dark fantasy than an out-and-out horror film. The director's idiosyncratic obsession with clockworks and insects was initially realized in the cronos device, a metal bug-like machine with a living insect at its core. Working with a modest budget, del Toro employs real-world locations, such as the funeral parlor and crematorium, to create a semi-documentary look to the film, yet is also able to conjure a brooding gothic mood of fantasy in the midst of reality. The film also marked the beginning of the director's artistic collaborations with Argentine actor Federico Luppi and American thespian Ron Perlman. Although *Cronos* received critical accolades in Mexico, it received very limited release in the United States and didn't make a great deal of profit.

Cronos is a very different kind of vampire film, one that focuses primarily on the humanity of the vampire, as Gris is beaten, stabbed, killed and almost cremated. His ordeal depicts the true horror of being undead. Once again, vampirism is related to drug addiction as Gris becomes more and more dependent on the machine's regenerative effects. The real departure from vampire mythology, however, is in the cronos device itself, an uncanny melding of mechanism and organism that confers both immortality and a thirst for blood. For the first time, a machine transforms human beings into vampires. The device is linked to alchemy, a blend of science and occultism that flourished during the Middle Ages and was the precursor of modern chemistry.

In 1971, after a change in censorship codes allowed comic books to explore horror themes that were previously prohibited, Marvel Comics brought out a comic book entitled *The Tomb of Dracula*, which updated the characters from Bram Stoker's novel into the present. In 1973, an African American nemesis of Dracula named Blade, the Vampire Slayer, was introduced and soon became a fixture of the series. The Blade character, created by Marv Wolfman and Gene Colan, appeared in a number of incarnations in several different Marvel titles over the decades; in the late 1990s he was brought to the big screen in a trilogy of vampire superhero action movies starring Wesley Snipes. Blade is a half human–half vampire hybrid who hunts down and destroys vampires because of a blood vendetta. Referred to as a "daywalker," he has most of the vampire's strengths and none of their weaknesses, but must use a serum to maintain himself in his quasi-human state.

The first film, *Blade* (1998), opens with a brief prologue set in 1967, in which Blade's pregnant mother, Vanessa Brooks (Sanaa Lathan), is admitted to a hospital emergency room after being bitten by a vampire. A baby boy is delivered while the mother dies. Cut to 1998 Los Angeles, where the hapless Dennis (Kenny Johnson) is lured into a weird underground rave club by the seductive Racquel (Traci Lords). As the dancers gyrate under the strobe lights to the electronic house mix, blood starts gushing from the sprinkler system on the ceiling, grotesquely covering the dancers. They are revealed as vampires who are about to drain their human victim when Blade

Mutant vampire hunter Blade (Wesley Snipes) in his secret lair in *Blade* (1998).

(Snipes) arrives. The daywalker wears a long black coat over black Kevlar armor and sports a pair of dark glasses. Panic ensues as the vampire slayer cuts a wide swath through the vamps with his silver sword and other anti-vampire weapons, leaving the badly burned body of the club owner, Quinn (Donal Logue), behind as the LAPD arrives to quell the mêlée.

Quinn's "corpse" is taken to a hospital, where hematologist Dr. Karen Jenson (N'bushe Wright) notes odd anomalies in its blood during an autopsy. Suddenly the vampire comes alive and bites Karen's throat. Blade arrives to drive Quinn off, but the vamp escapes as the police show up looking for him. The vampire hunter flees the hospital, taking Karen to his secret headquarters, located in a factory building, where she is introduced to Blade's mentor, Abraham Whistler (Kris Kristofferson). Whistler is a grizzled old guy with a gray beard, long gray hair and a bad attitude who cooks up all manner of hi-tech anti-vamp munitions for Blade to use in the field. The vampires are vulnerable to sunlight or UV light, silver and garlic, but are not affected by crosses, holy objects or mirrors.

Blade explains to Karen that the vamps have established their own underground subculture completely unknown to humans and have secretly amassed great power and influence over society. "They own the police," he tells her, "they've got their claws into everything," which is the reason he and Whistler must operate outside the law. Having been bitten by Quinn, Karen is in danger of becoming a vampire herself, and is therefore motivated to use her medical expertise to find a cure. She finds that the anticoagulant EDTA reacts strongly with vampire blood and may be the answer she is looking for.

In the meantime, during a meeting of vampire honchos, brash young upstart Deacon Frost (Stephen Dorff) proposes that the vampires should emerge from the shadows and enslave humanity, but he is chastened by the elders for his radical views. Unknown to them, Frost is secretly working on decoding the Book of Erebus, the "vampire Bible," an ancient text that will enable him to release the vampire god La Magra and usurp the power of the elders. He begins his coup by killing Gitano Dragonetti (Udo Kier), the leader of the Vampire Council, and imprisoning the others. While Frost is hatching his plot, Blade and Karen invade the vamp's records facility and discover clues about what the young upstart is up to, and learns that Frost intends to sacrifice Blade and the remaining elders to La Magra during a ceremony in the vampires' Temple of Eternal Night.

Racing against time to forestall becoming a vampire, Karen continues her hematology research and uses a retrovirus to alter vamp DNA and cure herself. Unfortunately, while Blade is absent, Frost invades his lair, takes Karen hostage and bites Whistler, mortally wounding him. When Blade discovers this, he leaves Whistler a gun with which to commit suicide. He then arms himself with a large supply of EDTA ampoules and goes after Frost, but is taken captive within the vampire's hi-tech fortress. He is imprisoned while Frost sacrifices the twelve elders to the vampire god and gains the powers of La Magra. Meanwhile, Karen manages to free herself and revive Blade with her own blood. Blade engages in a swordfight with Frost, who is now invulnerable to his weapons, but kills the super-vamp by injecting him with EDTA. In the aftermath, Karen is cured of vampirism, but Blade refuses to become human again because he must continue to fight the vampires with their own powers.

Neatly directed by Stephen Norrington from a screenplay by David S. Goyer, *Blade* is a slick actioner that successfully captures the excitement of the comic book. The director makes skillful use of downtown L.A. locations to depict the gritty urban interzone of the vampires, who exist in a demimonde of underground rave clubs and strip joints. Action star Wesley Snipes conveys the physicality of the titular superhero character, but having to wear his signature dark glasses in most scenes makes Blade a distant figure who is somewhat lacking in emotional affect. By contrast, Kris Kristofferson's snarling performance as the grumpy old Abraham Whistler is funny and oddly endearing. Stephen Dorff is entertainingly irritating as the villainous vamp Deacon Frost, and his perfidy is given an able assist by Donal Logue as his psychotic sidekick, Quinn.

Blade was released near the beginning of the cycle of Marvel superhero screen adaptations that would eventually culminate in the enormously profitable Spider-Man and Iron Man franchises. With a budget of $45 million, the film was a well-produced, glossy effort that moved the vampire genre strongly in the direction of sci-fi action-adventure, a trend that would continue in movies like *Van Helsing* (2004), *Ultraviolet* (2006), *Against the Dark* (2009), *Priest* (2011), and the *Bloodrayne* and *Underworld* series of films, and may have provided inspiration for the black-clad martial arts superheroes of *The Matrix* (1999). *Blade* performed well at the box-office, grossing $200 million in domestic and foreign sales, and spawned two sequels.

The Blade character exemplifies the concept of the *dhampir*, an Eastern European term for a half-vampire who hunts down and kills other vamps. Like *Star Trek*'s half–Vulcan, half-human character Mr. Spock, Blade is a hybrid being with a divided identity. Abraham Whistler is a hi-tech version of *Dracula*'s Abraham Van Helsing, who devises sophisticated anti-vamp weaponry. The vampire society exists, not inside a gothic crypt, but in a science fiction realm of computers and futuristic technology. David S. Goyer's script adds another sci-fi element to the vampire myth, namely the theme of a conspiracy by a secret society of vamps aimed at world domination. The film's vampires resemble the alien invaders in the science fiction classic *Invasion of the Body Snatchers*, human-looking creatures who have secretly infiltrated society.

The sequel, *Blade II* (2002), was directed by Guillermo del Toro, who had kicked off his career with the quirky vampire melodrama *Cronos*, just nine years earlier. Wesley Snipes reprised his role as the sword-wielding vampire slayer, and Kristofferson returned as the crusty old Abraham Whistler. The action takes place two years later in the Czech Republic, where Blade is tracking down a coven of Euro-vamps who have reportedly turned Whistler into a vampire (after his suicide in the previous movie) and have been keeping him alive. Armed with updated anti-vampire weapons, such as an automatic pistol that uses silver-nitrate bullets, he blasts his way into a vampire halfway house and finds his mentor floating inside a tank of blood, attached to a gaggle of life-support hoses and cables. He frees his mentor from the tank and brings him to his local headquarters, where he administers an injection of "accelerated retroviral detox" that turns Whistler into a human once more after he's been "sucking blood clots for two years."

Blade has acquired a new tech guy in the interim, the irreverent, twenty-something, pot-smoking Scud (Norman Reedus), who has personality conflicts with the curmudgeonly Whistler. One night, Blade's domain is invaded by vampire ninjas who engage him in swordfights and martial arts contests. They are Asad (Danny John-Jules) and Nyssa (Leonor Varela), the daughter of the vamp Overlord, Eli Damaskinos. They have come to propose a temporary truce and a parlay with the Overlord. Escorted to the vampires' lair inside the futuristic Caliban Institute, Damaskinos (Thomas Kretschmann) informs Blade and his assistants that their help is being sought by the High Council of Vampires in combating a new strain of virus that is creating a mutant race of vampires called Reapers. The Reapers are impervious to silver, garlic, and the anti-coagulant EDTA, and are vulnerable only to ultraviolet light. When they feed, their entire lower jaw opens up and a tube-like organ emerges to siphon up blood. The

Reapers are extremely voracious, and their accelerated metabolism demands that they feed on both humans and vampires every few hours. They are bald, pale-skinned, pointy-eared and generally resemble the Count Orlok character in F.W. Murnau's *Nosferatu.*

Damaskinos convinces Blade and his crew to go after the head Reaper, Jared Nomak (Luke Goss), and his brood with the aid of a team of vampire warriors called the "Bloodpack," who are headed up by the burly Reinhardt (Ron Perlman). An uneasy alliance is formed as Blade and the Bloodpack seek out Nomak in a vamp hangout called the "House of Pain," while Whistler and Scud conduct surveillance outside. The anti–Reaper squad pursues Nomak through the building's extensive basement area, but the Reapers prove hard to kill, and their quarry escapes. Fortunately, Whistler and Scud manage to capture a Reaper, who appears to be half dead.

The team brings the creature back to the Caliban Institute, where Nyssa performs an autopsy on the now-deceased Reaper; the cause of death is that it hasn't fed recently. They also learn that the Reaper virus alters human physiognomy, dissolving the lower jaw to allow the mouth to open wide and extrude a barbed tongue containing a neurotoxin that paralyzes its prey. The Reaper's heart becomes encased in bone that is nearly impossible to penetrate. Only ultraviolet radiation seems to affect them, which poses a problem for the vampire members of the team for whom UV is also deadly.

Armed with UV guns, grenades and bombs, the Bloodpack, Blade, Whistler and the two vamp ninjas seek out the Reaper hive in sewers beneath the city. A fierce battle ensues with the Reaper hordes, most of which are taken out with the UV bombs, but casualties among the team are also heavy, leaving only Blade, Whistler, Nyssa and Reinhardt alive. Nyssa has been badly burned by one of the UV bombs, and Blade must give her some of his blood to ensure her survival. Then vamp squads arrive and, under Reinhardt's direction, stun Blade into submission with shock rods and take him and Whistler back to the Overlord as prisoners. Their quarry, Nomak, has eluded them once more.

Back inside the Overlord's fortress, Damaskinos explains to Blade and Whistler that the Reaper virus was not a natural mutation, but was genetically designed to produce a type of vampire that is immune to silver and garlic. He displays a cylinder holding sacs containing tiny vampire fetuses while conceding that his experiment was a failure because the upgraded vamps were not immune to sunlight. The Overlord intends to harvest Blade's blood in order to isolate the factors that make him resistant to UV radiation and create a new race of vampire daywalkers. Scud then reveals that he is a traitor who has been working for Damaskinos all along. Blade manages to kill him with a small bomb.

Blade is taken to an operating room where he is strapped to a table and his blood is extracted. Whistler, fortunately, manages to escape and free him. He then tosses Blade into a pool of blood, which fully revives the daywalker. As Blade takes on the Overlord's minions, Nyssa learns that Nomak is actually her father's son and her brother; she feels betrayed, realizing that Damaskinos sent her and the Bloodpack out

Blade (Wesley Snipes) strikes a samurai pose in this poster for *Blade II* (2002).

to die, while Blade gave her his own blood to save her life. Blade continues his rampage, slicing Reinhardt in half with his sword, when Nomak invades the sanctuary and begins to cut a wide swath through the Overlord's defenses. Seeking revenge on her father, Nyssa lets Nomak enter Damaskinos's sanctum sanctorum, where the Overlord and the Reaper share a brief moment of familial rapprochement before the prodigal son drains his father's blood and bites his sister out of spite.

Blade arrives to confront Nomak, and a tremendous battle ensues, which the daywalker wins by slipping his silver sword through the bone protecting the Reaper's heart. After the battle, Nyssa feels herself turning into a Reaper and implores Blade to let her look upon the sun one last time. As the morning sun rises, Nyssa's body fades away into a shower of sparks and Blade is left to savor his bittersweet victory.

Arguably the best entry in this Marvel series, *Blade II* surpasses its predecessor thanks to the cinematic artistry of director del Toro, who infuses the proceedings with his signature brand of visual fantasy. Filmed in Prague, the sequel has an old-world gothic look that contrasts with the real-world L.A. locations used in the first film. Exquisite production design by Carol Spier and imaginative costumes by Wendy Partridge realize del Toro's science-fantasy visions on the screen. The Reapers, with their hinged jaws that open the face into a gaping red maw, are particularly horrific and were created using animatronic robots.

The complex screenplay by David S. Goyer creates a new kind of vampire, a second-stage vamp who drinks the blood of other vamps. *Blade II* also introduced the notion of different clans of vampires involved in an internecine conflict. In his second go-round as the Blade character, Wesley Snipes is still having fun with the role and exudes superhero exuberance, while Kris Kristofferson's caustic portrayal of Whistler adds some grit to the mix. Although Luke Goss's Nomak is the nominal supervillain of the piece, del Toro repertory player Ron Perlman delivers a more delicious menace as the vampire warrior Reinhardt.

Blade II proved to be a seminal film that redefined the iconography of the science fiction bloodsucker. Its bestial, bald-headed, *Nosferatu*-like vampires would provide the visual template for the sci-fi vamps in *Underworld: Evolution* (2006), *I Am Legend* (2007), and *Priest* (2011). The concept of vampirism as a parasitic viral disease that causes extreme physiological changes in the human body would re-appear in del Toro's vampire novel *The Strain* and its sequels (see Chapter Two). The scene in which the Overlord displays rows of hybrid fetuses suspended in a hi-tech incubatorium is mirrored in similar narratives of genetically engineered children floating in artificial wombs found in alien abduction reports. Whistler's futuristic anti-vampire weaponry, including UV guns and UV bombs, are even more hi-tech and visually dynamic than those in the first movie.

The third film in the series, *Blade: Trinity* (2004), takes place six months after the events of *Blade II*. In a brief prologue, helicopters land near an ancient ziggurat structure deep in the Syrian Desert. Four vampires, wearing protective clothing against the sun, enter the structure, where they discover a secret chamber. A massive figure, wearing

Kris Kristofferson as Blade's technician and mentor, Abraham Whistler, in *Blade: Trinity* (2004).

a fearsome horned mask, arises from the ruins. It is Lord Dracula, the primordial vampire, who has been resurrected by the cult.

Blade and Whistler have returned to the United States, where they have resumed their vampire-hunting duties, but things have changed for the worse. The daywalker's vigilantism has been called into question by pop psychologist Dr. Edgar Vance (John Michael Higgins), who is leading a crusade to turn the public against him. One night, during a raid on a vampire-biker hangout, Blade is framed for the murder of a human and is accused of homicide by FBI agents Ray Cumberland (James Remar) and Wilson Hale (Michael Rawlins). FBI SWAT teams descend on Blade's sanctuary, but Whistler knows that vampires and their human "familiars" have infiltrated the power structure; he chooses to destroy their warehouse lab and all of their computer records rather than let the data fall into the wrong hands. Whistler detonates a bomb and is killed in the explosion while an emotionally devastated Blade is taken into custody at LAPD headquarters and placed under heavy sedation.

Whistler's fears prove to be well founded when a "transfer team" arrives to escort Blade to a more secure facility. In reality, they are a group of vamps led by Danica Talos (Parker Posey), her brother Asher (Callum Keith Rennie) and the hulking Jarko Grimwood (Paul Levesque). Before they can spirit Blade away, he is rescued by two vampire hunters, Whistler's illegitimate daughter, Abigail (Jessica Biel), and ex-vamp Hannibal King (Ryan Reynolds). Abby and King revive Blade with an inhaler containing his serum, and the trio manage to fight their way out of police headquarters and escape into the night in a van driven by Dex (Ron Selmour).

Blade is driven to the Honeycomb Hideout, where he is introduced to the rest of the vampire hunters, who call themselves the "Nightstalkers." In addition to Abby, King and Dex, the team consists of weaponeer Hedges (Patton Oswalt), blind biologist Sommerfield (Natasha Lyonne) and the scientist's young daughter, Zoe (Haili Page). Despite Abby's pedigree, Blade is not impressed with the motley crew, whom he considers a bunch of amateurs, or "rejects from a Saturday morning cartoon." The Nightstalkers inform him that Dracula, who is now known as "Drake," has been revived as part of a vampire master plan designed to subjugate the human race. In order to counter the threat, Sommerfield has been working on a bio-weapon called DayStar, a powerful virus that is capable of wiping out the entire vampire race; her research, however, has hit a snag, and the effectiveness of the weapon is unreliable. The team needs to obtain a sample of Dracula's blood, which contains the purest vampire DNA, to fully potentiate the DayStar virus.

Information gleaned from one of the vampire's familiars leads them to Dr. Vance, who is paid a visit by Blade, Abby and King. They find Vance dead inside his office, but are confronted by a second "Dr. Vance," a double who shapeshifts into Dracula/Drake (Dominic Purcell). Drake jumps out of a window and falls several stories onto the street, with Blade in hot pursuit. He follows Drake onto the roof of a nearby building, but the vampire now holds an infant in his arms. The lord vampire and the daywalker size each other up for a few moments while Drake explains that the modern-day vampires are striving to replicate his immunity to ultraviolet. Then Drake pitches the baby off the roof and Blade is forced to rescue the child and lose track of his quarry.

Back at the Honeycomb Hideout, Sommerfield believes she has located a vamp facility at a factory run by Biomedica Enterprises, where large quantities of polymerase, bone marrow growth supplement and genetic sequencing enzymes have recently been delivered. Blade and Abby stake out the company's giant warehouse and observe the arrival of an individual that they recognize as Chief of Police Martin Vreede (Mark Berry), whom they now know is one of the vampire's familiars. Using Vreede's ID, they gain entrance to the building and find that the vamps have constructed a blood farm. Rows of human bodies are suspended in hi-tech cocoons, festooned with tubes and wires for life support and blood extraction. Vreede explains that the vampires have decided this approach is preferable to hunting their human prey. The victims, who are culled from the homeless population, are brain dead and maintained in a vegetative state. There are similar industrial blood-farming facilities located in every major city in America, Vreede informs them, and this program represents the vampires' final solution for mankind. Revolted by this grim discovery, Blade kills Vreede and shuts down the blood farm.

In the meantime, Drake invades the Honeycomb Hideout, murders Dex, Hedges and Sommerfield and takes King and Zoe back to the vampires' lair. Fortunately, another scientist named Caulder (Christopher Heyerdahl) has intercepted a final mes-

(Left to right) Abigail Whistler (Jessica Biel), Blade (Wesley Snipes) and Hannibal King (Ryan Reynolds) prepare to clean house on a nest of vamps in *Blade: Trinity* (2004).

sage from Sommerfield just prior to her death. In the recorded message, Sommerfield tells them that she had perfected a new strain of the DayStar virus, which needs to be directly injected into Drake's body; she also warns that the virus may be so lethal it could very well kill the human/vamp hybrid Blade. She then explains that she transmitted the genetic code for DayStar to Caulder, who has cooked up a batch of the virus. The serum has been loaded into a projectile that Abby fastens onto the tips of several of her arrows.

Using a signal from a locator implanted inside King's body, Blade and Abby invade the vampires' lair and pump silver-nitrate gas through the building's ventilation system. They free King, who joins in the battle with Danica, Jarko and the other vampire warriors. Abby rescues Zoe while Blade engages in a swordfight with Drake, who shape-shifts into a fearsome demonic being. The power of the ancient vampire is too much for Blade, who is nearly overcome. At that moment, Abby arrives and pierces Drake with one of the DayStar-tipped arrows, potentiating the virus. The DayStar bug wafts throughout Drake's lair, killing him, Danica and all the other vampires. As he is dying, Drake lauds Blade's prowess, and hails him as being the new generation of vampire, saying, "The thirst always wins." Fortunately, Blade is unaffected by the virus, and lives to continue his war against the vamps.

Although it's a bit of a comedown from del Toro's elegant visuals in *Blade II*, the third installment in the trilogy is a slick and effective sci-fi action thriller. Writer-turned-director David S. Goyer does a competent job at the helm, but his screenplay is a bit of a disappointment. For one thing, killing off the Whistler character early in the proceedings deprives the film of his garrulous yet comic screen presence. The Nightstalkers are not well developed, and are a poor substitute for Whistler, and the Hannibal King character, played by Ryan Reynolds, is particularly irritating as he spouts his non-stop wiseguy patter and pseudo-witty dialogue.

The film's biggest flaw, however, is in its depiction of the most famous bloodsucker in vampire lore, Dracula. Sporting a leather vest and pants outfit, the beefy Dominic Purcell looks more like a professional wrestler than the dreaded king of the vampires. Jessica Biel is graceful and easy on the eyes as Abby, while Parker Posey's Danica Talos exudes mega-bitchiness as the film's femme fatale vamp. Star Wesley Snipes plays the role of Blade with the same violent exuberance as he exhibited in the two previous installments.

Like the other movies in the series, *Blade: Trinity* features a futuristic vampire lair and exotic weaponry such as an ultraviolet laser bow, capable of chopping vamps in half, and the hi-tech military detection gear used to locate Dracula's tomb. The depiction of the industrial blood farm is truly horrifying. The concept was first mentioned (but not shown) in Roger Corman's alien vamp flick *Not of this Earth* (1956) and would later re-appear in *Daybreakers* (2009). Once again, the vampire is associated with disease and plague, and is foiled by a genetically engineered virus created by a scientist.

Declining box-office receipts for the third installment of the series curtailed the production of further sequels in the *Blade* series. Snipes and Kristofferson sued the producers, claiming that their roles were abridged in order to provide more screen time to the Nightstalker characters. Another factor was Snipes's conviction for tax evasion, which took the actor out of circulation for three years. The three *Blade* films were single-handedly responsible for transforming the vampire into a sci-fi superhero action figure for the 21st century.

Horror maven Wes Craven, who had directed modern classics of the horror genre, such as *The Hills Have Eyes* (1977) and *A Nightmare on Elm Street* (1984), was the executive producer of *Dracula 2000* (2000), directed by Patrick Lussier. The film begins in London in Y2K, where a futuristic mega-building contains a small, archaic structure housing the firm of Carfax Antiquities. Carfax is run by the aged Matthew Van Helsing (Christopher Plummer) and his young assistant Simon Sheppard (Jonny Lee Miller). One night, while Van Helsing is upstairs performing a strange procedure involving bloodsucking leeches, his secretary, Solina (Jennifer Esposito) lets a team of thieves headed by her boyfriend, Marcus (Omar Epps), into the facility, where they hack into the firm's hi-tech security system and open up a huge vault leading to an underground chamber.

The cellar contains nothing of value except a sealed metal coffin. Reasoning that the coffin contains Van Helsing's true valuables, they knock down one of the walls and escape into an adjacent tunnel with their loot. The coffin is then loaded onto a twin-engine cargo plane bound for the United States. When Van Helsing discovers the theft he sets off for America in hot pursuit. On board the airplane one of the thieves opens the coffin, releasing the revived corpse of Count Dracula (Gerard Butler), who proceeds to drain the blood of the crew. The plane crashes in a Louisiana bayou, and Dracula heads for New Orleans.

Meanwhile, in the Big Easy, Mary Heller (Justine Waddell) lives with her roommate, Lucy Westerman (Colleen Fitzpatrick), while they are attending college. Mary is a virginal young woman who has been having disturbing dreams about a handsome yet terrifying man. Van Helsing and Simon soon arrive in the city and begin their quest for the coffin when Van Helsing reveals to his partner that he is the original Abraham Van Helsing who had defeated and imprisoned the Count back in 1897. He has kept himself alive all these years by injecting himself with Dracula's blood, which he obtains from leeches, to guard against the vampire's return because the Count is "beyond the reach of death," and cannot be destroyed. Their best chance, he explains, is to try to ascertain Dracula's origins in order to figure out why he abhors the cross and other holy objects.

He also reveals that Mary is his daughter, who was separated from him by her mother, and that Mary and Dracula share a telepathic link. Dracula has come to New Orleans, he believes, to seek out his daughter and exact his revenge on the Van Helsing lineage. Unfortunately, Dracula gets to Mary's house first, turning Lucy into a vampire who kills Van Helsing and takes Mary and Simon captive. On a rooftop presided over by a huge neon sign representing Jesus on the cross, Dracula reveals his secret: he is the biblical Judas Iscariot who betrayed Christ to the Romans and hung himself in despair afterward. God's punishment for this sacrilege was to live for two thousand years as a vampire. This explains his vulnerability to sacred objects and to silver, with which he was paid for his betrayal.

Simon and Mary do battle with the Count and his subordinate vamps on the rooftop. As Simon dispatches the other vampires, Dracula and Mary fall off the roof, but Mary manages to wrap a wire noose around the Count's neck, leaving him suspended beneath the neon crucifix. She survives the fall, but Dracula, hanged for a second time for his blasphemous misdeeds, is destroyed in a fiery conflagration as the rising sun's rays fall upon his exposed body.

Marketed to a youthful demographic, *Dracula 2000* featured a soundtrack with music by metal bands Slayer and Disturbed. With his shoulder-length hair and pretty-boy looks, Gerard Butler appropriates the iconography of Frank Langella's depiction of the character in Universal's remake of *Dracula* (1979). Butler is simply too young to be playing the immortal Count, and his performance in the role strains credibility. The rest of the twenty-something cast turn in mediocre, forgettable performances. Only veteran actor Christopher Plummer delivers any dramatic heft, in the role of Van Helsing, a performance that is an homage to Peter Cushing's many Hammer films as the character. The screenplay, by Joel Soisson and director Patrick Lussier, quickly abandons any pretense of being derived from Stoker's novel (à la Francis Ford Coppola's 1992 retread *Bram Stoker's Dracula*) and instead forges ahead into biblical territory. On the plus side, director Lussier makes effective use of atmospheric New Orleans locations and uses the Mardi Gras as a grotesque background for the proceedings.

Most of the film's science fiction content comes in the early reels, in which the thieves defeat the hi-tech security system at Carfax Antiquities in a sequence that seems to belong in a *Mission: Impossible* movie. A modern turboprop cargo plane has replaced the 19th century sailing ship as the Count's transportation of choice. In a later scene, Dracula visits a New Orleans nightclub and is fascinated with the big screen displays of sexual carnality projected on the walls, modern visual media that the Count finds impressive. The vampire is represented here as a supernatural creature with powers of levitation, invisibility, shape-shifting and telepathy that serve to confound the modern technological world. Two direct-to-video sequels followed, *Dracula II: Ascension* (2003) and *Dracula III: Legacy* (2005).

Underworld (2003) kicked off a four-movie series about a centuries-old war between vampires and werewolves. British actress Kate Beckinsale stars as Selene, the dark-haired, dark-attired member of a group of vampire assassins called the "Death Dealers." The vamps believe that they have exterminated most of the Lycans (their term for werewolves, derived from the word *lycanthrope*) along with their leader, Lucian, and Selene's job is to hunt down and kill the remaining members of the Lycan race. She is motivated by a personal vendetta against the Lycans because, she believes, they slaughtered her family six hundred years ago.

The Death Dealer has been shadowing a group of Lycans and follows them into a subway station, where a shootout ensues near their underground lair. Werewolves, like vampires, are immortal, although they can be dispatched by silver bullets. The Lycans manage to elude Selene, who then returns to her coven's mansion headquarters to report to the vamps' leader, Kraven (Shane Brolly). Selene produces a specimen of a new type of hi-tech anti-vampire ammunition: bullets containing an irradiated UV fluid. Later, while reviewing surveillance recordings of the incident, she discovers that the Lycans were following a human, Michael Corvin (Scott Speedman), for reasons unknown. Selene urges Kraven to attack the werewolves, but she is overruled due to the imminent arrival of the leader of another vampire clan in a ceremony that will unite the two noble houses.

Back at the Lycans' lair, it turns out that their leader, Lucian (Michael Sheen), is still very much alive and scheming with scientist Singe (Erwin Leder) to create a hybrid being that will unite the bloodlines of the two races of immortals and be more powerful than either. Singe is looking for the purest strain of blood from the ancient Corvinus family that will combine with vampire blood to create the hybrid. The man the Lycans have been following, Michael Corvin, is believed to be a descendant of Alexander Corvinus, a fifth-century Hungarian warlord, who was the first human to acquire the immortality virus that created both vamps and Lycans. Lucian intends to inject himself with blood from both Michael and Amelia, the reigning vampire elder, the mingling of which, he hopes, will transform him into the ultimate immortal.

Vampire assassin Selene (Kate Beckinsale) is armed and dangerous in *Underworld* (2003).

Selene gets to Michael just before Lucian and the werewolves attack, and the two manage to escape. The fact that Lucian is still alive makes Selene fear that Kraven has betrayed the coven, so she returns to the mansion and revives the ancient vampire elder Viktor (Bill Nighy) for guidance. Victor, who has been in suspended animation for centuries, is chagrined at having awakened prematurely and becomes even more upset when Selene captures Singe and has him reveal his plans to unite the races. Singe also tells them that Kraven is a traitor who is plotting with Lucian to obtain the blood of the arriving vamp elder, Amelia, and combine it with Corvinus-strain blood from Michael to make himself into the supreme hybrid being.

In the meantime, the Lycans have abducted Michael and taken him to their hideout. There, Lucian tells him that it was Viktor, not the Lycans, who murdered Selene's family in order to prevent Lucian from marrying her sister and birthing a combination of werewolf and vampire. When the train carrying Amelia (Zita Gorog) and her vamp delegation arrive, they are assassinated by a Lycan hit squad; Amelia is subsequently found with her blood drained. This act precipitates an all-out war between the vamps and the Lycans, as Selene, Viktor and the Death Dealers assault the Lycan stronghold.

During the battle, Kraven shoots Michael and Lucian with bullets impregnated with poisonous silver nitrate. Kraven then reveals the truth about Viktor to Selene and suggests that she bite Michael to save him from the effects of the poison. Selene does so, saving Michael's life and transforming him into the hybrid were-vamp. The powerful Viktor arrives and battles with Michael, but winds up having his head slashed off by Selene. With both Viktor and Lucian dead, Michael and Selene have now become fugitives who will be hunted by both vampires and Lycans.

The best thing about *Underworld* is the film's gothic cyberpunk ambience, a dark netherworld of hi-tech gang warfare waged in a city of perpetual night. European locations and Old World architecture do much to enhance the movie's Goth visuals. The vampires are slick and sophisticated, dress in sexy black-leather outfits like rock stars and inhabit a lush mansion, while the more proletarian Lycans lurk like sub-humans in a filthy underground lair. All the action takes place in a universe where the sun

Selene (Kate Beckinsale) pays obeisance to the resurrected vampire elder, Viktor (Bill Nighy) in *Underworld* (2003).

never shines and everything is lit in subdued blues, grays and greens. Director Len Wiseman keeps the action moving along smoothly enough, but the story by Danny McBride, Kevin Grevioux and director Wiseman is convoluted and hard to follow. Kate Beckinsale brings an icy British reserve to the role of Selene that serves to emotionally disengage the audience, making her a one-dimensional figure. The rest of the cast turn in colorless, forgettable performances, with the exception of Bill Nighy, who brings a Shakespearean malevolence to the role of the vamp elder, Viktor.

There's scant neck biting or bloodsucking in *Underworld*, where it is suggested that the vampires subsist on animal blood or on a synthetic substitute manufactured by a vamp outfit called Ziodex Industries. The film's vampires are not vulnerable to crucifixes or garlic, but only to ultraviolet, and they do not sleep in coffins. As in the *Blade* films, secret societies of vamps (and werewolves) exist alongside humankind, yet humans are blissfully unaware of their existence, a conspiracy-oriented theme that is a staple of many sci-fi flicks. The gunplay and gang warfare between the two groups of immortals recalls the insular conflicts in gangster movies like *The Godfather*, lending a double meaning to the film's title. Both clans have scientists hard at work devising exotic weaponry, such as silver-nitrate projectiles and UV-infused bullets, and the Lycans are hard at work concocting genetic formulas that will enable hybridization. Along with the *Blade* franchise, the *Underworld* films moved the concept of the vampire from the realm of supernatural horror into a sci-fi/action/superhero mode. It also originated the notion of a war between vampires and werewolves, a theme that would appear in *Van Helsing*, released in the following year, and would later become a major plot element of the *Twilight* saga.

The next film in the series, *Underworld: Evolution* (2006), begins with a prologue set in AD 1202 in which the three vampire elders of the Corvinus clan, Viktor (Bill Nighy), Marcus (Tony Curran) and Amelia (Zita Gorog) track Marcus's Lycan brother, William (Brian Steele), to a village that has been ravaged by werewolves. William Corvinus, the first and most powerful of the Lycan clan, is hunted down by the vampires and imprisoned, on Viktor's orders, in an undisclosed location, due to his excessive brutality.

Flash-forward to the conclusion of *Underworld*. Selene (Kate Beckinsale) and Michael Corvin (Scott Speedman) are on the run from coven leader Kraven (Shane Brolly) and take refuge in one of the coven's safe houses, while back at the vamps' manor, the elder Marcus has awakened from his state of hibernation. Now the most powerful vampire of all, Marcus can appear as his human-looking self or he can assume the form of a monstrous bat-winged creature. Marcus kills Kraven for his treachery, biting his neck and drawing out Kraven's memories along with his blood. Using the manor's computer system, the vampire traces Michael and Selene to the safe house.

Kate Beckinsale reprises her role as the Death Dealer Selene in *Underworld: Evolution* (2006).

Cut to the werewolf's lair, the scene of the vamp/Lycan battle from the previous film, where a squad of hi-tech military types are removing the bodies and loading them onto a jet helicopter. The helo transports the corpses to the landing pad of what appears to be an ultra-modern warship, where the crewmen take the dead vamps into the hold. The captain of the ship is an elderly gent named Lorenz Macaro (Derek Jacobi), who lays out the bodies in a morgue area where he examines the remains of the vamp elder, Viktor. He cuts open Viktor's chest and removes an ornately carved metal disc.

Marcus, in his man-bat form, flies after Selene and Michael as they try to escape in a truck. Michael transforms into the werewolf/vampire hybrid being and fights him in the back of the speeding vehicle and manages to drive him off. Selene intuits that Marcus is after a medallion she has in her possession, but she has no idea as to the artifact's significance. They travel to an ancient prison/monastery, where vampire historian Andreas Tanis (Steven Mackintosh) has been exiled for the past three hundred years by the vamp elders to learn more about the pendant.

Tanis recounts the origin of the vampires and Lycans, tracing their lineage back to the first immortal, Alexander Corvinus, who had twin sons, William and Marcus, both of whom inherited his immortality. Marcus was bitten by a bat and became the first vampire, while William was bitten by a wolf and became the first werewolf. When William was unable to return to his human form and started turning people into Lycans, Marcus turned dying warlord Viktor into a vampire who would create a vamp army to combat the werewolves. When William was taken captive by the vampires, Viktor entombed him in a secret prison built by Selene's father. To keep the location of the prison a secret, Viktor then killed the architect and his family, except for Selene, whom he turned into a vampire. The medallion, a gift from Selene's father, is part of the key to William's tomb. Tanis suggests they contact Lorenz Macaro, who may have more information about the artifact. After Selene and Michael leave, Marcus arrives and bites Tanis, learning the location of William's tomb as he drinks the dying vampire's blood.

When Selene and Michael confront Macaro he reveals that he is, in reality, the first immortal, Alexander Corvinus, who is neither vampire nor Lycan. He operates an organization of "cleaners" who have been obscuring the existence of both vamps and werewolves from humans throughout the centuries. Marcus, he explains, wishes to free William so that the two brothers will rule over a new world of vampires and Lycans. During their meeting Marcus arrives and wreaks havoc, mortally wounding Alexander and Michael and learning William's location when he partakes of Selene's blood. Having obtained both parts of the key to William's tomb, Marcus flies off to free his brother, while Alexander uses a bomb to blow himself up along with his ship. Selene commandeers Corvinus's helicopter and a group of his cleaners and sets off after Marcus, taking Michael's body along with her.

Marcus arrives at the site of William's entombment in the ruins of an ancient castle. He locates William's prison deep in the castle's dungeons and uses the two parts of the key to free his brother. Soon afterward, Selene and the cleaners arrive at the site with Michael, who has awakened from his deathlike state and regenerated himself during the flight. The cleaners are soon dispatched by the bestial William as Michael, in his hybrid form, joins the battle alongside Selene. A brutal struggle ensues, in which Michael kills William, and Selene kills Marcus.

Arguably the best of the series, *Underworld: Evolution* undoubtedly has the most memorable villains: the über-vamp Marcus and the super-lycanthrope William. The bat-winged Marcus is one of the most visually striking vampires in recent screen history,

Derek Jacobi as the Captain Nemo-like immortal Alexander Corvinus in *Underworld: Evolution* (2006).

his grotesque, demonic form artfully rendered by CGI, while Tony Curran, who plays Marcus in his human form, projects a dark malevolence into the role. Star Beckinsale struts about in her skin-tight black leather outfit once again but remains aloof and distant as Selene, while co-star Scott Speedman delivers a bland, colorless performance as her cohort, Michael. The distinguished English actor Derek Jacobi, however, shines in his role as Lorenz Macaro/Alexander Corvinus. Director Len Wiseman crafts a slick sci-fi actioner that is well paced and has a fine gothic ambience. The screenplay, by Danny McBride, delves a bit too deeply into the convoluted genealogy of the Corvinus clan and the vampire elders, which makes the narrative a bit hard to follow at times.

In contrast to *Underworld*, much more bloodsucking is depicted onscreen. As in the first film, the vamps exist within a technological milieu. In one scene, Marcus, in his bat form, inputs commands into a computer by using his wing talons to punch the keys on the keyboard. Alexander Corvinus employs a hi-tech warship equipped with sophisticated electronic and computer gear and a sleek, state-of-the-art jet helicopter to perform his mission of keeping the existence of vampires and Lycans a secret. His "cleaners" wear futuristic uniforms that sport infrared sensors and other hi-tech accouterments. Corvinus, who commands a private, technologically advanced warship on a private quest, recalls the charismatic Captain Nemo in Jules Verne's science fiction classic *Twenty Thousand Leagues Under the Sea*.

The third installment in the series, *Underworld: Rise of the Lycans* (2009) is a prequel set in the 13th century that provides historical backstory on the vampire and Lycan clans, but contains no science fiction elements. *Underworld: Awakening* (2012), the fourth *Underworld* film, resumes the story arc of the series. After the death of Alexander Corvinus in *Underworld: Evolution*, his efforts to hide the existence of the two races of immortals has ceased, and humans have discovered the existence of vampires and Lycans. World governments institute "the Purge," an all-out war of extermination designed to eradicate the two races of immortals. Attempting to escape the genocide, Michael and Selene are boarding a ship when the humans come after them. As Selene watches, Michael appears to have been killed; she is wounded and sinks into mental oblivion.

Selene awakens inside a cryogenic hibernation unit where she has been kept in suspended animation as "Subject 1" in the experimental laboratory of a biomedical firm called Antigen Corp. There is also an empty hibernaculum nearby that is designated for a "Subject 2." Selene wastes no time breaking out of the Antigen building, but soon learns that she has been kept on ice for twelve years, during which time the humans believe they have exterminated all Lycans in their interspecies war and are hunting the remaining vamps to extinction as they implement mankind's final solution. In retribution, she brutally attacks a truck driver and drinks his blood.

Selene starts to receive telepathic visions from another person's sensorium and follows the visions to a building where she encounters a young vampire named David (Theo James). She experiences another vision that leads her inside the building, where she and David discover an adolescent girl named Eve (India Eisley) hiding out. They learn that Eve is "Subject 2," a vamp/Lycan hybrid and the offspring of Selene and Michael (presumably the product of some artificial insemination and gestation process). It has been Eve's mind into which Selene has been tapping.

As they try to leave the building they are attacked by a group of degenerate Lycans, and Eve is gravely wounded in the battle. David insists that they take her to his coven, which is located in an underground tunnel near a hydroelectric plant. David's father, the vampire elder Thomas (Charles Dance), severely reprimands his son for bringing the girl and Selene to their secret location, but Eve is given treatment and quickly heals.

Thomas is concerned lest scientists from the Antigen Corp trace Eve to their hidden lair. What he does not know is that the head of Antigen, Dr. Jacob Lane (Stephen Rea) is secretly a Lycan and is working on a vaccine that will remove the werewolves' vulnerability to silver and enhance their physical capabilities. But the scientist needs to obtain samples of Eve's hybrid DNA to perfect the formula. Toward this end, Lane has been injecting his Lycan son, Quint (Kris Holden-Ried), with doses of the vaccine. Thomas's fears are soon realized when the vamp hideout is attacked by a group of Lycans. Selene is attacked by a mega-werewolf and is knocked unconscious. When she comes to, she learns that Thomas has given up Eve to the Lycans to prevent the total annihilation of the coven.

Looking for a way to infiltrate Antigen, Selene hooks up with police detective

Sebastian (Michael Ealy), who had previously conducted an investigation of the pharmaceutical corporation. Sebastian is sympathetic to her plight because his wife had become infected with vampirism and died during the Purge. Together, they formulate a plan to invade the corporate headquarters using silver-nitrate explosives. As Dr. Lane starts to perform the DNA-extraction procedure on Eve, Selene attacks and decimates the Antigen rent-a-cops. While hunting through the building for Eve, she discovers Michael, designated as "Subject 0," frozen in a cryogenic vault. She shoots a bullet into the cryo-chamber, releasing the super-cold gasses, and moves on.

Lane is forced to move the operation to a secure location and attempts to transport Eve, who is still hooked up to surgical equipment, in an ambulance van, but Sebastian interferes, causing the van to crash. Lane changes into werewolf form and fights with Eve, now awakened from anesthesia during the tumult. In the meantime, Selene is confronted by Quint, who has turned into the mega–Lycan. Eve overpowers Lane and kills him, while Selene manages to kill Quint by imbedding a grenade inside his body. After the battle, Selene looks for Michael, but finds that he has defrosted and escaped. In a voiceover postscript, Selene expresses her desire to find Michael and reassert the vampire's hegemony over humans and Lycans.

Clocking in at a brisk 78 minutes without end titles (although the official running time is 96 minutes), *Underworld: Awakening* is short and to the point, with little screen time wasted on character or plot development. Since many of the main characters had been killed off during the previous movies, the only link to the earlier films is Selene. Scott Speedman, who played Michael, is only depicted via digital superimposition on another actor's features, and many fans of the series bemoaned his absence. Beckinsale maintains her icy aloofness to the last as the icy Death Dealer Selene. "You're as cold as one already dead," Eve tells Selene in one scene, and this pretty much sums up her performances in all the *Underground* films. In this entry her behavior is even more brutal, as she avenges herself upon her human persecutors.

The film was very much a team effort, involving two directors (Måns Mårlind and Björn Stein) and no less than four screenwriters (Len Wiseman, John Hlavin, J. Michael Straczynski and Allison Burnett) that make the film seem like it was made by committee. Unlike the Old World locations that characterized the other entries in the series, *Awakening* was shot in Vancouver and has more of an urban American ambience. The new characters, Eve, David, Thomas and Dr. Lane, are much less interesting than Viktor, Marcus, Michael and Alexander Corvinus in the earlier movies.

Underworld: Awakening has the dubious distinction of being the first vampire film released in the 3D and IMAX formats (although 2011's *Priest* was hastily retro-converted to 3D in post-production) as 21st century cinema technology caught up with the ancient vampire myths. Like the first two films in the series, *Awakening* is set against a hi-tech backdrop of medical experimentation, computerized security systems and suspended-animation chambers, and much of the action takes place inside the futuristic Antigen Corporation building. The plot once again revolves around the idea of the hybridization of two inhuman races and genetic engineering designed to produce a master race that will one day control Earth. Like the *Blade* films, the *Underworld* saga did moderately well at the box office and further served to affect the transformation of the vampire from a 19th century, Old World gothic nobleman into a sci-fi super-vamp for 21st century audiences.

The trend toward vampire superhero movies continued with Universal's reworking of the Dracula legend, *Van Helsing* (2004). The brainchild of writer/producer/director Stephen Sommers, the idea was to create a homage to the studio's 1940s-era monster rallies like *House of Frankenstein* (1944) and *House of Dracula* (1945) with updated, CGI visual effects. The film had a budget of $160 million and starred Hugh Jackman, best known for his role as the Wolverine, a member of the popular super-team the X-Men, as the butt-kicking monster slayer "Gabriel" Van Helsing. His co-star was the athletic Kate Beckinsale, who played the vampire Selene in the *Underworld* movies.

The film begins in the year 1887, with a prologue, filmed in nostalgic black and white, in which Dr. Victor Frankenstein (Samuel West) and his assistant, Igor (Kevin J. O'Connor), are performing experiments on his Monster (Shuler Hensley) inside Castle Frankenstein in Transylvania. The scientist's laboratory area is immense and crammed with huge dynamo coils and electrical machinery that is emitting showers of sparks and lightning-like bolts of electricity. His patron, Count Dracula (Richard Roxburgh), arrives at the lab and announces he wants to use the Monster for his own experiments in bringing his undead children to life. When the doctor refuses, Dracula kills him, an act that angers the Monster, who breaks free of his restraints and puts Dracula out of the picture temporarily. The distraught creature picks up his creator's corpse and is chased into an old windmill by a mob of enraged peasants who are marching on the castle. They set the mill on fire and the Monster is thought to have been destroyed in the flames.

The locale shifts to Vatican City in Rome, where Van Helsing (Jackman) has been summoned by Cardinal Jinette (Alun Armstrong), leader of the Knights of the Holy Order, a secret organization run by the Church that is the world's "last defense against evil." Van Helsing, one of the Knights, is assigned by the cardinal to travel to Transylvania, where reports of vampires and werewolves have surfaced. Jinette assigns Vatican weapons expert Friar Carl (David Wenham) to accompany him on his journey. Carl shows Van Helsing around the Holy Order's extensive laboratory, where monks are working amid bubbling chemical flasks and scientific equipment on advanced weapons such as a Gatling gun, a gas-propelled crossbow, nitroglycerin and a light-emitting bomb.

Van Helsing and Carl arrive in Transylvania, where they are confronted by xenophobic villagers and the district's resident monster slayer, Anna Valerious (Beckinsale). But the men from the Vatican soon prove their worth when they help repulse an attack by Dracula's three wives, Aleera (Elena Anaya), Marishka (Josie Maran) and Verona (Silvia Colloca), who swoop down on the town in the form of bat-winged harpies. Anna joins forces with Carl and Van Helsing to combat the vampires, who have turned her brother Velkan into a werewolf. Van Helsing and Anna track Velkan to Castle

Frankenstein, where Dracula is experimenting on him, using the werewolf in place of the Monster to generate electrical power. Infiltrating the castle, the monster hunters find hundreds of slimy vampire egg sacs hanging from the ceiling in the dungeon. Each sac is connected to an electrical cable as power from the machines above transmit electricity through Velkan and into the sacs. The eggs are the undead spawn of Dracula and his wives that he is attempting to imbue with life in replication of Dr. Frankenstein's experiments. Unfortunately for the Count, his experiment is a failure and the fledgling vamps expire soon after hatching.

Escaping from the castle, they accidentally come across a hidden cave in which they encounter the Monster, who has survived the fire. "I am the key to my father's machine," the creature explains, "the key to life." Van Helsing decides to take the Monster to Rome, where he will be safe from Dracula's clutches. While they are transporting him by carriage, however, they are attacked by the vampire brides and Velkan in his werewolf form. Velkan is killed, but not before biting Van Helsing, while Aleera carries off Anna to the Count's summer palace in Budapest. Carl, Van Helsing and the Monster travel to the city, where Van Helsing rescues Anna from the palace, using one of Carl's photon bombs to incapacitate the vampires. Unfortunately, the Monster is captured and taken to the Count's hidden fortress at Castle Dracula.

Van Helsing discovers a magical portal into the castle and travels there along with Anna and Carl. Upon the rising of the moon that night, Van Helsing will transform into a werewolf; he has learned that Dracula has developed an antidote for lycanthropy because he can only be killed by a werewolf. With the Monster hooked up to the arcing electrical devices, Dracula is poised to instill life into another brood of vampire egg sacs. Switches are thrown, the giant dynamos emit bolts of artificial lightning and the current flows into the eggs. But, as the little vamps start hatching, Van Helsing confronts the Count and transforms into a werewolf in the light of the moon. Dracula assumes the form of a bat-man and battles the lycanthrope, while Anna and Carl go after the antidote. As Van Helsing, in his wolfen form, rips out Dracula's throat, Anna arrives to administer the antidote, but is killed by the werewolf before it can take effect. Deprived of their father's life force, the vampire hatchlings fade out of existence. In the final reel Anna is buried in a solemn ceremony, the Monster is given his freedom and Van Helsing and Carl ride off in the direction of a sequel.

In an odd reversal of roles, Dracula becomes a learned scientist while Van Helsing is made over into a younger, hipper character wielding James Bond–type gadgets. As film critic Leonard Maltin so succinctly put it, "Edward Van Sloan, R.I.P."[1] The film's chronology is skewed, as the events depicted supposedly take place in 1887, leaving only ten years until the narrative of Stoker's *Dracula* unfolds for Van Helsing to morph from an athletic young man into an aged scholar.

Apart from the general silliness of the concept, *Van Helsing* is overlong and poorly executed by director Stephen Sommers, who also wrote the screenplay. The emphasis on special effects and comic book adventure prevents the film-makers from building a horror movie mood of fear and dread. Hugh Jackman's Van Helsing has no depth

Steampunk vampire hunter Gabriel Van Helsing (Hugh Jackman) displays his buzz-saw nunchuks in *Van Helsing* (2004).

whatever, and has little to do except flex his muscles and look handsome, while co-star Kate Beckinsale's Anna resembles a sword-wielding swashbuckler from a pirate movie. Even more disappointing is Richard Roxburgh's bland portrayal of Count Dracula, who projects negligible screen menace in the role of the screen's most famous vampire. Ironically, Roxburgh and Beckinsale both read their lines in an ersatz Eastern European dialect, while Jackman's Van Helsing has no trace of a Dutch inflection in his speech. This overblown, cartoonish extravaganza grinds on for over two hours of grunting, groaning and screaming histrionics emitted by monstrous creatures with no sense of empathy. The elaborate and expensive special effects add little to the film's overall effectiveness.

While it's certainly a flawed film, *Van Helsing* continues the theme of supernatural vampires versus Victorian technology that was first put forth in Stoker's *Dracula*. Here, however, Dracula himself has become a scientist who supplants Dr. Frankenstein, a role the Count had not played since *Abbott and Costello Meet Frankenstein* (1948). *Van Helsing* definitely qualifies as an example of Steampunk; that is, science fiction set during the 19th century, and is one of a number of Steampunk-inspired sci-fi efforts that appeared during the passage to the new millennium such as *The Wild, Wild West* (1999) and *The League of Extraordinary Gentlemen* (2003). The digitally created laboratory sets are much more grandiose than any of the "mad labs" built for the classic Universal monster epics by Hollywood technician Kenneth Strickfadden. Giant dynamos glow with high-voltage electrical energy as Tesla-coil bolts of electricity arc through the air. Van Helsing's tour of the Vatican weapons shop early in the film also showcases exotic 19th century Steampunk gadgetry, such as a steam-powered crossbow and a pistol that shoots soporific gas.

Despite negative reviews in the American entertainment press, *Van Helsing* did healthy business at the box office, mostly in the overseas markets, garnering over $300 million in receipts worldwide. Numbers like these would generally spawn a sequel, as the ending of the film suggests, but all that emerged was a half-hour animated prequel entitled *Van Helsing: The London Assignment*, released in 2004 and featuring the voice of Hugh Jackman.

As the early years of the 21st century progressed, vampires began to contend not only with past or present levels of technology, but with the hi-tech worlds of the future. *Dracula 3000* (2004) was an attempt to bring Stoker's tale into the third millennium and into the realm of outer space. In the year 3000, the salvage vessel *Mother III* comes upon a derelict transport ship in an area of deep space called the "Carpathian Galaxy." The ship, the *Demeter* is on a heading toward Earth without any personnel aboard, and the crew of *Mother III* clambers aboard to claim salvage rights to the derelict. The crew consists of Captain Abraham Van Helsing (Casper Van Dien), science officer Arthur Holmwood (Grant Swanby), navigator Mina Murray (Alexandra Kamp), Vice Captain Aurora Ash (Erika Eleniak) and cargo specialists Humvee (Tommy "Tiny" Lister) and 187 (Coolio).

On board the *Demeter* the crew discovers the vessel's chief officer, Captain Varna (Udo Kier), tied to his chair in the ship's control room. The captain's video log reveals that his crew is dying off, one by one, from a mysterious degenerative disease. Then, for no apparent reason, *Mother III* undocks from the *Demeter*, leaving the crew stranded on the derelict without any means of communication. To make matters worse, fifty mysterious coffin-like containers are discovered in the ship's cargo bay. One of the boxes, naturally, contains the remains of the vampire, Count Orlock (Langley Kirkwood), who soon emerges from his resting place and commences to turn the crew members into vamps. Only Aurora seems to be immune from the plague, which arouses the captain's suspicions, so he orders her tied up while the rest of the crew fights the vampires. At this point she confesses that she is really a Proteus 4 android cop sent to spy on their salvage operation. Orlock is not interested in her because she's not a human being.

Going through the ship's historical databases, the captain learns that he is a direct descendant of Abraham Van Helsing, the famed vampire slayer of centuries past. Then, Orlock and his vampire minions attempt to wrest control of the *Demeter* from the remaining human crew members in a final struggle. In the climactic battle, Captain Van Helsing is killed by Orlock, who, in turn, gets his arm torn off. Soon, only Aurora and Humvee are left to stave off the vamps, who are staked with pool cues. After Orlock and the vampires have been destroyed, the *Demeter* is blown up by a bomb set by Captain Varna.

This low-budget, direct-to-video effort tries to boldly go where no Dracula flick has gone before, but instead dives down a cinematic black hole. Most of the blame can be assigned to the execrable screenplay, penned by director Darrell Roodt and co-scripter Ivan Milborrow, which attempts to meld elements of *Alien* and *Dracula* together and winds up with an inane mishmash of horror clichés. Plot elements borrowed from *Alien* include the discovery of a derelict ship with a deadly cargo, the gory elimination of each of the crew members, one of the crew being an android, and the destruction of the ship at the film's conclusion. Direction is tepid, dialogue is crude and the actors' performances are uniformly awful. Langley Kirkwood's Count Orlock (the name of the Dracula character in Murnau's *Nosferatu*), attired in operatic cape, a high collar and white lace cuffs, delivers one of the most ludicrous portrayals of the Count in screen history, and once again the Van Helsing character has been turned into an action hero. What might have been a promising idea gets lost in the film's poor execution.

A more satisfying take on futuristic vampirism was provided by *Ultraviolet* (2006), a film set in the future world of A.D. 2078, after a viral pandemic has swept through the general population causing symptoms resembling vampirism, including elongated canine fangs, a sensitivity to sunlight and the necessity of receiving frequent blood transfusions. Life expectancy after infection is twelve years, and there is no cure. Victims of the Hemoglophagic (blood eating) Virus, abbreviated as HGV, are being rounded up and exterminated by a militant organization called the Archministry, which is headed up by the autocratic Vice-Cardinal Ferdinand Daxus (Nick Chinlund).

The heroine of the piece is Violet Song Jat Shariff (Milla Jovovich), a survivor of one of the death camps, who was forced to undergo a series of torturous experiments by the Archministry before escaping to join a Hemophage resistance group. Violet manages to steal a weapon designed to destroy all remaining HGV-infected vamps from an Archministry laboratory facility, but when she opens the case she finds it contains, not a weapon, but a young boy ("flat space" dimensional compression technology enables the boy to be concealed inside a small, flat carrying case). Having lost her infant child during the experiments, Violet bonds with the youth, whose name, she learns, is Six (Cameron Bright). She will not allow Six to be killed or captured, either by Daxus or by a rival gang of Asian vamps, the Blood Chinois, who are allied with the Archministry. As Violet and Six undergo many violent ordeals together, she begins to have maternal, protective feelings for the boy.

Violet is contacted by Daxus, who tells her that Six is his son and that he is, in essence, a weapon, as his body is swarming with cultured antigens that will destroy all of the vamps if they are let out into the environment. Disbelieving, she takes the boy to the secret laboratory of her friend, the Hemophage scientist Garth (William Fichtner), who examines Six and finds that the opposite is true: the antigens in his body are designed to be fatal to humans, not vampires. He also tells her that the boy is radioactive, that he can be easily traced by the Archministry, and has only a matter of hours left to live. Another conversation with Daxus reveals that Six is not his son but his clone, and that since the HGV epidemic is over, the Archministry is looking for a new plague that will help maintain its power over the populace because humans will need a shot of the antidote every day in order to survive.

Knowing that the boy hasn't long to live, Violet takes the child to a playground where he can live out the last moments of his life in happiness. As he is dying, one of her teardrops falls on Six's face and is absorbed into his eye. Daxus arrives and takes the body away, but Violet, in a sudden flash of insight, realizes that the boy may still be alive. Arming herself with a variety of spatially compressed weapons, she invades the Archministry and defeats a small army of guards to arrive in the laboratory as Daxus is about to dissect Six. After a flaming swordfight in the dark she kills Daxus and escapes with the child's body. Six later revives due to antigens he received from Violet's tear, and she is optimistic about reverse-engineering the antigens in his blood to provide a cure for the HGV virus

Milla Jovovich as the vampire warrior Violet Song Jat Shariff in *Ultraviolet* (2006).

Obviously inspired by the *Blade* and *Underworld* vampire movies (as well as *The Matrix* and its sequels), *Ultraviolet* continues in the vein of futuristic action hero vamps. Written and directed by Kurt Wimmer, the film bears a number of similarities to his previous science fiction effort, *Equilibrium* (2002), in which a lone hero defies an authoritarian power structure in a future dystopia. Most of the film's settings are digitally generated, giving the sci-fi landscapes the surreal, two-dimensional quality of a video game, but somehow this works to the film's advantage. Wimmer employs bright primary colors and deeply saturated hues to create a dazzling, unique futureworld that is all the more believable due to its unusual visual textures.

While there's plenty of shoot-'em-up action, the plight of the characters also manages to engage the audience's sympathies. Milla Jovovich, who has made a career out of playing sci-fi femmes in films like *The Fifth Element* (1997) and *Resident Evil* (2002), not only displays the athletic qualities of an action heroine but also delivers a surprisingly effective dramatic portrayal of a woman deprived of motherhood by a totalitarian

Violet (Milla Jovovich) plays mother to the virus-infected Six (Cameron Bright) in *Ultraviolet* (2006).

state. Cameron Bright also turns in a noteworthy performance, as the enigmatic, laboratory-bred clone child Six.

The vampire element in the plot is somewhat downplayed, the more clinical term "hemophage" being substituted. Once again a highly contagious viral organism is responsible for the spread of vampirism. According to the film, the Hemoglophagic Virus (HGV) was originally found in Eastern Europe, where it was responsible for historical accounts of vampires, but was isolated and genetically engineered by a U.S. government agency trying to create soldiers with superhuman abilities. Unfortunately, the genetically modified virus became much more contagious and spread quickly among the general population. In order to prevent a panic over the epidemic, the government discourages the use of the word "vampire" in favor of the less disturbing term "hemophage." Like traditional vamps, however, the Hemophages have sharp canine teeth, they exist by ingesting blood, and they possess augmented physical strength, faster reflexes and enhanced senses. The plot element involving a lethal virus created in a U.S. government laboratory reflects conspiracy theories that the HIV virus that causes AIDS was the result of clandestine genetic research allegedly conducted by the CIA. The cure for vampirism being found in the blood of a Christ-like individual harks back to *The Omega Man* (1971).

Mutant viruses were responsible for an epidemic of vampirism once more in the

Steven Seagal vehicle *Against the Dark* (2009). The film takes place in a near-future world ravaged by a vampire apocalypse, where scattered groups of humans fight for survival against the animalistic bloodsuckers. Aging action star Seagal plays Tao, the leader of a group of ex-military warriors who have become vampire hunters. Most of the action involves a group of forgettable characters who, needing medication, have taken refuge in an abandoned hospital. The humans are then stalked through the building's hallways by the fiends. To make matters worse, local military commander Lt. Waters (Keith David) is planning to sterilize the entire area with an airstrike, but is temporarily dissuaded by State Department official Cross (Linden Ashby). Fortunately, the sword-wielding Tao arrives at the hospital with his badass vamp killers to rescue the refugees before the place goes up in smoke. The humans wander through the dark, decaying halls of the hospital, looking for a way out of the building, while getting picked off, one by one, by the vampires. In the end, only Tao and two others survive the bloodletting and escape to safety moments before the jet planes arrive to blow the place to smithereens.

An embarrassingly bad direct-to-video stinker, *Against the Dark* was filmed almost entirely in a dingy, decrepit hospital location with minimal lighting and low-end production values. There are seemingly endless scenes of the actors walking down dimly lit corridors, with ominous music on the soundtrack. Martial arts mystic Steven Seagal, in what is arguably the worst film of his checkered career, stalks around wearing a long, black leather coat and wielding a samurai sword like a poor man's version of *Blade*, his clumsy moves clearly revealing his advancing age. Direction by Richard Crudo is pedestrian at best, while the screenplay by Mathew Klickstein has Seagal mouthing such memorable lines as, "We're here to decide who lives and dies," "Kill anything that looks infected," and "Guess I'm still alive." There's not much in the way of science fiction content beyond the now clichéd viral disease leading to a vampire apocalypse.

Priest (2011) takes place in an alternate reality, where a war between humans and vampires has been going on for centuries. Humans have withdrawn to the protection of walled cities under the protection of the Catholic Church, which has developed the ultimate anti-vamp weapon—the Priests. These specially trained vampire slayers are warriors who possess the spiritual powers and martial arts prowess that enable them to hunt down and destroy the vamps. The Priests are all branded with the symbol of the cross on their foreheads as an indication of their piety. Their opponents, the vampires, are bald-headed humanoids who are without eyes, but who sport a mouthful of wicked-looking fangs. The vampires have a society resembling social insects, like ants or bees, and live underground in vast hives, honeycombed with passageways and chambers.

A flashback prologue introduces the protagonist, who is simply named Priest (Paul Bettany), during a mission with several members of his order to the Sola Mira hive in search of the "queen." A member is seized by a group of vamps and spirited deep into the hive as the others watch helplessly. The memory haunts Priest years after the war is concluded and the vampires defeated, after which the Church ordains that the order of priestly vampire slayers be disbanded. Priest now inhabits Cathedral City, a gloomy dystopian metropolis that exists in a perpetual night, where towering electric signs display the Church's propaganda slogans: FAITH, WORK, SECURITY; ABSOLUTION IS THE ONLY WAY; TO GO AGAINST THE CHURCH IS TO GO AGAINST GOD.

One day, Priest is paid a visit by Hicks (Cam Gigandet), the sheriff of a town named Augustine, in the wasteland outside the city. Hicks informs him that his brother and sister-in-law have been mortally wounded by vampires, and that his niece, Lucy (Lily Collins), has been abducted by the creatures. He has come to ask for Priest's aid in tracking down the vamps and rescuing Lucy. Priest pleads with his superior, Monsignor Orelas (Christopher Plummer), to be reinstated, but is refused and ordered not to leave the city. When he defies the order, Orelas sends four former priests after him to bring him back, dead or alive.

Hicks and Priest head out to the Nightshade Reservation, a prison facility that houses Familiars, humans who have been infected with a virus that makes them the vampires' slaves. They learn from one of the Familiars that the vamps have returned to the Sola Mira hive, the site of Priest's great battle years earlier. Priest and Hicks explore the hive, a grim underground lair littered with human bones and skulls. There they encounter Priestess (Maggie Q), one of the four members of the order dispatched by Orelas. The lady priest decides to defy the Church and join forces with them due to a personal bond with Priest, forged in the past. The three of them are attacked by a hive guardian, a troll-like vampire soldier, and manage to kill it. They then find a chamber that was recently occupied by a vamp army.

At sunset, an ominous armored train pulls into the station, in the wasteland town of Jericho. A horde of vampires pours out of the train to attack the populace, led by an enigmatic man wearing a black hat. As the three priests arrive in Jericho to quell the vampire uprising, they are defied by Black Hat (Karl Urban), who appears to have extraordinary powers. Priest, Priestess and Hicks enter Jericho the next day to find the town deserted and the three priests crucified. It becomes apparent that the vampire army from Sola Mira has been loaded onto the train and that the vamps are using it to move around during the daytime. Last stop on the line is Cathedral City, where the vamp army is ultimately headed. Using futuristic high-speed motorcycles left behind by the dead priests, the trio head off through the wasteland to intercept the train.

While Priestess speeds off ahead of the train to place demolition charges on the tracks, Priest and Hicks manage to board the train and go looking for Lucy. Hicks stumbles onto a railway car filled with slimy vamp egg sacs hanging from the ceiling. Meanwhile, Priest encounters Black Hat on top of the train and the two engage in a *Matrix*-like slow-motion display of martial arts. Black Hat reveals that he was the priest who was taken by the vamps in Sola Mira five years earlier, and was transformed into a human/vampire hybrid by the Queen. The fight is going badly for Priest, but Priestess saves the day by mounting an explosive device on her motorcycle and ramming it into the train. The blast destroys Black Hat and the vampire army, but Priest, Hicks and

Priest (Paul Bettany) and Priestess (Maggie Q) pursue vampires on their hi-tech motorcycles in this poster for *Priest* (2011).

Priestess all survive. In the aftermath, Priest returns to the city and delivers physical evidence—in the form of a severed vamp head—that the vampires have returned. He tosses the head at Monsignor Orelas's feet before riding off into the wasteland on his futuristic motorbike.

Based on a graphic novel by Korean artist Min-Woo Hyung, *Priest* continued the comic book-ization of vampire mythology. The screenplay, by Cory Goodman, altered several elements of the graphic novel and also incorporated ideas from recent sci-fi vamp flicks. The notion of "Familiars"—humans who cozy up to vampires—seems to have been appropriated from the *Blade* films, while bald-headed vamps living underground in hives were featured in *I Am Legend*. Elements from *Van Helsing* also crop up, including the cadre of vampire hunters recruited by the Catholic Church, and the vamps' hanging egg sacs. One flaw in the script is that the characters have vague names like Priest, Priestess and Black Hat, which only serve to distance them from the audience's emotional involvement. Paul Bettany comes off as suitably tortured in the title role and speaks his lines with a Clint Eastwood hard-guy inflection, while Maggie Q projects an ethereal screen presence as his female sidekick.

The film had a troubled production history, languishing in development hell for several years before being greenlighted. In 2010, the producers decided to convert the film to 3D, making it the first vampire film released in that format. Unfortunately, the conversion did little to enliven the visuals. Director Scott Stewart moves the action along nicely throughout the movie's eighty minutes of running time (*sans* end titles), but the film attempts to go off in too many directions and appropriates elements from too many genres. It starts out in a *Blade Runner*–like urban dystopian mode, then tries to incorporate motifs from the western genre along with cyberpunk, post-apocalyptic and horror themes. Director Stewart saw *Priest* as an homage to John Ford's classic western *The Searchers*, in which two men seek to rescue a woman kidnapped by Comanche Indians. Unfortunately, this melding of sci-fi, western and horror was not well received, and *Priest* performed poorly at the box office.

Despite these flaws and derivative elements, *Priest* presents some original takes on the science fiction vampire concept. The creatures represent an entirely distinct species who are able to reproduce normally without having to turn humans into vamps. Like social insects, they live in a hive and are divided into different castes, such as drones, warriors and queens. Although they do not possess speech or material culture, they seem to be linked into a telepathic hive mind. *Priest* is the first film to feature completely digital vampires, a technique that emphasizes their inhuman speed and agility and makes them seem more alien.

Vampires and high technology have been interacting since Stoker's bloodthirsty Count squared off against Professor Van Helsing's 19th century scientific acumen. In the eighty years between *Dracula* (1931) and *Priest* (2011), vamps and hi-tech have had a lively interplay in the cinema, with some vampires using their occult powers against science and others readily assimilating technology and using it to further their interests. The vampire hunters have changed as well, adopting hi-tech gadgets in their quest.

Everything from steam-powered crossbows to UV grenades have become part of the modern Van Helsing's arsenal.

The image of the vampire has also evolved over the decades, from the stage figure of a cultured nobleman attired in evening clothes and an operatic cape to computer-generated humanoid creatures without eyes and a horrid mouthful of fangs. High technology has propelled the vampire into new and exotic worlds. As cinema technology evolves, the filmic vampire will no doubt mutate into novel and fantastic forms as well.

CHAPTER SEVEN

Bloodsuckers from Outer Space

Aliens and vampires have a lot in common. They both have penetrating eyes that have the power to hypnotize. Both are at odds with humankind and victimize humans. They can both look like normal people and infiltrate society, going among us clandestinely as they tend to their nefarious business, even forming secret societies of which we are unaware. Both can appear and disappear at will and have other superhuman powers. And sometimes aliens, like vampires, drink blood.

As recounted in Chapter Two, the notion of vampires from outer space dates back to the granddaddy of all alien invasion stories, H.G. Wells's 1898 novel *The War of the Worlds,* which featured alien bloodsuckers from Mars. Other extraterrestrial vamps followed, notably Gustave Le Rouge's *The Prisoner of Planet Mars* (1908) and its sequel *The War of the Vampires* (1909), C.L. Moore's story "Shambleau" (1933), A.E. Van Vogt's "Asylum" (1942) and Colin Wilson's *The Space Vampires* (1976).

But aliens did not invade movie screens until the 1950s, when E.T.s began to descend from the skies in vast numbers. The reason for this sudden influx of extraterrestrials was the curious phenomenon of flying saucers. Beginning in the summer of 1947, unidentified flying objects, dubbed UFOs, began to be seen in the skies and caused much consternation in officialdom. The UFOs moved at such tremendous speeds and seemed capable of performing maneuvers that were impossible for earthly aircraft to duplicate, leading to speculation that they were spaceships from other worlds. While the Air Force grappled with the problem of defending the skies against alien invaders, the flying saucers would prove to be a box-office bonanza for the Hollywood film industry, which rushed in to exploit the sensational implications of the UFO phenomenon. The decade of the 1950s was the "happy time" for monsters and saviors from outer space, and the very first alien to arrive on planet Earth in a flying saucer was a vampire.

The Thing from Another World (1951) takes place at Polar Expedition Six, a scientific facility located near the North Pole and manned by a team of scientists, led by Nobel Prize–winner Dr. Arthur Carrington (Robert Cornthwaite). A report of a mysterious plane crash near the pole sends USAF captain Pat Hendry (Kenneth Tobey) and a group of airmen up to Polar Six to sort things out. Along for the ride is intrepid newshound Ned "Scotty" Scott (Douglas Spencer), who smells an important story and insists on joining the investigation.

Capt. Hendry flies Dr. Carrington and a scientific-military team to the crash site, where they find a flying saucer frozen under the ice. An attempt to melt the craft out of the ice with heat-generating thermite bombs causes the saucer to explode, but an occupant of the UFO is found nearby and chipped out of the ice. The block of ice containing the alien is transported back to Polar Six for study, and one of the airmen inadvertently melts the ice, releasing the monstrous creature from deep freeze. Fleeing into the Arctic wilderness, the Thing from another world encounters a group of sled dogs, and a battle ensues.

By the time the men reach the area, the Thing has fled into the darkness and two of the dogs are found dead, but the alien's severed hand and arm, chewed off by the dogs, is discovered under one of the animals. Carrington and the scientists examine the arm and find it is composed of plant tissue, leading Scotty to exclaim, "An intellectual carrot. The mind boggles." As they watch, the hand begins to move, leading to speculation that the body part was nourished by blood absorbed from the dead dog. "You mean it lives on blood," Scotty wryly observes. Carrington then extracts a number of vegetable seed pods from inside the hand and puts them aside for further study.

Even though the alien has shown itself to be a dangerous killer, Carrington pleads with Hendry not to destroy the creature before he can try to communicate with it. Hendry, however, is noncommittal, citing the safety of the base personnel as his primary responsibility. When Carrington discovers evidence that the Thing is visiting the base's greenhouse area, he conceals the information from Hendry, an act that leads to the deaths of two scientists when the creature returns to the area. A survivor of the attack relates how the men were suspended from an overhead beam with their throats cut, allowing the vampire to feed on their blood. Hendry and his posse corner the creature in the greenhouse, catching a glimpse of the monstrous being before they bar the door and the alien escapes out into the snow through a back entrance. The Thing (James Arness) is bald-headed, seven feet tall and bears more than a passing resemblance to Frankenstein's monster. It cannot speak to the humans; instead, it growls like an animal. The creature is clad in a garment that resembles a military uniform.

In the aftermath of their first close encounter, Carrington calls the scientists together to show them the latest development. Using seed pods obtained from the severed hand, he has grown a garden of monstrous alien plants, which he displays to his fellow savants. Realizing that blood was a primal factor in the cultivation of the seeds, he planted them and saturated the dirt with plasma stolen from the base's blood bank. The vampire plants resemble pulsating seed pods and are still being nourished by bottles of plasma suspended overhead. One of the scientists listens in on the pods with a stethoscope and describes the sound as being like "the wail of a newborn child that's hungry." Speculation arises that the Thing might be the advance guard of an invasion, but Carrington discounts the idea.

The creature lays siege to the base and the humans respond by trying to burn it to death, but neither flames nor bullets can kill it. Given its vegetative nature, the scientists are hard pressed to come up with a way to destroy the alien. It has even regenerated the severed arm torn off by the dogs. Their predicament becomes even more

Future *Gunsmoke* star James Arness poses with an unidentified stunt double (used in the scene in which the creature melts into nothingness) in this publicity photograph for *The Thing From Another World* (1951).

dire, however, when the creature shuts down the base's heating system, forcing the humans to destroy the creature in order to survive. Other methods having failed, the base personnel hit on the idea of trying to electrocute it and set to work building a high-voltage electrified walkway.

The Thing makes its move, breaking into the base and stalking down the main passageway toward the humans in a menacing manner. Suddenly, Carrington runs up to the creature and delivers an impassioned plea for cross-species communication, but the alien contemptuously swats him down like a bug and resumes its advance. When it gets onto the electrified walkway, Hendry throws the switch and the creature is zapped by lightning-like bolts of high-voltage electricity. The Thing is burned to ashes in the electrical barrage and Scotty sends his story to the world press, but first delivers a warning. "Tell the world," he rants. "Tell this to everybody wherever they are. Watch the skies, everywhere. Keep looking! Keep watching the skies!"

Adapted from the classic John W. Campbell science fiction novella *Who Goes There?* by screenwriter Charles Lederer, *The Thing* takes a number of liberties with the original story, including making the alien into a vampire. While directorial credit is given to first-timer Christian Nyby, most film historians insist it was actually directed by Hollywood veteran Howard Hawks, who was the film's producer. The director of such manly fare as *The Big Sleep* (1946) and *Red River* (1948), Hawks imbues the tale with large quantities of postwar self confidence as the seasoned military men successfully cope with the unearthly situation. The polar base, with its darkened, maze-like corridors, provides a creepy, neo-gothic environment for the alien vamp to romp through, and the howling winds and snowbound wasteland of the film's Arctic location contribute to the mood of fear and claustrophobia. Dimitri Tiomkin's aggressive, take-no-prisoners score featured the theremin, the world's first electronic musical instrument, whose eerie tones would become a fixture of 1950s science fiction films.

Kenneth Tobey is perfectly cast as Captain Hendry, the military officer whose fortitude defeats the first alien invasion, while Robert Cornthwaite is properly frosty as Dr. Carrington, the icy Nobel laureate with a death wish. Margaret Sheridan has a juicy role as Carrington's assistant, Nikki Nicholson, a typically Hawksian tomboyish heroine and the first in a long line of female scientists that would appear in '50s-era sci-fi flicks. Douglas Spencer provides comic relief as the wisecracking newsman Scotty, while the hulking James Arness, future star of the TV series *Gunsmoke*, delivers the chills as the titular Thing.

Although the word "vampire" is never used in the film, the alien clearly uses blood, not only for sustenance, but as part of its reproductive process. A scene showing the Thing biting the neck of one of the slaughtered scientists was originally planned, but later dropped. One of the film's tag lines was, "Natural or Supernatural?" indicating an ambiguity regarding the creature's origin. Like Count Dracula, the Thing rises from a cold grave, cannot be killed by bullets or other conventional means, needs humans to reproduce and possesses superhuman strength and great cunning. The alien is actually an amalgam of the two Universal icons: Dracula and Frankenstein's Monster. Vampires from the vegetable kingdom date back to H.G. Wells's 1894 story "The Flowering of the Strange Orchid," but outside of *The Thing*, this idea never caught on as a theme in science fiction films. The window box full of pulsating vampire plants feeding from bottles of blood plasma is an especially horrific touch.

The Thing from Another World would prove to be a seminal work in the history of science fiction films, its influence pervading many of the essays in sci-fi horror that followed. In a direct line of descent were *It! The Terror from Beyond Space* (1958) and John Carpenter's 1982 remake. The Carpenter version is a more faithful adaptation of the John W. Campbell novella that dispenses with vampirism and makes the alien into a shapeshifter instead. But the film's most profound influence was on Ridley Scott's sci-fi/horror mega-hit *Alien* (1979), which cribbed many plot elements: the confining locale; the finding of a deadly extraterrestrial in a downed spaceship; a machine with a blinking light that heralds the presence of the alien; and a scientist who wants to keep the creature alive at the expense of the humans who want to kill it.

Earth was invaded by the forces of extraterrestrial vampirism once more in writer-producer-director Edward D. Wood, Jr.'s, loopy *Plan 9 from Outer Space* (1959). Wood's name has become synonymous with bad film-making, and *Plan 9* has long been ridiculed by critics as being the Worst Film Ever Made. Although Wood's eccentric space vampire epic has many serious cinematic flaws, it still manages to entertain in spite of itself.

Bela Lugosi, in his final film role, stars as the Old Man, whose wife of many years has just passed away; he is shown grieving for her at her funeral in the San Fernando Cemetery. Meanwhile, in the skies above Los Angeles, Captain Jeff Trent (Gregory Walcott) is piloting American Airlines flight 812 into Burbank Airport when the plane has a close encounter with a flying saucer. The UFO comes in for a landing in the graveyard and soon afterward the Old Man's wife (Vampira) is resurrected by some alien force and is seen roaming around the cemetery.

The Old Man, deep in mourning, absent-mindedly steps in front of a car and is killed. "First his wife, then he," laments one of the mourners at his funeral. During the burial, the bodies of two gravediggers are discovered, and the L.A.P.D. is called in to investigate the double homicide. Detective Inspector Daniel Clay (Tor Johnson) leads the investigative team. While he is trolling through the graveyard looking for clues he is attacked and killed by the Old Man, who is now a reanimated ghoul, and his undead wife.

The action shifts to Space Station 7, the alien mothership in near–Earth orbit, where Space Commander Eros (Dudley Manlove) and his cohort Tana (Joanna Lee) are meeting with their bored-looking superior, His Excellency (John "Bunny" Breckenridge) to discuss the latest strategy for subjugating the earthlings. Eros explains that he has attempted to contact Earth's leaders, but "they refuse our existence." His Excellency therefore gives the go-ahead to implement "Plan 9," which involves the resurrection of dead bodies to create armies of corpses that will assail the world's cities and bring them to ruin. The alien duo then flies back to the cemetery and proceeds to res-

Tor Johnson, as Inspector Clay, and Vampira (Maila Nurmi), as Vampire Girl, aboard the alien spaceship in cult director Ed Wood's infamous invasion opus *Plan 9 from Outer Space* (1959).

urrect Inspector Clay with their "electrode guns." Clay, the Old Man and his wife become the vanguard of the extraterrestrial's army of the living dead.

The Hollywood UFO flap elicits a reaction from the saucer busters at the Pentagon, causing the Air Force brass to dispatch field investigator Colonel Tom Edwards (Tom Keene) to Tinseltown to look into the strange goings-on at the San Fernando Cemetery. Col. Edwards confers with Captain Trent and his wife, Paula (Mona McKinnon), who just happen to live next door to the graveyard, about the UFO sightings. As Edwards is questioning the couple, Eros decides to send the Old Man to the Trent residence and then disintegrate him as a demonstration designed to intimidate the humans. The vampire creature invades their home and is zapped by a ray from the saucer that turns him into a caped skeleton before their wondering eyes.

Edwards, Trent and the police go looking for the landed saucer in the cemetery and are guided to it by the craft's pulsating light. The wily Eros lets the earthmen enter the ship thinking to trap them inside, while the zombified Clay is sent to abduct Mrs. Trent and bring her to the saucer. Eros confronts the humans, revealing his fellow aliens' fears that mankind will discover an explosive substance called "solaranite" that makes the H-bomb look like a firecracker. This must not be allowed to happen, because "all you of Earth are idiots," whose "juvenile minds" will cause the annihilation of the entire universe due to our self-destructive foolishness. Trent responds by decking Eros, and setting the ship's equipment afire, while the others manage to open the door to the craft. The saucer struggles to take off with Tana at the controls, but blows up in a fireball, causing Clay and the vampire woman to instantly disintegrate.

Much ink has been spilled by writers analyzing the hilarious shortcomings of this offbeat exercise in low-rent cinema. The litany includes daffy dialogue, laughable special effects, grade-Z production values, confusing lapses in continuity and a kooky cast of characters. All of this is indeed true, but anyone who thinks that *Plan 9* is the worst film of all time clearly hasn't screened *They Saved Hitler's Brain*, *Zontar: The Thing from Venus* or dozens of other truly awful sci-fi/horror cheapies that aren't half as entertaining. While his direction is pedestrian, Wood's screenplay, larded with unintentionally hilarious one-liners, keeps the laughs coming.

These immortal lines of dialogue are spoken by such neophyte actors as the film's narrator, celebrity psychic Criswell, openly gay actor "Bunny" Breckenridge and pro-wrestler Tor Johnson. Although she does not have a speaking part, Los Angeles TV horror hostess Vampira (whose real name is Maila Nurmi), delivers a memorable performance as the movie's creepy female ghoul. Former radio announcer Dudley Manlove has some of the best lines in the film, including a rambling monologue about the perils of the dread "solaranite." The film was built around some footage Wood had shot shortly before Bela Lugosi's death in 1956 that were integrated into the finished product, including shots of Lugosi attired in full Dracula regalia stalking through the graveyard. After his death, a double (reportedly Wood's chiropractor Tom Mason), who was obviously much younger and taller than Bela, replaced him in the role.

The film's storyline is augmented with dire pronouncements about the existence of UFOs and military/political cover-ups of the alien presence that are as paranoid as anything in *The X-Files*. Alien invaders from "a planet in our galaxy," are paradoxically portrayed as enlightened beings who have harnessed high technology and butchers who wish to destroy humankind with an army of corpses simply because they think people are stupid warmongers. It's not clear whether Tor, Vampira and Lugosi are actually vampires or merely graveyard ghouls, but they are clearly members of the "undead."

Paul Birch as the alien vampire Paul Johnson in Roger Corman's *Not of This Earth* (1957).

Lugosi, in some of his brief appearances, dons the Dracula cape and presents the iconography of the screen's most famous vampire, while Maila Nurmi's Vampira would provide the inspiration for Morticia Addams on the popular television series *The Addams Family*; her sexy vamp look would later be appropriated by TV horror hostess Elvira.

Los Angeles was subjected to an alien vampire invasion of a very different sort in cult director Roger Corman's *Not of This Earth* (1957). The film opens on a quiet suburban street in L.A., where a young woman is returning home after a date and unexpectedly encounters a portly middle-aged man wearing a dark business suit and dark glasses. The man removes the glasses, causing a strange crackling sound that renders the girl unconscious. He then opens a metal suitcase containing a suction pump apparatus and attaches a syringe to the girl. Her blood starts to flow through a system of tubes, filling bottles inside the case.

The next day the man in black pays a visit to the medical office of hematologist Dr. Fredrick Rochelle (William Roerick) and introduces himself as Paul Johnson (Paul Birch). Johnson claims to be dying of a rare blood disease and requests that the doctor give him a blood transfusion at once. Dr. Rochelle takes a sample of Johnson's blood and finds he is suffering from a degenerative blood disorder that he has never before encountered. Johnson then places the physician in a hypnotic trance and speaks to him telepathically, explaining that he is an alien from the planet Davanna, a world that has been ravaged by a blood disease caused by a prolonged nuclear war. He has come to Earth to determine whether human blood is suitable for consumption by his race. The alien gives Rochelle a post-hypnotic command to study the blood sample and not to discuss his research with anyone else. He also arranges to have the doctor's nurse, Nadine Story (Beverly Garland), move into his home to administer the blood transfusions he requires.

Nadine moves into Johnson's place, a comfortable but slightly creepy old L.A. mansion, where she is introduced to his sleazy chauffeur-valet Jeremy (Jonathan Haze). That night, Johnson telepathically communicates with "The Courier," his superior on Davanna, using a matter transmitter machine hidden in his closet. The Courier (who appears as a disembodied talking head), discusses the Davannan master plan to subjugate the "second stage sub-humans" and turn Earth into a blood farm for the alien vamps. Johnson's mission is to send blood samples and living human specimens back to the home world for future study via the matter transmitter.

Following the Courier's orders, Johnson teleports blood samples obtained from various Angelinos to Davanna, and burns the bodies in an incinerator in the basement. Eventually, Nadine and Jeremy become suspicious of the weird disappearances at the mansion, and Nadine communicates her anxieties to her boyfriend, L.A.P.D. cop Harry Sherbourne (Morgan Jones). One day, Johnson encounters a black-clad Davannan female (Anne Carroll) on the street, and the two aliens engage in a telepathic exchange. She explains that there is great anarchy on Davanna and that she has escaped from the carnage via the teleportation device. Seeing that she is badly in need of blood, Johnson escorts her to Dr. Rochelle's office, but mistakenly transfuses her with blood from a rabies victim, which proves fatal. When Rochelle discovers the corpse, he calls the police and Sherbourne arrives for the post-mortem, which indicates that the dead woman is of extraterrestrial origin.

Fearing that the authorities are closing in on him, Johnson animates a grotesque bat creature that flies to Dr. Rochelle's office and kills him, then eyeball zaps Jeremy when the chauffeur confronts him with a skull discovered in the basement furnace. Johnson drives around the streets until he locates Nadine and gives her a hypnotic command to return to the mansion and teleport herself to Davanna. Sherbourne arrives on a motorcycle and, spying Johnson, turns on his police siren and chases his limo. The loud noise causes the alien to crash his car, freeing Nadine from his mental control before she can complete her one-way trip to Davanna.

One of producer/director Roger Corman's most memorable low-budget sci-fi horror efforts of the 1950s, *Not of This Earth* is well paced, well acted and conveys a genuinely eerie mood. Without resorting to expensive special effects, Corman crafts a superior alien-invasion thriller using economical means, such as a refrigerator stocked with bottles of blood and mental telepathy simulated by reverb-laden dubbed dialogue. The screenplay, by Charles Griffith and Mark Hanna, is wonderfully inventive and conveys a sense of the otherworldliness of the Davannans and their vampire society through the exquisite use of dialogue. "Time narrows, there is death upon Davanna," the Courier announces, "the conquered enemies dwindle in the pens of pasture and time constricts." Later, the Davannan woman tells Johnson, "The Courier is dead, murdered for his blood." The stolid Paul Birch is sinister yet somehow sympathetic in the role of the alien Mr. Johnson, while the incomparable Beverly Garland is perfectly cast as the plucky Nurse Nadine. Jonathan Haze, who would later star in Corman's horror/comedy *The Little Shop of Horrors* (1960), provides a light touch as Jeremy, Johnson's sleazebag gofer/chauffeur, while Anne Carroll delivers a strong performance as the pathetic Davannan woman. Ace monster maker Paul Blaisdell designed the creepy-looking alien bat creature that makes a brief appearance.

The alien vampires depicted in *Not of This Earth* are an entirely original concept. Dispensing with rubber masks and elaborate costumes, Corman's space vamps walk among us while concealing their identity behind dark glasses and a stony attitude. The film's Hollywood gothic setting is a novel and decadent environment for an updated tale of nouveau vampirism. Like Count Dracula and other screen vamps, the Davannans can exert hypnotic and telepathic control over their human victims, although fangs have been replaced by a more efficient, hi-tech means of blood extraction. Unlike sexually passionate terrestrial vamps, however, these space vampires are cold and unemotional. The notion of industrial blood farms run by vampires originates here and would later be fully realized in *Blade II* and *Daybreakers. Not of This Earth* may have provided inspiration for the mysterious "Men in Black," the enigmatic black-suited individuals of hit science fiction movies.

Mr. Johnson (Paul Birch) menaces Nurse Nadine Story (Beverly Garland) in *Not of This Earth* (1957).

Not of This Earth was remade twice, with Corman acting as executive producer both times. The first remake was released in 1988, and directed by Jim Wynorski from a screenplay by R.J. Robinson, which follows the plot of the original fairly closely. Arthur Roberts plays Mr. Johnson, the black-suited alien vampire from Davanna, but the film's real attraction was former porno starlet Traci Lords in her first straight role as Johnson's nurse, Nadine Story. The retread is considerably trashier than Corman's original version as the focus of the narrative shifts from sci-fi horror thrills to displaying the charms of Ms. Lords. In keeping with the R-rating, Johnson's blood donors and test subjects are prostitutes and strippers who aren't shy about appearing topless in front of the camera. Wynorski's remake is unnecessary, poorly executed, and demeans the fine qualities of the original film.

The second remake was a 1996 made-for-TV movie, directed by Terence A. Winkless from a script by Charles Philip Moore, which is much closer in tone to Corman's original concept. British actor Michael York portrays space vampire Paul Johnson, while the nurse (named Amanda Sales in this version) is played by Elizabeth Barondes. Television tough guy Richard Belzer is cast as Jeremy, Johnson's sleazoid chauffeur. The '56 remake expands the scope of the original by utilizing special effects provided by Media Magic and John Carl Buechler. In this version Johnson can emit fireballs from his eyes, Paul Blaisdell's gothic bat-creature from the 1957 original has been replaced by a geometric computer-generated lifeform and a tentacled, alien blob is ensconced in Johnson's private quarters.

Michael York, best known today as spy chief "Basil Exposition" in the *Austin Powers* comedies, easily carries the film in his portrayal of the otherworldly Mr. Johnson, whose alien monicker is "Sidal 2." York creates a quirky screen persona that seems continually perplexed at being a stranger in a strange land and recalls a similar portrayal of an alien being by fellow Britisher David Bowie in Nicholas Roeg's *The Man Who Fell to Earth* (1976). He cocks his head to the side like a lizard or bird inspecting its environment and converses in odd speech patterns, mannerisms that effectively communicate his extraterrestrial otherness. Richard Belzer is perfectly cast as the slimeball Jeremy, while Elizabeth Barondes is properly photogenic in a nude shower scene. The third version updates the alien vampire theme into the age of AIDS, as the virus contained in the alien's blood is likened to HIV. Johnson ruminates about how humankind is "like a virus that is killing the planet" and that the alien vamps represent a "vaccine against the human virus." In one hilarious scene Johnson is watching a Dracula movie on TV and inquires about the character. "Who is this Dracula?" he asks. "He interests me. He I would like to meet."

In the late 1950s the American space program was in its infancy. The Russians had launched the first Earth-orbiting satellite, *Sputnik*, in 1957 and America was trying hard to catch up. Outer space was a mysterious, uncharted realm, and scientists did not know for certain if human beings could survive in the alien environment. During this time, the U.S. Air Force was testing a series of rocket-powered airplanes such as the X-1, in which Chuck Yeager broke the sound barrier, and the X-15, the fastest manned aircraft that ever flew. The X-15 actually reached an altitude of fifty miles above Earth, which is at the threshold of outer space. This was the historical backdrop for the British science fiction/horror film *First Man into Space* (1959).

The story takes place in at a U.S. Navy missile range in New Mexico, where Colonel Chuck Prescott (Marshall Thompson) is in charge of testing a high-altitude rocket aircraft called the Y-13. The rocket plane seems to work fine, but the colonel's biggest headache is his younger brother Dan (Bill Edwards), the hotshot test pilot of the Y-13 program, who is stuffed so full of the right stuff that he has a hard time obeying orders. Chuck and Dan try to put their sibling rivalry aside, but during the maiden flight of the Y-13 Dan can't resist being "the highest man in the world" and, disobeying orders, takes the aircraft to an altitude of 250 miles, making him the first man in space. Unexpectedly, Dan runs into a freak cloud of meteorite dust and all radio contact with the Y-13 is lost.

The rocketship's escape capsule comes down in a rural area of New Mexico, but Dan is not inside. Examining the capsule, Col. Prescott and project scientist Dr. Von Essen (Carl Jaffe) find that the exterior is coated with some kind of alien gunk, the residue of Dan's passage through the cloud of meteorite dust. The capsule is brought back to the lab for study. Before long, livestock are found dead, drained of blood. A monstrous creature makes an unauthorized withdrawal from a local blood bank and kills a nurse. A baffling series of brutal murders follows, in which the victims are found drained of blood through a jagged wound in the neck. "It seems to like the taste of

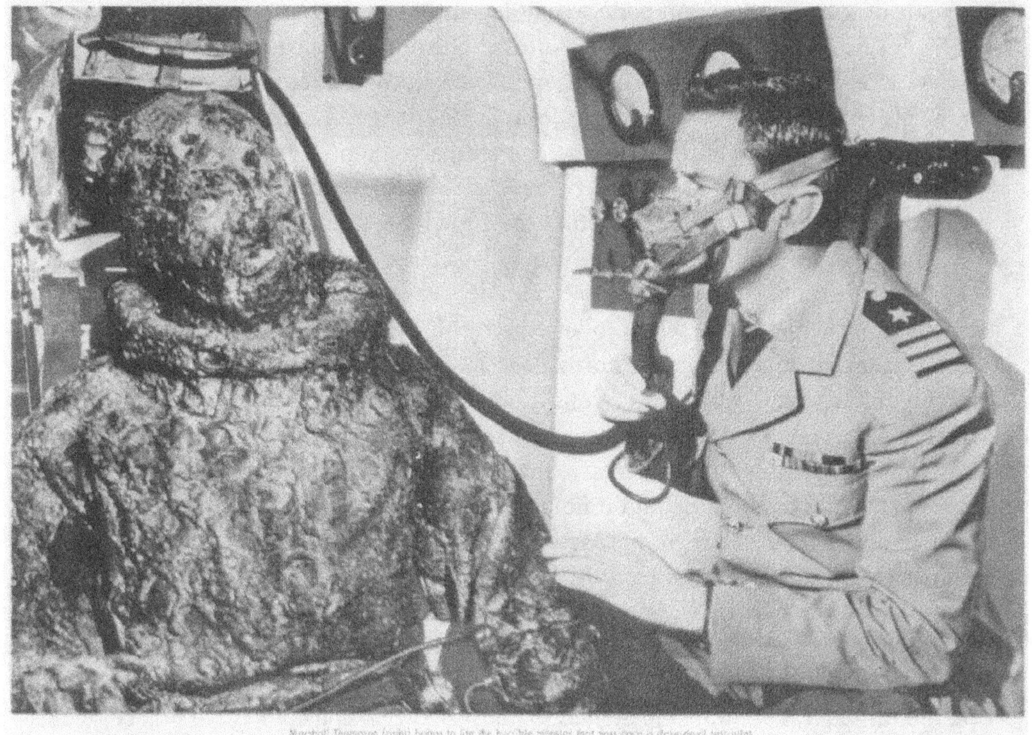

Vampire astronaut Dan Prescott (Bill Edwards, left) converses with his brother, Colonel Chuck Prescott (Marshall Thompson), inside the high-altitude chamber in *First Man into Space* (1959).

blood," Col. Prescott observes at the site of one of the killings, where he finds material in the victim's wounds that resembles the matter found on the escape capsule.

Back at the lab, Dr. Von Essen has analyzed the coating on the capsule and found that it forms a protective barrier that counters the destructive effect of cosmic rays. He theorizes that, if Dan has also been covered with the alien material, it might have adapted his metabolism to survive in outer space. Consequently, Dan's body may be starved of blood and may feel the constant need to replace it. Von Essen's theories prove to be accurate as the vampiric astronaut invades the space center, his body covered with the space sludge. Dan's face has been horribly disfigured in the crash, and the scientist describes him as being transformed into "a great big lumbering deformed monster." Clinging to the shreds of his humanity, Dan convinces Prescott to place him in the facility's high-altitude test chamber, hoping that he will be able to survive in the simulated space environment. Tragically, he dies anyway because he cannot replenish his blood supply. "I just had to be the first man into space," he says before expiring.

Lensed by British director Robert Day, who helmed mature horror fare, such as *The Haunter Strangler* (1958) and *Corridors of Blood* (produced in 1958; released 1962), this tale of space exploration gone wrong is a neat little creature feature that exploits 1950s-era anxieties about the great unknown. The film is rife with stock footage of Air Force rocket-powered X-planes being launched, lending a documentary verisimilitude to the proceedings. The screenplay, by John C. Cooper and Lance Z. Hargreaves, seems to have borrowed plot elements from the similarly themed 1956 Hammer film *The Quatermass Xperiment* (see Chapter Four). The acting is earnest and workmanlike, but the film's attempt to make the murderous "great big lumbering deformed monster" into a sympathetic figure in the final reel falls flat.

The infected astronaut in *First Man into Space* represents a novel twist on the science fiction theme of vampirism being the result of some exotic disease. The nature of the "meteorite dust" that transforms Dan into a bloodthirsty fiend, or just why this space gunk acts to adapt him to conditions in outer space, is never explained. Still dressed in his muck-covered space suit without its helmet, with a single eye glaring out from his horribly disfigured face, the tragic vampire astronaut in *First Man into Space* presents a frightening and unique take on the sci-fi vampire concept.

Anxieties about the perils of space exploration continued in another space vampire monster mash, *It! The Terror from Beyond Space* (1958). In the future year of 1973, the first manned mission to Mars has crash-landed on the Red Planet, but a mysterious fate has befallen the crew. All of the astronauts have perished except for the expedition's leader, Colonel Edward Carruthers (Marshall Thompson from *First Man into Space*). Six months later, a second ship arrives to take Carruthers back to Earth to face a court martial for murdering the crew, but the colonel insists that his fellow astronauts were killed by an unseen monster. As they prepare to depart, a hulking, shadowy figure sneaks through an airlock and hides itself inside the rocketship as it blasts off.

Flight Commander Van Heusen (Kim Spalding) and the majority of the crew disbelieve Carruthers's story about an unknown creature, but they are forced to re-evaluate their skepticism when several crew members are attacked and killed by the alien. They soon have a close encounter with the Martian stowaway, a big ugly monster with a homicidal attitude (played by stunt man Ray "Crash" Corrigan in a rubber suit). Autopsy analysis of the victims reveals that all of the blood and other bodily fluids have been sucked out by the It creature.

The alien proves hard to kill as the crew systematically tries every method conceivable to exterminate it. Bullets, gas grenades, electricity and even radiation are tried, but as one crewman laments, "It won't die!" To make matters worse, Commander Van Heusen gets wounded by the creature and contracts an infectious disease that requires frequent transfusions, but the blood is stored in an area of the ship made inaccessible by the alien. Finally, the surviving crew members are barricaded in the command center of the ship, awaiting the creature's next assault, when Carruthers happens to notice that oxygen levels on the ship are lower than normal; he theorizes that the Martian's enormous lungs have been taking in the extra oxygen. Donning their spacesuits as the It monster crashes through the last barricade, they open the airlock and asphyxiate the creature as all of the spacecraft's oxygen rushes out into the vacuum of space.

A fine example of '50s-era sci-fi horror, *It! The Terror from Beyond Space* is a rousing monster movie, well crafted by science fiction luminary Jerome Bixby's script and Edward L. Cahn's steady direction. The plot, in which a group of humans are caught in an enclosed environment and must battle a seemingly indestructible alien creature, borrows heavily from *The Thing from Another World* and also from A.E. Van Vogt's classic short story "Black Destroyer" (1939). Many critics have pointed out the film's influence on Ridley Scott's 1979 megahit *Alien*.

Stuntman and former cowboy star Ray "Crash" Corrigan steals the show as the titular It creature, combining his enthusiastic athleticism with the hideous rubber suit, designed by monster maker Paul Blaisdell, to create one of the most memorable sci-fi vamps of the period. Unlike the upfront bloodsucking antics of the alien in *The Thing*, this film does not emphasize the vampiric nature of the creature, although an alternative title was *It! The Vampire from Outer Space*.

By the end of the 1950s the Hollywood wave of science fiction movies that had flourished during the atomic age of anxiety had abated as fears of alien invasion, space exploration and atomic mutation began to lessen in the public mind. The end of the decade also heralded the end of the low-budget, black and white sci-fi horror thriller as color films became the new standard. As a consequence, science fiction films began to be produced outside of Hollywood, in Europe and Japan where production costs were less expensive.

The acclaimed Italian director Mario Bava is best known for his exquisitely photographed gothic horror films *Black Sunday* (1961) and *Black Sabbath* (1963). Bava's *Planet of the Vampires* (*Terro nello spazio*, 1965) was the director's attempt to create a gothic science fiction film in a color idiom. As the film opens, deep space exploration ships *Argus* and *Galliott*, in a distant quadrant of the galaxy, detect an anomalous signal emanating from the planet Aura. Thinking that there may be intelligent life on Aura, the ships go into orbit around the mysterious planet, but instead of being able to land normally, the *Argus* and *Galliott* are forcibly pulled down to the surface of the alien world by a massive tractor beam.

Argus touches down on Aura without mishap, but for some unknown reason the crew begins fighting with each other. After the fracas dies down, Captain Mark Markary (Barry Sullivan) the ship's commanding officer, leads a team across the desolate, fog-bound landscape of the unexplored planet to locate their sister ship. Upon reaching the *Galliott*, the team finds that the crew members have slaughtered one another. In addition, someone has sabotaged the ship's vital equipment so it can no longer fly in space. The dead crewmen are buried in futuristic-looking graves with metal headstones, but soon return as the undead. In one of the film's most memorable sequences, the resurrected space explorers emerge from the graves and work their way out of their clear plastic shrouds to stalk off into the foggy alien landscape.

Exploring the planet's surface, Captain Markary and female crew member Sanya (Norma Bengell) discover a derelict spaceship of unknown origin that crashed on Aura centuries earlier. They find a giant skeleton still at the controls of the ship, the remains of one of the alien crew. Poking around the ship's controls, Markary accidentally activates recorded voices of the dead creatures, a mournful basso droning that echoes eerily through the ship. Markary and Sanya are temporarily trapped when automatic doors close around them, but they soon manage to escape and return to the *Argus*.

Two of the crewmen of the *Galliott* suddenly arrive and are admitted inside the *Argus*, but are soon revealed to be undead zombies animated by the Aurans, energy beings who are inhabiting their dead bodies. The Aurans tell Markary that their sun is dying and they are desperate to migrate to another planet, but because they are pure energy, they must rely on manipulating carbon-based lifeforms to accomplish tasks in the physical world. The beacon signal was merely a ruse to draw their ships down from space, and now they want to use the *Argus* to escape from their dying world while possessing the crew's bodies. When Markary refuses, the undead zombies attack, and the battle ends with the ship damaged, the entire crew dead except for the Captain and Sanya, who have fallen under the domination of the Auran body snatchers. Unable to venture far into space, the Aurans set course for the nearest habitable planet—Earth.

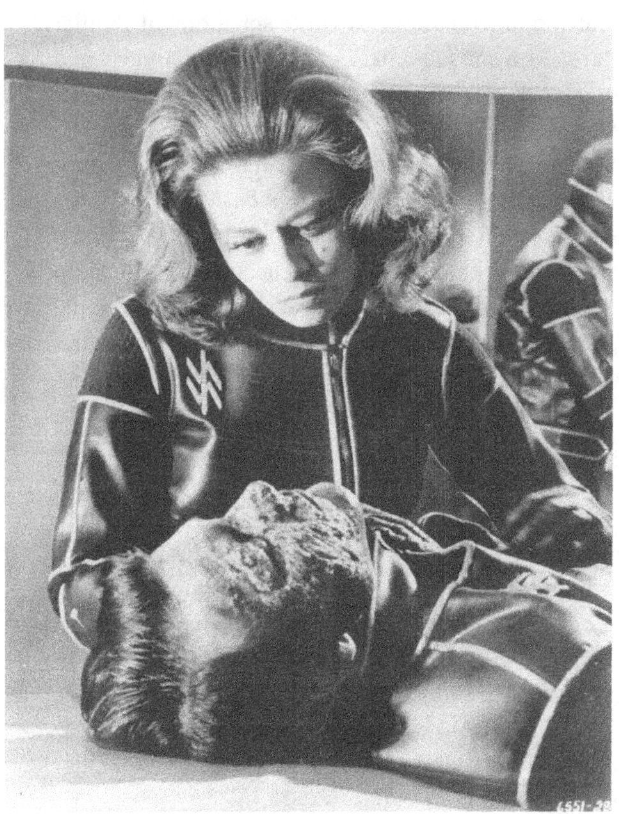

Cosmonaut Sanya (Norma Bengell) contemplates the mutilated corpse of one of her fellow crewmembers in Mario Bava's space gothic *Planet of the Vampires* (1965).

The great Bava neatly transposes the cinematic universe of gothic horror into an outer space setting, substituting spaceships and an alien planet for the goth churchyards and ruined castles of the traditional vampire film. Bava makes evocative use of fog and shadow, and a deep, saturation of colors on the bleak phantom planet of Aura, creating an ambience of fear and mystery. Sound is used to great effect to create a futuristic setting, including a tense electronic score composed by Kendall Schmidt. The screenplay by Ib Melchior, Antonio Roman, Alberto Bevilacqua, Rafael J. Salvia, Catillo Cosulich and Lewis M. Heyward, adapted from the story "One Night of 21 Hours" by Renato Pestoriniero, makes the film resemble a nightmarish episode of TV's *Star Trek* series, which would come a year later.

Note that the undead crea-

Captain Mark Markary (Barry Sullivan) and Sanya (Norma Bengell) discover the petrified remains of a giant humanoid inside a derelict ship in *Planet of the Vampires* (1965).

tures in the film are not actually bloodsucking vampires, although they are resurrected zombies who rise from their graves to stalk the living. The crew members of the two spaceships wear form-fitting, black leather uniforms with high collars that suggest futuristic vampire costumes. Like *The Thing* and *It! The Terror from Beyond Space*, *Planet of the Vampires* provided plot elements that would later appear in *Alien*, including the space beacon that lures ships onto a bleak world, and the discovery of a derelict vessel containing the skeleton of a long-dead extraterrestrial crewman.

In the mid–'60s, the ever-resourceful producer Roger Corman acquired the rights to a Russian science fiction epic entitled *Niebo Zowlet*, that contained lots of stylish color footage of rocketships and outer space scenery. Corman decided to convert this exercise in Soviet socialist realism into a low-budget, exploitation horror flick by patching in new footage shot in America. Cult film-maker Curtis Harrington was called in to write and direct a cast that included Basil Rathbone in one of his last roles, leading man John Saxon, and the up-and-coming young actor Dennis Hopper. The result was a tale of vampirism in outer space entitled *Queen of Blood* (a.k.a. *Planet of Blood*, 1966).

The story is set in the future world of 1990, in which mankind has established bases on the moon and is exploring interplanetary space. An alien spacecraft from another galaxy, passing through the solar system, issues a distress call and jettisons a lifeboat somewhere in the vicinity of the planet Mars. The International Institute of Space Technology, headed by Dr. Faraday (Basil Rathbone), sends a team of astronauts to Mars to rescue any survivors. The recovery team consists of Alan Brenner (John Saxon), Anders Brockman (Robert Boon), Laura James (Judi Meredith) and Paul Grant (Dennis Hopper). They locate the lifeboat on the Martian moon Phobos and rescue the sole survivor, a mute, green-skinned alien woman (Florence Marley), then set a return course for Earth.

During the voyage home Paul makes an attempt to communicate with the E.T., but gets no response. One night the femalien stalks Paul, hypnotically immobilizes him, and feeds on his blood. The next day Paul's drained corpse is discovered and the alien is found to be in a somnolent state after having gorged herself on his bodily fluids. Brockman, the mission commander, insists that the creature be kept alive, even if the crew has to take turns feeding her, but ironically he is the space vampire's next victim. Soon only Alan and Laura are left alive, and when the alien vamp goes after Alan, Laura manages to inflict a wound on the creature, who promptly bleeds to death because she comes from a race of alien hemophiliacs. Laura and Alan make it back to Earth, but discover that their spacecraft is infested with hundreds of alien eggs. It turns out that the space vamp was a brood queen whose mission was to bring her eggs to Earth. In the ominous ending, Dr. Faraday orders the ship to land as the red, pulsating vampire eggs are offloaded and taken to the lab for study.

The combination of Corman's ingenuity and Harrington's writing and directorial skills elevate *Queen of Blood* above the dismal standards of most low-budget sci-fi fare of the period. Corman's editors flawlessly integrate the Russian space footage from *Niebo Zowlet* into the film's continuity, the arty special effects lending a poetic tone to the finished film's outer space panoramas. Harrington's direction, shooting in deep red and purple tones, builds a palpable aura of horror and suspense aboard the doomed spaceship. The interesting cast includes the aged Basil Rathbone and the youthful Dennis Hopper, whom Harrington had previously directed in the mermaid fantasy *Night Tide* (1963), but it is Florence Marley's haunting performance as the alien Blood Queen that dominates the film. Having green-colored skin and sporting an enormous beehive hairdo, her extraordinary screen presence conveys a sense of the space vampire's otherness without resorting to dialogue. The alien vamp, while mute, possesses the hypno-telepathic powers of her supernatural brethren and uses humans as part of her reproductive strategy.

While Japanese culture is not one to embrace vampirism themes, during the 1960s their movie industry was busy cranking out science fiction films, most of which were in the sub-genre of *kaiju eiga*, or "mysterious monster" movies, featuring humongous creatures such as Godzilla and his oversized ilk. Hajime Sato's *Goke, Body Snatcher from Hell* (*Kyuketsuki Gokemidoru*, 1968) departed from this formula to create an eerie tale of extraterrestrial invasion and vampirism. As the film opens, Japan Airlines Flight 307 is en route from Tokyo to Osaka, when anomalous phenomena are observed. The sky has turned from blue to a baleful reddish color and crows are hurtling themselves against the aircraft's windows, becoming harbingers of evil. To make matters worse, a radio message is received from air traffic control that there may be a bomb aboard the plane. JAL 307 is ordered to return to Tokyo at once.

Co-pilot Sugisaka (Teruo Yoshida) is assigned to check the passengers' baggage for a bomb, but when he finds a rifle inside one piece of luggage, its owner (Hideo Ko) pulls out a gun and orders the pilots to divert the plane to Okinawa. As the airliner is changing course, it has a close encounter with a flying saucer that disables the plane's systems, causing it to crash in a desolate area. Miraculously, only the pilot is killed while the rest of the passengers and crew survive, but they have no idea where they are. Guided by some strange instinct, the hijacker bolts from the plane and is telepathically directed to a landed UFO. Entering the glowing craft in a trance, he stands motionless before a pulsating light, while a blue, blob-like creature crawls toward him. A wound opens in the middle of his forehead and the blob crawls inside his head.

The alien blob has turned the terrorist into a vampire, who begins stalking his fellow passengers, one by one, and drinking their blood. For their part, the passengers, deprived of food and water, are at each other's throats. During the night, the hijacker escorts one of the women, Noriko (Yuko Kusunoki), to the saucer, where she, too, is possessed by the alien force. The next day, the passengers go looking for Noriko and find her staring down at them from the top of a high cliff. She speaks to them in an alien voice, telling them that the Gokemidoru race has targeted the planet Earth for invasion, and that humankind is to be exterminated. When her message is completed, Noriko hurls herself off the cliff to her death, and her corpse dissolves into dust.

One by one, the passengers succumb to the Gokemidoru bloodsucker, until only the co-pilot, Sugisaka, and the plane's stewardess, Kuzumi (Tomoni Sato), are left. The couple decides to abandon the downed airliner and take their chances in the wilderness. Before long, they leave the desolation of the crash site and come upon a road with a line of stationary cars seemingly caught in a traffic jam; on closer inspection, they find that all the drivers are dead. Following the road, they reach a city filled with corpses, victims of the Gokemidoru final solution. The film ends with fleets of saucers flying through outer space on their way to Earth.

Reportedly one of *Pulp Fiction* writer/director Quentin Tarantino's favorite films, *Goke*'s heady mixture of UFOs, vampirism, antiwar sentiment (grisly photographs from the Vietnam War are periodically inserted into the movie for no particular reason), apocalyptic nightmare and terrorism straddles the film somewhere between the art house and the grindhouse. Director Sato shoots in highly saturated, even gaudy, colors and frequently frames his actors in extreme longshots that create an uneasy feeling of isolation, as the tiny human figures struggle through vast, desolate landscapes. Susumu Takahashi and Kyuzo Kobayashi's screenplay has a *Lord of the Flies* flavor, as it follows a group of formerly civilized people in an isolated environment as they descend into madness and anarchy. The Japanese cast displays an earnestness that makes this bizarre material believable.

But it is Hideo Ko's portrayal of the terrorist hijacker-turned-vampire that drives the film. Attired in a white suit, shoes and gloves, and sporting a nasty-looking vertical scar in the middle of his forehead, the actor projects a uniquely malignant screen presence, as he sinks his teeth into the role and into several members of the cast as well. The scenes in which the alien blob enters and exits the opening in Ko's forehead are particularly memorable. Oddly, *Goke* harks back to *Plan 9* in connecting an alien invasion with a plague of vampirism, but the film never explains why the extraterrestrials need to possess a human body and send it out to suck people's blood. The blue blob that invades the hijacker's body is, presumably, a member of the Gokemidoru race, but this plot point in similarly unclear. In any event, *Goke, Body Snatcher from Hell* presents a unique Japanese vision of the science fiction vampire.

Perhaps the most ludicrous sci-fi vamps in the history of cinema appeared in shlockmeister Al Adamson's bizarre pastiche *Vampire Men of the Lost Planet* (1970), a.k.a. *Horror of the Blood Monsters, Creatures of the Prehistoric Planet, Horror Creatures of the Prehistoric Planet, Space Mission to the Lost Planet, Flesh Creatures of the Red Planet, Horror Creatures of the Lost Planet, Blood Monster, The Flesh Creatures, Horror Creatures of the Prehistoric Planet, Creatures of the Red Planet* and other lurid titles too terrifying to be mentioned here. Producer/director Adamson had acquired the rights to a black-and-white movie about vampire cavemen, lensed in the Philippines, and combined it with new material he shot about a space voyage to a primitive planet and effects footage of dinosaurs and other prehistoric beasts from the silent version of *The Lost World* (1925) and Hal Roach's caveman epic, *One Million B.C.* (1940). Because the Filipino material was in B&W, it was tinted in a variety of hues to match the new color footage, using a process advertised as "Spectrum X."

A brief prologue by a narrator doing a terrible Bela Lugosi imitation informs the audience, "The infected blood of the vampire was carried to Earth millions of years ago by the Tuberton vampire men of a distant galaxy far beyond this solar system." Meanwhile, vampires (including director Adamson) are shown attacking various people at random. Cut to a launch pad, where spaceship XB-13 is blasting off for the "Spectrum solar system," with a crew that includes Commander Steve Bryce (Bruce Powers), Captain Bob Scott (Fred Meyers), Willy (Joey Benson), Linda (Britt Semand) and the brilliant scientist Dr. Rynning (John Carradine). En route to their destination, the XB-13 is damaged by a radiation storm and the crew is forced to set down on an unknown planet to make repairs.

They land on a world that is virtually identical to Earth, so no oxygen tanks or space suits are needed to venture out onto the planet's surface. While Dr. Rynning stays on board the ship, the rest of the crew goes outside to explore. They encounter dinosaurs and other prehistoric fauna (including the time-honored conflict between a finbacked alligator and a monitor lizard, posing as dinosaurs from *One Million B.C.*, that had been used in countless low-budget sci-fi flicks), and watch a battle between a group of vampire cavemen with fangs and a human tribe of troglodytes. Suddenly, we see a human female who is being chased by three of the vamp cavemen. The crew rescues the girl and implants a translator chip in her head that enables her to talk to the Earthlings.

The cavewoman, whose name is Lian Malian (Jennifer Bishop), fills them in on a blood feud being waged between the vampire Tubaton people and her tribe, the peace-loving Tagani. She relates her tribe's quest for "firewater," a flammable liquid used to keep the primitive Tubatons at bay, which is shown in extended flashbacks as the Tagani are attacked by monstrous lobster men and bat men on the way to the cave, where the firewater is found. Commander Bryce thinks the fiery fluid must be a type of petroleum that could be distilled into rocket coolant for the XB-13, so he has Malian lead them to the cave to obtain some of the firewater. On the way back to the ship they are attacked by the Tubatons, and Bob is killed, but the rest of the crew members make it back alive. While Dr. Rynning is distilling the firewater, he tells them that their blood has been infected by a virus that has caused the Tubaton race to revert to savagery and will ultimately kill them, but the crew will be okay once they are back on Earth because the virus can't survive there. When the repairs are completed, the XB-13 blasts off for home, leaving the doomed Tubaton vampire men to their eventual fate.

Vampire Men of the Lost Planet is lively drive-in fare, although Adamson's combination of disparate filmic elements lacks continuity. Still, it's tastefully done, without resorting to gratuitous nudity or excessive violence. The space effects are chintzy and the costumes on the lost planet's lobster men and bat men are nothing short of hilarious. Ditto the fanged Tubaton cavemen, while the film's star, veteran hambone John Carradine, chews the scenery like a nest of termites. The cheapjack "Spectrum X" color process, which enables the mating of the color with the black-and-white scenes, does little to enliven the proceedings. Vampire cavemen represent a novel, if ludicrous, concept of the sci-fi vampire, and it's not clear whether the film's equally silly bat people are also alien bloodsuckers.

Occult writer Colin Wilson's 1976 novel *The Space Vampires* (discussed in Chapter Two), received the big-screen treatment in a British adaptation entitled *Lifeforce* (1985). It was directed by the able Tobe Hooper, who had been responsible for the cult horror classic *The Texas Chainsaw Massacre* (1974) and the big budget ghost story *Poltergeist* (1982). The film version was scripted by Dan O'Bannon, who had written the screenplay for *Alien* and featured special effects by John Dykstra, best known for his work on *Star Wars*, and a musical score written by the acclaimed film composer Henry Mancini, which was performed by the London Symphony Orchestra.

The film follows the plotline of Wilson's novel fairly closely. The space shuttle *Churchill* is on a joint U.S.-U.K. mission to explore Halley's Comet when they discover a 150-mile-long derelict spaceship of unknown origin, trailing the comet. A team of four astronauts is assigned to explore the creepy-looking ship. Spacewalking through the ship's cavernous and menacing interior, the scientists surmise that it has been blindly traveling through space for centuries. The team discovers the dead bodies of bat-like alien creatures, and in one chamber they find the naked but perfectly preserved corpses of three humanoids, two men and a woman, encased in transparent coffins. They bring the three bodies aboard the *Churchill*, which loses radio contact with Earth shortly thereafter. The shuttle is found drifting in near–Earth orbit a month later, with its crew dead or missing, its data tapes erased, and the three bodies still intact inside their protective chambers. The bodies are off-loaded from the shuttle and sent to the European Space Research Center in London for further study.

Once they arrive at the Space Research Center, the three corpses are placed in a laboratory environment, where they are studied by the Center's head scientist, Dr. Bukovsky (Michael Gothard), thanatologist Professor Fallada (Frank Finlay) and security chief Colin Caine (Peter Firth). One night, the female being (Mathilda May) awakens and, rising from her transparent coffin, stalks and kills a security guard by sucking the life force out of him, leaving him a dried-out husk. Afterward, she escapes from the center, walking out into the streets of London, stark naked. When an autopsy is being performed on the unfortunate guard, his desiccated corpse rises from the table to absorb the life force of the doctor. Bukovsky, Falada and Caine now know they have a zombie epidemic on their hands. To make matters worse, the two male aliens revive, escape from the center, and start spreading the zombie plague throughout the streets of London.

In the meantime, Colonel Carlsen (Steve Railsback), the sole survivor of the *Churchill* disaster, has returned to Earth in an escape capsule. Carlsen hurries to the Space Research Center, where he briefs his colleagues on what transpired aboard the doomed shuttle. It seems that the alien vampire girl awakened during the voyage to Earth and killed off the *Churchill*'s crew while forming a strange erotic/symbiotic relationship with Carlsen. Because he has a telepathic link with the alien vamp, he thinks he may be able to locate her via remote viewing. Going into a trance state, Carlsen remote views the alien, who has switched her consciousness into another female body, and traces her to a mental asylum north of London.

Caine and Carlsen, hot on the trail of the alien vamp, are airlifted to the asylum in a helicopter. They meet with the facility's director, Dr. Alexander (played by *Star Trek: The Next Generation*'s Patrick Stewart), who, Carlsen intuits, is inhabited by the consciousness of the femalien. After a struggle, they manage to restrain the doctor and load him into the chopper for the return trip to London. On the way, however, the girl's essence reconstitutes itself and escapes. When Caine and Carlsen arrive in the city, they find it in the grip of a zombie apocalypse as the plague of the undead spreads anarchy, violence and death across London. Martial law has been declared as British troops battle with the zombies through the streets.

They return to the besieged space center, where they confer with Professor Fallada about the situation. The professor tells them that human life forces are being collected and beamed up to the alien ship orbiting in space. These life forces are visible as a line of light emanating from St. Paul's Cathedral and streaming into the sky. Fallada also informs him that the vampires can be killed by being pierced with an ancient sword made of leaded iron. Carlsen, realizing that he alone can destroy the alien menace, takes the sword and fights his way through the undead hordes to St. Paul's, where he finds the vampire girl stretched out on the altar, her body providing the focal point for the life energy streaming upward into space. He joins her on the altar, and as the two are making love, he thrusts the leaded iron sword through both of them. The transmission of the life energy ceases and the alien ship becomes deactivated and drifts away from Earth into the depths of space.

On paper, *Lifeforce* has everything going for it. Hooper's direction, Wilson's source material, O'Bannon's screenplay, Dykstra's effects, Mancini's orchestral soundtrack and a decent budget should have produced a masterpiece of horror/sci-fi cinema, but this is not how things worked out. The main problem is that, like much of literary science fiction, the work is heavy on ideas and concepts, but light on characterization. There are no characters in *Lifeforce* with whom the audience can identify. Lacking any emotional resonance, the film falls flat despite all the frenetic action and sophisticated special effects. The movie's focus shifts too radically from space exploration epic to police procedural to zombie apocalypse for the audience to get a handle on the plot.

On the plus side, the early scenes inside the derelict alien ship are scary and evocative, and Hooper's artistic use of full frontal female nudity still has the power to shock. Although she doesn't get a lot of screen time, Mathilda May's portrayal of the alien vampire woman is the most memorable performance in the film, her statuesque figure and dominatrix-like imperiousness project an otherworldly, overwhelming force of vampiric femininity.

Regardless of its cinematic virtues, or lack thereof, *Lifeforce* contains some interesting ideas about the nature and origins of vampirism. These concepts are expressed by the scientist Prof. Fallada, who acts as a kind of Van Helsing figure. At one point, Fallada muses, "In a sense, we're all vampires. We drain the energy from other life forms. The difference is one of degree." Later on, he theorizes about the aliens having visited Earth in ages past. "It is my belief," he lectures, "that the vampire of legend came from creatures such as these, perhaps even from these very creatures." It is also Fallada who figures out that the alien vamps can be destroyed by being pierced by leaded iron. Like the novel, the film's plot owes a debt to A.E. Van Vogt's 1942 short story "Asylum," but there are also a number of similarities with Stoker's *Dracula*, including the ghost ship, with all the crew dead on board, that transports the vampires to London; the learned professor who skewers the vampire's weaknesses; and the telepathic mind-meld between the vampire and its human lover.

As discussed in Chapter Two, the very first extraterrestrial invaders were also vampires. H.G. Wells's classic alien invasion epic *The War of the Worlds* (1898) featured Martians who subsisted on the blood of humans and other creatures. When Wells's novel was brought to the screen by science fiction producer George Pal in 1953, the Martians' vampirism was omitted, but their vampiric nature was restored in Steven Spielberg's big-budget remake *The War of the Worlds* (2005).

The novel's locale has been changed from 19th century England to early 21st century New Jersey, where blue-collar everyman Ray Ferrier (Tom Cruise) is struggling

An alien war machine harvests humans for their blood in Steven Spielberg's invasion epic *The War of the Worlds* (2005).

with a recent divorce and sharing custody of his little girl, Rachel (Dakota Fanning), and teenage son, Robbie (Justin Chatwin), with his estranged wife. An alien invasion intrudes into the midst of this family drama as humongous tripod war machines emerge from beneath the ground and begin vaporizing the populace with death rays. The invaders have also utilized an electromagnetic pulse weapon that renders all electronics inoperable and disables all motor vehicles. Ray and his children escape the carnage in a car that has just had its solenoids replaced and is in working condition. The family witnesses horrifying scenes of devastation and slaughter as the tripods hunt down any remaining humans. Their car is taken from them at gunpoint by a mob gathered at a ferry terminal, where the family watches as the machines start picking up people with their mechanical tentacles and stowing them inside the tripods. They continue on foot until they run into a battle between army forces and the tripods, during which Justin is separated from the family.

After surviving the battle, Ray and Rachel are given shelter in an isolated house by kooky survivalist Harlan Oglivy (Tim Robbins), who wants to enlist Ray's aid in a guerrilla war against the invaders. From their concealment, they watch the machines spew out large amounts of what appears to be blood over the landscape. The influx of blood causes a creeping red vine to grow everywhere, as if the aliens are "terraforming" Earth to make it more like their own environment. Ray and Rachel manage to remain undetected in Oglivy's cellar until they observe a tripod in the act of extracting blood from a man with a needle-like probe.

The horrible sight terrifies Oglivy. He starts chanting the phrase, "Not my blood, not my blood," over and over again. "They drink it," he frantically intones, "then they spray it like fertilizer." Fearing that Oglivy's erratic behavior will reveal their presence to the invaders, Ray is forced to kill him with his bare hands. But, despite Ray's best efforts, the aliens discover their hiding place, and Rachel is hauled up by a metal tentacle and placed into a collection basket with other humans slung underneath the tripod's head. Fortuitously, Ray happens to find a string of hand grenades in an empty army humvee, then calls attention to himself so that he will be captured. The tripod duly hoists him up and places him in the basket beside Rachel. A tentacle periodically emerges from a sphincter-like orifice in the bottom of the machine to seize human victims and drag them inside the machine, but when Ray is picked up, he cleverly manages to set off a brace of hand grenades within the mechanism. The stricken tripod falls to Earth, breaking open the specimen basket and leaving Rachel and Ray unhurt and free.

Father and daughter head for Boston with vague hopes of finding Ray's wife. The army has taken charge of the city, where the alien death machines are behaving erratically. As Ray watches, troops employ a shoulder-fired missile launcher to take down one of the tripods, which appears to be in a weakened state. One of the aliens attempts to emerge from the ruined war machine and promptly dies on the spot. In fact, all of the invaders are dying off, their immune systems having been compromised, as in Wells's novel, by earthly germs against which they have no defense. The creeping blood vines are likewise unable to survive in Earth's environment, and simply wither away. At the film's happy ending, Ray is reunited with his ex-wife, Mary Ann (Miranda Otto), and with Justin, who has somehow survived the alien holocaust.

Spielberg has shown a knack for directing big budget, hi-tech science fiction blockbusters, such as *Jurassic Park* (1993) and *Minority Report* (2002), and brings the same "Spielberg touch" to the H.G. Wells alien invasion classic. All through the firestorm of special effects, provided by Industrial Light & Magic, the director never loses sight of the human dilemma or the characters. Fine performances by principals Tom Cruise, Dakota Fanning and Tim Robbins add poignancy to the sci-fi spectacle of horror, death and destruction. The screenplay, by Josh Friedman and David Koepp, neatly transposes the novel's Victorian setting to contemporary America, while preserving the book's apocalyptic immediacy. Whereas the 1953 version dispensed with Wells's tripod war machines, the remake brought them to terrifying life. *The War of the Worlds* is sometimes an unpleasant film to watch as mankind's much-vaunted defense weapons are destroyed by the superior technology of the invaders. Devoid of any humorous elements, it's much darker in tone than the similarly themed alien invasion epic *Independence Day* (1996) and reflects an American angst in a post–911 world of uncertainty and terrorism.

Little is seen of the invaders themselves, who are no longer Martians, but hail from parts unknown. Their menace is expressed mainly by their hi-tech war machines, the towering tripods that rain death upon a hapless humanity. The aliens are not actually shown drinking blood as they do in the novel, and it's unclear how the blood extracted

Harlan Oglivy (Tim Robbins, left) and Ray Ferrer (Tom Cruise) hide from the invaders in *The War of the Worlds* (2005).

from their victims serves as fertilizer for the red vegetation, which appears to be a vampire plant. These red weeds appear in Wells's novel, but they are not explicitly linked to the Martian's vampirism. Spielberg has stated that the monstrous aliens in *The War of the Worlds* were meant to present a counterpoint to the benign off-world visitors who graced his earlier films *Close Encounters of the Third Kind* (1977) and *E.T.: The Extra-Terrestrial* (1982).

Alien vampires do not necessarily have to come from outer space. In Christopher Hutson's *Bled* (2009), an inhuman bloodsucker is transported into our world from another dimension. Sai (Sarah Farooqui) is a talented young artist whose paintings have a weird, otherworldly quality. At an exhibition of her work in a Los Angeles gallery she meets a mysterious European gentleman named Renfield (Jonathan Oldham), whose seductive qualities encourage her to invite him to her apartment after the show. His seduction, however, is of a different kind. He offers her a hallucinatory experience, induced by the sap of a rare bark called *strigoi* (an Eastern European term for vampire), which was used by such visionary artists as Gustav Klimt and Aubrey Beardsley. Only one person can breathe the *strigoi* fumes at a time, he explains, because, "one goes in, one stays out," so she will have to undergo the experience alone. Sai is intrigued and agrees to use the *strigoi*, so Renfield picks off a pea-sized piece of red stuff from a piece of bark and heats it in a spoon. As Sai inhales the vapors she goes into convulsions and Renfield walks out the door, leaving her to her fate.

Sai finds herself transported to a shadowy netherworld, a twilight realm, where she is stalked by a monstrous being. The pale-skinned humanoid creature is bald, pointy-eared and has clawed hands and can assume human form at will. Sai falls under the spell of the vampire creature and allows it to drink her blood before the effect of the *strigoi* drug wears off. She rhapsodizes about the visionary effects of the plant to her boyfriend, Royce (Chris Ivan Cevic), and her friends Eric (Alex Petrovich) and Kerra (Michele Morrow), all of whom are curious enough to try the *strigoi* vapors themselves. One by one they are drawn into the mysterious dimension and encounter the vampire creature, who begins to cross over the barrier between the worlds by invading their minds. It ultimately bleeds Kerra to death.

Becoming addicted to the visionary vapors, Sai takes too much of the drug and is trapped in the alien dimension. When Royce takes the *strigoi* to cross over into the other world and rescue her, the vampire genuinely materializes and goes after Eric. Encountering Sai in the other dimension, Royce realizes she has become a bloodsucker herself, and he stakes her. In the meantime, in the real world, as the vampire attacks Eric, Renfield suddenly reappears and wounds the creature, collecting some of its blood in a syringe. This causes the vampire to dematerialize, while Royce returns to reality without Sai. An epilogue shows Eric going off with Renfield, who now appears much younger after using the vampire's blood as a youth elixir.

Bled is a surrealistic mood piece that largely takes place in the eerie, fog-bound landscape of the film's nightmarish alien dimension, an evil, enchanted realm where vampires lurk. Christopher Hutson's direction is visually stylish, shot in dark, saturated color tones that give the proceedings an aura of fear and mystery. This modestly budgeted effort makes excellent use of a small, intimate cast of unknowns, who acquit themselves well, especially Jonathan Oldham as the evil manipulator Renfield. All in all, the film has a haunting, dreamlike quality that, at times, conjures up the visionary ambience of a hallucinogenic drug trip.

The film's screenplay, written by Sxv'leithan Essex, presents an entirely original take on the science fiction vamp concept by creating an inter-dimensional vampire being. *Bled*'s grotesque, inhuman bloodsucker (played by Ivan L. Moody) is, in appearance, a cross between a gothic goblin and an extraterrestrial, and it's unclear exactly where in the space-time continuum its misty realm is located. Like the traditional vampire, the creature has the powers of mental telepathy and the ability to appear in different forms to its victims. The film makes an explicit linkage between vampirism, drug addiction and artistic creativity.

Alien vampires are arguably the scariest of all varieties. Devoid of all human emotion, they are not sympathetic and have motivations unknown to Earthlings. They can assume monstrous, quasi-human forms, such as the hulking creatures appearing in *The Thing from Another World* and *It! The Terror from Beyond Space*. Conversely, they sometimes assume the appearance of seductive females, such as the alluring femaliens in *Queen of Blood* and *Lifeforce*. They can possess human bodies, as in *Plan 9 from Outer Space*, *Planet of the Vampires* and *Goke, Body Snatcher from Hell*, or even look like ordinary members of society, as in *Not of This Earth*. They can use superior technology to slake their thirst, as in *The War of the Worlds*. Not having a supernatural origin, they are not constrained by wolfbane, garlic, the cross or any of the traditional deterrents. They are the cutting edge of the science fiction vampire concept.

EPILOGUE

The Vampires We Need

Although vampire legends extend back into antiquity, the literary vampire emerged during the Victorian Era, at the same time that human reality was being transformed by modern science and technology. Bram Stoker's Count Dracula, a figure of supernatural menace, was defeated by the powers of late Victorian science, while H.G. Wells's blood-drinking extraterrestrial invaders were undone by their ignorance of immunology.

During the intervening decades, as technology came to have an increasing influence on our lives, the vampire has become ever more tech savvy. Today's techno-vamps have little in common with their gothic predecessors. As our society has become increasingly secularized, vampires have abandoned their ruined castles and graveyards in favor of spaceships, futuristic cities and time machines. They now wield hi-tech weaponry and utilize Jedi-like powers of mind. As our lives have become increasingly bound up with computers, the Internet, biotech and nanotech, we demand that our concept of the vampire evolve into the technological world as well. In this brave new world of consumer tech, we must create the vampires we need.

As science fiction cinema and literature have progressed, they have assimilated the vampire myth and mutated it into new and vibrant forms. Science fiction has produced cyber-vamps ("The Stainless Steel Leech," "Marid and the Trail of Blood"), time-traveling bloodsuckers ("Blood," *Dracula Unbound*), vegetable vampires ("The Flowering of the Strange Orchid," *The Thing from Another World*), psychic vampires ("The Parasite," *Trilby*, *The Cabinet of Dr. Caligari*, "Carrion Comfort"), and alien vampires (*The War of the Worlds*, "Asylum," *Lifeforce*). Vampires have been created by mad science (*Blood of Dracula*, *The Vampire*, *Atom Age Vampire*), discovered during travel in outer space (*Planet of the Vampires*, *Queen of Blood*, *Dracula 3000*), and inhabit futuristic cities (*Ultraviolet*, *Priest*). In an age of AIDS, SARS, and other virulent viral diseases that are still evolving, vampires have continued to be associated with plague in works such as *I Am Legend*, *Rabid*, and *Daybreakers*.

There is one type of science fiction that is popular in literary SF but has not translated well onto the silver screen, namely the "alternative world" concept that speculates about what reality would be like if key historical events had transpired differently. A well-known example is Philip K. Dick's novel *The Man in the High Castle*, which imagines what daily life would be like in America if the Axis Powers had defeated the Allies in World War II. In Kim Newman's novel *Anno Dracula* (1992), the historical Dracula,

Vlad the Impaler, has conquered England, married Queen Victoria, and presides over a decadent, vampire-infested London. A more recent example of an alternate world vampire story is Seth Grahame-Smith's 2010 novel, *Abraham Lincoln, Vampire Hunter*, filmed in 2012 by Timur Bekmambetov, which posits a scenario in which vampires fought alongside the Confederacy during the Civil War in order to procure a separate nation of their own. The vamp army is defeated at the battle of Gettysburg, using silver ammunition hastily collected and melted down by Union forces. Although these examples stray from SF into fantasy, the alternative world concept may provide a fertile field for the imagination of future science fiction vampire stories.

Another recent trend has been the "superhero-ization" of the science fiction vampire. After the success of Tim Burton's *Batman* (1989), films featuring the exploits of superheroes became wildly popular in American culture. By the early 2000s, these superhero blockbusters would come to dominate the science fiction movie genre in general, and the sci-fi vampire film in particular. This is hardly surprising, as Count Dracula may be considered the first super-villain in literature and the Batman character is, in some ways, associated with the vampire. With the relaxation of the long-standing Comics Code censorship in the 1970s, sci-fi vamps such as Vampirella, Blade, Morbius and Man Bat began to appear in comic books. The film adaptation of *Blade* (1998), based on the Marvel Comics vampire slayer character, cemented the filmic union of superhero and vamp. The *Blade* sequels were followed by the derivative *Underworld* series of films, along with sci-fi actioners such as *Van Helsing*, *Ultraviolet*, and *Priest*. Even the romantic/fantastic vampires of the *Twilight* saga became superheroized by the conclusion of that popular series. As the superhero trend in sci-fi cinema seems to have finally run its course, this aspect of the science fiction vampire may diminish.

Another permutation of the vampire myth involves a thematic confluence between vampires and reported contacts with UFO occupants reportedly encountered during alien abductions. The UFOnauts, frequently referred to as "Grays," have many traits in common with the vampires of legend: nocturnal bedroom visitations; being able to pass through closed doorways; pale skin; compelling eyes with hypnotic and telepathic powers; the ability to summon people by placing them in a somnambulistic trance, and, subsequently, inducing amnesia. The Grays also reportedly extract blood and other bodily fluids from their victims. Perceptions of both vampires and UFO aliens in the bedroom may be related to the phenomenon of sleep paralysis (as discussed in Chapter One), in which hypnagogic or hypnopompic hallucinations appear to the dreamer in a state between dreaming and waking. One of the leading proponents of the abduction phenomenon is novelist Whitley Streiber, author of *The Hunger* and other works of vampire fiction. If the reality of UFO abductions is ever proven, it could provide a factual basis for vampire legends as well.

Vampires and science fiction have had a close association from the beginning, as savants like Dr. Hesselius and Prof. Van Helsing matched their scientific acumen against the supernatural menace of the *nosferatu* and bloodsucking Martians. Over the years they have changed their forms, like the shapeshifters they have always been reported to be. The future may bring android vampires, nanotech vampires, genetically engineered vampires, virtual-reality vampires, or other science fiction vamps that are currently beyond our level of technological comprehension.

Filmography

Abbott and Costello Meet Frankenstein (1948) Director: Charles Barton. Producer: Robert Arthur. Screenplay: Robert Lees, Fredric Rinaldo, John Grant. Cast: Bud Abbott, Lou Costello, Bela Lugosi, Lon Chaney, Jr., Lenore Aubert, Glenn Strange, Jane Randolph. USA (Universal). B&W. 83m. DVD: Universal.

Against the Dark (2009) Director: Richard Crudo. Producer: Phillip B. Goldfine. Screenplay: Matthew Klickstein. Cast: Steven Seagal, Tanoai Reed, Jenna Harrison, Linden Ashby, Emma Catherwood. USA (Sony Pictures). Color. 93m. DVD: Sony Pictures Home Entertainment.

L'Atlantide (*Mistress of Atlantis*, 1932) Director: G. W. Pabst. Producer Screenplay: Herbert Rappoport, Laszlo Vajda, Pierre Ichac, from the novel by Pierre Benoit. Cast: Brigitte Helm, Pierre Blanchar, Tela Tchai. Germany (Nero-Film). B&W. 83m. DVD: Mill Creek Entertainment.

Atom Age Vampire (*Seddok, L'erede Satana*, 1960) Director: Anton Giulio Majano (Richard McNamara). Producer: Mario Bava. Screenplay: Piero Monviso, Gino di Santis, Alberto Bevilacqua, A.G. Majano, John Hart. Cast: Alberto Lupo, Susanne Loret, Sergio Fantoni, Roberto Berta. Italy (Topaz) B&W. 87m. DVD: Alpha Video.

The Bat People (1974) Director: Jerry Jameson. Producer/Screenplay: Lou Shaw. Cast: John Beck, Marianne McAndrew, Michael Pataki, Stewart Moss, Paul Carr. USA (American-International). Color. 95m. DVD: MGM Midnight Movies.

Bats (1999) Director: Louis Morneau. Producers: Bradley Jenkel, Louise Rosner. Screenplay: John Logan. Cast: Lou Diamond Phillips, Dina Meyer, Bob Gunton, Carlos Jacott. USA (Destination Films). Color. 91m. DVD: Destination Films.

Blade (1998) Director: Stephen Norrington. Producers: Peter Frankfurt, Wesley Snipes, Robert Engelman, Andrew J. Home, Avi Arad. Screenplay: David S. Goyer. Cast: Wesley Snipes, Kris Kristofferson, Stephen Dorff, N'bushe Wright, Donal Logue. USA (New Line/Marvel). Color. 119m. DVD: New Line Cinema.

Blade: Trinity (2004) Director/Screenplay: David S. Goyer. Producers: Peter Frankfurt, Wesley Snipes, David S. Goyer, Lynn Harris, Avi Arad. Cast: Wesley Snipes, Kris Kristofferson, Jessica Biel, Ryan Reynolds, Parker Posey. USA (Marvel/Amen Ra Films). 113m. DVD: New Line Cinema.

Blade II (2002) Director: Guillermo del Toro. Producers: Peter Frankfurt, Wesley Snipes, Patrick Palmer, Avi Arad. Screenplay: David S. Goyer. Cast: Wesley Snipes, Kris Kristofferson, Ron Perlman, Leonor Varela, Norman Reedus. USA (Marvel/Amen Ra Films). Color. 117m. DVD: New Line Cinema.

Bled (2009) Director: Christopher Hutson. Producers: Brigit Allard, Jeffrey Allard, Christopher Hutson, Kent Jones, Chris Kazmier, Julie Newsome, Scott Rettberg, Joe Vetrano,

Gregg von Thaden. Screenplay: Sxv'leithan Essex. Cast: Sarah Farooqui, Chris Ivan Cevic, Alex Petrovich, Jonathan Oldham, Ivan L. Moody. USA (Grindstone). Color. 95m. DVD: Grindstone Entertainment Group.

The Blood Beast Terror (*The Vampire Beast Craves Blood*, 1967) Director: Vernon Sewell. Producer: Arnold L. Miller. Screenplay: Peter Bryan. Cast: Peter Cushing, Robert Fleming, Wanda Ventham, Vanessa Howard. UK (Tigon/Pacemaker). Color. 88m. DVD: Redemption Video.

Blood of Dracula (1957) Director: Herbert L. Strock. Producer: Herman Cohen. Screenplay: Ralph Thornton. Cast: Sandra Harrison, Louise Lewis, Gail Ganley, Jerry Blaine. USA (American-International). B&W. 70m. DVD: Lion's Gate Home Entertainment.

Blood of the Vampire (1958) Director: Henry Cass. Producers: Robert S. Baker, Monty Berman. Screenplay: Jimmy Sangster. Cast: Sir Donald Wolfit, Victor Maddern, Barbara Shelley, Vincent Ball. UK (Universal). Color. 87m.DVD: Dark Sky Films.

Bloodrayne III: The Third Reich (2010) Director: Uwe Boll. Producers: Uwe Boll, Dan Clarke. Screenplay: Michael Nachoff. Cast: Natassia Malthe, Michael Pare, Brendan Fletcher, Clint Howard. USA/Canada/Germany (Boll Kino Beteiligungs). Color. 76m. DVD: Phase 4 Films.

The Cabinet of Dr. Caligari (*Das Kabinett des Dr. Caligari*, 1919) Director: Robert Weine. Producer: Uncredited. Screenplay: Carl Meyer, Hans Janowitz. Cast: Werner Krauss, Conrad Veidt, Lil Dagover, Fredrich Feher, Rudolf Klein-Rogge. Germany (Decla-Bishop). B&W. Silent. 71m. DVD: Kino on Video.

Captain Kronos, Vampire Hunter (1974) Director: Brian Clemens. Producers: Albert Fennell, Brian Clemens. Screenplay: Brian Clemens. Cast: Horst Janson, John Carson, Caroline Munro, Shane Briant. UK (Hammer). Color. 91m. DVD: Bruton Films.

The Climax (1944) Director/Producer: George Waggner. Screenplay: Curt Siodmak. Cast: Boris Karloff, Susanna Foster, Turhan Bey, Gale Sondergaard, Thomas Gomez. USA (Universal). Color. 86m. DVD: Universal.

Cronos (1992) Director/Screenplay: Guillermo del Toro. Producers: Arthur H. Gorson, Bertha Navarro, Alejandro Springall. Cast: Federico Luppi, Ron Perlman, Claudio Brook, Margarita Isabel, Tamara Shanath. Mexico (Instituto Mexicano de Cinematografia). Color. 91m. DVD: October Films.

Daybreakers (2009) Director/Screenplay: Michael Spierig, Peter Spierig. Producers: Chris Brown, Sean Furst, Bryan Furst. Cast: Ethan Hawke, Willem Dafoe, Sam Neill, Michael Dorman, Isabel Lucas. Australia/USA (Lionsgate). Color. 98m. DVD: Lionsgate.

The Devil Bat (1940) Director: Jean Yarbrough. Producer: Jack Gallagher. Screenplay: John Thomas Neville. Cast: Bela Lugosi, Dave O'Brien, Suzanne Kaaren. USA (PRC). B&W. 69m. DVD: Kino Classics.

Dracula (1931) Director: Tod Browning. Producer: Carl Laemmle, Jr., Tod Browning. Screenplay: Garrett Fort, from the novel by Bram Stoker. Cast: Bela Lugosi, Helen Chandler, David Manners, Dwight Frye, Edward Van Sloan. DVD: Universal.

Dracula AD 1972 (1972) Director: Alan Gibson. Producer: Josephine Douglas. Screenplay: Don Houghton. Cast: Christopher Lee, Peter Cushing, Christopher Neame, Caroline Munro, Stephanie Beacham. UK (Hammer/Warner Bros.). Color. 95m. DVD: Warner Home Entertainment.

Dracula 2000 (*Wes Craven Presents Dracula 2000*, 2000) Director: Patrick Lussier. Producers: W.K. Border, Joel Soisson. Screenplay: Joel Soisson. Cast: Jonny Lee Miller, Justine Waddell, Gerard Butler, Christopher Plummer, Jennifer Esposito, Omar Epps. USA (Dimension Films). Color. 99m. DVD: Dimension Home Video.

Dracula 3000 (2004) Director: Darrell Root. Producer: David Wicht. Screenplay: Ivan Milborrow. Cast: Casper Van Dien, Erika Eliniak, Udo Kier, Tom Lister, Coolio. USA/South Africa. Color. 86m. DVD: Lionsgate Films.

Dracula's Daughter (1936) Director: Lambert Hillyer. Producer: E.M. Asher. Screenplay: Garrett Fort. Cast: Gloria Holden, Edward Van Sloan, Otto Kruger, Marguerite Churchill, Nan Grey. USA (Universal). B&W. 80m. DVD: Universal.

First Man into Space (1959) Director: Robert Day. Producers: John Croydon, Charles F. Vetter, Jr. Screenplay: John C. Cooper, Lance Z. Hargreaves. Cast: Marshall Thompson, Marla Landi, Bill Edwards, Carl Jaffe. UK (Anglo-Amalgamated). B&W. 77m. DVD: Criterion Collection.

Goke, Body Snatcher from Hell (*Kyuketsuki Gokemidoru*, 1969) Director: Hajime Sato. Producer: Takashi Inomata. Screenplay: Kyuzo Kobayashi, Susumu Takaku. Cast: Teruo Yoshida, Tomoni Sato, Eizo Kitamura, Hideo Ko. Japan (Shochiku). Color. 84m. DVD: Criterion Collection.

House of Dracula (1945) Director: Erle C. Kenton. Producer: Paul Malvern. Screenplay: Edward T. Lowe. Cast: John Carradine, Lon Chaney, Jr., Onslow Stevens, Glenn Strange, Jane Adams, Lionel Atwill, Martha O'Driscoll. USA (Universal). B&W. 67m. DVD: Universal.

The Hunger (1983) Director: Tony Scott. Producer: Richard A. Shepard. Screenplay: Ivan Davis, Michael Thomas, from the novel by Whitley Strieber. Cast: Catherine Deneuve, Susan Sarandon, David Bowie, Dan Hedaya, Cliff DeYoung. USA (MGM). Color. 94m. DVD: Warner Home Entertainment.

The Hypnotic Eye (1959) Director: George Blair. Producer: Charles B. Bloch. Screenplay: Gitta Woolfield, Read Woolfield. Cast: Jacques Bergerac, Allison Hayes, Joe Patridge, Marcia Henderson. USA (Allied Artists). B&W. 79m. DVD: Warner Home Entertainment.

I Am Legend (2007) Director: Francis Lawrence. Producers: Akiva Goldsman, James Lassiter, David Heyman, Neal H. Moritz. Screenplay: Mark Protosevich, Akiva Goldsman, from the novel by Richard Matheson. Cast: Will Smith, Charlie Tahan, Alice Braga, Salli Richardson. USA (Village Roadshow Pictures). Color. 100m. DVD: Warner Home Entertainment.

It! The Terror from Beyond Space (1958) Director: Edward L. Cahn. Producer: Robert E. Kent. Screenplay: Jerome Bixby. Cast: Marshall Thompson, Shawn Smith, Kim Spalding, Ann Doran, Ray "Crash" Corrigan. USA (United Artists). DVD: MGM Home Entertainment.

The Last Man on Earth (1964) Director: Ubaldo Ragona, Sidney Salkow (U.S. Version). Producer: Robert L. Lippert. Screenplay: Logan Swanson, William P. Leicester, from the novel by Richard Matheson. Cast: Vincent Price, Giacomo Rossi-Stuart, Francoia Bettoia. Italy (American-International). B&W. 86m. DVD: MGM Home Entertainment.

Lifeforce (1985) Director: Tobe Hooper. Producers: Menahem Golan, Yoram Globus. Screenplay: Dan O'Bannon, Don Jakoby, from the novel by Colin Wilson. Cast: Steve Railsback, Peter Firth, Mathilda May, Frank Finlay, Patrick Stewart. UK (TriStar). Color. 100m. DVD: MGM Home Entertainment.

Mill of the Stone Women (1960) Director: Giorgio Ferroni. Producer: Gianpaola Bigazzi. Screenplay: Remigio Del Grosso, Ugo Liberatore, Giorgio Stegani, Giorgio Ferroni. Cast: Wolfgang Preiss. France/Italy (Parade Pictures). Color. 90m. DVD: Mondo Macabro.

The Night Stalker (*Kolchak: The Night Stalker*, 1972) Director: John Llewelyn Moxley. Producer: Dan Curtis. Screenplay: Richard Matheson. Cast: Darren McGavin, Carol Lynley, Barry Atwater, Simon Oakland, Ralph Meeker. USA (ABC-TV). 73m. Color. DVD: Universal.

Nightwing (1979) Director: Arthur Hiller. Producer: Martin Rensohoff. Screenplay: Steve Shagan, Bud Shrake, Martin Cruz Smith, from his novel. Cast: Nick Mancuso, David Warner, Kathryn Harrold, Strother Martin. USA (Columbia). Color. 103m.DVD: Sony Pictures Home Entertainment.

Nosferatu (1922) Director: F.W. Murnau. Producer Screenplay: Henrik Galeen. Cast: Max Schreck, Gustav von Wangenheim, Alexander Granach, Greta Schroeder, Ruth Landshoff. Germany (Prana-Film), B&W. Silent. 94m. DVD: Kino International.

Not of This Earth (1957) Director/Producer: Roger Corman. Screenplay: Charles Griffith, Mark Hanna. Cast: Paul Birch, Beverly Garland, Jonathan Haze, Morgan Jones, Anne Carroll. USA (Allied Artists). B&W. 67m. DVD: World Beyond Video.

Not of This Earth (1988) Director: Jim Wynorski. Producers: Jim Wynorski, Murray Miller. Screenplay: Jim Wynorski, R.J. Robinson. Cast: Traci Lords, Arthur Roberts, Lenny Juliano, Roger Lodge, Ace Mask. USA (MGM/UA). Color. 82m. DVD: New Concorde Home Entertainment.

Not of This Earth (1996) Director: Terrence H. Winkless. Producer: Roger Corman, Lance H. Robbins. Screenplay: Charles Philip Moore. Cast: Michael York, Parker Stevenson, Elizabeth Barondes, Richard Belzer, Arthur Roberts. USA Color. 91m. DVD: New Concorde Home Entertainment.

The Omega Man (1971) Director: Boris Sagal. Producer: Walter Seltzer. Screenplay: John William, Joyce H. Carrington. Cast: Charlton Heston, Anthony Zerbe, Rosalind Cash. USA (Warner Bros.). Color. 98m. DVD: Warner Home Video.

Plan 9 from Outer Space (1959) Director/ Producer/Screenplay: Edward D. Wood, Jr. Cast: Bela Lugosi, Tor Johnson, Vampira, Criswell, Joanna Lee, Gregory Walcott, Mona McKinnon. USA (DCA). B&W. 79m. DVD: Image Entertainment.

Planet of the Vampires (*Terrore nello Spazio*, 1965) Director: Mario Bava. Producer: Fulvio Luciano. Screenplay: Catillo Cosulich, Antonio Roman, Alberto Bevilacqua, Mario Bava, Rafael J. Salvia. Cast: Barry Sullivan, Norman Bengell, Angel Aranda, Evi Marandi, Fernando Villena. Italy/Spain (American-International). Color. 86m. DVD: MGM/UA Home Entertainment.

Priest (2011) Director: Scott Stewart. Producers: Michael DeLuca, Joshua Donen, Mitchell Peck. Screenplay: Cory Goodman. Cast: Paul Bettany, Karl Urban, Lily Collins, Maggie Q, Cam Gigandet. USA (Tokyopop). Color. 87m. DVD: Sony Pictures Home Entertainment.

The Quatermass Xperiment (*The Creeping Unknown*, 1956) Director: Val Guest. Producer: Anthony Hinds. Screenplay: Richard Landau, Val Guest. Cast: Brian Donlevy, Richard Wordsworth, Margia Dean, Lionel Jeffries. UK (Hammer/United Artists. B&W. 78m. DVD: MGM Home Entertainment.

Queen of Blood (*Planet of Blood*, 1966) Director/Screenplay: Curtis Harrington. Producer:

George Edwards. Cast: Basil Rathbone, Florence Marly, Dennis Hopper, John Saxon, Judi Meredith. USA (American-International). Color. 80m. DVD: MGM Home Entertainment.

Rabid (1977) Director/Screenplay: David Cronenberg. Producer: John Dunning. Cast: Marilyn Chambers, Frank Moore, Joe Silver, Howard Ryshpan. Canada (Cinepix/Dybar). Color. 91m. DVD: Warner Home Video.

The Return of Doctor X (1939) Director: Vincent Sherman. Producer: Brian Foy. Screenplay: Lee Katz. Cast: Humphrey Bogart, Wayne Morris, Rosemary Lane, Dennis Morgan. USA (Warner Bros.). B&W. 62m. DVD: Warner Home Video.

The Return of the Vampire (1943) Director: Lew Landers. Producer: Sam White. Screenplay: Griffith Jay. Cast: Bela Lugosi, Matt Willis, Frieda Inescort, Nina Foch, Miles Mander. USA (Columbia). B&W. 69m. DVD: Sony Pictures Home Entertainment.

The Satanic Rites of Dracula (*Count Dracula and His Vampire Bride*, 1973) Director: Alan Gibson. Producer: Roy Skeggs. Screenplay: Don Houghton. Cast: Christopher Lee, Peter Cushing, Michael Coles, Freddie Jones, Joanna Lumley. UK (Hammer). Color. 84m. DVD: Echo Bridge Home Entertainment.

The Shout (1978) Director: Jerzy Skolimowski. Producer: Jeremy Thomas. Screenplay: Michael Austin, Jerzy Skolimowski. Cast: Alan Bates, Susannah York, John Hurt, Tim Curry, Robert Stephens. UK (Rank Organization). Color. 87m. DVD: Films Incorporated.

Svengali (1931) Director: Archie Mayo. Producer: Uncredited. Screenplay: J. Grubb Alexander, from the novel *Trilby* by George du Maurier. Cast: John Barrymore, Marian Marsh, Donald Crisp, Bramwell Fletcher, Carmel Myers. USA (Warner Bros.) B&W. 81m. DVD: Alpha Video.

The Thing from Another World (1951) Director: Howard Hawks/Christian Nyby. Producer: Howard Hawks. Screenplay: Charles Lederer. Cast: Kenneth Tobey, James Arness, Margaret Sheridan. USA (RKO). B&W. 87m. DVD: Warner Home Video.

Thirst (*Bakjwi*, 2009) Director: Park Chan-wook. Producers: Park Chan-wook, Jeong Seo-Kyeong. Screenplay: Park Chan-wook, Ahn Soo-Hyeon. Cast: Song Kang-ho, Kim Ok-vin, Shin Ha-kyun, Kim Hae-sook. South Korea (Moho Films/Focus Features). Color. 134m. DVD: Universal.

Ultraviolet (2006) Director/Screenplay: Kurt Wimmer. Producers: John Baldecchi, Lucas Foster, Tony Mark, Pauline Chan. Cast: Milla Jovovich, Cameron Bright, Nick Chinlund, William Fitchne, Sebastian Andrieu. USA (Screen Gems) Color. 94m. DVD: Screen Gems.

Underworld (2003) Director: Len Wiseman. Producers: Tom Rosenberg, Gary Lucchesi, Richard Wright. Screenplay: Danny McBride. Cast: Kate Beckinsale, Scott Speedman, Michael Sheen, Shane Brolly, Bill Nighy, USA/UK/Germany/Hungary (Lakeshore Entertainment). Color. 134m. DVD: Sony Pictures Home Entertainment.

Underworld: Awakening (2012) Directors: Mans Marlind, Bjorn Stein. Producers: Tom Rosenberg, Gary Lucchesi, Len Wiseman, Richard Wright. Screenplay: Len Wiseman, John Hlavin, J. Michael Straczynski, Allison Burnett. Cast: Kate Beckinsale, Sandra Holt, Theo James, Michael Ealy. USA (Lakeshore Entertainment). Color. 88m. DVD: Sony Pictures Home Entertainment.

Underworld: Evolution (2006) Director: Len Wiseman. Producers: Tom Rosenberg, Gary

Lucchesi, Richard Wright, Len Wiseman, Kevin Grevious. Screenplay: Danny McBride. Cast: Kate Beckinsale, Scott Speedman, Bill Nighy, Derek Jacobi, Tony Curran. USA (Lakeshore Entertainment) Color. 106m. DVD: Sony Pictures Home Entertainment.

The Vampire (1957) Director: Paul Landres. Producers: Arthur Gardner, Jules Levy. Screenplay: Pat Fielder. Cast: John Beal, Coleen Gray, Kenneth Tobey. Mexico (United Artists). B&W. 74m. DVD: MGM Midnight Movies.

The Vampire Bat (1933) Director: Frank Strayer. Producer: Phil Goldstone. Screenplay: Edward T. Lowe. Cast: Lionel Atwill, Melvyn Douglas, Fay Wray, Dwight Frye, Robert Fraser. USA (Majestic) B&W. 71m. DVD: Alpha Video.

Vampire Men of the Lost Planet (*Horror of the Blood Monsters*, 1970) Director/Producer: Al Adamson. Screenplay: Sue McNair. Cast: John Carradine, Robert Dix, Vicki Volante, Joey Benson, Jennifer Bishop. USA (Independent International). Color. 85m. DVD: Alpha New Cinema.

Van Helsing (2004) Director/Screenplay: Stephen Sommers. Producers: Stephen Sommers, Bob Ducsay. Cast: Hugh Jackman, Kate Beckinsale, Richard Roxburgh, David Wenham, Will Kemp. USA (Universal). Color. 131m. DVD: Universal.

The War of the Worlds (2005) Director: Steven Spielberg. Producers: Kathleen Kennedy, Colin Wilson. Screenplay: Josh Friedman, David Koepp, from the novel by H.G. Wells. Cast: Tom Cruise, Dakota Fanning, Miranda Otto, Tim Robbins. USA (Dreamworks/Paramount). Color. 117m. DVD: Dreamworks Home Entertainment.

Chapter Notes

Introduction

1. Melton, J. Gordon, *The Vampire Book: The Encyclopedia of the Undead* (Detroit: Visible Ink Press, 1999), 606.
2. Mark Collins Jenkins, *Vampire Forensics* (Washington, D.C.: National Geographic, 2010), 13.
3. Raymond T. McNally and Radu Florescu, *In Search of Dracula: A True History of Dracula and Vampire Legends* (New York: Warner Paperback Library, 1974), 168.
4. Ibid., 170.
5. Brian Aldiss with David Wingrove, *Trillion Year Spree: The History of Science Fiction* (New York: Athenium, 1986), 25.
6. David J. Skal, *Screams of Reason: Mad Science and Modern Culture* (New York: W.W. Norton), 83.
7. Nina Aurebach, *Our Vampires, Ourselves* (Chicago: University of Chicago Press, 1997), 145.
8. Matthew Beresford, *From Demons to Dracula* (London: Reaktion Books, 2008), 154–155.

Chapter One

1. Mark Collins Jenkins, *Vampire Forensics*, 111.
2. Beresford, *From Demons to Dracula*, 100.
3. Aldiss with Wingrove, Brian, *Trillion Year Spree*, 144–145.
4. David J. Skal, *Hollywood Gothic: The Tangled Web of Dracula from Novel to Stage and Screen* (New York: Faber & Faber, 1990), 74.
5. Jenkins, *Vampire Forensics*, 76.
6. Bram Stoker, *Dracula* (New York: Tor Books, 1989), 69.
7. Ibid., 83–84.
8. Whitley Strieber, *The Hunger* (New York: Pocket Books, 1981), 115.
9. David Hufford, *The Terror That Comes in the Night: An Experience-Centered Study of Supernatural Assault Traditions* (Philadelphia: University of Pennsylvania Press, 1982), 88.
10. Ibid., 93.
11. Stoker, *Dracula*, 275.
12. Hufford, *The Terror That Comes in the Night*, 237.
13. Skal, *Hollywood Gothic*, 49.

Chapter Two

1. J. Sheridan Le Fanu, *Carmilla*, in Otto Penzler, ed., *The Vampire Archives* (New York: Vintage, 2009), 108.
2. George Du Maurier, *Trilby* (London: J.M. Dent & Sons, 1977), 54.
3. Ibid., 57.
4. Ibid., 58.
5. Skal, *Hollywood Gothic*, 48.
6. Arthur Conan Doyle, "The Parasite," in Penzler, ed., *The Vampire Archives*, 487.
7. M.E. Braddon, "Good Lady Ducayne," in Penzler, ed., *The Vampire Archives*, 6.
8. Stoker, *Dracula*, 228.
9. Ibid., 290–291.
10. H.G. Wells, *The War of the Worlds* (New York: Scholastic Books, 1974). 182.
11. Ibid., 194–195.
12. Ibid., 200.
13. Ibid., 209–210.
14. Ibid., 194–195.
15. Hanns Heinz Ewers, *Alraune*, trans. S. Guy Endore (New York: J. Day & Co., 1929), 330.
16. Algernon Blackwood, "The Transfer," in Penzler, *The Vampire Archives*, 432.
17. Ibid., 434.
18. Fritz Leiber, "The Girl with the Hungry Eyes," in Penzler, ed., *The Vampire Archives*, 801.
19. Ibid., 809.
20. Ibid., 809.
21. C.M. Kornbluth, "The Mindworm," http://www.lesvampires.org/mindworm.html.
22. Richard Matheson, *I Am Legend* (New York: Orb Books, 1997), 88.
23. Ibid., 169.
24. Strieber, *The Hunger*, 265.
25. Whitley Strieber, "Pain," in Dennis Etchison, ed., *Cutting Edge* (New York: Doubleday, 1986), 281.

26. Ibid., 273.

27. Whitley Strieber, *Communion: A True Story* (New York: Abon Books, 1987), 78.

28. Ibid., 100.

29. Ibid., 24–25.

30. Dan Simmons, "Carrion Comfort," in Penzler, ed., *The Vampire Archives*, 896.

31. Brian Aldiss, *Dracula Unbound* (Poughkeepsie, NY: House of Stratus, 2001), 173.

32. George Alec Effinger, "Marid and the Trail of Blood," in Effinger, *Budayeen Nights* (Urbana: Golden Gryphon Press, 2003), 111.

Chapter Four

1. Susannah Clements, *The Vampire Defanged: How the Embodiment of Evil Became a Romantic Hero* (Grand Rapids: Brazos Press, 2011), 131–132.

2. David J. Skal, *V is for Vampire: The A-Z Guide to Everything Undead* (New York: Plume Books, 1996), 1–2.

Chapter Five

1. John Baxter, *Science Fiction in the Cinema* (New York: Paperback Library, 1970), 78.

Chapter Six

1. Leonard Maltin, *Leonard Maltin's 2007 Movie Guide* (New York: Plume, 2006), 1426.

Bibliography

Aldiss, Brian. *Dracula Unbound*. Poughkeepsie, NY: House of Stratus, 2001.

_____, with David Wingrove. *Trillion Year Spree: The History of Science Fiction*. New York: Athenium, 1986.

Ashley, Mike. *Who's Who in Horror and Fantasy Fiction*. New York: Taplinger, 1977.

Aurebach, Nina. *Our Vampires, Ourselves*. Chicago: University of Chicago Press, 1997.

Baxter, John. *Science Fiction in the Cinema*. New York: Paperback Library, 1970.

Beresford, Matthew. *From Demons to Dracula: The Creation of the Modern Vampire Myth*. London: Reaktion Books, 2008.

Butler, Ivan. *Horror in the Cinema*. New York: A.S. Barnes, 1970.

Clarens, Carlos. *An Illustrated History of the Horror Film*. New York: Capricorn Books, 1967.

Clements, Susannah. *The Vampire Defanged: How the Embodiment of Evil Became a Romantic Hero*. Grand Rapids: Brazos Press, 2011.

Clute, John. *Science Fiction: The Illustrated Encyclopedia*. London: Dorling Kinderly,1995.

Davis, Wade, *The Serpent and the Rainbow*. New York: Warner Books, 1985.

Del Toro, Guillermo, and Chuck Hogan. *The Fall*. New York: William Morrow, 2010.

_____, and _____.*The Night Eternal*. New York: William Morrow, 2011.

_____, and _____. *The Strain*. New York: William Morrow, 2009.

Du Maurier, George. *Trilby*. London: J.M. Dent & Sons, 1977.

Effinger, George Alec. *Budayeen Nights*. Urbana: Golden Gryphon Press, 2003.

Etchison, Dennis, ed. *Cutting Edge*. New York: Doubleday, 1986.

Everman, Welch. *Cult Science Fiction Films*. New York: Citadel, 1995.

Ewers, Hanns Heinz. *Alraune*. Trans. S. Guy Endore. New York: J. Day & Co., 1929.

Hufford, David. *The Terror That Comes in the Night: An Experience-Centered Study of Supernatural Assault Traditions*. Philadelphia: University of Pennsylvania Press, 1982.

Jenkins, Mark Collins. *Vampire Forensics: Uncovering the Origins of an Enduring Legend*. Washington, D.C.: National Geographic, 2010.

Lee, Tanith. *Sabella, or, the Bloodstone*. New York: Daw Books, 1980.

Maltin, Leonard. *Leonard Maltin's 2007 Movie Guide*. New York: Plume, 2006.

Matheson, Richard. *I Am Legend*. New York: Orb Books, 1997.

McNally, Raymond T., and Radu Florescu. *In Search of Dracula: A True History of Dracula and Vampire Legends*. New York: Warner Paperback Library, 1974.

Melton, J. Gordon. *The Vampire Book: The Encyclopedia of the Undead*. Detroit: Visible Ink Press, 1999.

Penzler, Otto, ed., *The Vampire Archives*. New York: Vintage, 2009.

Skal, David J. *Hollywood Gothic: The Tangled Web of Dracula from Novel to Stage and Screen*. New York: Faber & Faber, 1990.

_____. *The Monster Show: A Cultural History of Horror*. New York: W.W. Norton, 1983.

_____. *Screams of Reason: Mad Science and Popular Culture*. New York: W.W. Norton, 1998.

_____. *V Is for Vampire: The A–Z Guide to Everything Undead*. New York: Plume, 1996.

Stanley, John. *Creature Features: The Science Fiction, Fantasy and Horror Movie Guide*. New York: Boulevard, 1997.

Stoker, Bram. *The Bram Stoker Companion: Classic Horror Stories*. New York: Taplinger, 1979.

_____. *Dracula*. New York: Tor Books, 1989.

Strieber, Whitley. *Communion: A True Story*. New York: Abon Books, 1987.

_____. *The Hunger*. New York: Pocket Books, 1981.

_____. *The Last Vampire*. New York: Pocket Books, 2001.

Wells, H.G. *The War of the Worlds.* New York: Scholastic Books, 1974.

Von Gunden, Kenneth, and Stuart H. Stock. *Twenty All-Time Great Science Fiction Films.* New York: Arlington House, 1982.

Welson, Michael J. *The Psychotronic Encyclopedia of Film.* New York: Ballantine, 1983.

Wilson, Colin. *The Space Vampires.* New York: Random House, 1976.

Index

www.ingramcontent.com/pod-product-compliance
Lightning Source LLC
Chambersburg PA
CBHW081332090726
47907CB00011B/2453

* 9 7 8 0 7 8 6 4 7 4 8 7 5 *